BarnYard Heroes:

The Havarti Travel Bureau Conspiracy

or

How I Learned to Stop Worrying

and

Love the Cow Zombie Apocalypse

by Samuel A. McAdams

Cover by Iconic Team

Third edition: January 2026

eBook ISBN: 978-1-963968-04-0

Paperback (5x8) ISBN: 978-1-963968-03-3

Paperback (5.5x8.5) ISBN: 978-1-963968-05-7

Contents

Some are born into greatness. A few have greatness thrust upon them against their will, while many arrive at greatness via hard work, determination, and perseverance. Then there are those who are brought to greatness through a series of incredibly painful operations, multiple genetic modifications, and a fair number of bizarre scientific and chemical experiments performed by a purple-skinned space alien.

This is THEIR tale ...

CONTENT WARNING: This novel contains tobacco and alcohol use, graphic violence, death, and a brief conversation about interspecies sex which the author hopes is enough to get the book banned from libraries in the state of Florida.

1: We're All Gonna Die

THE ABSURDITY OF BARNYARD animals providing perimeter surveillance never occurred to me. I focused on positioning the other animals around the church grounds and neighboring cornfields, a job akin to herding squirrels. Everyone, except the pig, kept leaving their posts to ask me inane questions like, "What should we do if it rains?" or "Can we eat the corn?" Once I finally got them set, I suppressed my worries, for the others would be far from the action. The human agents would handle the raid, though I couldn't fathom what dangers lurked inside the country church. If not for the half dozen cars in the gravel parking lot, I would have assumed the church to be abandoned. The wood siding of the hundred and fifty-year-old church needed a fresh coat of white paint two decades ago. Moss grew on the shingles of the steeple-less roof. From the outside, only the stained-glass windows differentiated the tiny church from a farmhouse.

I shifted my focus to my next assignment: reconnaissance. Crouching outside a giant stained-glass window, the best a cow can do, I took a deep breath, rose, and peered inside. No one sat in the pews or roamed the aisles. I stretched my neck to view the empty altar.

I trotted behind the church, enjoying the sun beating on my leathery back. A whiff of the corn's floral greens, underscored by a hint of natural fertilizers, harkened me back to my days of grazing on lush pastures. My new life left no room for such leisure. I checked the rooms behind the sanctuary. The pastor sat in his office studying his laptop screen, while a small group of gray-haired ladies occupied the neighboring classroom.

"Cow, do you have a visual on the church interior?" asked Agent Orange, the director of Global Intergalactic Bureau of Defense, commonly known as GIBOD.

To respond, I needed to tap my earpiece. Easy for Agent Orange and the human agents to do, but not me. I scrunched my shoulder up but came nowhere near my ear. I lifted my right front hoof, but it only stretched to my knee.

"Cow! Do you copy?" asked Agent Orange.

I smacked the side of my head against the windowsill. "Thhir, I'm here." Dr. Hash Browns provided me and the other animals with a multitude of amazing enhancements, but he never completely got rid of my lisp. He blamed my enormous tongue.

"Give me your report."

I positioned myself between the windows of the classroom and office. "I'm not sure what you expected to find inside a church on a Tuesday afternoon. The pastor is at his desk and there'thh a group of old ladies knitting."

"How many old ladies are there?"

"Five or thhix." Dang that lisp.

"Cow, I need an exact count."

"They're old ladies. What difference doethh it make how many?"

"Need I remind you this is a training mission? Your performance is being evaluated. Now, give me an exact count on the old ladies."

I pictured the red marks on our evaluation form. Shut up and take orders. That's how he trained us. Luckily, the other animals didn't understand English. They would be unaware of my blunder. Except the pig. He'd know.

I raised my head and took another look inside the classroom. "Five. There are five old ladies knitting."

"Cow, return to your position on the side of the church. Agents, it's time."

I made my way back to the large stained-glass window as oversized military trucks roared to life and lurched down the quiet country road. It's a mystery how no one inside the church heard them coming. For that matter, they should have seen them coming. Flat cornfields and grazing pastures spread out for miles in all directions, without a tree or a building to provide cover.

The trucks approached from opposite directions and simultaneously turned into the church parking lot like Shriners in a parade. Agents in black military uniforms poured out of the trucks. Agents Burgundy and Maroon positioned themselves outside my window, while others paired up outside the other windows of the church. A dozen agents lined up on either side of the giant wooden front doors.

Agent Burgundy raised an eyebrow. "Cow, why aren't you invisible?"

"That's your one superpower. That's why they sent you to case the joint," said Agent Maroon.

"It only lastthh a few minutes," I lied. I had forgotten to activate it. "It must have worn off."

"Cow, go invisible. And everybody cut the chatter," said Agent Orange, as I glimpsed his black Suburban pulling onto the church's front lawn.

In a hushed tone, Agent Burgundy asked, "How is he hearing us?"

Agent Maroon pointed to my earpiece.

"Thhorry," I said, as I smacked my head against the windowsill to turn off my mic. I closed my eyes, let out a deep breath, and concentrated on activating my invisibility. With the buzz of a moth frying in a bug zapper, my cloaking power expanded across my hide.

Agent Maroon cocked his head as he stared at me. "Do you realize your outline is still visible?"

"It'thh more of a cloaking power. It'thh better if I stay still." Immobilizing my torso had never been a problem, but I struggled to keep my ears from twitching and my tail from swishing.

Agent Maroon held up his index finger. "You remind me of the Predator." He clicked off the safety of his weapon as he turned to Agent Burgundy. "Remember that movie?"

Agent Burgundy cocked his head in the same manner as Agent Maroon but added a chin scratch and an eye squint. Eventually, he mimicked Agent Maroon's finger point and said, "You're right. She does look like the Predator. That's pretty cool."

"Thankthh," I said, with an overwhelming sense of déjà vu. The rabbit and duck had brought this movie up at least a dozen times.

"Of course, the Predator could go fully invisible," said Agent Burgundy as he readied his weapon.

"What are you talking about, bro?" asked Agent Maroon, both verbally and facially. "The Predator had an outline, just like hers. You saw the movie, right?"

"The outline was a cinematic convention, so the viewers saw the Predator. In reality, it could go completely invisible."

"Bro, your argument makes no sense. In reality, the entire movie is made up."

Agent Orange thankfully put an end to the conversation, before I quoted the rabbit's argument, that the reactions from the other characters clearly indicated they didn't see the Predator, not even an outline.

"Agents, if you're not in position, get there now," said Agent Orange, getting out of his military-grade Suburban. He surveyed the troops through his dark sunglasses. He and his number one, Agent Periwinkle, were the only agents dressed in black dress suits. The others wore black military uniforms. The rabbit and duck insisted GIBOD was actually

Men in Black, arguing Agent Orange could easily pass as Agent K. He was a middle-aged white man, with short black hair, who walked as if he was in a military parade, never smiled, and spoke with a tone which made even casual conversation sound like a command.

On the other hand, the gray-haired, wrinkled faced Agent Periwinkle, whose feet never shuffled an inch off the ground, was no Agent J.

"This might not be the best time, but I've wanted to talk to you about your lisp," said Agent Burgundy as he peeked into the church. "I've noticed it's not consistent. Sometimes you pronounce your s's just fine."

"What'thh your point?" I asked, annoyed he'd brought this up now.

"You blame it on your enormous tongue, but I think it's more mental than physical."

"I had a lisp when I was a kid," said Agent Maroon. "After some coaching from a speech therapist, I got rid of it."

Agent Burgundy gave Agent Maroon a nod. "Exactly. With a bit of therapy, you can lick this."

"Thankthh, guys. I'll take that under consideration." I had no intention of taking it under consideration. They had no idea how much "therapy" Dr. Hash Browns had put me through in his attempt to correct my lisp. "We better focus on the mission."

Agent Orange tapped his earpiece. "Agents. On my mark... Advance!"

Windows and doors on all sides of the church flew open, as agents poured in.

Knitting needles clinked on the tile floor.

Pews skidded into each other like a multi-car pileup.

A man screamed.

The old ladies watched the tiny red dots bounce around their chests and bob up and down their faces, as agents herded them across the stage toward the choral risers in the back. One lady sat down on the first step of the riser with her knitting bag resting next to her and returned to knitting her shawl.

"ON YOUR KNEES!" said Agent Crimson as he whacked the needles and shawl out of her hands.

The old woman smiled at Agent Crimson as she flexed and stretched her fingers. "Honey, I don't know what this is all about, but I haven't been able to get down on my knees since the Clinton administration, and I ain't about to start now. So, I'm going to sit right here until you boys finish up whatever it is you came here to do." She picked up her needles.

The eyes of the tiniest old lady darted from Agent Crimson, to her friend knitting, to the red dots that danced on her blouse. "Marjorie," she said, "I don't think it's wise to provoke these gentlemen."

"Oh, relax, Blanche," said Marjorie, as she reached for her knitting bag. "I'm sure these fine men and women are not here to arrest the evil Town and Country Baptist Church Knitting Club."

Agent Crimson narrowed his glare and raised his weapon as she fumbled through her bag. He lowered it once she pulled out a new ball of yarn. Marjorie returned to her knitting while the rest of the ladies gasped. A pair of agents dragged the pastor out of his office and deposited him by the altar. Behind them, agents streamed into the back rooms like a mob of looters.

I remained at my post outside the stained-glass window as Agent Orange strutted up the altar steps.

"What is the meaning of this?" asked the middle-aged pastor, running fingers through his hair. A pointless act, since despite being dragged out of his office and tossed to the floor, his hair remained perfectly groomed. He raised to his knees and straightened his back. "This is a place of worship. What could you possibly want with us?"

I had the same question. A briefing on mission objectives would have been nice, but Agent Orange insisted the information was classified.

"Yes, a place of worship. What a perfect cover." Agent Orange paced to the organ next to my window to play an ominous cord.

Agent Orange strolled up to the pastor's prone position and lorded over him. "Pastor Johnson, would you care to explain why a tiny church in the middle of farm country needs three enormous satellite dishes?"

I ducked as the director gestured toward my window. The three industrial-sized satellite dishes formed a Charlie's Angels-like pose on the edge of the church grounds, visible from the window I cowered under. I felt ashamed for not noticing them earlier. An agent must be fully aware of their surroundings and note any out-of-place objects. If Agent Orange knew of this lapse in observation, it would be another red mark on my score card.

The pastor cleared his throat. "We have no right to restrict God's message of salvation to Earth, so we beam our sermons to the cosmos for intelligent life-forms across the universe to hear."

"You're not fooling anybody," said Agent Orange. "We know those satellites are used to communicate with the intergalactic terrorist organization known as the Havarti Travel Bureau. We intercepted the transmissions. Transmissions you will decode for us."

"This is some kind of joke, right? Where's the hidden camera crew?"

I peeked into the church to see the pastor scanning his ransacked sanctuary for a camera crew.

"I assure you, Pastor Johnson, regarding matters of the Havarti Travel Bureau, I do not joke."

"Look, I have no idea what you're talking about. We broadcast into space. We don't receive messages." The smugness had drained from the pastor's face and his shoulders slumped.

A door at the back of the sanctuary sprang open. Everyone turned to watch a teenage boy stroll up the side aisle, absorbed in the glow of his smartphone. He controlled it with one hand and adjusted his earbuds with the other. He stopped a step away from my window. His eyes looked up from the device. His perpetually drooped mouth shifted to a gape. He yanked an earbud out. "What the–?"

"Nick," said the pastor, with pleading arms extended. "You're part of the tech team. Tell them we're not receiving any messages on those satellites."

The boy's eyes darted around the sanctuary. He took a single step in multiple directions before backing up against the wall. "I, um..., I don't know what you're talking about." His eyes rested on the emergency exit door.

The agents stopped flipping pews and raised their weapons.

His eyes popped wide open as red laser dots danced on his chest. He raised his arms above his head.

A faint pew-pew came from the choral risers. So faint, it would have gone unnoticed, if not for the fireworks-level explosion that followed. The blast obliterated the church organ, spraying wood and ivory splinters across the church like an exploding volcano. The last cords wheezed out of the pipes as organ shards rained to the floor.

"You're gonna die," cackled a little old lady. "You're all gonna die."

I searched the gang of old ladies, stunned that one of them carried a weapon of such destruction, but found no bazooka or rocket launcher.

Pew-pew. Pew-pew.

Juicy explosions, like microwaved tomatoes, preceded the pastor shrieking like a teenage Elvis fan. Agents dove behind the toppled pews, but Agent Crimson had no time to find cover. His headless body crumpled to the floor.

"He's dead now." It was Marjorie, the little old lady who had returned to her knitting. She had dropped her knitting needles and held what resembled a toy water gun. She grinned as she aimed the tiny gun at Agents Burgundy and Maroon, who had the boy cornered. "Now you're all gonna die."

The pew-pew came before I could verbalize words of warning. I ducked just in time to avoid a face full of Agents Burgundy and Maroon's brains. Spitting up cud from my first and second stomachs is a normal part of my digestion, but the sight and sound of the agents' heads splattering across the stained-glass window like the contents of a pail of slop, coupled with the stench of their laser-roasted brains brought remnants from my third and fourth stomachs. I spit the nasty bile flavored cud out on the church lawn.

She had me believing in her catchphrase. *What were we thinking? We're a bunch of misfit lab animals who should have stayed in our laboratory. Why did we want to be special agents? We're all gonna die on our training mission.*

Marjorie broke from her catchphrase. "What are you waiting for? Run, Nick, run." She hadn't looked at the teenager as she lined up her next target, Agent Orange.

The boy's shadow panned over me as he sprinted toward the emergency exit.

Pew-pew.

I contemplated sprinting for the cornfields, yelling it was every animal for themselves.

BLAM! BLAM!

The old woman winced.

Agent Orange marched toward her with his pistol aimed at her head. "Don't even think about picking that weapon up," he said, kicking her laser gun off the altar stage.

She responded with a mild groan and clutched her wounded hand.

The exit door flew open.

"Cow, it's time for your team of animals to put your training to use. I want that boy alive."

The team had trained hard for this moment and desperately wanted to showcase their skills. I couldn't run away and let them down. I took a deep breath and smacked my ear into the side of the church. "We're on it, thhir. We won't let you down."

2: Let the Field Test Begin or The Pursuit of Nick La Conn

AGENT ORANGE CALLED OUR outside surveillance a perfect first assignment, where we could demonstrate our training, with a low risk of action coming our way. So much for that logic. He now relied on *us* to capture the prime suspect. But, with a good performance, we would become agents of GIBOD.

Nick bolted out the emergency exit near the back of the church. He turned the corner and disappeared. His rapid footsteps crunched on the gravel of the back parking lot.

I prepared to whack my ear against the side of the church to activate my mic before remembering it was already on. In Cheddarian, I said, "Team! The suspect is sprinting through the back parking lot. Does anyone have a visual?"

The chicken poked her head out of the cornfield behind me. "My sense of sight is still working. Why would you think otherwise?"

"What's a, um…, what's a suspect?" asked the dog, who insists he does not stutter, but instead has an endearing Jimmy Stewart stammer.

"You idiots," said the pig, patrolling the field on the other side of the church, along with the fish. "The cow wants to know if anyone sees the boy who ran out of the church. Cat, you should see the suspect. He's coming right at you."

"If what you refer to as 'the suspect' is a slender built adolescent male humanoid sprinting across the church's back parking lot, then yes, I have a visual," said the cat.

"Yethh, that'thh him! Stop him!"

"Cow, the adolescent male humanoid is over ten times my mass. How am I supposed to, as you say, 'stop him'?"

"Just get in his way and slow him down," said the pig, "so I can catch him before he reaches the cornfield."

I galloped around the corner of the church as the cat sprinted out of the cornfield and under the Old West style wood fence that marked the edge of the church property. She scampered into Nick's path. He weaved to avoid her, but she kept getting in his way. I winced and briefly stopped my pursuit when, without breaking stride, he kicked the cat into the cornfield.

"Cat, are you ok?" I asked as I raced across the gravel parking lot.

"I am surprisingly unharmed."

"I got him," said the chicken as she broke into her hyperspeed. Her blur whizzed past me and straight at Nick. Her image briefly appeared when she slowed down to peck at the young man's face. He flailed his hands in the air as if swatting a swarm of gnats. The blur of the chicken swooped around his arms, delivering pecking blow after blow.

"Duct tape him," I said.

The blur dissolved into the chicken. "Did you say something?" she asked, perched on top of Nick's baseball hat.

"DUCT TAPE HIM!" I said.

Nick, whose face resembled someone who had lost a knife fight, wiped away blood with one hand as he reached for the chicken with the other.

The chicken hopped to avoid Nick's reach and fluttered to the ground. "Well, I didn't bring any duct tape. I'm working on new attack methods."

Nick glared at the chicken, showing no signs of surprise that a hyperspeeding chicken had attacked him or that said chicken spoke in a screechy alien language. He raised his foot to chicken stomping height.

She hopped from side to side, casually avoiding Nick's Converse high-top. "That duct tape bit was getting old, don't you think?"

"No, it wasn't getting old. I loved the duct tape attack."

"Thank you. I'm glad you like it. Now I wish I had brought a roll."

I couldn't believe the chicken didn't bring her primary weapon on our test mission. I should have spotted this and corrected it earlier. This would be another red mark on our performance evaluation. *No time to worry about it now.* "Forget about it. Go back to what you were doing."

"Sure thing, boss." But before she jumped back into hyperspeed, Nick swooped down and grabbed her by the neck. He spun around and tossed the chicken into the cornfield in a manner akin to the track and field hammer throw.

The cat and chicken's efforts slowed the suspect. I was only a few gallops away from pouncing on him. The pig approached from the opposite direction, running as fast as a waddling goose on his tiny hind legs. Dr. Hash Browns' experiments turned the pig's forehooves into karate-clench hooves, a virtual equivalent of hands, which forced him to walk on his hind legs. As he shuffled toward me, I remembered how glad the rest of us were when he started wearing pants.

Nick glared at me and then at the pig. He shifted into a boxer's pose. "Bring it on, you mutant freaks."

We closed in on him from either side.

I readied myself for a final gallop.

The pig jumped.

I lowered my head.

Nick calmly took a step backward.

The pig and I both tried our best to pivot and change directions. Hooves and gravel don't mix. Rocks and dust sprayed into the air as we skidded into a collision. The pig's forehooves pushed off my chest, sending the two of us tumbling in opposite directions. Thankfully, we didn't wear body cameras, so there would be no video record of us slamming into each other for Agent Orange to critique in the post mission meeting.

The boy chuckled. "Later, losers." He hopped the waist-high wood fence and disappeared into the tall corn of the neighboring farm.

"Cow, you idiot. I had him dead to rights."

He didn't. *I* had him dead to rights. But I didn't get the chance to argue my point. The low rumblings of an enormous engine vibrated my chest, diverting my attention. I surveyed the farmland. Several hundred yards into the field, the largest piece of farm equipment I had ever seen chewed a path in the corn.

"Cow! I'm hearing a lot of static on the line, but it's not that ear-piercing chatter you call Cheddarian," said Agent Orange. "What's your status?"

"We have visual on the suspect and are in pursuit, thhir."

"Visual is not good enough. I need to hear 'we have the assailant apprehended.'"

"Yethh, thhir."

"I'm on it, sir." The pig sprung back to his hind legs and restarted his chase. "Assuming no further interventions by the other animals, I'll have him in a couple of seconds."

I groaned and shot a glare at the pig, which he never saw. I resumed my pursuit, determined to make this a team win and not a showcase for the pig. In Cheddarian, I said, "Rabbit. Duck. He's heading into the cornfield behind the church toward your position. Do you copy?"

There was no response.

"Rabbit! Duck! Report!"

Still no response.

"I've got him in my sights," said the fish. "He's coming right at me." The fish's assertion that he had him did not fill me with confidence. Dr. Hash Browns engineered the fish with the ability to swim through the air and solid objects, the same as ordinary fish swim through water. Unfortunately, this power provided no help in apprehending a fleeing suspect. The fish hovered in the air directly in the boy's path. I could only surmise the fish planned to use his other power: hypnotism. I groaned at the thought. Seventy-five percent of the time, the fish hypnotized himself instead of his target.

The roar of the farm machinery grew louder as it lumbered in our direction.

The pig and I entered the rows of corn. We weaved through the stalks, scanning for the boy.

The pig pointed with a forehoof. "There he is. Don't get in my way this time."

Nick looked back at us as he ran. He never saw the fish.

The fish hovered firm and passed straight through the boy's head.

Nick wiped his face and shook off the sensation of running through a cobweb. I knew the experience well.

"Yeah, I don't have him," said the fish.

"Rabbit! Duck! Where are you?"

Still no response. *Perhaps they couldn't hear me over the increasing engine roar. I hope they're not in its path.*

"I've, I've...I've got him," said the dog, who is usually afraid of everything from beady-eyed stuffed animals to moldy cheese. He sprang out of the corn stalks to my right and tackled Nick. The two tumbled, snapping cornstalks. They wrestled and rolled, creating a tiny crop circle. Nick grabbed the dog by the throat and tossed him off.

The pig and I fought through the depths of the corn forest as the cat and chicken effortlessly weaved between the stalks.

Nick and the dog scrambled to their feet.

Despite my height advantage, I could no longer see the farm machinery, but the engine chugged louder, like a slow approaching train.

Nick squatted in the classic wrestler's pose.

The engine roar drowned out the dog's growls.

The pair rotated slowly in the patch of fallen corn.

Nick faked a couple of hand moves.

The dog lunged for Nick's ankle. His fangs dug into the boy, who screamed as he tried to fling the dog off. The dog continued to growl as he flopped from side to side until he lost his grip and tumbled into the corn. He sprang right back to his paws.

By this time, the rest of us caught up. The pig, cat, chicken, dog, and I formed a circle around the boy. We had him. And we'd done it as a team. "We have him surrounded, thhir."

"Cow, I can't understand you. Too much interference," said Agent Orange.

We could ignore the blaring engine no longer.

"It's a combine! Run!" said the pig in Cheddarian as he grabbed the cat and the dog.

We scrambled and dove out of the way, except Nick. He stood there motionless, staring at the giant combine. As the gigantic rotating blades of death made their final approach, he raised his arms to the sky and tilted his head back as if in prayer.

I turned my head, which, for a cow, is not an effective method to look away. So, I closed my eyes. I expected to hear the hideous snapping of bones and be splattered with the blood and guts of the teenage boy. I braced for gasps from my barnyard friends and a blood-curdling scream from the young man.

None of that happened.

"Did you see that?" said the chicken.

"What?" I asked as I opened my eyes, expecting a gruesome sight of mangled body parts tumbling in the spinning blades, but the blades were clean.

"That black blur," said the chicken.

"I witnessed no black blur, but did observe the human adolescent male's disappearance in the fraction of a second before his dismemberment by the combine would have occurred," said the cat.

"Where did he go?" I looked around the cornfield for pieces of Nick.

"Excellent question. His whereabouts are unknown," said the cat.

"Nobody else saw that blur?" asked the chicken. But before we could answer, she blasted into hyperspeed, only to arrive back in less than a second. "Nobody saw that?"

"No," I replied.

The chicken took off again.

Inside the cabin of the combine, the rabbit and duck hopped and flapped around, smacking buttons and turning knobs, but the blades kept spinning and the combine kept moving. Their only accomplishment was turning the radio on full blast to a Christian radio station.

"Idiots." The pig grabbed the backend of the combine and lifted the massive tractor off the ground.

I wished he had used his superstrength before the spinning blades of death reached the boy. Then maybe he wouldn't have disappeared.

The pig tipped the combine. The rabbit and duck rolled out like dice from a cup. He set the running combine down and climbed in. After he whacked a couple buttons and spun a couple of knobs with his karate-clench forehooves, the giant blades of death slowed to a stop. He stomped on the pedals and pulled a lever. The enormous farm equipment jerked to a halt. Only the soothing melody of Bill Gaither's

'Because He Lives' remained, which the pig quickly silenced.

The pig jumped down. "Are you two complete morons? What were you thinking? Why'd you take a joy ride in the middle of a mission?"

"Dude, we just saved the day," said the duck as he brushed himself off.

"We spotted this runaway tractor coming toward us and took action, man," said the rabbit.

"And we were about to get it stopped before you dumped us out. Not cool, dude," said the duck.

"Yeah, man. Not cool."

"Morons. You were not even close to turning it off. And you made us lose our suspect," said the pig.

The blur of the chicken streamed back toward us. She stopped right in front of me and rocked back and forth like the cartoon Road Runner. "No sign of the suspect in the cornfields, sir."

"Great. We lost him," I said.

"Yes, we have, but I don't understand how that is great. Considering this is our training mission, I don't think the loss of the suspect will give us good grades."

"Chicken, you do remember the definition of sarcasm?" said the fish as he swam up to her.

"Yes, I remember, but it's very confusing."

"I used sarcasm to express my irritation," I said.

"Why didn't you yell and cuss? Lots of people do that when they're irritated. It's much easier to understand," said the chicken.

BLAM!!

A shotgun blast ended the conversation, for which I was thankful. The other animals and I scrambled toward the church.

"Cow! Was that a gunshot I heard?" asked Agent Orange in my earpiece.

"Yethh, thhir." The tinier animals led the way, weaving through the rows of corn with the fish and duck skimming the corn tassel. I galloped behind them with the trotting pig in the rear.

BLAM!!

"DUCK!" I yelled, serving the dual purpose of getting the duck's attention and getting him to duck into the cover of the corn.

"Who's shooting?" asked Agent Orange.

"I don't know, thhir."

"It's the farmer," said the pig in English.

"Great," said Agent Orange. "Just what we needed. Did you at least get the boy?"

"No, thhir. We lost him."

"WHAT?"

"He disappeared, thhir. Vanished right in front of our eyes."

Agent Orange went silent while we broke out of the corn, hopped the short fence, and scrambled across the back parking lot. Human agents rushed past us and entered the corn.

I surmised Agent Orange had put us on mute while he unleashed a steady stream of expletives. Finally, he spoke. "Cow, get your team to the truck. We will discuss your failures later."

"Sir," said the pig in English, "you'll have my full report by evening."

Agent Orange hadn't asked me to provide a report. *Did he have the pig spying on us?* The pig had grown increasingly critical of our performance over the last month. His report would sink our hopes of becoming agents. I closed my eyes and took a deep breath of the country air.

Agent Orange thanked the pig before doling out other orders. "Periwinkle, control the farmer situation. Take Agents Eggshell and White with you. The rest of you, we have a suspect on the loose. Our suspect's name is Mr. Nicholas La Conn. You know the drill. Let's get those checkpoints set."

With my eyes back open, I began the walk of shame. As we approached our truck, I rationalized this might be for the best. We weren't cut out to be secret agents. Best to leave the dangerous work to humans.

3: The Waiting Game

FOR THE NEXT THREE days, my stomachs churned as I relived every second of the mission and every mistake we made. I should have prepared the team better. If we could get one more chance, we would catch the boy. Our mission grades would be bad, but why hadn't we heard a single word from Agent Orange yet? I wished he'd just fail us and ship us off to the safety of a secluded farm. That would be for the best, anyway.

A year had passed since Dr. Hash Browns' company canceled his project and threw us out with the trash as failed experiments. We fought back, found our way to Earth, and saved the planet's cow population from the company's thieving corporate executive. Our heroics caught the attention of GIBOD, and they asked us to join their agency. After decades of being cooped up in Dr. Hash Browns' lab, the others couldn't wait to join. Except the pig, who insisted joining would be a death sentence for us all.

"Within a matter of minutes, we will all end up on autopsy tables next to the Area 51 space aliens." That's what he said then. Now, he loves the secret agent life and the humans more than any of us.

My eyes burned, and I wished for hands to rub them. The same paragraph of Warren Bennis's *On Becoming a Leader* stared at me. I had read it a dozen times but hadn't comprehended a word. After slamming the book closed with my tongue, I stared at my cowbell. Though not the original bell bestowed upon me, it still symbolized the honor of once being the bell cow. My farmer saw leadership potential in me when I was but a calf. I became the youngest heifer in herd history to wear the bell. As soon as I strapped it around my neck, the herd trusted me to lead them to the barn for milking and out to the fields for grazing. *Why was I concerned about my leadership skills? I didn't need books to teach me how to become a better leader. I was born to lead.*

My stomachs churned at a milder rate as I strolled out of my office with renewed confidence and my head held high. I surveyed the shared living space of what we call the BarnYard Heroes Academy. In reality, I walked into the large open area in the center of the barn where the agency housed their "special" animals. They insisted we keep a low profile. We weren't supposed to refer to ourselves as the BarnYard Heroes or call the barn the BarnYard Heroes Academy.

Despite our renovations, the barn maintained its rustic motif, especially the open space. The wood framing remained unfinished, and we hadn't replaced the dirt floor. Our renovations focused on the private living spaces. On the second floor, the wheels of the rabbit and duck's skateboards raced through their obstacle course. Dust rained down on me. I have only seen photos of their makeshift course. It's impossible for me to climb the rickety ladder and fit through the small opening to the second floor.

The main floor housed six stalls and an office. We claimed the stalls as our bedrooms, while the cat converted the office into a computer lab. I missed the office. It gave the barn and our team some class and a sense of professionalism. So, I turned my stall into an office. Plus, I loved the antique metal desk and office chair that had been in the old barn office and didn't want to see them trashed.

I strolled past the stalls. The cat's room was directly across from mine, with the fish's next to hers. The cat spent the majority of her time in her computer lab, working on the translator, but retreated to her stall for her frequent power naps. A cat tree large enough for a party of eight dominated her space, with a couple of blankets and cat beds scattered about. The agency originally installed an automated litter box, which she found demeaning and disgusting. She demanded they remove it.

The fish made no changes to his stall. He didn't see the point of having furniture he couldn't sit or sleep on. He wasn't in his stall, because I'd sent him to spy on Agent Orange to learn anything he could about our mission review.

The chicken's stall came next, with the dog's across from hers. They converted the chicken's space into an art studio/board-game room and used the dog's room for relaxing and sleeping. The cat had summoned the pair to the computer lab, where she continued to bark orders at them.

Home gym equipment took up most of the pig's stall, which sat between my stall and the dog's. I sneered at the dust accumulating on the equipment he hadn't used in months. He preferred doing his workouts in the agency's weight room. I assumed he did this to show off his super strength in front of the humans, whom he now spent most of his free time with. In fact, we hadn't seen him since the raid on the church. My cheeks burned, remembering he provided a report to Agent Orange on our training mission performance. I hadn't seen it. All he told me was he didn't candy-coat the truth. But I'm sure he gave himself high marks.

I walked away from his stall and stood in front of my office, thus completing my loop past the empty stalls.

"Hello."

The sudden appearance of the fish triggered a stationary gallop flinch. "Geez! Where'd you come from?"

"Sorry." He dropped his chin down. "I swam through the walls. I forget that can startle folks."

"It'thh okay. Thho, what did you learn?"

Before the fish answered, the rabbit and duck bounced down from the second floor and rushed toward us.

"Dude, you're back. What's the news?" asked the duck.

"Yeah, when are we becoming agents, man?" asked the rabbit.

Our miserable performance outside the church failed to curb the rabbit's and duck's excitement. As soon as we got back to the barn, they put on tailored tiny black suits they'd ordered from the internet and still had them on three days later. Somehow, they believed we deserved excellent ratings on the mission and insisted that the two of them saved the day.

"Well, they just completed a senior-level meeting," said the fish.

"Was Agent Orange there, man?"

"I said senior-level, so yes, Agent Orange, the *director* of GIBOD, was there." The fish prepared to say something else, but didn't get the chance.

"Dude, was Agent Orange's creepy manservant there?"

"What?" The fish snapped his squinty eyed head back. "Agent Orange does not have a manservant."

"Sure, he does, man. That grandpa that's always following him around." The rabbit pantomimed an old man walking with a cane.

"That's not his manservant, and he doesn't walk with a cane. That's Agent Periwinkle. And yes, he was at the meeting, because he's a senior agent."

"Emphasis on the senior, if you know what I mean, dude."

"Was the pig's girlfriend there, man?"

"The pig has a girlfriend?" I asked.

"Yeah, man. That's why he doesn't hang around the barn anymore."

"He's busy making googly eyes with Agent Lavender, dude."

"I cannot confirm her romantic involvement with the pig, but I can confirm she was at the meeting," said the fish.

"The pig wasn't at the meeting, was he?" I worried he had been promoted to our leader.

"He wasn't."

"Dude, stop keeping us in suspense and tell us what happened."

The fish opened his mouth, but before he could speak, the rabbit asked, "They were talking about us, weren't they?"

The fish narrowed his lips. "Well, I'd love to tell you all about it, but I couldn't understand a word they were saying. When is the cat going to get that translator contraption working?"

When we'd first arrived on Earth, Hector Spector, a human scientist and eccentric cow enthusiast, kidnapped me along with over forty regular cows. He experimented on us in his underground mad-scientist lab, hoping to accomplish his life's goal of talking to cows. He created a contraption that had zero effect on regular cows, but somehow meshed with my enhancements, instantly allowing me to understand English. The cat had spent the past year attempting to adapt Hector's device into a universal translator that would download English into the rest of us animals. The agency even dragged Hector in to assist, but he couldn't fix it.

I looked at the computer lab, as the blur of the chicken zoomed out, circled past us, and zipped back to the lab in less than a quarter second, leaving behind a dust cloud trail. I stomped over to the lab. This did not look to be translator related work.

The others flew, hopped, and swam into the office. I poked my head through the doorway. Three rows of tables piled high with computers filled the room, leaving no space for me.

"Cat! What are you doing?" I asked.

She sat on top of a second-row table tinkering with electronic equipment. "Testing my hyperspeed detector." She never took her eyes off her work.

"Thho, not working on the translator," I said.

"Affirmative." The cat typed commands into a computer, turned a few dials on what looked like an old stereo receiver, tapped a button on a handheld device and said, "Go." The white blur of the chicken blasted past me and circled the open center space of the barn in a fraction of a second. After the chicken reappeared in front of her, the cat shook her head and let out a quiet sigh as she glared at her laptop.

"We don't need you playing gamethh with the chicken. We need you to get that translator working."

"First of all, as I am sure you are well aware, my progress on the translator is, and has been, blocked for the past week due to the fact this agency's IT department is incapable or unwilling to fulfill a simple request for a basic cloud computing environment."

"What are you talking about?" I asked.

"I copied you on all of my email inquiries to this most incompetent of organizations."

"We have email?" I asked.

The cat sighed, rolled her eyes, and continued to scroll through some computer log files. "Yes, we have email. Something our IT department has managed to not screw up, *yet*. Now, to address your other statement; I do not play games. For your information, I am working on a solution to find our lost suspect, which is infinitely more productive than sulking over our poor performance at the church raid, which is all you've done for the past three days."

"I haven't been sulking. I've been... Okay, maybe a bit." I'd hoped the others hadn't noticed.

The cat finished scrolling through the log files, entered a couple of commands, and said, "Go."

The chicken hypersped through the barn.

"Thhorry, but what are you doing?"

"Moments before the disappearance of the suspect, known as Nick La Conn, multiple sources reported an anomaly." She adjusted the dials and typed another command into the computer.

"By multiple sources, you mean the chicken and the fish?" I asked.

"Affirmative. The anomaly these two described resembled the white streak observed by those of us in standard time mode, witnessing the chicken travel at her time-shifted hyperspeed." The cat smacked the stereo-like machine and tapped the handheld device. "Go!"

Once again, the chicken zipped around the barn.

The duck's eyes rolled into the back of his head. "But, dude, the streak was black, not white."

"Naturally. My theory is that another creature possesses the same time-shifting hyperspeed ability Dr. Hash Browns engineered into the chicken. I surmise this other creature to be primarily black, making the anomaly black instead of white."

"I guess that makes sense, but what are you building, man?" asked the rabbit.

"As I mentioned previously, I'm creating a hyperspeed detector. I suspect this is not the first time this creature has time-shifted into hyperspeed. More importantly, nor will it be the last. Once I get this device functioning, we will be able to track the creature's movements. We locate this creature, and it will lead us to our prime suspect, a one Mr. Nicholas La Conn. Go!" The chicken streaked off and reappeared from the opposite direction less than a second later.

"That'thh clever. Nice job."

"Your gratitude and praise are unnecessary," said the cat. "The mental stimulation this project provides me far exceeds any gratification I experience from the accolades of other creatures."

"Fine. It'thh a stupid idea, and you did a lousy job with it."

"Your attempt to irk me with mean-spirited sarcasm has no effect on me." Her grumpy tone suggested otherwise.

I silently chuckled, pleased with myself. "Let'thh get back to discussing the translator. Agent Orange made it clear that we all need to learn English. What can we do to get this translator working that doesn't require IT's help?"

"You know what the pig would say." The fish dropped his voice to baritone levels and rocked his shoulders. "Of course there is. You could all learn English the old-fashioned way, by studying, like I did."

"You know, I remember every sound and word the humans say," said the chicken. "But this English language is messed up." The cat said go, and the chicken sped through the barn, returning so fast she continued talking without a pause. "I think I figure out what a word means, then I hear that same word again, and it can't possibly mean what I thought it meant. It's like the same word has two different meanings."

"They do that a lot. In fact, I'd say most words in the English language have multiple meanings," I said.

"That's crazy. Why would they do such a thing?" asked the chicken.

"If you think that'thh crazy, there are also homonyms like there, they're and their."

"Dude, you just said the same word three times in a row. What are you trying to do? Summon a demon?"

"It'thh three different words. They're spelled different and have different meanings, but sound the same."

"Humans have no concept of how to design a proper language," said the chicken. "There is no way I'll learn English on my own. Their language is impossible. It's like they're making it up as they go."

The duck turned toward the cat with open wings. "Dude, you've got to get the translator working. A big dump of the language into my brain is the only way I'll speak English."

"Chicken, you can take a rest. I have enough data at this time," said the cat, scrolling through a series of graphs on her computer.

The south doors clanked open with authority. The pig marched into the barn with his front hooves folded behind him, back straight, and chest puffed out. He'd swapped his gym shorts for the black shorts and gray T-shirt worn by the human recruits.

The duck flew to greet the pig. "Dude, what can you tell us?"

The rabbit hopped in the air as he asked, "Our sources say your girlfriend was at some big important meeting. Did she tell you anything?"

"Did she tell you when we're becoming agents, dude?"

"Guys, for the umpteenth time, she is not my girlfriend." The pig's pink face turned darker as he power-walked past the pair.

"You sure spend a lot of time with her, dude. Are you sure she's not your girlfriend?"

"She sure acts like your girlfriend, man."

"I'm not doing this with you two again." The pig's cheeks had gone full rosy by the time he approached me. His stern expression and mini eye-roll hinted that anger caused the flushness, but I believed embarrassment was the reason. "Cow, get everybody assembled. Agent Orange is on his way."

4: And the Envelope Says...

Agent Orange's bodyguards, Agents White and Eggshell, slid the double barn doors open for him and his second-in-command, Agent Periwinkle. I'd seen and talked with Agent Periwinkle on numerous occasions and simply considered him an experienced agent. But as he shuffled behind his boss, the words of the rabbit and duck ran through my head. His black shoes scraped the dirt floor with every short stride he took. A noticeable limp suggested a hip replacement to be well overdue, and I wondered how he managed without a cane. His hair appeared grayer and his face more wrinkled. For the first time, I pictured him in the role of Batman's butler, Alfred.

"Attention. Director in the room," said Agent Eggshell.

The pig snapped to attention in the center of the barn. The rabbit and duck stopped mimicking their old-man-with-a-cane walk, then scrambled to line up next to the pig. With a huff, the cat sauntered into her customary regal sitting position, a safe distance from the rabbit and duck, who purposely bumped into each other.

Agent Orange stomped to a halt in front of our in-progress line construction. He closed his eyes and squeezed the bridge of his nose with the index finger and thumb of his right hand. He opened them with a groan.

The dog and chicken fidgeted from side-to-side, and back and forth, increasing the jaggedness of our ill-formed formation. As I took my position at the start of the line, the fish swam through my head. I shook off the sensation of having a cobweb dragged across my brain and cleared my throat with an authoritarian tone. The others paid no attention. The wiggling and pushing continued.

Agent Periwinkle shuffled up next to Agent Orange. His perpetual frown curved further down as he eyed our row.

The pig growled and shouted, "ATTENTION!!"

The dog and chicken stopped fidgeting, the rabbit and duck ceased roughhousing and the fish settled into position. I scanned our ranks. Of course, the pig demonstrated the perfect legs together, forelegs at his side, chest out, head held upright posture, while the rest of us either slouched or straightened into uncomfortably stiff statue poses.

Agent Orange ran his eyes down the lineup. His angry squint increased along the way, and he ended with a quick eye-roll. "At ease."

The pig took a precise step to his right and folded his front hooves behind him. The rest of us wiggled into slightly less uncomfortable positions.

Agent Orange took a deep breath before saying, "The raid on the church was not just a key component of your training. It was an important mission for this agency. I cannot begin to describe my disappointment in the outcome; in particular, your failure to apprehend the suspect, Nicholas La Conn."

"Cow, what's he saying?" asked the fish.

Agent Orange groaned and gave me the stink eye. "When will you have the translator fixed?"

"IT has the cat blocked, thhir. We could use your help to escalate her equipment request."

"I don't want to hear about that right now." Agent Orange paced toward me. "Just paraphrase what I said. Tell them they all stink and wrecked an important mission."

"He thhaid we ruined a very important mission," I said in Cheddarian.

"Why was, why was the mission so important?"

"Dog, I don't know. He didn't thhay."

"And, and, there's something that's been, that's been bugging me. What's the deal with the, with the Havarti Travel Bureau?"

"Dog, thithh is not the time. You had three days to ask me that."

"Cow, are we ready to continue?"

I heard Agent Orange but couldn't see him. I turned my head and there he was, his face inches from my snout. Agent Orange used invasion of personal space as intimidation, but he failed to understand that in my case, he entered my blind spot. This ruined the intimidation factor and bordered on comical.

"Yethh, thhir."

"Okay, here's the deal. When you all joined the agency, I envisioned an elite team of super beings. A team with amazing superpowers that couldn't fail. I was a fool." Agent Orange had walked away from me and paced in front of our irregular line.

The others looked at me, waiting for the translation. "He said we're an elite fighting force."

"The dude's got that right." The duck gave the rabbit a webbed foot to paw fist bump.

"That's not what he said," grumbled the pig out of the corner of his mouth.

Agent Orange stopped us with a hand gesture. "No more translating. Fill them in when I've finished." He paused for a deep breath. "Your collective performance at the church proved you are far from invincible and far from a team. I have concluded I cannot keep your team together.

I have assigned a majority of you animals to manual labor or desk jobs. If, and I'm not promising anything, but if we deem it necessary to call upon one of your special talents, we may individually call on you to join a mission. Agent White will provide your assignments. Do you have any questions?"

"Thho, does this mean we're agents?"

He backed up and shot a glance at Agent Periwinkle, who shrugged his shoulder. Through puzzled squinted eyes, Agent Orange muttered, "Well..., technically, yes."

"We're agents!" I said in Cheddarian.

Except for the pig, the others pumped wings, paws, and fins into the air.

The rabbit and duck did a chest bump.

"We did it, dude!!"

"Time to pop the champagne and spark up the stogies, man."

"Dude, do we get to pick our agent color names now?"

With a furrowed brow, Agent Orange took a step back and examined our celebration. "I think I've given you the wrong impression."

The pig broke out of his at-ease pose and stormed up to me. In English, he said, "You're not telling the full truth!" He turned to Agent Orange. "Sir, I don't think you meant to say all of us have become agents. What about the rabbit and duck?"

Agent Orange gave a nod to the pig. "Right. Thank you." His forehead relaxed as he addressed me. "I need to clarify. Not all of you have become agents. Not the rabbit and duck. The rabbit and duck will never become agents of GIBOD."

"What? Why?"

Agent Orange snapped his head back. "You ask why?" His furrowed brow returned, but this time with narrowed eyes. He took a step toward me. "Were you not paying attention during the church raid? They left their post, nearly killed the rest of you, and single-handedly led to the loss of the suspect. And then there's their training record. They failed every test, every evaluation, and every exercise. Yet, you ask why they are not becoming agents?"

The rabbit poked my ankle. "Are you asking about our color names, man?"

I shooed him away with my hoof. "Thhir, you will find nobody more excited and dedicated to becoming agents than the rabbit and duck. Sure, they've made mistakes, but no one tries harder than those two."

Agent Orange backed away. "Enthusiasm alone does not make an agent."

The pig waddled into the vacated space. "Cow, why do you keep covering for them?" he said in English. "They're a menace. They just about killed us all."

I turned my head so I could glare at him with a single eye. "You knew this already? I bet you lobbied to make sure they didn't become agents."

"This is for the best, and you know it. If we take those misfits out on another mission, they *will* get somebody killed."

"You're not denying it. You lobbied for this."

The others stopped their celebrations. With quizzical expressions, they gathered around the pig and me. They didn't understand our words, but they recognized the tone.

"They sealed their fate on our mission."

My jaw tightened as I scuffed my forehoof in the dirt and contemplated clobbering the pig. Dr. Hash Browns taught me to count to ten in moments like this. I got to two, then glimpsed Agent Orange and Agent Periwinkle heading for the door. I bumped the pig aside and caught up to them. "Thhir, you said you gave the rest of us desk jobs. Isn't there a desk job you can assign to them? That'thh not dangerous."

Agent Orange stopped at the open barn doors. "Cow, what kind of desk job could they do? They don't have hands. They don't understand English. They can't type. They don't sit still. Give it up."

I blurted out their one skill he could not dispute. "They're excellent pilots."

"Any aircraft small enough for them to pilot already fly themselves. We call them drones. Heck, even our larger planes practically fly themselves nowadays. We have no need for pilots anymore." He and Agent Periwinkle exited the barn.

Agents White and Eggshell remained by the doors.

"The director has left the building," said Agent Eggshell.

Without hesitation, I rushed out of the barn. I needed answers about what to say to the rabbit and duck. "Wait! What are they supposed to do?"

"I told you." Agent Orange did not turn or slow his pace. "Agent White has your assignments."

I rushed in front of him and Agent Periwinkle, forcing them to stop. "I mean the rabbit and duck."

"They don't have assignments. Why are you struggling with this concept? Those two are a menace. They will not be agents."

I flared my nostrils at him. "That'thh my point. If they don't have orders, what are they supposed to do? Where are they supposed to go? What am I supposed to tell them?"

"I don't care. Tell them they're free to do as they please." He tried to sidestep past me.

I slid my behind around to block his escape. "You can't just kick them out into the streets. They have no place to go."

"I don't have time for this. I'm too busy cleaning up the mess you made." Agent Orange shoved my butt out of his way.

Agent Periwinkle grabbed his boss's arm.

Fire brewed in Agent Orange's eyes, as his gaze slowly rose from Agent Periwinkle's grabby hand to his cloudy old man eyes.

"Sir, she brings up a good point. We can't let those two loose on society. We've seen how that goes. Remember how they almost wiped out Maple Park?"

"Those two tell a different story. They claim they fixed the tornado siren just in time to save the town."

"That's not what the video showed," snapped Agent Orange. "Stop defending them like they're your children."

"My point, thhir, is that it would be best if they stayed in the barn, where we can keep a close watch on them."

Agent Orange groaned and crossed his arms. "Fine. The rabbit and duck can stay in the barn, but we're not paying for any more modifications to their obstacle course or their skate park thing."

"Yethh, thhir. Thank you, thhir." I stepped out of their way and trotted back toward the barn, happy the rabbit and duck would continue staying with us, but worried about how they would take the news about not becoming agents.

Agents White and Eggshell still stood by the barn entrance, as if they were guarding it. Agent White attempted to hand me a stack of manila envelopes.

I reached to grab them with my mouth, but the agent pulled them away. "You're slobbering."

"I don't have hands. This is how I grab things."

"How about we email them to you?" said Agent Eggshell.

"Give them to me," said the pig as he walked up and snatched the folder from Agent White with his karate-clench hooves. Agents White and Eggshell ceremoniously clicked their heels, spun, and left the barn.

The pig read off the assignments one by one. I heard the words, but none of it registered. My thoughts focused on how to break the news to the rabbit and duck in a compassionate manner, that added a positive spin.

Once the pig finished, the room went silent.

The rabbit and duck exchanged glances.

"Dude, what about us?"

"Yeah, man, what's our assignment?"

The question registered. I had run out of time. I needed to tell them.

The pig scoffed and chuckled.

I cleared my throat and prepared to deliver the news in a straightforward yet compassionate manner.

"You both failed basic training, failed the entrance exams, and nearly got us all killed on our training mission. Neither of you became agents, nor will you ever become agents."

Of course, that wasn't me speaking. The pig delivered the news.

The rabbit's mouth and the duck's bill hung open, as their heads, in unison, slowly turned from the pig to me.

"You said we were agents, dude."

"We all celebrated. What gives, man?"

"Sorry. I misunderstood Agent Orange'thh initial statement. But even though you're not agents, you can stay here in the barn. Which is nice."

Their mouths closed, but their bottom lip and bill quivered. Their eyes watered and reddened.

"Is what the pig said true?" asked the rabbit.

"We'll never become agents?" asked the duck.

Neither used their customary man or dude.

"I know that'thh what the director said, but I don't believe it. I'm sure if you continue to work hard, they'll give you another chance at the tests."

The rabbit loosened his black tie. "But we worked so hard."

The duck used his bill to remove his black suit coat and whipped it to the floor. "We saved the people of that town. We're superheroes. This agency should be honored to have us in their ranks."

The pig gave the pair a sideways stare. "That's not what the video shows."

The rabbit wiped away his tears and stepped up to the pig. "The video shows us fixing that emergency siren speaker."

"What I see in the video is you two numbskulls trashing that speaker. And then there's our mission. What were you two idiots thinking when you took that combine for a joyride?"

The duck waddled up to the pig. Fire raged in his beady eyes. "The combine started by itself."

"Lucky thing we were there to take action to stop it."

"But you didn't stop it." The pig pointed a hoof at his own chest. "*I* stopped it."

"We slowed it down." The rabbit removed his tie and let it drop to the floor as he walked away from the pig.

"Pig! Take it easy on them." I should have stopped the tactless pig the moment he opened his mouth. "This is a tough moment for them."

The pig's stern eyes and tight face softened a bit. "Look, I'm sorry about how this played out, but we're just trying to keep everyone safe. GIBOD field work can be dangerous. We've seen how our special powers don't always save us."

It annoyed me that the pig might be right, and his show of genuine compassion surprised me. But none of that mattered. I focused on his use of *we*. "Thho you admit it. You were part of the decision to ban the rabbit and duck from the agency!"

"They asked for my input, and I provided it, but Agent Orange made the decision."

The rabbit spun, hopped twice, and lunged at the pig. "You betrayed us!!!"

The duck flew behind him. "And you knew all along we wouldn't be agents and you didn't tell us!"

The pig casually sidestepped their attack. As the pair rolled across the dirt floor, the pig said, "I know you're both angry, but I believe this is in your best interest."

"We're a team. They can't split up the team and cast two of uthh away like yesterday'thh stale bagels. I will not stand for this. I thhay we all quit.

We don't need this agency. We'll be fine on our own. Who'thh with me? Who'thh ready to start a new chapter in our lives?"

The pig raised an eyebrow. "What's your plan? Open a bar?"

The dog looked up from his assignment papers. "I, I kind of, I kind of agree with the pig. Secret agent work is, is dangerous. And, and they..., they offered me a job. I, um, I get to dig post holes. I'm, I'm great at digging holes, so, I'm, I'm kind of looking forward to that."

"They have me delivering the mail," said the chicken as she flipped through the pages from her folder. "I bet I can break records with how fast I can deliver the mail. Plus, it says if they ever need my superspeed, I'll get to go on a mission. That's exciting."

"I, I..., I hope they don't, don't send you on any dangerous missions."

"They want me to inspect the interior walls, looking for water leaks," said the fish, as he flopped around on top of his folder, trying to flip a page. In what resembled a poltergeist manifestation, he sprawled the papers across the floor. He darted down. His tail wiggled as he hovered above the documents. "And I might go on missions as well. They might need me to do reconnaissance assignments, like checking out a building before they attack." He glanced at me, his eyes gleaming. "I can do that."

"But we're a team. We can't split up." I needed an ally. "Cat, surely you think we should stay together as a team?"

She fiddled with a handheld device. "Can't you see I'm busy?"

"We're discussing whether we should stay or leave the agency. I would like to hear your opinion."

"Cow, where do you propose we go?"

"Perhaps a quiet farm in the country?"

"Will we have high-speed internet? And let me be clear, high-speed means 10-Gig minimum." She still hadn't looked up from her device.

"I'm sure we can arrange something," I said, having no idea if it was possible.

"Your tone lacked conviction and confidence. I will remain here."

"Is no one else ready to make a stand?" I stomped my front hoofs, creating a mini dust cloud.

The rabbit and duck trudged over their discarded tie and black suit to hug my leg.

"It's okay." The watery shine had disappeared from the rabbit's eyes. "At least we get to stay in the barn."

"And that means we stay together," said the duck.

"Plus, if we leave now, we'll never become agents," said the rabbit, as he removed his jacket.

I appreciated the sentiment of their words, even if they still did not use their patented 'dude' and 'man'.

The pair's dragging feet left lines in the dirt as they trudged for the loft ladder with their heads down and shoulders slouched, leaving a trail of their disrobed black suits along the way.

The pig's eyes shifted from animal to animal. "I have an announcement."

The rabbit and duck stopped their procession to the ladder and turned to listen.

"Despite my initial reservations about this agency, I now believe I have found my home. This is where I belong. They offered me a position as a field agent. I will no longer be staying in the barn. I'll be moving into the human barracks."

My pulse spiked. My cheeks flared. A vein in my forehead throbbed. "How convenient. You recommended cushy *safe* jobs for the rest of us and suggested kicking the rabbit and duck out of the agency. Meanwhile, you lobbied to get yourself a full-fledged field agency job."

The pig rubbed the back of his neck with a forehoof. "It's not like that. I didn't expect them to offer me a field position."

I circled around him, like a lion toying with his fallen prey. "But you don't deny that you've been working against uthh from the start."

"I'm not working against you. I only have your safety and well-being in mind." He held his karate-clench hooves out palms up, as if praying for me to believe him.

"Fine! Go! Get out of here! Play with your precious humans. See what we care."

With eyes popped wide open, the chicken, dog, rabbit, duck, and fish formed a mini arc a few feet from the pig and me.

The pig's hooves still pleaded for understanding. "Cow, you need to look at the bigger picture. This is all for the best."

I stepped up to him and exhaled a hot breath into his face. "I told you to leave the barn." My teeth mashed and my upper lip quivered.

I feared he'd clobber me. But his face remained placid while he searched for allies among the others. They responded with tightened mouths and narrowed eyes. He pivoted away from me and marched to the door. He paused. "Someday, you'll all realize I'm on your side and still a part of the team."

Once he slid the door closed behind him, I turned with a huff. "I'll be in my office." The others gawked but remained silent and still as I stomped into my office. I shoved my chair out of the way and clomped a couple laps around my desk. The pig had left my assignment papers on the desk. I stopped and read far enough to see they'd given me the title of supervisor when a realization hit me. The assignments were written in Cheddarian. Only one other being besides me could have done that translation. "PIG!!"

"Are, are, you, are you okay?"

I spun to face the chicken, dog, fish, rabbit, and duck, who had assembled outside my stall like a group of carolers. "No. I'm not okay. Were all of your assignments written in Cheddarian?"

The dog backed away while the others stood still, but their heads jerked back and their eyes widened. They nodded yes.

"None of the humans know Cheddarian, so who do you think wrote our orders?"

I needed no verbal confirmation. I saw the realization on their faces.

They scattered as I stormed out of my office. I kicked up dirt as I thumped in circles in the barn's open area.

The fish swam above the dust cloud and hovered in front of me.

I stopped clomping and snarled at him.

"Cow, we all feel a bit betrayed, but I do believe the pig has our best interests in mind. Sure, our dreams of becoming field agents saving the world have suffered a setback, but we're all safe and healthy. We have a roof over our heads. And we have each other. Things could have ended up a lot worse."

Being lectured by the fish poured gasoline on my internal flames of anger. But it reminded me that as their leader, I needed to project calmness in times of high stress, not act like an adult male human whose team just lost because of a bad call by the officials. I took a deep breath to compose myself. "Yethh, at least we're still together," were the only words flowing through my head which portrayed calmness, though I had to bite my lips to prevent myself from adding 'except the pig.' "That'thh what matters. We'll get through this together."

"I apologize for interrupting your personal growth moment, but I require another test of the hyperspeed detector." The cat sauntered into the open space and tapped her handheld device. It hummed like an old refrigerator.

I slid over to get a view of the cat's handheld screen, thankful for any distraction.

The cat toyed with a set of buttons on the side of her device. The hum lessened. "Chicken, please blast into hyperspeed."

The blur of the chicken circled the room. As she came to a halt, the cat's handheld device beeped.

"Perfect. I received a clear signature. Now it's time to cast the net." She tapped the side buttons. The hum crescendoed as she waltzed back to her office. A second after crossing the threshold, her device beeped.

"I have a confirmed anomaly. Calculating coordinates."

"You've detected another hyperspeed already?" I asked, leading the others toward the computer room.

"Precisely. Somewhere in the Southern Hemisphere." The cat tapped and swiped.

"How are you able to detect hyperspeed activity that far away?" the fish asked.

"The agency's satellites and microwave relays cover the globe. Narrowing the anomaly to the country of Bolivia."

"And you have permission to use their equipment?" I asked.

"Last I checked, I'm an agent of GIBOD and I say that gives me permission." The cat nodded toward her assignment file. "Shall I inform Agent Orange of my findings?"

"No. No, I don't think we will." I smiled and held my head high as I backed away. "We found this information, thho I thhay this is our mission. It'thh time to show this agency what we're capable of. Show them we're ready to be full-fledged agents. Let'thh go to Bulgaria, find this Nicholas La Conn, and arrest him ourselves."

"It's Bolivia. Not Bulgaria," said the cat.

"Bolivia. Bulgaria. What'thh the difference?"

"Bolivia and Bulgaria are two different countries. Bolivia is in South America, while Bulgaria is a part of Europe. The official language of Bulgaria is Bulgarian, while Bolivia has multiple official languages, including Spanish, Quechua, Aymara, Guarani–"

My jaw locked and through gritted teeth I said, "Chicken, that'thh enough. I am aware they are two different countries. It was an expression." I loosened my corner mouth muscles and forced my smile to reappear. "My point is we're going to go get this kid, and we will prove to Agent Orange and the pig that we're more than post hole diggers and mailmen. We will prove that we are agents. Who'thh with me?" I did a mini buck of my forehooves and galloped past our stalls to the back door exit.

The rabbit and duck scurried behind me, snatching their discarded clothes along the way.

"I'm in, dude," said the duck as he dusted his jacket off and put it back on.

"Me too, man," said the rabbit as he re-tied his tie.

The chicken hypersped past them and rocked to a stop near the door. "I'm in too. This sounds like fun."

"Chicken, please refrain from hyperspeeding. It contaminates my readings," yelled the cat from her office.

The dog trotted up. "I guess, I'm, I'm in if everyone else is going, but, but Agent Orange isn't gonna to like this."

The fish swam up to join us. "What Agent Orange doesn't know won't hurt him. I'm in."

"Cat, what about you? Are you in?" I asked. "We'll need you and your magic tracking device."

"Cow, your plan, if one can call it a plan, is preposterous. To begin with, what is your proposal for getting to Bolivia?"

"I say we ride the rails, man. Hop from freight train to freight train all the way down to Bolivia."

"Rabbit, that would take months. We're not doing that," I said.

"I got it. We stowaway on a cargo ship, dude."

"Equally bad idea," I said, happy to hear their inane suggestions and thrilled they returned to their overuse of dude and man. "I thhay we commandeer one of the agency'thh planes." I slid the back barn door open, revealing the two planes parked on the base's runway.

"But, I don't, I don't think we have permission to take one of the agency's planes," said the dog.

"Last I checked, we're agents of GIBOD, well, most of uthh, and I say that gives uthh permission. Start packing your supplies. We're going to Bulgaria."

"Bolivia, boss," said the chicken.

"Right. Thank you. Now don't forget to bring your duct tape."

"Sure thing, boss. Should I get the pig?" asked the chicken.

"No! We're not including the pig. He'thh no longer one of uthh. He'thh no longer a BarnYard Hero." I wanted to lead the charge, but I looked at the sunny daytime sky and slid the door close. "We leave at midnight."

5: What's Wrong with These Caterpillars?

AGENT ORANGE WASN'T KIDDING about the planes flying themselves. Once the cat entered the coordinates, the plane did the rest. The others raced through the plane, checking out the stateroom, office, conference room, kitchen, command center, and living space. I could only squeeze into the command center and living space, and after whacking my shins on a coffee table, I headed to the cargo bay. Besides, I wanted some quiet time to contemplate the mess I'd gotten us into.

My clumping echoed off the metal walls as I searched for a spot to lie down. I chose the closest corner, but before I got there, the fish popped through the wall.

"Ah, there you are." The fish swung his head from side to side. "I've been wanting to catch you alone. You do realize that even if we find this hyperspeeding creature, there's no guarantee that boy will be with him."

"Yethh, I am aware." The stupidity of going rogue and stealing an agency plane had already taken me to darker realms. The consequences of failing to apprehend the boy would be severe. Yet the fish bringing up this obvious flaw in the plan gave my stomachs another turn and had me snapping at him.

"Okay. Just making sure. You seemed confident when you told the others."

"Of course I did. They have to believe this will work. Everything is riding on this. We have to catch the boy."

"I have an idea for a plan B."

I didn't process the fish's attempt to help. Images of me and the others shackled to walls in the depths of a dungeon consumed my mind. The rabbit and duck bounced into the cargo bay and the memory of the fish having a plan B disappeared.

"Dude, these robots will give you whatever you want." The duck held a bag of chips under one wing and clutched an energy drink with the other.

The rabbit had a bag of popcorn and, of course, an energy drink. "So, where do y'all think this hyperspeeding creature came from, man?"

"These Earth dudes ain't got technology like that."

"It's got to be extraterrestrial, man."

I hadn't contemplated this prior to convincing everyone to come on this fool-hearted mission, but once airborne, it wrestled with my fear of failure for brain processing time. I'd come to the same conclusion as the rabbit and duck. The creature had to be extraterrestrial or at least extraterrestrially enhanced.

The fish swam over to the rabbit and chicken. His elevated position gave an aura of superiority, as if he spoke from the pulpit. "It's been a year since Mr. Steak&Eggs sold Dr. Hash Browns' equipment and notes, presumably to Dr. Hash Browns' lifelong rival, French Toast. It is conceivable that French Toast has enhanced a creature with this hyperspeed ability by now."

"Dude, that's what we were thinking." Chips billowed out of the duck's mouth as he talked.

I did a quiet sigh. Thankfully, the others didn't notice. I was ten steps behind them all, yet they followed my lead.

The chicken and dog were the next to join us in the cargo bay.

"Hey, where did, where did you get food? And, and drinks?" asked the dog.

"The robot waiters, man."

"They are here to serve, my dude."

"Do they, do they have meals?"

"The robot waiter dude said something about beef, chicken, or fish dinners. But then he mentioned chips."

"And popcorn." The rabbit poured ten pieces into his mouth.

"I'm, I'm literally salivating like, like one of them dogs in that Earthling's experiment with the bell."

The chicken held her wings up. "What's with all of you? Dr. Hash Browns engineered our bodies to reuse our natural energy and survive off solar power. We don't need to eat."

"It's not about *needing* to eat, man."

The duck nodded his bill toward his bag. "Dudes, these sriracha chips are awesome."

The two returned to chomping on their snacks and slurping their drinks.

The fish swam down to their level. "Did they say what type of fish?"

"Dude, you want to eat fish?"

"That's gross, man."

"It's like the cow eatin' a steak, dude." The duck opened his mouth wide and mimed jabbing a wing down his throat.

The fish rolled an eye. "Fish eat other fish. There's limited options in the sea." He licked his lips. "I haven't had fish in a long time. I'm not passing up the chance." He swam through the wall, presumably headed toward the kitchen.

Their inane chatter pushed its way to the forefront of my consciousness. "Why are you all thho obsessed with this plane's food?"

"It's free, dude."

"And all you can eat, man."

"Don't you know GIBOD has a mess hall? You can go *there* and eat all you want." Agents raved about the prime rib special and the all-you-can-eat burger bar. That's how I heard about it. It's also why I decided to never step a hoof in the place. I guess I never told the others about it.

"Dude, we've got a mess hall?"

The jaws of the rabbit and duck dropped as their heads whipped to face each other.

"How did we not know about this, man?"

The dog cocked his head. "What's a, what's a mess hall?"

The fish returned with a frown on his face. "What a disappointment. They serve the tilapia deboned, degutted, and broiled. Disgusting. Humans ruin everything."

"Dude, we need to take you to a sushi bar."

The dog's head snapped toward the fish. "Do they, do they cook the beef?"

"I assume so."

The dog scrunched his lips to the right. "I, I, prefer raw, but cooked will do." He took a step toward the door, then stopped. He whipped his head toward me. His eyes had popped wide, and his mouth hung agape. "I ah, I ah, mean no, no disrespect. It's, it's, it's…"

I stopped the dog before he said anything that made matters worse. "It'thh okay. You're a carnivore. I understand."

The dog bolted toward the kitchen, bumping the cat as he rushed by.

The cat sauntered into the cargo bay, surveyed the crowd, and then assumed her regal position. "I have been monitoring GIBOD communications. They are aware of the stolen airplane and have dispatched a subsequent plane in pursuit of us."

***

THE PLANE MADE A smooth landing, despite using a field of brown grass clumps and scraggly leafless shrubs as a runway. We walked down the descending ramp. Dust kicked up by the plane hung in the air, adding haze to the morning sunrise. The cool air that greeted us did not match the dusty terrain, which lacked trees or even tall shrubs. The absence of cacti made me question whether they classified it as a desert.

"Those are the ancient ruins of Tiwanaku," said the fish, nodding to the west.

Time had reduced this once thriving ancient city of a hundred thousand people to crumbling stone walls and low-standing ruins that outlined where full buildings once stood.

"Talk about your fixer-uppers, dude." The duck waddled down the ramp. I had insisted he and the rabbit remove their suits, so they could blend in as regular animals.

The fish swam up next to the duck. "Actually, the walls and monuments of this ancient city have held up quite well, considering they are at least a thousand years old and built without the use of mortar. It's a testament to the precision cuts of the fitted stones used in the construction."

"I guess that's cool, man, but why do we care about these ruins?"

"The cat'thh device has detected hyperspeed activity in and around those ruins. We find this hyperspeeding creature, we find Nick La Conn. But we need to do this fast. The agency plane tailing us will be here in thirty minutes." This tight window heightened my concerns. I had planned on having days to track down and capture the boy, and even then, I figured the odds were slim. Capturing him in thirty minutes seemed impossible.

This reality had not dawned on the rabbit and duck. They hopped and waddled up to me, their butts wiggling with excitement.

"Let's do this, man."

"Dudes, it's time to prove we're the best agents ever."

"What do we do first, man?"

I turned to the cat. "What'thh the last known location of this hyperspeeding creature?"

"The last hyperspeed anomaly detection occurred in the mountain range north of our current position." She pointed back through the plane which landed facing due north.

"I'm on it. I'll find this creature." The chicken bolted for the mountain, leaving a dust cloud path in her wake.

The rabbit and duck cheered on the chicken as the rest of us meandered around the ramp.

When the dust settled, the duck turned to me. "So, dude, what do *we* do?"

"I guess we start walking toward the mountains." I had no better plan than that.

The others started walking without an argument.

The cat's device beeped a couple of seconds later. "A new hyperspeed activity occurred 2.8 kilometers south."

"Which way, um, which way is south?" asked the dog.

"The opposite direction the chicken went," I said.

We turned and walked south. As we weaved through the brown grass clumps, I became unsettled by how the ground wiggled. I tilted my head down for a closer look. Hundreds of caterpillars wiggled out of the grass clumps.

The chicken zoomed up to us, with a dust cloud trailing her. "I found nothing in the mountains."

"Since your departure, a new hyperspeed anomaly has been detected in the foothills of the small mountain range to the south." The cat silenced her device, which had alerted when the chicken returned.

"Got it." The chicken blasted off again.

The cat's device let out only a short beep before she killed it.

We took a few more paces south before the cat's device beeped again. "A hyperspeed anomaly has been detected in the ancient ruins to the west."

We turned right and headed for the ruins.

We were several hundred yards outside the ruins when the chicken returned. "I found nothing in those mountains, either."

The duck pointed a wing toward Tiwanaku. "Now the dude is in the ancient ghost town."

The chicken rocketed toward the ruins.

Seconds after the cat cleared the alert from the chicken, her hyperspeed detector beeped again. "Hyperspeed anomaly detected in the city of La Paz." The cat turned and pointed behind us.

As we changed directions, the duck kicked at the dirt, launching a half dozen caterpillars along with a cloud of dust. "This is pointless. That dude will be gone long before the chicken gets there."

"And we'll certainly never get there in time to catch him, man."

"Agreed," said the cat. "The city of La Paz is over sixty kilometers away. On foot, it would take us approximately five-point-eight hours to reach this location, assuming no breaks."

The cat preferred the metric system because, in her opinion, it was the most logical form of measurement. She used kilometers instead of miles and invented a universal metric clock and calendar that, as far as I know, only she used. She had a website that explained the insanity. The important thing to know is that one of her hours is equivalent to two-point-four Earth hours, so when she said it would take five-point-eight hours, it actually means it will take almost fourteen hours. Leave it to the cat to complicate something as simple as tracking time.

I let out a muffled snort, partially out of frustration at having to recalculate the cat's time, but mostly because we were running out of time. But something else bothered me as well. "Why are you all assuming the hyperspeeding creature is male?"

The duck preened his wing feathers. "In my defense, I call everybody dude; males, females, asexual beings, single-celled organisms, it doesn't matter. I use dude in a non-gender and non-species-specific fashion. You're all dudes to me."

"The same goes for my use of man, man."

"We lack data to identify a gender, or if the object even has a gender, let alone preferred pronouns. Therefore, I have refrained from specifying the form of the object creating these anomalies or attaching a pronoun," said the cat.

"Never mind. Forget I mentioned it. Besides, we need to speed this up. The agency plane will be here soon. We need a new approach."

The rabbit stopped. "I'm not taking another step until we decide on this new approach, man."

The cat paused and scratched her chin with a paw. "Remaining in a stationary location has merit. The anomaly demonstrates a repeated pattern of returning to locations in and around the ancient ruins of Tiwanaku."

The rabbit scanned the surrounding ground. "I'd sit down, but there's worms everywhere."

"Those aren't worms, dude. They're maggots."

The cat glanced down. "You are both incorrect. Those are caterpillars." Her device beeped again. She deactivated it. "Anomaly detected in the fields to the east."

As if on cue, the chicken returned. We pointed east without saying a word and the chicken took off.

The dog scanned the dusty ground. "Is it, is it just me or are they, are they all crawling toward us?" With his paw, he poked at a wiggling caterpillar.

He had a point. The ground pulsed in all directions.

"Dude, they're so cute." The duck stuck his wing out and let one crawl on.

"And, and another thing. There, there seems to be something, something wrong with these caterpillars."

The duck stared at the caterpillar crawling up his wing. "They look normal to me, dude."

"But, aren't they, aren't they walking funny?"

"Caterpillars don't walk. They slither, man."

"They don't slither. That's snakes, dude. Caterpillars crawl."

"Well, whatever you call it, they're, they're doing it weird." The dog cocked his head as he stared at the caterpillars gathering around him.

"What do you mean, weird?" I asked, though I worried more about how the numbers had increased.

"It's like they're, they're limping."

"That doesn't make sense, man," said the rabbit.

"Dude, the one crawling up my wing looks normal." The duck looked ready to give the caterpillar inching toward his face a kiss. "It's doing the typical caterpillar crawl, pushing its midsection up in the air and then stretching out."

"It'thh not how they move that worries me. Why are there thho many of them?" There couldn't have been that many in the grass clumps, and they had no place to hide in the leafless shrubs. Yet, more and more squirmed toward us. A million or more had us surrounded.

"Well, the, the ones by me aren't moving like normal caterpillars. It's like they're dragging the back half of their bodies. It looks more like a slither than a, than a crawl."

"See, man, they're slithering. Like I said, caterpillars slither."

"Dude, stop it. We've already been over this. Snakes slither. Caterpillars crawl."

The fish swam down to better observe the caterpillars. "The dog may be on to something. A few years back, the US government created a special breed of caterpillars as part of their war on drugs. They bred caterpillars to eat coca plants. The plan was to dump billions of these genetically engineered caterpillars on Bolivia and Columbia and have them eat all the coca plants, thus wiping out the source of cocaine."

"Dude, you've got to be kidding."

"I thought the US government didn't follow through with the plan, but perhaps they did, because this sure looks like an army of coca leaf-eating caterpillars struggling to crawl straight. I think they're all stoned out of their tiny little caterpillar minds." As the fish brought his face close to a caterpillar, it raised its head and lunged at him. The caterpillar fell through the fish's jaw.

"Dude, did that little bugger just try to bite you?" asked the duck.

"That's what it looked like." The fish flinched as the caterpillar lunged and passed through him again.

The dog poked at the caterpillars still limping along in front of him. A pair wiggled and twisted their bodies toward the dog and lunged at his paw. Their tiny little caterpillar mouths latched onto the dog's foot. "Ow! Ow! Get 'em off! Get 'em off!" The dog hopped around, flapping his front paw in a desperate attempt to get the bugs off him. "Dang. These suckers got sharp teeth. Ow!"

"Dude, I don't think caterpillars have teeth."

"YES, they do! Now, get 'em off me. Get 'em off me." The dog spun around in circles, smacking his paw on the ground, but the caterpillars hung on.

We didn't have time for this. I needed to get these caterpillars off the dog, so we could return our focus to finding this creature. "Dog, stand still and stick your foot out. I'll stomp on them."

He stuck out his paw but pulled it away as I stomped my hoof down.

"Dog, keep it steady."

He did, and I came straight down on his paw.

"OW! You idiot. That's the wrong foot. I'll, I'll take care of this myself." The dog raised his paw up to his mouth and bit the caterpillars off. He turned his head and spat the caterpillars into the dirt.

"Save those specimens. I would like to examine them," said the cat.

I figured if she wanted cocaine-crazed caterpillars, she could grab them herself. "We need to move. Get away from these stoned caterpillars."

"Dude, I think you're overreacting." The duck tried to twist his head to peck at his caterpillar. It scurried farther up his neck and plunged its mouth into the duck's neck. "OW! The dog is right. They have teeth!" He swatted at it with a wing. "It's going for the jugular. Dude, it's trying to kill me."

"I'll save you, man." The rabbit jumped on the duck and started yanking on the determined caterpillar with his front paws. With one big yank, the rabbit ripped the bug off his friend. The force of the pull sent the rabbit tumbling head over paws into a patch of brown grass. He emerged covered in orange and black caterpillars, resembling a tiny leopard.

"Ouch," is all he said before he fell flat on his face, disappearing in a billow of dust.

The dog ran up to help the rabbit, but once the dust settled, he stopped and gagged. He stopped short of losing his mid-flight meal. "Call 9-1-1. Call 9-1-1."

The duck scurried over. He reached to pick up his friend but recoiled. "Dude, they're like sucking the life out of you." He wobbled backwards and threw up in the grass.

The chicken reappeared and surveyed the scene. "What did I miss?"

"We're, we're getting attacked by drug-crazed caterpillars," said the dog.

"I'm being eaten alive. Somebody do something, man!" The rabbit sat up, appearing to be covered in orange and black dreadlock extensions. His pupils dilated, then disappeared with his irises into his eye sockets. He groaned like a dying HVAC system, which harmonized with the hum of munching caterpillars.

"I'm on it." The chicken darted toward the rabbit, unphased by the grotesque scene. She hopped around him like popcorn in a hot air popper. Caterpillars and blood flew out in all directions.

I tried to look away, but my near three-hundred-and-sixty-degree vision kept the image in view. My stomachs churned.

The chicken stopped. "This is taking too long."

This reminded me that the agency's plane was only minutes away. "Cat, where'thh the agency plane?"

"The aircraft has begun its descent. The estimated arrival time is 3.6 minutes."

"What'thh that in regular time?"

"Metric time is the closest to regular time in the known universe," said the cat.

"Just tell me in freakin' Earth time!"

"We have a little over five minutes in your precious Earth time before the plane lands."

Meanwhile, the chicken had mummified the rabbit in duct tape. I yelped at the sight of him. "Chicken, what did you do that for?"

"When I pull the duct tape off, the caterpillars will come off with it." But instead of pulling on the duct tape, she whipped her head toward the ruins.

The cat's alarm blared.

"Did you see that? Did anyone see that?" The chicken blasted off toward the ruins before any of us answered.

"Anomaly detected in the ancient ruins of Tiwanaku," said the cat.

"We should follow," said the fish, already swimming toward the ruins.

"Absolutely. This is our chance. Let'thh move out." I took a stride toward Tiwanaku. The cat and dog followed.

The duck staggered away from the grass. "Dudes! What about the rabbit?"

I froze. I stared at the ruins only a short field away. I'm not sure I blinked, but I know my mouth gaped and I'm pretty sure I drooled.

What was I thinking? Why did I lead them into this death trap? And for what? We had no chance of catching this Nick kid before the wrath of Agent Orange descended upon us. Without the kid, we'd never become agents. In fact, this would land the lot of us in the stockade. I had doomed us all. But that wasn't the worst of it.

I closed my mouth and turned my head. Drool may or may not have dropped onto the dusty Bolivian soil.

The rabbit wobbled as his eyes stared aimlessly toward the mountains. "They just keep chewing."

It was my fault he was here, covered in flesh-eating drug-crazed caterpillars. I had to save him.

"I'll help the rabbit. The rest of you race to the ruins and find that kid." I took several deep breaths before approaching the rabbit.

"Dude, I'm not going anywhere." Using his bill and a webbed foot, the duck found the end of the tape and peeled it back.

I shot a glance at the dog, chicken, and fish, who had huddled around the rabbit and duck. "GO!! The two of uthh will take care of this. Get to those ruins!"

They hesitated for a moment, but after a firm furrow of my brow, they sprinted and swam off toward the ruins.

I tapped the ground with a hoof. "Put the end of the tape here."

The duck stretched the tape to where I pointed. I planted a hoof on it. "Now spin him around."

The duck started slow. The first couple of spins pulled duct tape off duct tape, but by the third spin, it started pulling off the caterpillars, along with a considerable amount of fur and a small amount of rabbit skin.

"HOLY MOTHER OF EARTH. OOOOOWWWW! We should have agreed on a safe word. OWWWW! STOP! FOR THE LOVE OF

ALL THAT'S HOLY, STOP!"

The duck halted the rabbit's spinning.

"Why did you stop? Keep spinning me again. And don't stop. No matter what I say."

The duck restarted the spinning.

"OOOOWWWW!!"

After a half dozen spins, the rabbit's screams subsided slightly, and he wobbled.

"He'thh getting dizzy," I said. "We can't let him fall. He'll get covered in caterpillars again."

The duck slowed down, but the rabbit's wobble increased.

I leaned my face into his view. "Rabbit, do what dancers and ice skaters do. Stare at one spot as long as you can and then snap your head all the way around."

"I don't understand, man. All I know is I think I'm gonna be sick."

"Rabbit, look at me. Keep your eyes focused on me." I made rapid swirls with my hoof.

The duck got the message and sped up the duct tape pulling.

"Focus on me. Keep looking at me. Now, whip your head around until you see me again." I repeated this on every spin. The rabbit followed my instructions. He still wobbled, but it didn't get worse.

The duck quickened the pace some more. The rabbit's screams rose several decibels, as did my commands for him to keep his focus on me.

It took two dozen more spins to remove the duct tape. The tape had pulled off caterpillars, fur, and skin. The rabbit looked as though someone sheared him with a weed whacker.

He staggered to his right.

"Duck. Grab him. Don't let him fall."

The duck grabbed him just before he toppled over. The rabbit collapsed in his friend's wings and puked over his shoulder. This triggered a minor chain reaction, as the duck puked, and I gagged.

One remaining caterpillar dangled from the rabbit's ear. He clutched it with a paw and yanked it off.

The shadow of the approaching agency plane rolled over us.

Through snarled lips, the rabbit said, "Let's go get that kid."

6: The Agents are Coming! The Agents are Coming!

With the duck flying above and the rabbit on my back, we raced toward the Tiwanaku ruins. My loping strides left a trail of dust and uprooted grass clumps. I saw no sign of the dog, fish, or cat. Presumably, they had already reached the ruins and hopefully found the chicken, the hyperspeeding black blur, and our primary target, the teenager from the church, Nick La Conn.

As we drew within two football fields of the ruin's outer wall, the reversing jet engines rumbled behind us. I glanced back at the dirt cloud in the wake of the landing agency plane. When the engines quieted, I spotted an additional threat. Security vehicles from the left and right hugged the outer wall. They converged and screeched to a halt. Doors flew open and uniformed personnel in riot gear poured out. The only man in a suit and tie barked out orders. The others scurried into positions behind the dozen SUVs, forming a gauntlet between us and the ruin's outer wall. They cocked their weapons and took aim.

I motioned with my snout and eyes for us to veer off to the left, but as I changed direction, the duck continued to fly straight at the heavily armed police detail. A clearing of my throat finally got his attention, and he followed my path. The officers' aim didn't follow us. They remained fixated on the taxiing agency plane. With time at a premium, I didn't swing us too far over. Several officers glanced in our direction. A couple pointed at us. A discussion ensued. Shoulders shrugged. Then their attention returned to the incoming agency plane.

I jumped the three-foot stone wall marking the start of the ruins. The duck guided us to the main square of the ancient civilization. The doorway to the square framed an ancient statue of a boxy humanoid creature resembling a giant Lego® man. We gravitated toward this ten-foot statue perched in the middle of the square, oblivious to the rest of our surroundings.

"Who's this dude?" asked the duck.

"It's the Ponce Monolith."

The voice of the fish startled me. It also reminded me to scan the surroundings of my newly entered environment. The dog and cat sniffed the edges of the square, which was barren aside from the statue.

"It's believed to represent a race of stone giants that in pan-Andean mythology first populated the Earth," said the fish.

The rabbit hopped off my back and up to the Ponce Monolith statue. In the short jog to the ruins, I had forgotten the recent ordeal. The rabbit's hairless patches and still bleeding scars triggered a gag reflex.

The rabbit carried on, oblivious to his condition. "I bet these stone guys were ancient aliens, man."

The duck smacked his forehead with a wing. "Dude, knock it off with the ancient alien stuff."

"How can you deny the existence of extraterrestrials? You've met some, man."

"Dude, that has nothing to do with it. My point is that show has poisoned your brain. It claims every ancient event and statue on Earth is proof of ancient aliens. It's ridiculous."

"Enough about the statue," I said. "Focus. And remember, when entering an unfamiliar place, survey your surroundings for potential threats. Identify your exits."

After counting the openings in the crumbling twenty-foot walls that formed the square, I wondered why no tourists milled around, examining the tiny faces embedded in the wall. As I approached one of the carved faces, the black blur whizzed by my head, followed closely by the white blur of the chicken. The streaks of black and white circled the ruins before spiraling into the sky.

The duck's bill hung open as he followed the action. "Dude, it's like I'm watching Goku versus Vegeta. We've gotta get a picture of this."

"Personally, I'm thinking Goku versus Frieza, man," said the rabbit. "But agreed. We need a picture. Who's got a camera?"

It did resemble a battle from the rabbit's and duck's all-time favorite show, but the countless Dragon Ball Z fight scenes looked the same to me.

They corkscrewed back down, and the black blur paused momentarily on the top of the Ponce Monolith. I expected the black blur to be a mysterious alien creature or a small mechanical orb. Instead, a run-of-the-mill black crow stood atop the stone monument. Its ordinary nature disappointed me. It calmly removed a strip of duct tape dangling off his tail before the white stream of the chicken plowed into it. Small chunks of the Ponce Monolith's hair or hat or whatever that block on his head represented tumbled to the ground.

The white and black streaks blurred together as they twisted and turned before smacking into the stone wall. A small section of the wall crumbled, but the rest stood strong. I caught a momentary glimpse of the chicken with her wings around the crow's neck before the two blasted off again, spinning into the air like a lopsided firework. The blurs stopped in midair, gifting us another brief image of the chicken battling the crow before the crow rocketed off. The chicken streamed after it.

I did my best to follow the action, as I heard Agent Orange's booming voice via the aid of a megaphone. "No one needs to get hurt. We're here for the animals. Nothing more. Help us collect them and we'll be on our way."

He spoke in Spanish, which, to my surprise, I understood. I granted myself less than a second to contemplate why, which provided enough time to conclude Hector Spector's device must have downloaded Spanish as well as English into my brain.

With the agency at the edge of the ruins, we needed to act fast. I glanced at the others. All of them sat with their heads tilted up, watching the hyperspeed battle. "We need to find that boy! If Agent Orange arrives and we don't have him, we'll never become agents. Thho, stop watching the fight and search for him."

Swiveling heads comprised the extent of their search efforts. No feet, claws, or paws moved.

"He'thh not in the square. We need to search the rest of the ruins."

They had only taken a step or two when the crow and chicken streamed full hyperspeed into the head of the Ponce Monolith statue.

A jagged crack weaved across its neck.

The box-shaped head teetered.

But settled into a slight lean.

Equilibrium had been reached.

But then it slid a smidge. Then another. Then off the neck, crashing to the ground.

The chicken and crow lay motionless atop the now headless statue for the briefest of moments before the battle raged anew.

"Alright. Let'thh get back to searching–"

A gunshot cut my order short and froze us all.

"Now you made me mad."

I had been on the receiving end of Agent Orange's wrath many times. I heaved a sigh. The consequences for the Bolivian security detail would be swift and harsh.

An ear-shattering explosion shook the ground. Pebbles and dust cascaded down the grooves of the stone walls. A side mirror catapulted into the square. After a couple of hops, it wobbled to a stop against the headless Ponce Monolith. Gunfire erupted, followed by a second massive explosion. A hood toppled over the wall and a tire rolled past the square entrance way.

"We surrender. We surrender," chanted the Bolivian security detail in Spanish. Their weapons thudded to the dirt as the sand cloud billowed over the walls.

The short outer wall provided the only remaining obstacle between us and Agent Orange.

I had no time to worry about that. The crow and the chicken raced straight toward me, their tiny faces barely visible at the heads of the black and white blurs. I barrel-rolled out of the way. They shot past me and blasted through a stone wall.

Me and the other animals fought each other in a mad scramble to get through the opening and follow the action. The chicken jumped on the crow's back. The pair twisted and spun like a missile, and smashed a hole in a stone tomb. They blasted back out together, rocketing into the clear skies in a braided pattern of black and white blurs.

The rabbit tapped my ankle. "Look at that, man." He pointed at the tomb.

An endless streak of orange and black poured out and twisted in the air like a gentle stream. The Halloween colors swooped toward us, revealing itself to be a kaleidoscope of butterflies. When it weaved closer, I realized the butterflies had issues. Most had only one good wing and flew forward by bumping into each other. A balance of butterflies with lame right wings versus lame left wings kept the kaleidoscope moving forward instead of in a constant circle.

One butterfly split from the pack, fluttering like a ribbon attached to a fan. In an act of equal parts desperation and luck, it landed on the dog's nose.

He crossed his eyes at it.

We collectively sighed over the cuteness. Someone should have snapped a photo.

Then it bit him. I didn't know it at the time, but that shouldn't have been possible. Butterflies don't have lips or teeth, just long coiled tongues.

The dog growled, shook his head, and swatted it off.

It crash landed, then limped in a circle.

A flashback to the rabbit covered in caterpillars triggered an epiphany. "RUN!!"

Everyone's head twisted toward me. But nobody ran. No one stepped back from the butterflies. That included me.

The butterfly stream dammed up above us.

The duck exchanged glances with the rabbit, then addressed me. "Dude, you okay?"

"NO! Do you know what caterpillars turn into?"

The rabbit and duck cocked their heads.

The dog scratched his ear, then tilted his head up. "They, um, they turn into, into butter, butterflies?"

"YETHH!"

The fish had floated up close to the swarm. He swam back down. "There's something wrong with those butterflies."

The duck scanned the rabbit's patchwork fur and countless scars. His eyes bulged wide. He took a peek at the swarm, which descended upon us like an open umbrella. "Drug crazed butterflies! Dudes! Run for your lives!"

This finally got everyone moving. The others scampered out from under the butterfly dome before it descended to their height. I, on the other hand, had to plow through the kaleidoscope. Dozens latched on. They chomped my ears, face, back, and tail. Ear wiggles, head snaps, and tail flicks failed to shake them off.

I had to wait for the rabbit, duck, and dog to scramble through the hole as butterflies gnawed my leathery hide.

The swarm reformed into a stream and weaved toward us. I poked my head through the hole, then stopped. *Where's the cat?* I pulled my head back and scanned the enclosure. No sign of the cat. The frontrunners of the butterfly stream nipped at my tail. I pushed through the hole and galloped up to the others. I didn't have to yell for help. They saw the butterflies clinging to me and took action. The rabbit and duck stomped on the ones chomping on my back. I dropped my head so the dog could bite the butterflies affixed to my ears and face. The fish pointed out the ones they missed. As they converged on my tail and finished clearing the butterflies, a chorus of guns cocked.

***

IF I'D FOLLOWED MY training, I would have scanned my surroundings as soon as I re-entered the ancient central square. Apparently, the other animals forgot their training as well. I could blame the crazed butterflies munching on my hide or the thousands, perhaps millions, swarming toward us, but it would have taken only a fraction of a second to survey the square and notice it crawling with GIBOD agents.

Agent Orange's snarled upper lip greeted me. He aimed his narrow-eyed glare and his semi-automatic rifle right between my eyes. I expected a Clint Eastwood quote but instead got a Star Trek Admiral Pike line. "Cow, do you have any idea what a pain in the butt you are?"

"Yethh, I do, and I can explain," Thanks to my wide range of vision, I addressed Agent Orange while keeping an eye on the drug-crazed butterflies streaming through the hole in the wall behind me. They dispersed into the square like slow-motion footage of confetti blasted from a cannon. The space cushion between us and the swarm would soon disappear. "But first, we've got to get out of here."

"Sure, because we shouldn't be here in the first place!"

Agents formed a semi-circle around me and Agent Orange, starting with Agent Eggshell, who clutched the cat by the scruff of her neck in one hand and held her device in the other. Though sad about her capture, I was relieved butterflies had not mauled the cat. To Agent Eggshell's right stood Agent Lavender. She restrained the rabbit with an extended arm, keeping his bloodied and mostly hairless body at a safe distance. Next to her, Agent White tugged a leash attached to a collar he had slipped around the dog's neck. Agent Cranberry handed Agent Orange a horse collar, then moved into position along with Agent Coral to complete the semi-circle. The others wrangled and swiped their claws, paws, and wings in failed attempts to free themselves. I admired their fight, but had they not realized how badly we'd lost?

I sighed and told myself to not dwell on the failure and pending consequences. "We'll go peacefully, but we need to go now and put thhome distance between uthh and those butterflies."

When I nodded toward the butterflies, the heads of the agents, including Agent Orange, shifted in unison towards the fluttering mass of orange and black. The butterflies had regrouped and billowed up as a collective to sniff the air, no doubt seeking the scent of blood.

Agents Cranberry and Coral broke from the semi-circle to inspect.

Their departure revealed the pig. He had the duck by the throat. With a snort, the pig stepped forward.

The duck's web feet swayed like the pendulum of a grandfather clock.

Thoughts of warning Agents Cranberry and Coral had disappeared from my consciousness.

The pig fixed his intense stare on me.

I returned the glare, adding a lip snarl.

"Cow, I never took you for a fool, *until* now. Words fail to describe the depths of your stupidity. You even brought the halfwit twins with you? And look, you nearly got the rabbit killed."

The rabbit twisted to face the pig, prompting Agent Lavender to tighten her grip, while extending her arm further out.

"It looks worse than it is, man. And it wasn't her fault."

The duck strained to look up at the pig. "But dude…" Thanks to the pig's grip, the duck could only speak a handful of words at a time. "We're all gonna… look like him… if we don't… run."

I ground my teeth, snorted, and stepped up to the pig. I didn't need a condescending lecture from this traitor. The stupidity of my plan was already quite clear to me.

Agent Orange stepped between us, yet his sneer remained fixed on me. "We'll discuss the levels of your idiocy later." He pushed the pig and me apart, then slid the horse collar around my neck. He tugged the rope tied to the collar. "Let's move out. Back to the planes, everyone."

As the pig and I unlocked our mutual glares, my attention returned to the butterflies. Agents Cranberry and Coral had wandered up to the swarm with their weapons lowered and their heads cocked.

"Get away–"

A beep from the cat's hyperspeed detector interrupted my warning, followed immediately by the chicken and crow crash landing at Agent Orange's feet. He sprang backwards, dropping the rope.

The chicken and crow became visible for a moment before blasting back into the air. As I tilted my head to watch the white and black blur, it occurred to me that the crow was a bigger prize than the boy. If the chicken captured the crow, it would justify our mission.

"What the heck was that?" asked Agent Orange.

"That'thh why we're here. That'thh the black blur."

"The what?"

"The black blur that saved the boy at the church. The chicken is going to capture him."

Agent Orange's mouth hung open as he followed the blurs swooping through the air. "You mean your cockamamie story about how Death snatched our prime suspect away just before he got fileted by the combine?"

"Yethh, except it wasn't Death. It was that crow. It has the same hyperspeed ability as the chicken."

Agent Orange's mouth snapped shut. First, he turned to Agent Eggshell, who held the still beeping hyperspeed detector. "Silence that thing!"

Agent Eggshell had been swiping and tapping to no avail. The cat stretched her back paw and tapped the screen. The beeping stopped.

"Thank you." Agent Orange then whipped his head around to scowl at me. "Let me get this straight. You located a creature with hyperspeeding superpowers and instead of alerting the agency to this threat, you stole an agency plane and flew to South America with your band of misfit mutants to apprehend this creature on your own. What part of this plan sounded like a good idea?"

I'd imagined the conversation going in a different direction, with Agent Orange ordering everyone to help capture the crow. He'd then heap praise upon me for my quick and decisive action. With my hope for redemption crushed, my thoughts shifted to minimizing repercussions for the others. "Sorry, thhir. The entire idiotic plan was my idea. The others just followed my orders. I take full responsibility for this incident."

"You will take full responsibility, but that won't get the rest off the hook." He snatched the rope out of the dirt and yanked me toward the planes.

I stumbled a couple of steps before a blood-curdling scream stopped both of us in our tracks. We turned to see a waterfall of butterflies pouring onto Agent Cranberry. She swiped them off her head and shoulders, but as soon as a spot cleared, new butterflies filled in. Within a couple of seconds, Agent Cranberry disappeared under a pulsating blob of orange and black wings.

Agent Coral fought her own battle. She'd taken a few steps backward as she swatted at the onslaught. When she noticed Agent Cranberry's peril, she pushed through the swarm.

"Agent Coral! Get out of there," yelled Agent Orange.

Several agents took steps toward the troubled pair, but Agent Orange held up his hand and they stopped.

Agent Coral turned her head. A shimmering ball of orange and black had replaced her face. She screamed as she peeled streaks of orange and black off her face.

Two agents, who'd stepped forward to help, slowly backed away, with their eyes bulging and mouths gaping. Another agent puked behind the headless Ponce Monolith.

Agent Cranberry collapsed to the ground.

Butterflies engulfed Agent Coral's hands. She tried to shake them off as an orange and black stream descended upon her.

Agent Bronze stepped forward. "Sir, we've got to help."

Agent Orange shook his head. "It's too late."

Despite a grumbling groan, Agent Bronze didn't take another step.

"I told you we needed to run, but you didn't listen." The conviction in my voice faded during the course of my statement. I had warned them, but then let myself get distracted.

I expected Agent Orange to blame me, which would have been fair. Instead, he asked, "How did you know these butterflies were deadly?"

The fish swam into view above us. "We surmise they metamorphosed from the drug crazed caterpillars, which the US government airdropped into the region to consume the coca plants."

"Watch out for those caterpillars, dude."

"They're the ones who got me, man."

"I'm sorry I asked." Agent Orange's face fumed into a deep red hue.

Instead of running, we stood motionless as Agent Coral screamed and fell to her knees, resembling an autumn colored bush instead of a human being.

With a jab of his finger into my neck, Agent Orange snapped me out of my trance. "Cow, this is on you."

My only surprise was it took him this long to say it. I had no response. Their deaths *were* on my hooves.

An unsettling murmur overtook the fading screams of the two agents, who no longer fought back. I turned my head, but because of my exceptional peripheral vision, the image of fluttering butterflies fighting for feeding positions remained in my line of sight.

Agent Orange handed the rope to Agent Bronze. "Get her and these other idiots back on the plane. Periwinkle, tell anyone still on the planes to grab any fire extinguishers they can find and get to these ruins ASAP. Everyone else, back to the planes."

Agent Bronze tugged at my harness. "Cow, let's go."

I staggered toward the planes, emotionally and physically numb. Then the cat's hyperspeed detector beeped. I dug my hooves into the sandy dirt. "The chicken is still up there fighting the crow. We can't leave without her."

The chicken and crow hung stationary in the sky, but still a blur to the naked eye.

Agent Orange rolled his eyes and his head. "Well, call her in."

I lifted my snout to the sky and yelled, "Chicken! We've got to go!"

Agent Orange grabbed my horse collar and wrenched my neck around so he could examine both ears. "Have you learned nothing? Never go on a mission without communicators."

Add another offence to the list. I shook off this additional failure. I raised up on my hind legs and waved my front hooves. "CHICKEN!!

CHICKEN!!"

This got her attention. She broke out of hyperspeed and hovered above us. The black blur seized the moment and smacked the chicken upside the head. He spun and smacked her on the other side of her head. The crow circled the chicken twice and then kicked her in the gut. The chicken hung in the air in classic cartoon fashion, then plummeted, crash landing next to the Ponce Monolith, but fortunately on the opposite side of the puke. Wasting no time, the crow streaked off toward the mountains. Agents opened fire but failed to hit the fast-moving bird.

The dog ripped the leash out of Agent White's hands and rushed to the chicken's side.

Most agents fled for the planes, including the pig, with a firm grip on the duck's neck, and Agents Lavender and Eggshell, who carried the cat and rabbit.

The bodies of Agents Cranberry and Coral had become engulfed in a dust cloud of butterflies that tumbled toward the statue.

I broke free from Agent Bronze's grip and ran to the aid of the chicken.

Agent Bronze threw his hands in the air and raced for safety.

The approaching wave of flesh-eating butterflies kicked dust into my eyes as I stood over the chicken. She lifted her head only a fraction of an inch and said, "Sorry, boss. I failed. I couldn't get him. He was just too fast."

"It'thh fine. It'thh fine. The important thing is, are you okay?"

She examined herself. A small amount of blood dripped from her beak. She had a swollen left eye, but her wings and skinny chicken legs were unbroken. "I'll survive."

Agent Orange arrived behind us. "Cow, pick up your little friend, and let's get moving."

The butterfly wave had crested and was about to cascade upon us. An early arriver landed on the chicken. Without hesitation, the dog snatched it with his teeth, chomped twice and spat out its remains. He then wound up his tail and unleashed a tailwhip, a power Dr. Hash Browns had enhanced him with. Dr. Browns insisted the dog could bring down a skyscraper with a single tailwhip, but the best I'd ever seen him do was knock someone off their feet. Until that moment. Granted, it was only butterflies. Nevertheless, the dog's tailwhip dispersed the wave, sending the entire kaleidoscope cloud backward.

Agents Orange and Periwinkle jumped in the gap between us and the swarm. They opened fire. Butterfly wings exploded and rained down, but the swarm regrouped. "Pick her up and let's go," said Agent Orange.

I grabbed the chicken in my mouth and tossed her onto the dog's back. As she landed, a small glass vial bounced loose from her right claw. The chicken reached for it with her wings. She tapped it into the air twice before her and the vial toppled to the ground. The chicken scrambled toward her dropped object, but Agent Periwinkle got there first.

"What's this?" he said.

"I'm not sure," said the chicken.

I picked her up and placed her back on the dog.

"The crow had it," she said. "It's empty now, but I saw him pour it on a pile of caterpillars."

Agent Periwinkle stared at the vial. "That's my handwriting. I remember filling out this label. What is it doing here?" He smashed a butterfly that landed on his neck and stuffed the vial into his jacket pocket. "We've got to go."

7: What's the Deal with That Vial?

A TEAM OF AGENTS, which included the pig, corralled me and the other animals into the cargo bay of the plane we'd stolen. We'd come along peacefully, yet the agents maintained firm grips, or kept poking us with their rifles. I kept my distance from the pig, but we still had a couple of angry-eyed exchanges.

Agent Orange directed a band of agents congregated at the bottom of the ramp. "I want every single butterfly and caterpillar in a five-mile radius exterminated. Burn the entire countryside if you need to."

The agents dispersed as Agent Orange stomped up the ramp, followed by Agent Periwinkle. As the cargo door closed, agents released us and vied for the pulled-down seats that lined the walls. After tossing the duck away from him, the pig took a seat next to Agent Lavender.

The other animals and I assembled in the middle of the cargo bay. The pig never looked in our direction.

The duck shook his bill. "It's like the dude doesn't even know us."

His betrayal was complete. I no longer considered him a BarnYard Hero.

The plane started rolling. The dog broke from our pack and jumped on the nearest seat. He grabbed the seatbelt in his mouth and buckled himself in.

I watched Agent Periwinkle whisper to Agent Orange, whose perpetual scowl grew grumpier with every word delivered. When Agent Periwinkle finished, Agent Orange whipped his head toward me. "Cow. Chicken. Dog. You're with Periwinkle and me."

Any hope for a respite prior to facing punishment for my ill-fated rogue mission disappeared. I had proven to be incompetent and reckless. In my final act as team leader, I planned to protect the others. "Thhir, I take full responsibility for this disastrous and criminal act. I accept the consequences of my actions, but plead that you spare the others. They merely followed my orders."

A vein zigzagged across his forehead, like a mountain range on a 3-D map. "Cow. Shut up and tell those two to follow us."

As I did for the rest of our discussion with Agents Orange and Periwinkle, I translated the message to the dog and the chicken.

"But, but, the plane, it's, it's…it's taking off. We need to remain in our seats with our seatbelts buckled, our tray tables up, and our seats in the upright and locked position."

I sighed and briefly closed my eyes. *Had the dog not seen the fire in Agent Orange's eyes? Didn't the dog see Agent Orange's pulsating temple vein? We're in deep trouble and he's worried about tray tables?*

Despite these concerns, I relayed the dog's response to Agent Orange. His eyes locked onto the dog. "If the plane crashes, you'll be just as dead whether you're buckled in or not. Now move it." Agent Orange marched out of the cargo bay with Agent Periwinkle at his heels.

My translation didn't come close to matching Agent Orange's tone, but the dog got the message. He fumbled with his seatbelt. I attempted to push the dog's seatbelt release button, but my hoof was too big. The chicken pecked the button with her beak, and the buckle clicked free.

As the three of us scampered for the cargo bay exit, the chicken asked, "Why is the director so mad? I thought he only hated the rabbit and duck."

"We did withhold valuable information and steal an agency plane to go on an unsanctioned mission," I said, happy *she* had read his body language and tone.

"Well, sure, we, we, we shouldn't have done that, but, but why is he blaming the three of us?" The dog angled his head up at me, paying no attention to where he was going.

"I don't know," I said, "and watch out for the wall." The dog didn't turn his head in time, and smacked into the wall. He acted like nothing had happened, and scurried through the doorway.

"What's he, what's he going to do to us? Will I, I still dig holes? Is he, is he going to kick us out of the barn? Are we going, going to be arrested?"

Good. The dog understood the gravity of our situation. But expressing my darker thoughts regarding our future would send him into panic mode. Time to lie.

"Not sure." He still didn't have his head looking forward. "Watch out. Couch."

The dog missed banging his head into the couch, but slammed his butt into an end table, sending a stack of magazines sprawling. He stopped looking back at me and navigated his way out of the lounge and past the communication station and kitchen. He cowered under me as we caught up to Agent Orange outside the conference room.

I backed up and nudged the dog into the room. I attempted to follow, but only my head fit through the conference room doorway. Agent Orange grunted and pushed me back so he could enter the room.

Agent Periwinkle and the chicken waited for us seated at opposite ends of the oval conference table. The dog paced behind the chicken.

"Cow," said Agent Periwinkle, "make sure no one is in the lounge or kitchen."

I pulled my head out and looked. "No one out there."

"Good. I've got an important question to ask you all," said Agent Periwinkle as I poked my head back in. "Did anyone else see the vial?"

"I don't think thho," I said. "Everyone else was heading to the plane by then."

"Did you tell anyone about it?" asked Agent Orange.

"I didn't."

"What about them?" Agent Orange nodded toward the chicken and then strained his neck.

I looked down to see the dog at my feet. "Should, should we start, start groveling for mercy?"

"No. He just wants to know if we told anyone about the vial," I said in Cheddarian.

"What, what vial?"

"The vial the chicken grabbed from the crow."

"Were we supposed to tell others about it?" asked the chicken.

"No. He'd prefer we hadn't told anyone."

"Oh," said the dog, "is that ah, is that what he's mad about? He thinks we told people about the vial?"

"Why would he be mad if we told someone about that?" asked the chicken.

"He doesn't seem that mad, actually."

The return of his throbbing forehead vein contradicted my assessment. "Cow, what's taking so long? It's a simple yes or no question. Did they or did they not tell anyone else about the vial?"

Blood thumped across my temples. *Had my forehead vein popped to the surface?* In Cheddarian, I asked, "Did you tell anyone about the vial?"

"No," said the chicken. "I had no time to tell anyone."

"I didn't, I didn't tell anyone either. Will that make Agent Orange happy now?"

I turned to Agent Orange without answering the dog. "They didn't tell anyone."

"Good, let's keep it that way. The news of us finding this vial stays with the five of us. Don't mention it to anybody. Not the fish. Not the pig. Not the cat. And for God's sake, don't mention it to the nitwit twins. Got it?"

"Yethh, thhir." I turned to the chicken and dog. "That appeared to make him happier."

"He doesn't, um...he doesn't look happier," said the dog, as he scooched under my legs.

Agent Orange had his usual frown and narrow-eyed stare, but his forehead vein had receded. "He'thh returning to normal grumpy Agent Orange. He wants to make sure we don't tell anyone. Understood?"

"Sure, no problem," said the chicken.

"I don't plan to tell anyone. I mean, I won't bring it up. But, but what, what if someone asks me about it? I'm a terrible liar." The dog had moved so far under me I couldn't see him.

"Just thhay you know nothing about it," I said.

"Okay, I, I can, I can do that. I guess."

"Cow, do they understand?" asked Agent Orange.

"Yethh."

"Good." Agent Orange planted his hands on the armrests, signaling the end of the conversation.

We didn't get yelled at. He hadn't read off a litany of charges. A wave of calm rolled down my throat and pacified my stomachs. With my mind relaxed, questions surfaced. "Thho, why the secrecy? What was in the vial?"

"The vial contained a zombie virus. A caterpillar zombie virus," said Agent Periwinkle.

"That'thh an oddly specific virus."

The forehead vein reappeared as Agent Orange focused his angry eyes on Agent Periwinkle. "It doesn't matter. The important thing is to make sure those two…" He bolted up from his chair. His eyes swept across the room. He pounded his fist on the table. "Get that dog back in the room."

The dog had crawled past my hind legs and toward the kitchen. I gave him a stern glare. "Dog, back in the room."

With his head lowered and his tail between his legs, he slunk back into the room.

After a couple of composing breaths, Agent Orange said, "Tell these two the official explanation is that the US government unleashed millions of genetically altered caterpillars to eat the coca plants. The story is plausible. The state department will deny it, which will convince everyone it's true."

I translated the message to Cheddarian.

As the dog started his, "But, but, but…" I closed my eyes and let the regret of relaying Agent Orange's message flood in. "But isn't that what happened?"

I should have kept my mouth shut. The chicken, the dog, and all the other animals already believed the cocaine-crazed caterpillar story to be the truth. I feared being stuck in an endless circular discussion, hopelessly trying to explain how they should believe what they already believed. I opened my eyes. The dog and the chicken stared at me with their mouths cracked open. "Well, that'thh not what happened, but pretend that'thh what happened."

The dog looked at the chicken, shrugged his shoulders, and said, "I get it. I, I, I just keep believing what I already believe. That's easy."

The chicken curled a corner of her beak. "The dog told me all about the drug-crazed caterpillars. That's the only story I know."

The corners of my mouth curled up. A long, frustrating conversation had magically been averted.

"Cow! Are we good here? They'll stick to the story?" asked Agent Orange.

"Yethh, thhir."

Agent Orange clapped his hands. "Then we're done here."

Instead of leaving, the chicken turned to me. "So, what *was* wrong with those caterpillars and butterflies?"

A fair question, but I should have ignored it or lied. Instead, I told the truth. "They were infected with a zombie virus. That'thh what was in the crow's tube."

A mild whimper came from the dog. His eyes, twice their normal size, darted between the rest of us in the conference room. "Those were...those were, were zombie caterpillars?" The dog looked down at the gauze bandage Agent Lavender wrapped around his caterpillar bites. "A couple of them bit me. I'm infected." He ripped the bandage off and held his paw up to me. "You've got the biggest mouth here. Suck out the blood. Get the poison out of me."

"I'm not sucking your paw. Besides, you're practically healed already. Now stop it."

Agent Orange waited to get past us and out of the conference room. "What's wrong with the dog?"

"The zombie caterpillars bit him. He thinks he'thh infected."

"It's not possible. The virus only affects caterpillars and the butterflies they turn into," said Agent Periwinkle. "He has nothing to worry about."

"Dog, Agent Periwinkle thhays the virus only works on caterpillars and butterflies."

The dog scurried about, sniffing us all. "He's wrong. I'm already turning into a zombie. I crave meat. Raw flesh. A bone to gnaw on."

The chicken rolled her eyes. "Dog, you're a carnivore. You always have those cravings."

The dog snapped his head toward her. "Don't patronize me. You weren't bitten by a caterpillar."

"Correct. But a butterfly bit me."

"That's, that's right. And then I, then I chomped on it to save you.

That thing was in my mouth." The dog spit on the floor. "I've got the zombie virus for sure. I need to throw up." He hunched his back and hacked like a cat coughing up a hairball. "This isn't working. The cat knows how to make herself throw up. I need to talk to her. Forget that. I don't have time. I need to throw up now."

He zipped under me and into the kitchen.

Agent Orange poked my chest. "Get him under control, or we'll need to sedate him." He pushed past and headed for the plane's executive office.

By the time the chicken and I caught up to the dog, he had the robot wait staff cornered. "Bananas and Sprite. Bananas and Sprite. I need it now."

"Sorry, we did not understand your request," said the robot closest to the dog. "Please try again."

"Cow, tell them, tell them what I need. They'll understand you. Bananas and Sprite."

The chicken hypersped around the kitchen. She wobbled to a stop and presented the dog with three bananas and a can of Sprite.

The dog grabbed a banana in his front paws and wiggled it until he dropped it. "I, I, I can't peel this. I need it peeled. Cow, get the robots to do it."

The robot staff computed the situation. They peeled the bananas without me saying a word. They also opened the can of Sprite and poured it into a bowl.

The dog gobbled down two bananas and lapped up the Sprite. "Why isn't this working? Why am I not throwing up? This banana and Sprite thing is a stupid urban legend, isn't it?"

Agent Periwinkle poked his head into the kitchen. "Seriously, the dog has nothing to worry about. The lepidopteran zombie virus has no effect on mammals."

"Enough!" Agent Orange stomped toward us. "Agent Periwinkle. Get a sedative."

Agent Periwinkle departed as Agent Orange arrived and stood guard at the kitchen entrance with his arms crossed.

"Do I look pale? I feel pale." The dog scrambled past the robot waiters to the stainless-steel dishwasher. He cocked his head from side-to-side as he stared at his blurry reflection. "I have icky, white, zombie eyes. Shoot me. Shoot me now before I eat you all." His stammer had disappeared, which only happens when he gets extremely riled.

"Dog, your eyes are fine." The chicken placed a wing on the dog's shoulder.

He brushed off her wing and pointed a paw at his reflection. "No, they're not. Look at them."

"It's a dishwasher, not a mirror. It's a distorted reflection." She pointed with a wing. "See, I have washed-out eyes, too."

"OH, NO!! You're turning into a zombie, too. The rabbit! The caterpillars mauled the rabbit. He's a zombie for sure. He's probably chowing down on everyone in the cargo bay." The dog grabbed the chicken's head with his front paws. "We need to be quarantined. Forget that. Blow up the plane." He turned to me. "They need to blow up the plane. We need to stop the zombie apocalypse."

"This is ridiculous." Without turning his head, Agent Orange yelled down the hallway. "Periwinkle! What's taking so long?"

"Almost ready."

I walked up to the dog. "You're not a zombie. Agent Periwinkle has assured uthh that none of uthh are zombies."

"How can he be sure? We need to do a blood test. Or test my spit. I spit on the floor over there. We can use that sample, or I can spit again."

Agent Periwinkle returned with a long needle.

"Fine. Agent Periwinkle will administer the test now," I told the dog, ecstatic I had a plausible explanation why he was going to stick the dog with a needle.

"Needles. I hate needles." The dog closed his eyes tight and turned his head. He let out a mild whimper when the needle pierced the skin. A second later, the dog collapsed on the kitchen floor.

Agent Orange groaned and shook his head. "I never should have brought you animals into the agency." He poked a finger at my snout. "Cow, when we return to the base, you and the rest of your gang are confined to the barn until further notice. Is that understood?"

"Yethh, thhir."

His tone indicated confinement to the barn, an equivalent to house arrest, to be harsh punishment, but it paled compared to the images I had of us shackled to dungeon walls. I tightened my lips to make sure I didn't smile.

He glared down at the dog and pinched the bridge of his nose, huffed, and stormed off.

The chicken got my attention with a peck of my ankle. "Was that an actual test they gave the dog?"

We watched the robot wait staff lift the dog onto my back.

"No. A sedative."

She scratched her chin with a claw and then shrugged. "Makes sense. Question, though. Why do we need to stick to the story of chemically altered caterpillars running amuck versus zombie caterpillars running amuck? What's the difference?"

"I don't know," I said.

"How do they know what was in the vial?"

"I don't know."

"Is the Havarti Travel Bureau behind the zombie caterpillar virus?" asked the chicken.

"I assume thho." A robot waiter patted me on the butt to signal they had finished draping the dog over my back.

"Why a caterpillar virus? I thought the Havarti Travel Bureau wanted to wipe out humans, so they can take over the planet and turn it into their high-class vacation paradise."

"That'thh a good question," I said, though my concentration focused on backing out of the tiny kitchen without letting the dog slip off my back. "But we should stop talking about this."

"Right, but why is it so important we don't mention this to anyone?"

"I don't know, just stop talking about it." I'd finished backing out of the kitchen. We headed for the cargo bay.

"But there's so many unanswered questions. Can't you ask Agent Orange or Agent Periwinkle?"

"This is not a good time to ask them questions."

"Who can we ask? Should we ask the pig?"

"What part of we're not supposed to talk about this to anyone else, do you not understand?"

The chicken cocked her lower beak to the side. "Fine. But we can talk about the crow, right? He didn't forbid us from that."

"I suppose thho."

But why hadn't he asked about the crow? He never mentioned her. I still held to my assumption the crow was female. *Isn't he curious about how the crow got her superpowers? He didn't yell at us for not telling him about the crow. He didn't ask how we tracked her. He didn't even ream us out for stealing the plane or for me almost getting the rabbit killed. House arrest. Could we get off that easy?*

This train of thought should have put my mind at ease and squelched the fire in my gut. Instead, my breath shortened into hyperventilation, and furnaces blazed in my stomachs.

I eased the dog into a pull-down seat. The chicken fastened his seatbelt, as I retreated to a corner, the best available option for solitude. As I focused on slowing my breathing, the pig approached. I spun around, intending to run away, but I'd worked myself into a corner. I had no escape route.

8: The Interrogation of Grandma Marjorie

As the pig sauntered up, I turned my backside to him. I meant it as a symbolic gesture, but as he approached, I fought the urge to buck him across the cargo bay.

"What did Agent Orange want?"

His perpetual scowl made it difficult to read his demeanor. I assumed him to always be angry. But his eyes didn't have the piercing glare, and his voice, though still gruff, didn't have the bite I expected. He seemed genuinely interested in what Agent Orange had said to us, bordering on being concerned. Plus, he spoke in Cheddarian, which he rarely used since learning English. All of this threw me. In the time it took him to cross the room, I had prepared for an argument, not a discussion. I struggled with how to respond. Plus, Agent Orange ordered us not to talk about it. "Nothing really. He told uthh the crazed butterflies were a byproduct of a US government initiative to spread genetically modified caterpillars across Bolivia to eat the coca plants."

The pig's piercing glare returned. "Humph. Why wouldn't he announce that to everyone?"

"Um, good point." I wanted to add something to cover the lie, but nothing came to me.

"What did he say about that hyperspeeding creature fighting the chicken?"

"Nothing. He didn't talk about the crow," I said, glad to answer a question without worrying about covering for the lie.

The pig wrinkled up one side of his mouth. "Doesn't that strike you as odd?"

"Yethh. Yethh, it does." I instantly regretted my enthusiastic agreement with the pig, the betrayer of our tribe.

"Secrets. It's always secrets with this guy."

My recent encounter with Agent Orange matched the pig's observation, but this time I restrained myself from enthusiastically agreeing.

The pig glanced around. "You may not be happy with me right now, but you need to understand that the safety of you and the other animals has and always will be my top priority. I've been talking with other agents who are not happy with Agent Orange's leadership. They're very concerned with the wall of secrecy that surrounds him. No one understands the purpose of their missions."

"Sure, but isn't that standard operating procedure for a secret agency or any military organization?"

He initially responded with a grunt. I could not decipher whether this meant frustration or agreement. He then leaned in closer and lowered his voice. "The point is, we need to trust each other and stay in close contact. Keep me informed of any suspicious or secret activities he's up to."

The conversation had jumbled my thoughts. At a loss for words, I nodded my agreement, and the pig departed. *Did the pig just offer an olive branch? Are we on speaking terms again? Were we ever not on speaking terms? Am I okay with this? And what is the deal with Agent Orange and the secrecy regarding the vial? Had he already forgiven us for our rogue mission?*

The questions fired all the way back to base. I had no answers for any of them. The cat, dog, fish, rabbit, and duck departed the plane ahead of me. A squadron of agents greeted them and escorted them toward the barn.

When the chicken and I reached the bottom of the ramp, Agent Orange stepped in front of us. "You two are with me." He marched off toward the base's office building. I motioned to the chicken to follow Agent Orange. She shrugged and obeyed.

Agent Orange never glanced back to confirm we'd followed him.

"Where is he taking us? Why just us two? I don't understand?"

I shrugged. The same questions ran through my head, along with images of agents waterboarding the chicken, while they strapped a cage full of rats onto my snout.

When he reached the base's office building, Agent Orange finally looked back. He waited for us before stepping forward to activate the automatic door. We headed straight for the elevator. Agent Orange took a position by the control panel, shuffling closer to it as I turned my head, twisted my torso, and squeezed myself in. Agent Orange pushed his back into my butt until he had enough room to pull his hand up and work the buttons.

The panel had way more buttons than a two-story building needed. Agent Orange pressed the one labeled B8, the meaning of which didn't dawn on me until we started moving down. The B stood for basement. *Do they actually have a torture chamber?*

"Thhir, where are we going?" I asked, surprised I hadn't stammered worse than the dog.

His eyes remained fixated on the changing floor number. "An interrogation room."

I managed to take a breath, but my shoulders remained tight. Though better than a dungeon, this still had me concerned. "I don't think that'thh necessary, thhir. We'll tell you everything we did, and everything we know."

"We're not interrogating you." He rubbed his forehead and eyes as he craned his neck to look at me. "It's agency policy to have at least three agency personnel present at all interrogations."

My shoulders relaxed, but my eyes rolled into the top of my eye sockets. "Why uthh? I mean, we're not agents, and I thought we were being disciplined."

He pressed the emergency stop button. The elevator came to a bouncing stop between basement levels six and seven.

The chicken's eyes bulged and zipped between me and Agent Orange. She mouthed, "What's happening?" If any sound came out of her, Agent Orange's stern voice drowned it out.

"Believe me, you and the chicken are not my first choice. Let me make this abundantly clear. You are by no means off the hook. You stole one of our planes. You violated dozens of agency regulations. Worst of all, you brought tweedle dee and tweedle dum with you. They do not go on missions. Your punishment will be swift and severe." He would have pointed a finger at my snout if he could have gotten his arm free.

"Understood, thhir."

"Good." He looked away from me. "*But* things have gotten complicated. The agency has a mole or perhaps multiple moles. Besides Agents Periwinkle, Eggshell, and White, I can't trust anyone."

"But you trust me and the chicken?"

He started the arduous process of turning back around by digging an elbow into my ribs. "I trust that you and the chicken didn't steal the zombie virus vials from the agency vault."

Consistent with the past couple of hours, the answer spawned more questions. "What zombie virus vials?"

He reached the buttons and restarted the elevator. "The vial your chicken took from that superpower crow."

"Right. That makes sense." I felt a bit embarrassed I hadn't figured that out, but a bigger and more intriguing question occupied my consciousness. "Why does the agency have zombie viruses stored in their vault in the first place?"

"It's our evidence fault. We confiscated them from the Havarti Travel Bureau. They had dozens of animal types, from salamander to elephant to whale. We put an end to whatever their evil plan was back then, but now several of the caterpillar zombie virus vials, along with vials of the chipmunk, swallow, and rhino zombie viruses are missing."

"Why do they want to spread a bunch of animal zombie viruses?"

"That's what I intend to find out in our interrogation, along with who the traitors are." The elevator dinged and Agent Orange stumbled out as soon as the doors opened wide enough.

****

THE HALLWAYS OF THE basement-level eight reminded me of the hospital corridors in the pirated medical TV dramas Dr. Hash Browns loved to watch. But the heavy metal doors, with a single mid-level flap opening wide enough to slide a tray, indicated the rooms housed occupants against their will.

Agent Orange marched away from the elevator at a brisk pace, once again trusting we would follow, which we did.

As we walked side-by-side, several steps behind Agent Orange, the chicken looked up. "I didn't interrupt your discussion in the elevator in fear of angering Agent Orange. But where are we going?"

I told her we would be a part of an interrogation to discover traitors in the agency. I stopped myself from mentioning the stolen vials of zombie virus, assuming this would lead to questions I didn't want to answer or had no answer to.

"So, who are we interrogating?"

Good question. I trotted up to Agent Orange and asked.

"The old woman from the church. The one with the laser gun." He stopped. We'd reached our destination. He motioned for me to enter the interrogation room.

I squeezed inside, knocking over the room's two chairs while sending the rectangular army surplus metal table screeching into the wall opposite the two-way mirror. I stood with my snout smashed in the corner, scraping against the cinder-block walls, trying to stay out of the way, while occupying a third of the room's free space. "Thhorry."

Agent Orange huffed and picked up the fallen furniture, as the chicken bounced from a chair to the table, before squatting on top of a filing cabinet tucked in a corner.

I took a tiny step away from the corner, as flashbacks of the tiny old lady unleashing her reign of horror in the church raced through my brain. "Thho, what do you want the chicken and me to do?"

"Stay out of the way, and keep your mouths shut," said Agent Orange, re-centering the table.

I wanted a better view of the interrogation, so I attempted to turn around. In doing so, I bumped into the table, screeching it across the floor again.

Agent Orange glared at me as he reset the table. "Stay still!"

I locked my legs in place and kept my neck stiff. I didn't even take a breath. But nerves triggered an involuntary tail swish, which banged a chair.

"Argh," he said, adjusting the chair back to the middle of the table.

I pressed my butt against the wall to prevent further swishing.

A distant shuffling of chains snapped Agent Orange's head. He rushed to the door and glanced both ways. "She's almost here." He scurried back to adjust the table and chairs, though neither had moved since his last adjustment.

He glared at me. "Go invisible. I don't want her to see you."

"You know it only lasts a few minutethh?"

"No worries. This shouldn't take long." He poked his head into the hallway.

"And I don't go completely invisible?"

He pulled his head back into the room. No visible vein pulsed across his forehead, but his narrowed eyes and furrowed brow foreshadowed its arrival. "Yes, I'm aware there's still an outline. Don't worry about it. The old woman has cataracts. She won't notice the outline."

"What about the chicken?"

Agent Orange glanced at her standing atop the filing cabinet, staring at the ceiling panels. Her beak rhythmically opened a fraction of an inch. "What is she doing?"

"I believe she'thh counting the dots on the ceiling panels." Counting things was one of her favorite pastimes.

He puffed his cheeks with an exaggerated exhale. The rattling chains grew near.

"Whatever. Go invisible and tell her to stay quiet."

I relayed his order as my invisibility cloak buzzed across my hide. The process completed just as Agent Periwinkle escorted the old woman into the room.

The sight of her didn't retrigger the nightmares of her laser blasting agents into exploding goo. I only saw a lovable grandma, who got mistaken for Betty White on a regular basis, despite Betty's passing.

They'd dressed her in an oversized orange jumpsuit, requiring her sleeves and pant legs to be rolled up multiple times. Jingling chains dangled off her as she shuffled into the room. Ankle-cuffs restricted her movement, but I don't think she would have moved any faster without them. She smiled at Agent Orange, and waved her fingers, the best she could do with her hands cuffed and locked to a harness around her waist. Agent Periwinkle yanked a central chain that served as a leash. He pointed at the chair opposite the mirror.

Her smile flattened as she shot sideways dagger eyes at Agent Periwinkle. "Relax, Bradley. I know where I'm supposed to sit. I'm just old and slow."

Agent Periwinkle grabbed her leather neck collar and directed her into the wooden chair. "My name isn't Bradley. I'm Agent Periwinkle." He unhooked the handcuffs from the waist harness and locked them to the ring in the table's center.

Her smile curled up as she shuffled and wiggled into as comfortable a position as she could. "Periwinkle? Seriously? You went with Periwinkle? I like Bradley much better."

Agent Periwinkle huffed. "Enjoy your visit with Agent Orange," he said, and stormed out of the room.

The old lady shifted her attention to Agent Orange as he pulled out the chair opposite her. I let out an audible grunt when the back of the chair dug into my ribs. He shot me a quick glare before attempting to sit down. After ramming the chair into my ribs a couple more times, he conceded he couldn't create enough room. He slammed the chair back into the table and paced near the door.

"Now, Joey, is this necessary?" With wide cat-begging eyes, she lifted her hands until the chains stopped her. "I'm a 78-year-old woman. You're a trained agent of GIBOD. You can't be worried about me overpowering you." Her open-mouthed smile exposed her top row of teeth, and her pleasant tone gave no hint of a mass murderer. "Besides, you have your big invisible cow bodyguard behind you and that cute little super-fast chicken over there."

She could see my outline, so calling me the invisible cow made sense. But how did she know the chicken had superspeed? Plus, she called Agent Orange and Periwinkle by names I assumed they had before taking their color-themed names. Renouncing their previous life was part of the indoctrination process. It protected their true identity. No one was supposed to know their real names, not even other agents. She knew too much. She had to be working with someone inside the agency.

Agent Orange stretched his neck and straightened his black suit jacket. "We've seen what you're capable of and have taken all necessary precautions. And there is no Joey here. I'm Agent Orange."

"As you wish, Joey, but I wish you'd given me a heads-up about this get-together. I would have baked cookies and brought some grain for your chicken."

The chicken continued to stare at the ceiling tiles, counting dots. No clue she had been mentioned.

Agent Orange snarled and opened a manila folder lying on the table. "I'd wipe that grin off your face, because you're in a lot of trouble. The rap sheet on you goes way back." He casually flipped pages. "Racketeering, bribing a senator, money laundering, drug kingpin. Do I need to go on?"

"I prefer the term drug queenpin." She turned her head and gazed into the distance as if posing for a glamor shot.

"The authorities would love to get their hands on you."

Her head snapped back toward Agent Orange as a sideways smirk replaced her friendly grandma's grin. "You mean you're not the authorities? Then who are you? And what gives you the right to lock me up?" She waved her arms in the air, rattling the chains.

He closed the folder and waved it in the old woman's face. "You know very well who we are, and we have enough evidence to lock you up for good."

She leaned back and attempted to cross her arms, but the chains prevented her. She rested her arms on the table, as if that's what she had planned from the start. "Lock me up for good, Joey. See what I care. I ain't gonna be on this planet much longer, anyway. My time has passed. But even while we speak, I'm securing my grandchildren's futures. So, go ahead. Take your phony trumped-up charges to the so-called authorities."

With his arms folded behind him, he strolled around the table, moving closer to his suspect. "Let me make this clear. You will tell us what we want to know. The only question is, are we doing this the easy way, or the hard way? The choice is up to you." By the time he finished, he'd leaned into her face, with his palms flat on the table.

She returned his glare with a chuckle. "Seriously? You just gave me the 'we can do this the hard way or the easy way' line? Joey, I think you've been watching way too many cop shows. And what's with you jumping right to torture?"

"Enough!" He pounded a fist on the table, causing my shoulders to flinch. "Don't call me Joey again. That's not my name anymore."

Her eyes popped wide. Her eyebrows raised. So did mine, though hidden by my cloak.

"So, you admit Joey used to be your name?" Her eyes narrowed and her eyebrows furrowed as she eased up, placing her palms face down on the table. She met the agent's menacing stare. "We know who you really are. We know who your friends, family, and loved ones are, and where they live. You've put them all in danger."

I expected this to send Agent Orange over the edge, and braced for the table to come flying at me. Instead, he broke away from the stare down and backed up. "Idle threats, old woman. If you truly know who I am, you'd know I have no family or loved ones. Now, we know you're working with the Havarti Travel Bureau. What we want to know is who you're working with inside the agency. They took a few items we'd like back."

"Oh, I'm so scared, Agent Orange. Let me tell you my entire evil plan." She grinned and relaxed as best she could, considering the chains, cuffs, and uncomfortable wooden chair.

Agent Orange backed up to the wall with the two-way mirror. A sinister smirk emerged, one I recognized, and triggered a mild shiver down my neck. "Here's the deal, old woman. You might not care what happens to you, but I bet you care what happens to one of your friends." He flipped a switch, and the mirror changed to a window. In the next room sat a lady in a barber's chair with her arms and legs strapped down. Agent Periwinkle, wearing a surgical mask and latex gloves, sat in a rolling chair behind her.

Grandma Marjorie leaned forward. "Is that Blanche?" Her chair rocked as she flopped backwards, laughing. "It is. You took Blanche prisoner. Did you take the entire knitting club prisoner?"

Agent Orange refused to look at her. A grimace replaced his smirk.

Her chains rattled as she pointed at Agent Orange. "HA! You did. You're dumber than I thought. How are you going to explain arresting and detaining a group of old ladies for ... how many days has it been? Four, five days?" Her chains danced across the tabletop as she waved her hands around with delight. "Their families have to be furious. I can smell the unlawful imprisonment lawsuits from here. There'll be criminal charges. Oh, this is precious. You'll be serving more jail time than me."

Agent Orange snapped his head, and took a step toward her. Again, I braced for flying furniture. "That is none of your concern. Your concern is with your dear friend Blanche and the unnecessary dental procedures Agent Periwinkle is about to perform."

I held back a chuckle as she smiled in the angry man's face. "Now you're going to torture an innocent old lady? Oh my, this is rich. You're a riot, Joey. A riot."

He leaned in with a snarl. "Stop calling me that!"

He pulled himself back and straightened his suit jacket again. After a deep breath and a crack of his neck, he nodded to Agent Periwinkle, who grabbed a dental drill and gave it a couple of menacing pumps. "In all the years you've been on this planet, old woman, have you ever seen someone have their tooth drilled down to the root without novocaine?"

"Can't say I have. This will be a first. But I take it this is an average day for you."

"This is your final warning. Who are you working with?"

She shrugged and looked away from the mirror. "Go ahead. Shred her teeth into pieces. I'll enjoy it. I grew tired of her constant bragging about her children long ago." Her usual cheerful face had disappeared, and her tone turned snarky. "Have you met my sons? William is a high-powered attorney, and Richard is a doctor. And you can't forget about little Susan. She's a United States Congresswoman, don't you know?" Her head dropped. I thought she might spit on the floor. After a mini huff, she raised her head and stared into the adjoining room. "I'm sure she's telling Bradley all about them. Well, let me tell Blanche something; it doesn't matter, because they're all gonna be dead soon." Her happy grandma's smile returned. "Anyway, carry on, dear. Have Bradley drill her teeth off. Are you selling popcorn for the show?" She moved forward in her chair and rested her arms on the table.

Agent Orange's eyes burned with fury. He gave Agent Periwinkle a nod, who fiddled and tested his drill. Agent Orange's eyes narrowed as he gave a sterner nod.

After lowering Blanche's backrest and raising his own chair, Agent Periwinkle glanced at his boss one more time.

Agent Orange didn't nod this time. Instead, he just gave him a glare.

Agent Periwinkle wiped his forehead and pushed up his sleeves before reaching toward Blanche's mouth. He backed off and checked the drill again.

"Get on with it!" Grandma Marjorie's chains rattled on the table as she flailed her arms. She caught Agent Orange's eye. "You want me to go in there? I'd be happy to. I'll drill her teeth off. That should shut her up for a while." She slouched back in her chair.

Agent Orange glared into the other room and threw his hands up. Agent Periwinkle took a deep breath and reached for Blanche's mouth. The drill intensified and reached a hideous high-pitched whir that reminded me of tools Dr. Hash Browns used on us. Blanche's arms and legs yanked and tugged at the restraints. Agent Periwinkle stood to get a better angle. He lowered the whirling drill into the old woman's mouth. A shrieking wail, like that of a colicky child, pierced above the shrill of the dental drill.

The corners of Agent Orange's mouth curled up as he rubbed his palms together.

Grandma Marjorie grimaced and turned her head.

I wanted to avert my eyes, but my extensive peripheral vision continued to soak in the scene. I prepared to close my eyelids when we collectively realized the source of the scream. The baby-with-gas scream came from Agent Periwinkle, not Blanche.

He dropped the still-running drill. It wiggled across the floor like a hissing cobra that had chugged an energy drink. Agent Periwinkle grabbed his drilling hand and lifted it over his head. Blood dripped down his arm as he scoured the room for something to wrap around his wound.

Agent Orange groaned. His victory palm rubbing morphed into clenched fists as he glared into the adjoining room.

Grandma Marjorie laughed and laughed and laughed. If she hadn't been chained to the table, she would have fallen to the floor. "Thank you, Joey. That's the best laugh I've had in years. You and Agent Periwinkle should take this show on the road."

Agent Orange's neck disappeared into his raised shoulders. With his anger fixated on Agent Periwinkle, he stomped into the adjacent room.

Muffled yelling and considerable hand-waving followed.

Grandma Marjorie turned toward me. A serious expression had replaced her kind grandma smile. "Sweetie, you can drop the invisibility trick. Your outline has been showing this whole time." She maintained a caring tone, but it lacked the sweetness she'd used with Agent Orange.

My hide tingled as my cloak phased off. "That'thh about as long as I can hold that cloaking power, anyway."

She leaned back with a smile. "I'm impressed with your English."

"Thank you. It was downloaded into me. I didn't learn it on my own, like the pig. I probably shouldn't be telling you thithh."

"It's okay, sweetie. Who am I going to tell?" She rattled her chains, then curled a single lip. "Bummer about that lisp."

"Yethh, but it'thh a miracle I can talk at all with this enormous tongue of mine. Dr. Hash Browns did the best he could. And again, I should stop talking." I closed my mouth tight and focused on the other room, where Agent Orange shoved Agent Periwinkle into the hallway. He glanced at Blanche, shook his head, and stormed back to the interrogation room.

He slammed the door closed and paced without glancing at us.

Grandma Marjorie politely cleared her throat. "I should have warned you. Blanche is a feisty one. I'd get your boy checked for rabies."

Agent Orange glanced at her, then whipped his head toward me. "Why aren't you invisible?"

"The power only works for so long, thhir."

Agent Orange groaned and whacked the switch that turned the window back into a mirror.

"Give your cow a break. I saw her outline the moment I walked in. Why are her and the chicken here in the first place?"

Agent Orange spun. His brow furrowed. His nostrils flared. His eyes blazed. "Don't tell me how–"

A blaring siren cut him off. His hands sprang to his face. A massage of his temples progressed to scraping his fingers through his hair, untidying his gentleman's cut.

The siren stopped as a public address microphone came to life. After a blow into the microphone, a male voice said, "Intruder alert. Intruder alert. All personnel, be on the lookout for a ... wait, this can't be right. Be on the lookout for a crow? Is this some kind of joke? The crow may appear as a black streak. Okay. That's it. I'm silencing the alarm.

Vantablack, this isn't funny. You're gonna get in serious trouble for submitting a false emergency." The voice continued muttering before the microphone clicked off.

"Now, Joey, you know that ain't no joke. You know very well what that is." She folded her hands together and rested them on the table. She winked at me and stood up, free of her handcuffs, ankle cuffs, harness, and chains. "Well, it's been fun, but I believe my ride has arrived." She checked herself in the mirror. "I'll keep the collar. I like the look."

Agent Orange gaped at Grandma Marjorie, with his hands crushing his skull like a vise. "How did you do that?"

"Joey, you already know the answer to that. I'm working with someone in your agency."

He released the grip on his head.

Grandma Marjorie shuffled toward the door.

He beat her there and slammed the door shut. "Cow, secure the exit!"

I made my move. The table skidded into Grandma Marjorie. A chair spun to the floor. I pinned Agent Orange to the wall as I scrambled to press the door closed with my butt.

She smiled and batted her eyes. "Sweetie, you're fighting on the wrong side. Why do you care about humanity? All they've ever done is butcher your kind." Her lips turned down. She placed a palm on my ribs. "Honey, have you seen how hamburgers are made?"

"All I know, is you're not leaving this room," I said. I saw this as an opportunity to get back into good graces with Agent Orange.

The chicken, still fixated on the ceiling tiles, asked, "What's going on?"

I answered in Cheddarian. "He'thh here."

"Who's here?"

"The crow."

The chicken's head dropped and jerked back and forth, scanning the room. "I don't see him."

"He'thh not in the room. He'thh somewhere on the base."

"Let me at him. I'll find him. I'm getting him this time." She hopped down from the filing cabinet and adjusted her feet into a sprinter's position. "Open the door."

I stretched my snout toward the door handle.

"Stop!" yelled Agent Orange. "What are you doing? Do not open that door."

The chicken blasted into hyperspeed on my first movement, and rocketed into the door.

"Ow." She hung in the air for the briefest of moments, then fell backward, stiff as a two-by-four.

Agent Orange glanced at the chicken, rolled his eyes, and pushed her under the table with a foot. He clapped his hands and turned his attention to Grandma Marjorie. "So, your little friend comes to rescue you. We have the bait, now we just need to spring the trap."

"What trap, thhir?"

"We lure that crow here and trap it in the room."

As if on cue, there came a rapid tapping on the door. For the second time in a week, Agent Orange smiled. His devilish grin, the only kind his face formed, frightened me. "There came a tapping." He slid over to the door. "As of someone gently rapping, rapping at my chamber door. Quoth the raven, 'Nevermore'."

"I think it'thh a crow, thhir, not a raven. And I wouldn't call that a chamber door. And what does quoth mean?"

"It's a poem. Never mind. Just move. I need to open the door."

I moved forward without bumping into anything as Agent Orange flung the door open. The black streak streamed into the room and circled around the ceiling. Agent Orange slammed the door shut and stood guard. "We've got you now, raven."

"Crow, thhir."

The crow rocketed into Agent Orange's gut. He gasped for air as he slammed into the door. A zigzagged pattern of black streaks engulfed him. The familiar sound of pulling tape bounced off the walls.

I spun around, sending the table, chairs and even the filing cabinet sprawling.

Once the furniture settled down, the crow stood on the table with his wings crossed. Behind him, Agent Orange hung duct taped to the door.

I nudged the chicken with my hoof. She staggered to her feet and looked at Agent Orange. "Did I do that?"

"No. It was him." I pointed a hoof at the crow.

The chicken's beady eyes narrowed, as did the crow's. She began a slow circle around the table. The crow followed her every move.

"You stole my patented duct-tape attack." The chicken blasted toward the crow. I tried to keep track of the action as they bounced from wall to wall and from ceiling to floor. They became briefly visible when the crow grabbed the chicken and whipped her across the room. The action mesmerized me, but I should have been monitoring Grandma Marjorie. With eyes on opposite sides of my head, I could have monitored her while watching the fight. Instead, the moan of Agent Orange and the door smashing into the wall alerted me to her escape. I bolted out the door, followed by a streak of black and white.

Grandma Marjorie stopped a few strides down the hall. She stood still. Her lips rolled into a kind grandmother's smile. "Cow, it's not too late to join the winning team."

I positioned myself sideways in the hallway. With my left eye, I watched the crow and chicken drop out of hyperspeed and become visible. The crow pecked at the chicken, who blocked the attacks with her wings. I kept my right eye on Grandma Marjorie. A door opened behind her. Agent Periwinkle appeared, with a mass of paper towels wrapped around his right hand. He gave me a wink and the finger over the mouth 'shh' gesture. He tiptoed up behind the old lady.

Meanwhile, my left eye watched the fight. They landed in the middle of the hallway. The crow nailed the chicken with a right-wing cross to the head. He followed up with a double clawed kick to her gut. The chicken staggered backward. With separation created, the crow blasted into hyperspeed.

With my right eye, I saw Grandma Marjorie give me a cute grandma-style wave.

Agent Periwinkle stood right behind her. As he reached out to grab her, the crow streaked from my left-to-right eye. The stream of blackness sucked up the old woman, streaked down the hallway, and disappeared around the corner.

"No, you don't. You're not getting away this time." The chicken took off after them. Agent Periwinkle and I ran to catch up. We turned the corner to an empty hallway, no sign of the crow, the chicken, or Grandma Marjorie.

Agent Periwinkle sighed and turned to me. "We need to get up top. We need to stop that thing before it leaves the base."

9: Where Have You Gone Grandma Marjorie

I FLATTENED AGENT PERIWINKLE against the back wall as he attempted to reach over me to push the button.

"Relax. I've got it." I pressed the lobby button with my tongue.

Agent Periwinkle yanked his hand back. His head recoiled into a grimace as slobber dripped from the elevator control panel.

As the elevator crawled toward the surface, his right heel jittered, and his eyes bounced from the doors to the illuminating floor number at least three times per floor. When the ding announced we'd reached the lobby, he slid under me and sprinted for the exit, waving for me to join him.

We blasted out the door and staggered into the street. We searched the skies. No black or white streaks. We twirled around, scanning the empty compound streets. Agent Capri strolled out of the warehouse. Agent Periwinkle sprinted toward her, shouting, "Have you seen the crow?"

She tilted her head up and pointed. "I think it's a hawk, sir."

Agent Periwinkle and I glanced up. Sure enough, a hawk circled above the camp.

Agent Periwinkle threw his hands in the air. "NO! The hyperspeeding crow from Bulgaria."

"Bolivia, thhir."

"Whatever. The point is, that creature infiltrated the base. We need to catch it."

Agent Capri's mouth scrunched to her left. "You mean the false alarm was real? We figured it was just some joker scared of his own shadow."

"It wasn't a shadow. We need to get that alarm reactivated." He spun and stormed back to the office building.

I wondered if I should follow him. Then a thought popped into my brain. "Thhir, I'll check if the cat can locate the crow and chicken with her hyperspeed tracker."

He was already at the office building door.

"Thho, I'm heading to the barn."

He charged inside, providing no confirmation that he'd heard me.

Agent Capri shrugged, peeked at the hawk, and then headed for the barracks.

As I made the final turn toward the barn, the public-address system crackled to life. The announcer cleared his throat and said, "Apparently, that wasn't a joke. This crow, which may appear as a stream of black, is a real thing. I understand some of you have already encountered this crow, slash, stream of black thing. Who knew? The point is, the intruder alert is real. I'm reactivating the alarm."

The public-address microphone snapped off with a harsh electronic clunk, thankfully putting an end to the blaring siren.

The dog sat outside the barn entrance, staring into the sky. He appeared not to notice me walk past, but then he followed me into the barn. We closed the doors. The blaring siren dampened. I stretched my neck and soaked in the reduction of noise pollution.

"You can, you can tell them to turn that stupid alarm off," said the dog. "The crow left, he left the compound. So did the chicken." The dog dropped his head. A single tear splashed on the floor. "I've got, I've got a bad feeling about this."

I did too, but smiled, hoping this hid my concern and frustration with the chicken giving chase on her own. A clear violation of agency protocol. "It'll be fine. You know that. You've seen the future."

His eyes narrowed and his jaw tightened. "You're, you're, you're talking about my vision? My visions are garbage. I've seen the same vision since we've gotten here. Rainbow rain. That's what I see. That's my vision of the future. No one knows what that's supposed to mean."

I regretted mentioning the subject. I should have known better. Little could be deciphered from his previous visions, which included wavy greenness and a giant mushroom. The topic had become triggering for him, especially since he'd stagnated on this rainbow vision. I attempted to recover from this misstep. "Seeing a vision of a rainbow has to be a good thing."

"It's, it's, not *a* rainbow. It's rainbow rain. Actually, more like, more like a rainbow hailstorm. Tiny pellets of colored ice pouring out of the sky. And, and there's lightning. It's terrifying."

"Well, that soundthh pretty cool to me. Anyway, no need to worry. The chicken is determined to capture the crow this time. You'll see. She'll be back soon enough with that crow in tow."

"I, I hope so, cause I, I don't like that crow."

"Me either. Now, let'thh have the cat locate where they've hypersped to."

"She's in the computer room. She's been, she's been looking for you."

The cat came out as we approached.

"Cow, I am pleased for your return. I am in need of your assistance in submitting subsequent online requests to a ticket you submitted, on my behalf, to this agency's incompetent IT department."

I had no available brain processing capacity to comprehend cat-speak, but understood enough to identify her comment as irrelevant to our current situation. "Cat, we have bigger problems to solve."

She had turned her back and sauntered to the computer room doorway. "Why the initial request for a basic cloud computing environment took this IT department over 120 days to complete is beyond my comprehension. They claim the environment is finally available, but refuse to provide me with root access, rendering the computing resources useless. But it gets worse."

Enough words registered for me to know she still talked irrelevant nonsense. "Cat, we need to locate the chicken."

"You have to see what this moronic IT department has done." She sat in the doorway and motioned her paw to look inside.

I rolled my eyes and poked my head in. The previously filled tables contained only loose wires, random scraps of paper, and numerous dust-free squares where computers and other electronic devices once sat. The scene left me speechless. I assumed this was punishment for our actions, but the cat clarified.

"Apparently, now that they claim the cloud computing environment is available, albeit useless without root access, they inexplicably determined we no longer required the use of the servers, desktop, and laptop computing systems, so they confiscated said computing devices."

The explanation relieved my concern the agency planned to take away all our possessions. My brain refocused on finding the chicken. "Forget about the stupid computers."

"With no computing resources at my disposal, I am incapable of making progress on the English language translator, which Agent Orange stated is my highest priority."

I ground my teeth while she spoke. We didn't have time for this discussion. "Cat, do you hear the alarmthh? Do you know what it meanthh?"

"Of course. The announcement clearly stated there to be an intruder alert, and identified the perpetrator of the intrusion as the crow. This was not new information to me since my detector had already alerted me to the crow's presence in this compound. Several minutes ago, my device indicated the intruder vacated the premises, thus bringing the crisis to an end, so why the alarm persists to blare on is a mystery to me. I can only surmise the activating and subsequent deactivating of the alarm is under the control of this agency's IT department, and therefore we need to submit multiple online requests to have the alarm deactivated, and pray it gets turned off in less than thirty days."

"Just get that device fired up," I said. "We need to track the crow and chicken."

"So, you are indicating the tracking of the hyperspeed creatures known as the crow and the chicken takes precedence over ensuring the computing environment necessary to complete the English language translator?"

"Yethh, of course it does! Now, go get your device." I let out a snort of disgust. For a creature of her intelligence, her stupidity amazed me.

"As you wish." The cat promenaded into the office, opened a desk drawer, and pulled out her handheld device. She hopped up onto the desk, grabbed a small battery pack, and reinserted it into the device. "You're lucky the IT department didn't confiscate this."

"Why did you take the battery pack out?" I asked while we waited for her device to boot up.

"The constant beeping had become an annoyance." The cat poked and swiped at her now active device.

"Couldn't you just silence it?"

"Of course, but it continued to vibrate, which proved to be only slightly less annoying." She tapped a couple more times. "They are in New York, New York."

"The, the city or the state?" asked the dog.

"If one says New York, followed by another New York, this denotes the City of New York in the state of New York," said the cat.

The duck, along with the rabbit, pulled themselves away from their video game and came down from the loft. A patchwork of bandages covered the rabbit's caterpillar bites.

"Wait, dude, there's two New Yorks? Shouldn't the second one be called New New York?"

"To be clear, there were two simultaneous hyperspeed phase shifts detected in the City of New York. One can deduct from this information that this is the last known location of the two creatures known to have the hyperspeed ability, i.e. the aforementioned crow and chicken."

The dog sat at attention with his tail wagging. "So, we're, we're off to New York, New…We are off to New York city."

"Dude, let's do it. Let's steal a plane again."

"You mean, borrow, man."

The dog joined the rabbit and duck in a wing to two paws high-five.

"We're not doing that again. I'll talk to Agent Oran–… oh no." I galloped to the barn exit. As I clasped the handle with my teeth, the door slid open.

Agent Periwinkle walked in. "Cow, I've been looking all over for you. Doesn't the cat have a device to track that crow thing?"

"Yethh, she does. The crow and the chicken left the compound already. You can tell them to turn off the alarm."

"Good," said Agent Periwinkle. "Not that they're gone. That's not good. I mean, it's good that we can track them. And that we can turn off that stupid alarm." He relayed the message via his communicator and then said to me, "So, where are they?"

"They're in New York."

"New York? The city or the state?" asked Agent Periwinkle.

After a mild shake of my head, I said, "The city."

"Okay. Let's get a crew ready to head to New York." Agent Periwinkle reached up to tap his earpiece but stopped. "By the way, do you know where Agent Orange is? He's not responding on his communicator."

"Yethh." I knew exactly where he was, but I didn't want to say.

"Well, where is he?"

"He'thh, well, he'thh still duct-taped to the door in the interrogation room."

"What? And you left him there?"

"I forgot about him."

"We better move it," said Agent Periwinkle with a vigorous shake of his head. "This is going to be ugly."

10: It's not quite Stonehenge, but at least it's not in danger of being crushed by a dwarf

Agent Periwinkle ordered me and the other animals to stay in the barn while he peeled Agent Orange off the door of the interrogation room. While we waited in the cat's computerless office, the anomaly detector beeped four times. The chicken and crow hypersped from Ottawa to Greenland to the middle of the Atlantic Ocean, but the last detection on the cat's device only detected one anomaly in London.

"What doethh that mean? Only one signal?"

The cat silenced the detector. "It means that there is only one hyperspeed detection in London. I considered my statement to be clear.

Where did you find confusion?"

"Thho, only one of them is in London? Which one? And where'thh the other one?"

"The device detects hyperspeed phase shifts. It is unclear how you expect me or this device to answer your questions, beyond the fact that one of the two creatures known to have the capability of hyperspeed just shifted out of hyperspeed in London."

The dog's head remained down as he scratched the ground with his front paw. "So, why, would... why would the chicken go to London, unless the crow went there? She wouldn't stay in the middle of the Atlantic Ocean if the crow wasn't there anymore. So, what happened to the chicken?" He wiped his eye with his paw.

"The logical conclusion is whoever won the battle between the crow and chicken is the one who headed to London," said the cat.

"But if the, if the chicken won, she would have come back here, not gone to London."

"Very sound reasoning. So, who do you surmise won the battle?" asked the cat.

The dog plumped to the ground and blew the ensuing dust cloud away with a heavy sigh. "The crow... the crow won. Which means the chicken lost, and, and, she's stuck in the middle of the Atlantic Ocean, wherever that is. Or worse." The dog let out another sigh and then popped to his feet. "We can't leave her there. We need to save the chicken. Let's steal another plane."

"Dude, that's what we suggested."

"Let's do it, man."

"Guythh, we won't get away with stealing another plane. I'm surprised we got away with it the first time."

The rabbit and duck winked at the dog, then flew and hopped toward the barn exit.

I stomped a hoof. "I'm serious. We're not stealing another plane."

The rabbit and duck stopped. With heads drooped, they shuffled back toward me.

"Dude, where did this hyperspeeding crow come from, anyway?"

"He's pretty annoying, man."

The cat sat on one of the now empty tables. "Dr. Hash Browns had many rivals, including French Toast. Presumably, one of them obtained the Mambomatic 5000 and Dr. Hash Browns' notes during the fire sale of his laboratory equipment. It is not inconceivable that over the past year they have learned how to operate the equipment, and applied the chicken's hyperspeed enhancement to a crow."

"I, I don't, I don't care where that stupid crow came from. I just, I just want to find the chicken."

"Look, once we explain thithh to Agent Orange, I'm sure he'll send search parties for both the crow and the chicken."

As if on cue, Agent Orange and his entourage of Agents Periwinkle, White, and Eggshell barged into the barn. A strip of duct tape dangled on the back of his jacket, and splotches of sticky residue speckled his suit and tie. "Cow, where are the crow and chicken?"

"One signal stopped in the middle of the Atlantic Ocean. The other is in London."

Agent Orange scratched his chin. "The one who remained in the ocean lost the battle. They are of no importance. We proceed to London. You and the dog are with me." He turned toward the door, then stopped. "And the cat. She's coming, too. And make sure she brings that tracker." He motioned for us to follow as he marched out of the barn.

The rabbit and duck rushed up, hopping to keep up with me as I followed Agent Orange.

"Dude, what about us?"

"We want to help, man."

"Can we join the mission?" they asked in unison.

We caught up to Agent Orange and, against my better judgement, I asked if the rabbit and duck could join the mission.

He sneered at me. "I thought I made it clear. Those two will never go on missions. They stay in the barn."

I relayed a toned-down response. With heads hung low and feet scuffling through the dirt, the rabbit and duck headed back to the barn. Neither of them looked up as the dog and cat passed by.

***

THE DOG AND I stood outside the plane, shoulder to shoulder opposite Agent Orange and his bodyguards, Agents White and Eggshell. Agent Periwinkle had already boarded to prepare for departure. The dog refused to board, insisting on searching for the chicken instead.

"Cow, get the dog under control and on this plane."

I still fumed over Agent Orange's callous disregard for the loser of the hyperspeeding battle and brushed off his scolding. "I agree with him. We should send a second plane to search the Atlantic. It'thh possible the crow was the loser."

"Unlikely. Besides, this is not a democracy. And you are in no position to argue. In the past twenty-four hours, you've broken nearly every agency regulation, including stealing an agency plane. On top of that, you failed to prevent me from getting duct taped to a door and then left me hanging there!" Spit flew as he yelled. He took a deep breath, straightened his duct taped bespeckled suit, and then addressed Agents White and Eggshell. "Put a leash on that dog, drag him onto this plane, and tie him up in the cargo bay."

Although my anger still raged, I knew it was best to stop arguing with the boss. My thoughts shifted to the rabbit and duck sulking alone in the barn. The two always showed great resilience in the face of harsh criticism, but Agent Orange rejected their offer of assistance with extreme cruelty. Their sad walk back to the barn flashed into my brain.

It was the most dejected I had ever seen them. *Would the pig think of comforting them? Was he capable of comforting them?*

Begrudgingly, I boarded the plane, along with the cat. The robot flight attendants summoned us to follow them through the lounge, past the kitchen and conference room, to the door of a small, yet luxurious office near the plane's cockpit. Agent Orange stood in front of a desk, handing a cigar to Agent Periwinkle.

Agents White and Eggshell squeezed past me.

"The dog is on board and secured in the cargo bay," said Agent White.

"Good. We can take off." Agent Periwinkle exited the office.

Agent Orange handed cigars to the other two agents. "You know the rule."

"Of course," said Agent Eggshell, sniffing his stogie. "This isn't our first rodeo."

"We even came up with our own catch phrase," said Agent White. "Catch the bloke and then we smoke."

Agent Orange groaned, then waved us into the room. His unexpected enthusiasm annoyed me.

The cat strolled in, indifferent to all that had transpired.

I remained in the hallway. The narrow doorway prevented me from entering.

"You animals smoke?" asked Agent Orange as the engines roared to life and the plane rolled down the runway.

"No, thhir. Never." I knew little about the human habit of smoking other than it came with health risks. I considered stating these risks, but figured the agents were already aware of them.

"Well, once we complete this mission, you're in for a treat. Keep these puppies someplace safe." He walked over to hand me three cigars.

An anger ulcer sprouted in my third stomach. After the recent hostilities, how could this man, who hadn't exhibited joy in all the time I'd known him, be so gleeful over cigars? Regardless, I reached out to grab the cigars with my mouth.

He pulled them back as his face recoiled. "How about I keep them until the end of the mission?" He stuffed them back into his jacket pocket.

Agent Orange then explained his plan. There wasn't much to it. The dog would chase the crow into the open where Agents White and Eggshell would capture him with fishing nets. The ones which look like giant butterfly nets, not the blanket-like nets commercial fishermen use.

With the plan described, Agent Orange dismissed us.

Heat radiated out of my ears. I found Agent Periwinkle and cornered him in the lounge. "Why can't we send a second crew in search of the chicken? And why'thh the dog leading the attack? He shouldn't even be on this mission. And why do we have such a small crew?"

Agent Periwinkle stepped away from my invasion of his personal space. "I thought you already understood that we have traitors in the agency. This crew represents the entirety of Agent Orange's circle of trust. Mind you, he used the word trust loosely. He's confident you lot didn't steal the vials, but I wouldn't say he trusts your abilities. As for Agents White and Eggshell, he trusts their abilities, but don't tell them anything about the vials. They may be his personal guards and have demonstrated extreme loyalty on numerous occasions, yet he still wants them in the dark about the missing vials. Got it?"

"Yethh, thhir." Defeat dominated my tone. A couple of days prior, I longed to be in Agent Orange's circle of trust and now I felt used and at the whimsy of a tyrant boss.

"Good. Glad we had this talk." Agent Periwinkle grabbed a soft drink and took a seat on a couch. He motioned for me to join him.

I shrugged and remained standing. *How could he not realize couches were not built for cows?*

The cat also shrugged, then jumped onto the couch and curled up to take a nap.

After a few sips of his beverage, he turned to me. "So, what's the deal with the dog and chicken? He's really worked up about her missing. Are they like a couple or something?"

"They are good friends, as most of uthh animals are. I guess they are a little closer than most. They sleep together."

"Okay. That's enough information." Agent Periwinkle held up his palm. "Sorry I asked."

"I don't see what you're making a big deal about. They've got their own room, and they like to sleep together."

"Please stop talking." He popped off the couch and paced toward the kitchen. "I don't need to hear details of their inter-species fornication."

"I was just talking about sleeping. The thought of them having S E X never entered my mind. Until now." With a scrunched mouth, I stared at the floor, flashing through memories of intimacy between the chicken and dog. A hug here. A lick of the face there. A tender rub of cheek to beak.

"Enough. I don't want to hear any more about it."

Consumed with my own thoughts, his words didn't register. "You don't suppose they actually are, do you? I'm not even sure they can. Then again, there's no reason they couldn't. We are all anatomically correct and fully functional. It'thh plausible."

"Cow, I'm begging you to stop."

But I couldn't. The prospect of the chicken and dog being a couple engulfed me. "Maybe they are doing it. Can you imagine?"

"And there it is. Thanks. I'll never get that image out of my head."

"We can't be certain. I mean, it'thh not like dog-headed babies with wings and chicken legs have been popping out of the chicken's eggs. Actually, I don't think she lays eggs."

The cat's tracker beeped.

"Thank goodness." Agent Periwinkle rubbed his eyes.

The cat awoke and examined her device. "Hyperspeed anomaly

detected in Paris, France."

"The creature left London. It'thh in Paris now," I told Agent Periwinkle as the cat sat down at the ship's control panel.

"Paris it is." Agent Periwinkle pointed to the navigation screen. "Type in the new coordinates here."

"She's familiar with the airplane'thh navigational system," I said as the cat entered the new coordinates. The plane made a hasty shift to the right.

While in flight, the tracker beeped several times, detecting new hyperspeed anomalies in Munich, Oslo, Amsterdam, and Edinburgh. The plane made minor, but abrupt course corrections each time the cat entered the new coordinates. As we approached the European continent, the cat's hyperspeed tracker identified activity in Southern Ireland.

As we circled above the coordinates, the cat pointed at the screen display of the landscape below.

"She thhays the hyperspeed detection occurred around that circle of stones."

Agent White tilted his head. "Is that Stonehenge?"

"Stonehenge is in England, you idiot, and a lot more impressive," said Agent Orange. "This is Drombeg Stone Circle."

"Impressive," said Agent Eggshell. "How did you know the name?"

Agent Orange pointed at the bottom of the screen. "Because it says it right there." He backed away, shaking his head. "Everyone, into the cargo bay and prepare for landing."

***

AGENT EGGSHELL UNTIED THE dog's leash. He sniffed with purpose, scampering to the ramp door with his tail wagging. His sniffs intensified as the ramp lowered. and became more frequent until his head snapped toward a small stone circle atop a hill several hundred yards away. The dog leaped through the opening, down the ramp, and bolted into a rolling meadow leading to the hill.

"He's got the scent." Agent Orange eased onto the still lowering ramp. "Let's move out."

With the ramp parallel to the ground, the humans shuffled out. Agents Orange and Periwinkle had their usual black suits on, while Agents White and Eggshell wore full tactical gear. Besides being heavily armed, Agents White and Eggshell carried the fishing nets, which reminded me I was supposed to relay the plan to the dog, which I never did. Since the dog appeared to be executing the plan, I kept this information to myself.

Agents White, Eggshell, and Orange jumped off the ramp and sprinted after the dog, who was a hundred meters into the grassy field, with no sign of slowing down. Agent Periwinkle lumbered to the edge, sat down, and eased himself to the ground. He followed the others, jogging at a pace that kept him from falling farther behind.

The humans had had the luxury of walking out on a near level ramp. It had a sharp decline by the time I put a couple of unsteady hooves on it. I'd never jumped off a still lowering ramp. After a deep breath, I dashed out. My initial burst sent ripples and clanks across the ramp. It wobbled wildly. The ramp didn't lower as fast as I anticipated, so when I attempted a follow-up gallop, my front hooves pounded into the metal well before I expected to encounter a solid surface. My front legs curled down. My head dropped. I would like to say that instinct or training kicked in, and I performed a graceful somersault, sticking the landing like a gold medalist gymnast. But alas, I slammed flat on my back, bounced, twisted, and slid off the ramp. The impact with the ground took my breath away. I scrambled away before the ramp clunked my head. My breathing normalized as I stood up and checked if any agents saw me. Thankfully, they all continued racing forward, without noticing my act of clumsiness.

The ramp jerked to a stop, with the cat patiently sitting on the edge. She sauntered off and passed me. "Smooth move. I hope the plane's security cameras caught it."

I groaned like Marge Simpson. "We better catch up."

We ran faster than the humans, especially Agent Periwinkle, and caught up as they labored up the hill. When we reached the hill's summit, we all crouched behind a row of shrubs.

The dog sniffed each of the sixteen stones that formed a circle the size of a sumo wrestling ring. The stone at twelve o'clock lay on its side, presumably on purpose, so it could serve as a table. From three to four o'clock sat a tiny rock, a fat boulder, and a miniature monolith. Another tiny stone sat in the ten o'clock position. I wondered if they had once stood as tall as the rest of the seven-foot monoliths.

A rustling came from a garage-sized clump of bushes beyond the stone circle.

The dog's ears perked and his head snapped. He scurried behind the 5-o'clock monolith and bowed. His chin rested on his front paws, while his butt and wagging tail stuck up in the air.

Grandma Marjorie pushed between shrubs and waddled for the circle with the crow perched on her shoulder.

Agent's White and Eggshell readied their nets.

The dog stretched his neck to peek around the boulder.

Grandma Marjorie clutched a cloth bag the size of a sack of potatoes with both hands. She reminded me of a farmer heading out to feed chickens, except the bag wiggled with life.

As she and the crow neared the ring, the dog stopped his tail wag, holding it straight up. He pawed the grass with his front claws.

Agent Orange gave a nod. Agents White and Eggshell stayed low as they fanned out behind our hedge. The plan had come together as designed, despite me never telling the dog.

Grandma Marjorie plopped the bag onto the table rock and opened the top.

The crow glanced over his shoulder, hopped down, and then plunged his head into the cloth bag. He reemerged with a rodent in his mouth. He slammed it onto the rock. It squealed. It knew Grandma Marjorie and the crow had evil intentions.

She pulled the bag's strings, sealing the rest of its contents inside.

Agents White and Eggshell positioned themselves at the edges of our hedge row.

The dog crawled forward.

The trap was about to be sprung. I racked my brain trying to remember my role.

The crow pinned the chipmunk to the stone tabletop, as Grandma Marjorie pulled a vial from a coat pocket and placed a drop of its contents in the chipmunk's eye.

The dog sprang out.

Agents White and Eggshell charged, their nets held high.

I rose and watched the action, still wondering if I had a role to play. *Was the cat supposed to be doing something?*

The crow and Grandma Marjorie turned their heads and scanned their attackers.

Grandma Marjorie capped the vial.

The crow released the chipmuck, who scampered into the field.

The dog leaped, ready to pounce on the crow.

After snagging the sack, the crow disappeared in a stream of black.

The cat's hyperspeed detector beeped.

Agents White and Eggshell flailed their nets as the black stream whizzed by and zipped down the field.

Meanwhile, Grandma Marjorie smiled as she watched the dog skid across the stone tabletop and tumble across the grass.

The dog scrambled to his feet. He shifted his head from side to side faster than a spectator watching a robotic ping-pong match. Then he picked up the crow's scent and circled the ring of stones, sniffing the ground before ending at Grandma Marjorie's feet. The dog circled her and the boulder table four times, alternating between searching the sky and sniffing the ground.

The cat and I joined the agents in fanning out around the stone circle. We inched toward the old woman. Agents White and Eggshell had abandoned their nets, as all the human agents had drawn weapons.

"Aren't you the cutest little puppy?" Grandma Marjorie bent down to pet the dog. He snarled and snapped at her hand, then returned to his search. "A bit of a feisty one, I see." Her side-eyed glance at me revealed enough of a twinkle to make my heart skip a beat.

"DOG!! Get away from her!"

He didn't listen to me. He snarled and sniffed her feet again.

She gave us her patented grandma smile, then bent over and snagged the dog around the neck with one arm while pulling a laser gun out of her sweater pocket with the other. "Drop the weapons, boys, or I blow the dog's head off." The dog wiggled and squirmed, but could not break free from the old woman's amazingly firm grip.

"Drop the dog, you old hag, and hand over the vial of zombie virus," said Agent Orange, as he and the other agents inched closer, their weapons still aimed at Grandma Marjorie.

11: Standoff at Poor-man's Stonehenge

Grandma Marjorie stood in the middle of the Drombeg Stone Circle clutching the dog, her tiny, yet powerful, laser gun pressed against his head. "Unless you cooperate, I *will* shoot your dog."

I wrestled with the juxtaposition of the ruthless evil lurking inside this sweet Betty White figure.

She glanced over her shoulder and watched Agents White and Eggshell position themselves behind the eleven and one o'clock monoliths. Her attention returned to Agents Orange and Periwinkle. With their guns drawn and aimed at her chest, they marched in unison between the six o'clock stones, the tallest monoliths, which marked the ceremonial entrance.

She strengthened her grip on the dog. "Don't make me count."

I'd witnessed her cold-blooded murder rampage firsthand, yet I couldn't imagine she'd actually laser-blast the dog in the head.

The cat sat down behind the nine o'clock stone.

I settled in behind the fat boulder in the three o'clock position.

The old woman's eyes shifted between me and Agent Orange. "You leave me no choice. The dog gets it in five. Four…"

"Give it up, old woman. We have you surrounded." Agent Orange motioned for Agent Periwinkle to stay back as he continued his methodical advance. Only three paces separated him and Grandma Marjorie.

"Three."

Agent Orange stopped. His eyes narrowed. He twisted his pistol sideways, signaling his preparation for a kill shot.

Every muscle tightened as I braced for the roar of his weapon.

"Two," she said, then added, "Hmph." Her upper lip quivered as she stared down Agent Orange.

Agent Orange cocked his head. Full gangster pose.

"One."

In my head I screamed, *"SHOOT! SHOOT!"* as I closed my eyes and ducked behind my fat rock.

No gunshots rang out.

No faint pew-pew squeezed out of Grandma Marjorie's laser gun.

I peeked over the rock with a single eye open.

The standoff remained unchanged.

Perhaps in the world of intergalactic espionage and counterintelligence, the countdown ends at zero. In my world, reaching the number one indicated the end of the countdown. *Why hadn't she shot?* Not that I wanted her to, or even believed she would follow through with her threat. But I'd hoped Agent Orange wouldn't take the risk. I wanted him to shoot her just in case she really did plan on splattering the dog's head around the sacred circle.

Agent Orange and Grandma Marjorie locked eyes. He seemed to dare her to say zero.

Shoot her! Shoot her! What are you waiting for?

The dog twisted the lower half of his body and wound up his tail.

Grandma Marjorie snarled and intensified her focus on Agent Orange.

Had she finished counting? Or was she going to say zero?

Agent Orange winked.

I assumed this to be a signal to the dog, and even though he didn't appear to have seen it, he unleashed his coiled torso. His tail nailed the old woman in the back of the legs, sweeping her off her feet.

The dog dropped from Grandma Marjorie's grip as she landed butt first on the ground. He snarled at the old woman, splattering drool in her face. Agent Orange rushed in and kicked the laser gun out of her hand. It skipped across the rocky inner circle and over to Agent Periwinkle.

The rest of us emerged from behind the safety of our rocks and stepped into the circle.

"Well, congratulations," said Grandma Marjorie, wiping the slobber off her face. "It only took four agents and three superpowered barnyard animals to capture a little old lady. You should all be proud of yourself."

The cat's device beeped.

Grandma Marjorie did a side-eyed peek into the fields. An evil smile formed.

I knew that couldn't be good.

The black streak zoomed across the fields and up the hill. It took one lap around the top of the stones before breaking out of hyperspeed. The crow hopped around the circle's center, holding his sack of chipmunks, his head lurching from person to animal to person.

Wasting no time, the dog lunged for the crow, who casually stepped to the side and watched the dog skid past.

"Agents, what are you waiting for?" Agent Orange kept his gun aimed at the old woman. "Shoot that crow."

The crow dropped the sack.

Chipmunks scattered out of the circle like roaches fleeing a kitchen when the lights go on.

Bullets skipped off the rocky ground.

The crow dissolved into a billowy stream of black haze and zipped directly for Agent Eggshell.

The cat's detector beeped.

Agent Eggshell scrambled back to his abandoned net. As he reached down, black waves engulfed his head. His helmet clanged to the ground. He let out an endless scream and collapsed to his knees. His hands covered his face.

The black blur made a beeline for Agent White, who looked like an amateur baseball player swinging late on a major league fastball as he flailed at the crow with his rifle. The crow relieved him of his gun. As the black streak circled Agent White, a couple of handguns, three knives, a baton, and a taser flew out like popcorn escaping the pot.

His head disappeared in a blur of black.

He dropped to his knees, screaming.

His helmet clanked to the ground and rolled out of the circle.

The dog, several moves behind the crow, skidded past the collapsed Agent White.

The black blur swooped to Grandma Marjorie. When the blur cleared, the crow sat perched on her shoulder.

"Shoot that evil beast," shouted Agent Orange.

Before Agents Orange or Periwinkle fired a shot, the crow confiscated every weapon they carried, including the laser gun, which he placed back in Grandma Marjorie's hand. He then returned to her shoulder.

Grandma Marjorie patted his head. "Thank you, Crownos."

The dog positioned himself to pounce. Grandma Marjorie pointed her laser gun at him. "Don't even think about it."

"Where's the chicken?" The dog spoke without a stammer. Not that this helped anyone except the cat and I understand what he asked.

Grandma Marjorie motioned him to join Agent Orange.

"Where is the chicken?" This time, he added a growl.

Her eyes locked onto me. "Cow. Control your dog."

I returned her stare. "He wants to know where the chicken is."

"That's the least of your concerns at the moment. Now call your dog, and all of y'all, huddle together."

"Cow! Cat!" Agent Orange looked back and forth at us. "Unleash your superpowers."

The cat and I locked eyes. I wanted to comply with Agent Orange's command, but becoming mostly cloaked isn't an attack move, and I wasn't going to go Nuclear Moo on them. The cat's primary superpower of superior intelligence may work as a weapon for Doctor Who, but without a sonic screwdriver, the cat had no attack moves.

After glancing between the cat and me, Grandma Marjorie chuckled. "Y'all bunch together or I start blasting." She kicked the dog away, who snapped, but missed her foot.

I relayed Grandma Marjorie's command to the cat and dog. With my head held low, I shuffled to Agents Orange and Periwinkle, as did the cat and dog.

"Okay, it's time to meet the rest of my grandsons. Boys, it's safe to come out now."

Rustling came from the giant bushes by which Grandma Marjorie and Crownos had emerged. Nick led two other teenage boys out. All three dressed in jeans and concert T-shirts, with Nick fitting into a medium size, while the other two required extra-large; one because of his larger frame and muscular physique and the other to cover his belly. The trio radiated a mix of cheap body spray, garlic, and skunk. They all oozed of white boy farmer, but that's where the similarity ended. The variety of hair colors, facial features, and body shapes gave no indication of blood relationship.

They strolled into the stone circle and gathered up the agent's weapons.

With a lull in the action, our attention fell on Agents Eggshell and White. They remained on their knees, hands over their eyes. Blood oozed between their fingers, running down their arms.

"What has that crow done to them?" Agent Orange nodded toward them.

She flashed her patented smile. "Let's just say he's incapacitated them. For now, I'm sparing that fate for the rest of y'all."

With a grunt, Agent Eggshell dropped his hands. Pools of blood had replaced his eyes. He pawed the ground until he found his net. To my amazement, he found the strength to stand. He raised the net above his head.

I admired his determination, but closed my eyes, not wishing to watch, but reopened them when he screamed, "Huzzah!" He ran right past Grandma Marjorie and out of the circle without bumping into a stone. He flailed his net and tripped over Agent White.

The two new grandsons cackled at the blinded agent's desperate attempt to fight back.

"Enough, boys." Grandma Marjorie glanced at her chuckling grandsons just long enough for them to feel her anger.

Their shoulders still quivered, but their audible laughter ceased. I wasn't sure if Nick directed his slow eye-roll and stoic head shake at his teenage companions or Agent Eggshell's actions.

"Crownos, please deposit your victims at the nearest hospital," said Grandma Marjorie.

He rocketed off her shoulder, morphing into a black blur that swooped up Agents White and Eggshell and disappeared past the giant bushes.

With open arms, Agent Periwinkle held back the snarling dog and growling Agent Orange.

Grandma Marjorie gave a friendly wave of her laser gun.

As Agent Orange took a slow breath, his forehead creased, eyelids squinted, and his jaw clenched.

The evil old woman chuckled. "You're gonna give yourself wrinkles, Joey. Anyway, time to return to our regularly scheduled programming. Crownos, if you wouldn't mind retrieving those critters you worked so hard to bring here, that would be marvelous."

Crownos zipped into the fields.

The cat's detector beeped, which she promptly silenced.

Crownos returned in an instant with the sack re-stuffed.

"Let's speed this process up." Grandma Marjorie pulled out a vial and popped the cork off. She poured the entire contents into the sack, pulled the strings tight, and gave the sack a shake. "That should do it." She handed the sack to Crownos, who rocketed off.

The cat's device chirped.

Grandma Marjorie's eyes locked onto the device. "So that's how you tracked us." She signaled for the muscular teenager and pointed at the cat's device.

When he drew close, the source of the skunk smell became clear. He made a menacing move toward the dog and threw up his hands, causing the dog to spin and hide under me. I found no humor in his actions, but the boy found this hilarious.

"Noy Sum! Stop messing with the dog, and destroy that cat's device," said Grandma Marjorie.

"How did a white farm boy get the name Noy Sum?" The question flowed out my lips before my inner-filter could stop it.

"None of your business." Noy snatched the handheld tracker from the cat's paws and whipped it to the ground. A small piece broke off, but the device remained mostly intact. He stomped on it with his boot. He smiled at the cat as he twisted his foot.

The cat cleaned herself, ignoring the boy, and the crushing sounds of plastic and electronic components. I admired her calm demeanor.

Grandma Marjorie walked up to me. "Are you finally convinced you're working for the losing side? We could use a few more animals with your unique talents. Are you and your little friends ready to join the winning team?"

I had no intention of joining the side of evil and changed the subject. "What have you done with the chicken?"

She grabbed me under my chin and looked at both sides of my head. "I've seen your invisibility power. It's not the best. I think we can help with that."

I yanked my head out of her grip. "Where'thh the chicken?"

"Yes, yes, yes. I assure you the chicken is safe and sound. If you join our team, I'll be more than happy to bring you to her."

"I will never join your team." I contemplated punctuating my refusal by spitting in her face.

"Pity. I was looking forward to seeing how that Nuclear Moo of yours works."

I didn't stop to wonder how she knew about Nuclear Moo, or think to deny it. "Don't mess with Nuclear Moo. It is far too dangerous."

"Now I'm more curious than ever."

She snapped her fingers, and the third boy ran behind the bushes. With his disappearance came a reduction in the excessive body spray odor. A couple of seconds later, he reemerged, driving a military truck. He parked it outside the circle, with the back wedged between the ceremonial entrance stones. With Noy's help, he pulled a large metal cage off the back of the truck. They carried it into the middle of the stone circle and set it next to Grandma Marjorie. The body spray stench had returned.

"Noy. Bugbear. What are you doing?" she asked.

"We brought out the cage for the cow like you wanted," said Bugbear.

The old woman chuckled. "I can't wait to see the three of you scrawny boys try lifting that cage with the cow in it."

Noy stretched his neck. "We're gonna have to pick it up and put it in the truck one way or another. It'll be easier if it's in the cage."

"My little simpleminded Noy. We force the cow to get into the truck and then into the cage." She pointed the laser gun at my head. "Let's go. Get in the truck."

I stiffened my stance, making it clear I would not go easily.

"You want to play the defiant game. Fine." She pointed the gun at Agent Orange. "Get in the truck or I blast the head off GIBOD's director."

"Cow, don't do it. She's going to kill me no matter what."

I made no move toward the truck.

"Oh, for crying out loud. Fine. I'll shoot the dog." The dog snarled at her when she pointed the gun at him. "Are you going to make me count? You know how I feel about counting."

I snorted and took a couple of steps toward the truck. Bugbear followed me as Nick and Noy headed toward the empty cage.

I turned to glare at Grandma Marjorie, but the cat caught my attention. She still licked the same spot on her leg. I saw her do this before. Dr. Hash Browns gave her the power to create tornados. The licking helped her concentrate.

A tiny funnel cloud, no bigger than the cat, spun above us.

The door to the cage swung closed.

Everyone looked at the cage, then up at the now dog-sized tornado.

The cage rattled and hopped.

Agent Orange charged and kicked the laser gun out of Grandma Marjorie's hand.

The dog spun and delivered a devastating tail whip to Nick's midsection, knocking his gun loose.

I bucked and nailed Bugbear in his squishy belly with a double back leg kick, sending him, Nick, and Noy into one of the stone pillars.

Rocks, grass, and dust swirled as Agent Orange reached for Nick's rifle. The now pig-sized tornado grabbed it first and smashed the rifle against a boulder. Agent Orange ducked to avoid a pistol clobbering him in the head.

"I strongly advise we exit these premises immediately," said the cat, as she picked up a tiny square piece of her shattered device.

The now couch-sized tornado knocked over two stone pillars as it spun out of the circle.

"I incubated three in total." The cat pointed to the chipmunk and bird-sized tornados that hovered above us. "You are aware tornados are uncontrollable once formed?"

Dr. Hash Browns claimed he gave the cat the power to control the tornados she created, but the cat insisted this to be scientifically impossible.

I planned to alert Agent Orange, but he already waved his arm like a third base coach sending a runner home and pointed toward the plane. Agent Periwinkle had run out of the circle and down the hill. The cat and dog sprinted after him. A stone crashed down behind me and shocked me into a gallop.

Halfway through the field, I glanced back to see Grandma Marjorie motioning the teenagers to the truck.

I reached the plane last. The dog sat at the top of the cargo ramp, staring intently past me. The cat sat behind him. I looked back at the circle. Like battling spinning tops, the now shed-sized tornados tossed the ancient stones into the surrounding fields like they were very small rocks.

The army truck had escaped the devastation and bounced down the hill, with Grandma Marjorie at the wheel and the teenagers standing in the bed.

The dog didn't watch the destruction of the ancient monument or the approaching truck. His eyes focused on the ground, where the crow made pecking gyrations à la Mick Jagger. He stopped, looked up at the dog, and ran his wing across his neck. Then he returned to his moves like Jagger. Once more, he stopped the dance and ran his wing across his neck.

The dog cocked his head. "What, ah, what do you, do you suppose that's supposed to mean?"

"Who knows. He'thh crazy. Now, let'thh go." I motioned with my head for the two to finish boarding the plane.

The cat tilted her head. "I surmise the unorthodox pecking routine to be the crow's impersonation of the chicken, while the slashing of the throat motion is clearly the kill gesture. This indicates the crow intends to kill the chicken."

I shot angry laser eyes at the cat, who simply slow blinked at me. *Of course, that's what the crow was doing, but she didn't have to tell the dog that.*

The dog leaped off the ramp.

The crow stood firm as the dog sprinted toward him. With as much of a grin as a crow can do, he repeated his mocking dance and death threat gesture.

"Dog! Come here. Come right here." I clumped down the ramp.

The dog never slowed down. He launched toward the crow. The crow transformed into a streak of blackness directed straight at the leaping dog. The two collided with a muffled thud and a faint whimper, then disappeared in a stream of black.

12: Mad Cow on the Loose in Southern Ireland

I WATCHED THE BLACK contrail dissipate over the Irish countryside. A single tear dropped on the grass. With a couple hard blinks and some gnashing of my teeth, I converted my pain to determination. I vowed to find and save my friends and stop Grandma Marjorie from completing whatever evil plot she's hatched.

"Cow. We've got to go." The roar of the plane engines nearly drowned out Agent Orange's words. Regardless, I wouldn't have acknowledged him.

"Cow, he's gone," said Agent Orange. "You can't bring him back by standing there."

A flurry of bullets snapped me out of my trance. Grandma Marjorie bounced the military truck through the field with her grandsons hanging off the sides like a pack of bootleggers.

I spun toward the plane, which had already begun rolling away. I galloped as fast as a dairy cow can, but when I caught up to the plane, the cargo ramp had risen to chest level. Agent Orange lay on the edge of the ramp with an outstretched arm.

"What are you doing? Get out of the way," I said while bullets flew past me.

"Give me your hoof. I'll pull you in." He repositioned to extend his reach, touching my snout.

"I can't give you my hoof. I can't run on three legs."

Agent Orange shifted to his knees and grabbed the scruff of hair on the top of my head with both his hands. He let out a weightlifter grunt as he yanked.

"OW! You idiot. What are you doing?" I attempted to shake off his grip, with no concern over calling my boss an idiot.

"I'm pulling you in."

"You can't pull me in. I weigh over fifteen hundred pounds. Get out of my way. I'm gonna jump in."

He let go of my hair. "Fine. But hurry, or you'll be left behind." He rolled to the side.

With the ramp at eye level and me at full gallop, I leaped. One of my fondest memories as a calf was jumping Old Man Johnson's picket fence, so I figured I'd have no problem jumping onto the ramp. This proved to be a gross overestimation. The top half of my front legs clanged hard into the edge of the ramp. My head bounced off the ramp floor. I dropped to the ground. For a moment, I landed on my hooves, then momentum and lack of coordination got the best of me. By the time I stopped tumbling head over hooves, the cargo bay door had closed, and the plane's wheels no longer touched the ground.

A spray of bullets kicked up dirt and grass on either side of me. The old woman and her band of grandsons hurtled toward me. My cloaking power instinctively activated. With a lowered head, I scuffed my front hoof in the dirt. I was no longer a common dairy cow. I had become a bull. After a series of loud snorts, I charged at the truck.

The old woman's eyes focused on my visible outline. She leaned forward as she ratcheted the truck into high gear.

Neither of us backed down or swerved.

Rage had removed all rational thought. I should have come out on the losing end of the collision. I should have died, or at the very least ended up mangled, broken and bloody, with limbs bent in ways they should never bend. At worst, the impact could have triggered my Nuclear Moo. Instead, I made a life-size cow imprint in the truck's hood and engine. The back end of the truck popped into the air. Airbags exploded. Grandsons flew into the field. The truck stood vertical for a second before crashing down. It bounced a handful of times before coming to a rest. Smoke and steam billowed out from under the remains of the hood. Waterfalls of oil, gas, and radiator fluid created rivers in the pasture.

I didn't bother to check for cuts or bruises. With a deafening bellow, I leaped onto the crumpled hood. Grandma Marjorie pushed the deflating airbags away and glared at me as I kicked in the windshield.

"Are you seeing what I'm seeing?" said Noy from the field behind me. "The Predator is real, and he's gonna eat Grandma."

"Don't be an idiot," yelled his grandmother. "It's just the cow."

"Didn't you see what it did to the truck?" asked Noy.

"I'm the one driving the truck, you moron." She shook her head and reached under her seat.

Bugbear hid behind the truck. "It's a monster. It's indestructible."

"We'll see about that," she said as she pulled out a rifle.

I slipped, trying to reposition myself, and landed spread-eagled on the crushed hood. My left eye fixated on a saddle bag resting atop the dashboard. A small vial peeked out the top. Meanwhile, my right eye stared at the wrong end of a rifle barrel.

She pulled the trigger.

At such a close range, the probability of her missing me approached zero percent. Yet, the bullet whizzed over my forehead. I didn't dwell on my good fortune. Instinct kicked in. I grabbed the bag in my mouth, leaped down, and took off running.

"Boys, she's got the vials. Get her."

Bullets ruffled my hair as I serpentined into the field. The grandsons followed. I dropped my cloak to devote all my energy to running. The boys continued to draw closer. I quit serpentining. The boys still gained ground.

I plowed through a row of hedges into a manicured field. A whistle blew, and a soccer ball bounced off my nose, or should I call it a football? A vague memory of Dr. Hash Browns ranting about the Irish calling it soccer because of the popularity of Gaelic football made me think soccer was the right term.

The kids, parents, and refs all stopped playing, cheering, and refereeing to stare at me.

The grandsons pushed through the hedges. They did their best to hide their weapons.

Kids ran to their parents without taking their eyes off me or the heavily armed grandsons. Several parents and a ref exchanged glances before moving towards us.

Nick raised his rifle and said, "Mad cow. Back away. Mad cow on the loose."

I didn't give him a chance to fire. I bucked and kicked Nick into the other grandsons.

The crowd gasped.

"That cow's got the mad cow disease," said a dad.

I'm not frothing at the mouth or stumbling around. Obviously, I don't have mad cow. I wanted to verbalize my argument, but knew a talking cow would devolve the situation into an entirely different madness.

"Her unprovoked aggression is a telltale sign," said another dad.

Let me point a rifle at your head and see if that doesn't provoke *you?*

"Her eyes have gone wild," said a boy.

They have not!

"Mad cow wiped out O'Malley's entire herd last year," said a mom.

"And the McCarthy's herd," said another mom.

With fire in her eyes, the referee pointed at me. "We need to kill that cow before we lose every herd in the county."

I rolled my eyes and turned to flee. The grandsons had gotten back up. I charged, forcing them to dive out of the way before readying their weapons. I plowed through the bushes and sprinted back into the pastures.

The mob, which included the grandsons, moms, dads, children, and the referee, chanted, "Kill the mad cow! Kill the mad cow!" as they trampled through the bushes.

The crowd cheered as the grandsons opened fire on me. I picked up my pace after a bullet clipped off a piece of my ear. I weaved around the pastures with the mob close behind. An occasional bullet whizzed past. Annoying as that was, it paled in comparison to the referee's constant whistle blowing.

I rammed through a row of hedges and headfirst into a wood fence. My backside flung to the right through a bush and smashed into a post. I lost my grip on the bag of vials, which flew over the fence.

I crumbled to the ground, closed my eyes, and waited for the bullets.

No gunshot came, but the blare of that referee's stupid whistle persisted. I opened my left eye. No mob. No grandsons. Just the referee and her whistle. She stood motionless, staring past me. Her mouth dropped open, thankfully, ending the shrilling whistle blowing. It hung on her lip for a moment, then the whistle dropped. That's when I heard the train. Well, what I thought was a train.

Creaks from the tree branches above me escalated to screams. I opened my right eye. One of the cat's tornados, now five stories tall, filled my view. "RUN!"

The referee's mouth closed as she snapped her head toward me. "Holy crap, you talk."

I shrugged my shoulders. "It's a long story."

I stretched a hoof through the fence slots and dragged the bag back.

"What's in the bag?"

I didn't get a chance to answer. A massive tree branch crashed down on her skull.

***

I snatched the bag a second before the fence exploded. The next thing I knew, I became engulfed in a cloud of dirt, grass, and shrub branches. I glimpsed the referee rocketing toward me before the sandblasting dust forced me to close my eyes. Her limp body smacked into me as the tornado lifted us off the ground. I tightened my grip on the bag of vials as chunks of the wooden fence, tree branches, and small farm animals smacked me from all sides. My speed increased as I spiraled up the funnel cloud. The rabbit and duck called this tornado surfing. Although their first experience happened by accident, they enjoyed it and planned to do it again, on purpose. As dust filled my eyes and I couldn't tell up from down, I agreed with Agent Orange; they shouldn't be agents. The rabbit and duck are idiots.

I felt trapped in the spin cycle of a washing machine filled with construction debris. My cloak fizzled on and off as my consciousness faded. I welcomed the fade to nothingness, but then the tornado spit me out.

After a brief panoramic view of the rolling hills of the Southern Irish countryside being ravished by the cat's tornados, I crash-landed on a hilltop, leaving a huge divot before rolling into a pasture. A herd of cows greeted me with a smattering of "Moos" and returned to grazing.

I had no pain, and miraculously still held the saddle bag full of chipmunk zombie viruses in my mouth. I checked for broken limbs and major lacerations, but could not see my legs. My cloaking power had activated on its own. When I deactivated the cloak, the herd greeted me with another round of "Moos" before returning to grazing.

Two of the cat's tornados battled each other as they ripped paths of destruction in pastures to the south. The tornado that spat me out continued its destruction to the west. I took a deep breath and enjoyed what remained of the beautiful view. Then I saw the angry mob of soccer parents. They gathered atop a second hill to the west after having somehow found time to gather pitchforks and rakes.

Pushing into the middle of the herd, I attempted to blend in. I set the bag down and joined their grazing. The blades of tasteless grass formed a ball in my mouth that I could not swallow. I used to love grass, but after my enhancements, I hated it.

A soccer mom pointed at me. The mob raised their makeshift weapons high and charged down the hill. I wondered how they'd spotted me, but a glance at the grazing herd made me realize I was the only spotted dairy cow.

I grabbed the bag, slid away from the herd, and sprinted toward the nearest farmhouse. Then my heart exploded with delight. A familiar black plane hung low in the sky with its wheels down. They had come back for me! After changing directions to run toward the plane, I realized it would land close to the angry mob.

The wheels touched down as I galloped past the herd. Engines roared in reverse as the plane played chicken with the angry mob. I angled toward the rolling plane. The cargo door lowered. Rocks from the mob landed all around me. I quickened my pace. The plane slowed. The cargo door bounced off the ground. Agent Orange stood at the top of the ramp, stoic as ever. He waved me in, with no look of joy or anger on his face.

I stepped on the ramp, but it bounced me off.

A pitchfork landed at my hooves.

I regathered my gallop and leaped onto the ramp with a resounding clamor.

Hatchets and rakes bounced around me and clanged off the ramp.

I sprinted into the cargo bay.

A mob member hopped on the rising ramp. He stomped and screamed with his tongue wagging. He launched a shovel at us. It clanged harmlessly past Agent Orange, who then shoved the man off. The plane picked up speed. Garden tools banged off the closed cargo door as we roared away.

Agent Periwinkle pulled the saddle bag out of my mouth. "What's this?"

"It'thh the chipmunk zombie virus vials."

"Nice work," said Agent Orange, snatching the bag from Agent Periwinkle.

Agent Periwinkle walked around me, looking me up and down. "You okay?"

"I feel good, thankthh for asking. And thankthh for coming back for me." I wanted to give both of them a hug, but I'm a cow and that's not something we can physically do.

"You don't have a scratch on you."

"A bullet clipped my ear."

He pulled my head down. "Yep, one minor nick. That's it. Amazing."

"I know. Incredible. I'm sure I have Dr. Hash Browns to thank."

"No offense," said Agent Orange as he rummaged through the bag of vials, "but we would be halfway home if it wasn't for the fact we don't understand a word your cat says. She has something important to tell us, but it's all gibberish to me."

I ignored Agent Orange's callus explanation for why they came back for me. The mention of the cat triggered my anger with her. "Where is she?"

"She's in the bathroom. Go find out what's so important."

I stormed off toward the cargo bay's bathroom with no intention of discussing the so-called important information the cat wanted to share. I found the cat hunched over. Her tiny body bobbed and quivered with every gagging hack she made. It made me nauseous, even though spitting my food up and re-chewing it is part of my normal digestion.

I gathered myself and said, "Cat, what is wrong with you? Why did you tell the dog that the crow planned to kill the chicken?"

The cat let out one more hack before she said, "As I recall, the dog asked a question. I knew the answer, so I provided it."

"You had to know how he would react. You should have kept your mouth shut or said you didn't know."

"Are you suggesting I should have feigned stupidity? I doubt anyone would believe that."

"I believe it because it was your stupidity that got the dog captured."

The cat squinted and cocked her head slowly from side to side. "I cannot determine the logic you have used to conclude I am responsible for the dog's capture. The dog's irrational behavior due to his strong emotional attachment to the chicken is clearly the cause."

Agent Orange walked up next to me. "Cow, what did the cat want to tell us?"

The cat would never understand my point, so I dropped the argument and did Agent Orange's bidding. "Thho, he says you were trying to tell them something, and it seemed important. What was it?"

"I requested a laxative," said the cat.

"What?"

"I confiscated the memory chip from my mutilated hyperspeed detector prior to escaping the Drombeg Stone Circle. Unfortunately, I swallowed it during my sprint to the airplane. I wanted the laxative to induce–"

"Enough. Got it." I turned to Agent Orange, ready to translate.

The cat held up a paw. "I no longer require a laxative. Plan B is approaching completion." The cat made one last hideous gag. A blob of soggy cat fur plopped on the floor.

As the ooze of the cat's hairball spread, I swore I would never rechew my cud again.

Agent Orange turned his head away but kept the blob in his view with a side-eyed gaze.

She sniffed the hairball and then spread the soggy hair apart, revealing the pebble sized memory chip.

Agent Periwinkle walked up, took one look, and jerked his head back. "I'll alert the sanitation droids."

The cat snatched the memory chip in her mouth and scurried away.

Agent Periwinkle leaned farther back. His cheeks lost their rosy glow. "Did the cat just pick something out of her own barf and put it in her mouth?"

"Technically, it'thh a hairball, but yethh."

Agent Orange still observed via his side-eyed stare. "You animals are so gross. I pray she had a good reason for picking something out of her puke."

"Again, it'thh a hairball, not puke. And yethh, she had a good reason. That'thh the memory chip from her hyperspeed tracking device."

Agent Periwinkle reversed his recoil. His eyes opened wide. "That should have the crow's travel coordinates. We can send teams to those locations and eradicate the infected chipmunks before the virus spreads."

Agent Orange twisted his head to face Agent Periwinkle, though his eyes remained focused on the hairball. "Excellent. Let's get those coordinates."

When we got to the computer room, the cat already had the list displayed on a monitor.

Agent Periwinkle entered a set into the ship's navigation system. The map zoomed in on Antarctica.

"The cat's memory chip must be damaged. These coordinates don't make any sense. The first location is in Antarctica." He typed in the next set. The map shifted to the middle of the Pacific Ocean.

The cat smacked her forehead with a paw. "My apologies. I forgot to convert the Colbian coordinates." The cat typed a few commands on her computer and displayed a new list of numbers. "There. The coordinates are now translated to the traditional latitude and longitude humans use."

Agent Periwinkle typed in the first set. A pin popped up just outside of Paris. "Much better." He quickly entered the rest of the list. Pins popped up all over Europe. "Excellent." He clapped his hands and did a quick finger stretch. "I'll get these out to the boys."

"What was the deal with the first set of coordinates the cat gave us?" asked Agent Orange.

"Those were Colbian coordinates," I said.

"What does that mean?"

"The Colbians have a strange system of mathematics. It'thh akin to your English language, with all its exceptions and exceptions to the exceptions. You need to understand the entire context of the equation or problem to determine what rules apply. For example, the circumference of a circle is $2\pi r$ unless you're a restaurant owner calculating the circumference of a circular food item, such as pizza, then it's $2\frac{1}{2}\pi r$."

"That's the stupidest thing I've ever heard. Math doesn't have exceptions to its rules," said Agent Orange with a look of constipation on his face.

"I've heard of the Colbians before," said Agent Periwinkle, tapping away on his computer. "They do the Havarti Travel Bureau's accounting,"

"Not surprising. Colbian accountants are in high demand. But it can be a gamble. A good Colbian accountant can make you a fortune overnight. A bad one can lose your life'thh savings in an instant."

Agent Orange sprang out of his chair. "Wait. The hidden messages broadcasted from the church. We found what looked like coordinates, but they didn't make sense when we brought them up on the map."

On his laptop, Agent Periwinkle brought up the list of those coordinates.

"Cat, can you convert these coordinates?" I pointed at the agent's laptop.

"Of course I can." She stopped cleaning herself and snagged the laptop away from Agent Periwinkle. While typing, she said, "The question you should be asking is why can't Agent Orange and Agent Periwinkle convert the coordinates? They are the intergalactic protectors of this planet, but are incapable of doing a simple Colbian coordinate conversion." She tilted the screen to show me the revised coordinates and returned to her grooming.

Agents Periwinkle brought the revised coordinates up on a map. He pointed at pins that popped up outside the Quad Cities in western Illinois, in South America near the border of Peru and Bolivia, and the Southern tip of Ireland. "The church, the Tiwanaku ruins, and the Drombeg Stone Circle."

The next pin popped up in the African country of Zimbabwe. A final pin appeared in India.

Agent Orange slapped Agent Periwinkle on the back and said, "Reroute the plane. We're not going home yet, boys. We're off to Africa and India."

13: Off to Africa

I ATTEMPTED TO LIE on the leather couch in the plane's lounge, but even after tossing the six pillows and three back cushions on the floor, less than half of my torso fit. I headed into the cargo bay and curled up in a corner. It came nowhere close to the soft bed in Dr. Hash Browns' space station lab or even a nice pile of hay in the barn, but at least it provided solitude. Thanks to Dr. Hash Browns' enhancements, I didn't need sleep, but I still enjoyed it. I closed my eyes and took several deep breaths, but instead of seeing darkness, I saw a replay of the crow grabbing the dog by the scruff of the neck and blasting off. The clip ran over and over. A cackling laugh from the crow got added around the fourth replay. I shook off the image and drummed up happy thoughts of cute kittens and dancing goats. It worked long enough for me to get drowsy, then the images dissolved to visions of the dog, cat, and chicken chained to operating tables with their midsections sliced wide open.

My eyes popped open, and I sprang to my feet. *I had failed to keep the others safe. Why did I agree to include them on this mission? Why did I let us join GIBOD?*

I sighed away the negative thoughts. The past could not be changed. I needed to focus on the present. Agent Orange insisted we continue the mission despite losing three of the seven team members. A callous and reckless decision that was on brand for him. Regardless, I was glad we didn't head home. I didn't care if we stopped the spread of animal zombie viruses. Continuing the mission would lead me to the crow, Grandma Marjorie, and her annoying grandsons. And they would lead me to the chicken and dog.

I headed for the kitchen to see what the robot waiters had to eat. A bit of comfort food would help me sleep. I passed the cat asleep on a chair in the lounge, and Agent Orange snoring away on the couch. He had not bothered to replace the pillows.

Before reaching the kitchen, I spotted Agent Periwinkle sitting in front of a computer terminal by the navigation systems.

"Have you heard anything about Agents White and Eggshell?" I asked.

"They'll survive, but barring some miracle new tech, they'll never see again."

"Sorry to hear that, though I'm glad they're alive." His screen displayed an aerial view of crumbling ancient walls. I wanted to change the subject and asked, "Are those the Bulgaria ruins with the crazed caterpillars?"

"That was Bolivia, but yes, this is a satellite view of the Tiwanaku ruins. I'm observing the cleanup." He zoomed in on a group of agents executing a controlled burn on a multi-acre field.

"You know what'thh been bugging me? Why does the Havarti Travel Bureau want to spread a caterpillar virus?"

"I remember thinking the same thing when I labeled the caterpillar zombie virus vials all those years ago. I mean, how can you even tell the difference between a zombie caterpillar and a regular caterpillar? Besides the fact they bite."

"That'thh easy. They crawl funny. They kind of slither, dragging the back half of their bodies instead of the normal up and down caterpillar crawl."

"That's a good observation. I'll make a note of that. In fact, I'll relay that on to the cleanup crew. Thanks." Agent Periwinkle popped open a small window on the computer and typed in the message. He turned back to me. "Anyway, I now realize the true genius behind a caterpillar zombie virus. After the caterpillars complete their metamorphosis, the virus transfers to their butterfly form. Butterflies are extremely mobile. Some migrate thousands of miles. They're a perfect vehicle for spreading a virus across the globe."

"But why would the Havarti Travel Bureau spread a virus that doesn't work on humans?"

"It's all part of their evil plan. Back in the day, the Havarti Travel Bureau had a human zombie virus, but simply unleashing it would draw suspicion from the intergalactic community. They had to be clever about it. They planned to unleash multiple strands of the zombie virus before introducing the human form, so the intergalactic investigation into the demise of humans would conclude a logical progression of the zombie virus to a human form. No suspicion of foul play."

"Here'thh another thing that'thh been bugging me. Why would Grandma Marjorie help the Havarti Travel Bureau wipe out the human race?"

"The Havarti Travel Bureau will offer riches and rewards beyond your wildest dreams, and you'd be surprised how many humans will sell out their own kind for such rewards. In Grandma Marjorie's case, I suspect they've promised to spare her grandsons."

"You sure know a lot about the Havarti Travel Bureau."

"That's how we stay one step ahead of them." Agent Periwinkle brought up a new aerial view of ancient ruins.

"Is that still Bulgaria?"

"That would still be Bolivia, but no. This is where we're headed. They're nowhere near as old as the Tiwanaku ruins. And this," he said, clicking to bring up a new picture of crumbling old stone structures, "is the final set of coordinates, the Martand Sun Temple in India."

"What'thh the deal with all the locations being ancient ruins?"

"The Havarti Travel Bureau knew these historic landmarks would remain intact for decades, making them great locations to hide the vials." He pointed to the image of The Great Zimbabwe ruins. "We need to beat Grandma Marjorie and her grandsons to these vials."

***

AGENT ORANGE INSISTED WE land the plane in a small field away from the Great Zimbabwe ruins, claiming we needed to hide our arrival. The clearing was less than a half mile away. Even though the autopilot didn't need lights to land in the dark, I'm sure we hadn't hidden our arrival from anyone near the ruins.

We could have taken an easy nine-minute stroll down a dirt road/path to the ruins, but Agent Orange had us trooping thirty minutes through a forest in the dark. The tree canopy made it impossible to see the uneven terrain and random tree roots. Cows are built for leisurely strolls through open pastures, not blazing new trails through dense forests in the dead of night. I had multiple slips, trips, and stumbles, but remained vertical throughout the journey, though my hooves and ankles ached by the end.

The cat had no problem hopping across the terrain, so we made her lead. When we emerged from the trees, the moonlight provided ample light. An ancient stone wall stood only a few yards away.

Agent Periwinkle stepped in front of the cat. He glanced at his tablet. "There should be an entrance down a ways."

Despite its age, the outer wall stood over thirty feet strong in most parts. We followed the oval stone fortress until we found the opening. This side entrance lacked the grandeur of the main entrance, which featured a narrow passageway between the thirty-foot walls. Agent Periwinkle had shown me the videos. I'm glad we didn't go that way. It had a strong slaughterhouse vibe.

The years had been harder on the inner enclosures, reducing some walls to disorganized piles of rubble, making it difficult to determine the room divisions.

Agent Periwinkle marched straight toward an inner circular enclosure that stood mostly intact. We followed him through a mini passageway with walls just over our heads, too short to trigger slaughterhouse panic. Once inside the courtyard, he paced across the dirt to a grassy area in the middle. He glanced between his tablet and the surrounding ruins. "The vials should be right here."

Agent Orange walked the perimeter, shining a flashlight in every nook and crevice of the relatively featureless circle. "Are you sure? I don't see any hiding places."

"The coordinates pinpoint this room." Agent Periwinkle spun in a circle, shaking his head. "Do you think they buried the vials?"

"That's possible, and something we should have considered before leaving the plane without shovels."

"If the dog was with uthh, he could dig for the vials. He'thh great at digging holes. Or if the chicken were here, she could search the entire enclosure in seconds or zip back to the plane for shovels. Our skills and powers come in handy sometimes." I started my rant mourning the loss of my friends, but by the end, I became consumed with bitterness for Agent Orange's lack of compassion regarding their disappearance.

"They're not here. So, move on and keep looking for the vials."

His response increased my bitterness to dark chocolate levels. I kicked at the dirt as I strolled over to the wall. I moved a couple of stones around with my hoof. The agents both had large flashlights, and the cat had a light on her handheld. I searched in the dark.

Agent Periwinkle examined the ground. "It's got to be buried. This is a tourist location. They wouldn't risk leaving the vials where they could be easily found."

"We passed several stone piles on our way to this circular courtyard. They would be great hiding places." I surveyed the rest of the enclosure, spotting more excellent hiding places. "Or they could have hidden the vials in the stone silo, or that well, or in the trees." I dwelled on the trees, deciding they wouldn't be great hiding places, then wondered how long they had been there. *Were they part of the original architecture? If they came later, why hadn't the ruins become overrun by the forest? Someone must keep them under control. And what about that tiny new one? Why are they letting that grow?*

Agent Orange scanned the Great Enclosure. "I agree. There are dozens of great hiding places. We're going to have to do a thorough search of the entire enclosure."

"And we came unprepared." Agent Periwinkle punctuated his statement with a heavy sigh. "No shovels, no rope, no pickaxes. We don't even have water."

"You should have thought of this before we left the plane," said Agent Orange.

"But we were in a hurry to beat Grandma Marjorie here," said Agent Periwinkle.

"Let's head back to the plane. Cow, you and the cat stay here and start looking for those vials."

I explained the situation to the cat. We shuffled to an enormous pile of rocks a few paces outside the inner circle courtyard and half-heartedly shifted through the stones.

After only a couple of minutes, laughter and coughing came from the main entrance.

"Someone'thh coming."

"I surmise it to be the return of Agent Orange and Agent Periwinkle."

"Have you ever heard either of them laugh?"

"Excellent point. Neither are prone to merriment."

I took a long sniff. Garlic, body spray, and skunk. "Hide. It'thh that old woman and her grandsons."

The cat slunk behind a pile of rocks while I trotted behind a wall near the tallest tree.

Grandma Marjorie and her entourage emerged out of the main entrance passageway and plopped down duffle bags of equipment. Of course, *they* arrived prepared.

After a quick scan of the Great Enclosure, Grandma Marjorie said. "Nick, bring me my chair."

Nick slid the camping chair off his shoulder, unfolded it, and placed it next to her.

Grandma Marjorie sat and then wiggled into a comfortable position. "You know the drill boys. Start searching."

Nick unpacked the bags as the other two strolled around the enclosure, swiveling their heads.

Bugbear wandered toward me.

I activated my cloak.

At twenty paces away, he looked right at me. His head-swiveling stopped.

Despite constantly reminding myself I didn't need to breathe, my lungs insisted on rapid shallow breaths.

His expression remained stoic. He blinked. Then his eyes darted toward the well and he headed for it.

I exhaled and checked on the cat. As Noy circled the pile of rocks, she kept herself low and on the opposite side. She focused on Noy, failing to realize that two more steps would put her in plain sight of Grandma Marjorie.

She backed up the two.

Grandma Marjorie flipped her flashlight on. "Boys, she's right here."

The cat froze.

I galloped out, decloaking along the way. "Cat. RUN!!"

Bugbear sprinted alongside me. I banged him into a hill of rubble.

By this time, Nick and Noy had the cat cornered.

The cat hissed and dropped into a crouch. Her head swiveled between her approaching assailants.

Grandma Marjorie did her best to keep the spotlight on the cat.

I lowered my head preparing to ram Nick, but I was too late.

He reached for the cat. "Come here, little kitty. Nobody's going to hurt you."

The cat lunged and sank her teeth into his hand.

Nick circled his hand in the air with the cat attached, flying around like a rally towel. He smacked the cat against the stone wall like he was beating a rug.

The cat shrieked with every strike. After three whacks, she let go. She hung six feet in the air with her hair on end and all paws extended. The cat landed with a soft, high-pitched grunt right next to Grandma Marjorie.

She toppled out of her chair in an arm-flinging attempt to grab the cat.

I plowed into Nick, taking him to the ground. I slammed a hoof on his chest. "Enough!"

I shot a stare at Grandma Marjorie, who dusted herself off, and reset her chair.

"You will take me to the chicken and dog." Fuming over her casually ignoring me, I increased the pressure on Nick's chest.

Nick grunted out a barely audible, "Grandma."

"Relax, Nick. The crow is on his way."

As if on cue, the black stream circled above the Great Enclosure.

Nick grunted as I pushed off and sprinted toward the cat, who hid in the shadows of the inner courtyard wall.

After one loop, the crow spotted her and dove.

I pounded the dirt hard and took a leap.

As I flew, I watched the crow sink his claws into the cat's back and blast off in a blur of black. Then I slammed snout-first into the wall.

I popped up. With boiling blood pumping through my veins, I

stomped up to Grandma Marjorie. I snarled. "You were supposed to take me! Not the cat. Take no more animals except me." Spit flew in her face with every syllable.

She turned without wiping her face and began folding her camping chair. "Sorry. We just came for the cat. Capturing you is no longer part of our orders."

"I don't care about your orderthh. Take me!"

"Well, my boss cares about the orders, and if I want to keep my boys safe when the world burns, I need to follow them." She stuffed her chair into its bag.

I shuffled over and got in her face once more. "Where did the crow take them?"

"Sweetie, that's way above my pay grade." She pulled the string on her bag closed. "Good job, boys. Let's finish packing up and get out of here."

Nick had everything packed already. He tossed a bag each to Noy and Bugbear.

Grandma Marjorie walked up and patted the side of my snout. "I really do like you and fear I may never learn what Nuclear Moo is. But you have to understand. I'm just following orders."

I clomped in front of them and blocked the passageway to the main entrance. "You will not pass."

"Sweetie, I am sorry, but you've bigger things to worry about." She motioned to the top of the passageway walls.

I saw nothing, but got a powerful whiff of a squashed stink bug that had been smoking weed. Then I noticed motion atop the wall.

Grandma Marjorie and her grandsons backed away and headed for the side exit. As I stepped forward to head them off, two men jumped off the wall, landing in front of me. Another three strolled up behind me. Five more materialized out of the Great Enclosure shadows.

They resembled an eclectic biker gang. A heavily armed, multi-racial attack force wearing lots of denim, leather, and black T-shirts. They all carried personalized weaponry, such as a khopesh, a machete, a pistol, a whip, a rocket launcher, a shovel, or a flamethrower. Clothing, facial hair, and stench were the only similarities between the men.

By the time Grandma Marjorie and her grandsons disappeared via the side exit, the diverse gang had me encircled, with weapons drawn. My nostrils burned from their oppressive odor. I swear they had tried to cover the stench of skunk spray by rubbing themselves with elephant dung. Apparently, the reek is normal for unbathed humans. I read it helped you survive as a species. You humans stunk so bad, no creatures would eat you. I sure wouldn't eat you. Of course, being an herbivore makes my opinions in matters of flesh aroma worthless. Regardless, as the gang drew closer, my urge to vomit increased exponentially.

The tallest and beefiest of the gang, which I presumed made him the leader, raised his khopesh sword.

The rest stopped.

He stepped up to me and pointed his sickle-shaped sword at me.

I snarled. I should have been terrified. Instead, bewilderment clouded my mind. *What was this diverse group doing in Zimbabwe? Were they actually a biker gang? If they were a biker gang, where were their bikes? Why didn't they shower? Where did the leader get that Egyptian sword?*

What I didn't wonder was what they planned to do with me. I should have been worried about that.

14: A European Swallow Maybe, But Not an African Swallow

My panoramic vision allowed me to keep all but one of the eclectic biker gang in view. I searched beyond their encirclement. Agents Orange and Periwinkle had not returned to the Great Enclosure.

I stared down at the curved blade of their dark-skinned muscular leader's sword. My default flight response was nowhere to be found. Yet, my heart raced, and my legs jittered, but not from nerves. Anger and rage over the loss of my friends pulsed through my veins. I began a deep breath to calm myself, but stopped as soon as the fecal infused skunk fumes assaulted my nostrils.

When the leader spoke, a couple of things took me by surprise. For starters, he spoke Somali. I assumed the multi-national biker group to be Americans, or at the very least, expected them to default to English as a common language. And why Somali? We were in Zimbabwe.

But what surprised me the most was that I understood him.

"It looks like steak is on the menu tonight, boys."

The others cheered their approval.

The leader raised his blade, preparing to strike with a double-handed blow.

My cloak instinctively activated as I braced my hoofing.

Murmurs ran through the gang. The leader lowered his blade, put a couple of fingers in his mouth, and let out a deafening whistle blast.

This silenced the murmuration.

The leader strolled up and grabbed my chin. "Is it just me, or does everyone see an outline of a cow? I guess we get to eat magic beef tonight, boys. I bet it tastes just like chicken."

His men roared with laughter.

He raised his khopesh high above his head.

The laughter faded.

My brain shut off. Rage took over.

I started with a headbutt.

The burly leader staggered backward. He regained his balance, raised the khopesh blade once more, and charged.

I bucked up on my back legs and repeatedly pounded his head with my front hooves.

Their leader, the fiercest warrior in the gang, crumbled.

The others stood motionless, watching the blood pool around him.

I seized the distraction. The Asian biker with a rocket launcher concerned me the most. Like an angry bull, I rammed him, flipping him into the wall.

A flamethrower whirred to life behind me, right in my blind spot. No visual required. The sound gave away his position. I nailed the flamethrower's owner with a back hoof to the gut. I followed up with several blows to the Hispanic man's head.

One by one, the others waged their attacks, and one by one I destroyed them all, wondering why they never attacked all at once.

Ten men lay bloodied, bruised, and presumed dead. It took several deep breaths to relax and keep the veins in my head from popping out of my skin.

Finally, Agents Orange and Periwinkle waltzed in.

"Whoa. What happened here?" said Agent Orange as he dropped a ring of rope. "And what's that stench?"

Agent Periwinkle dropped the shovels, pickaxe, and flashlights he brought and ran over to the body of the gang's leader. "What are the Nile Crocodiles doing here?"

My hooves shuffled as I swung my head, searching for crocodiles.

With a scrunched face, Agent Orange scanned the bodies. "Is that some sort of aging Country boy band?"

"No." Agent Periwinkle slapped a palm to his forehead as he squatted down to examine the gang's leader. "These are members of the famed Somali biker gang, the Nile Crocodiles."

Agent Orange increased the scrunch of his face to a point where his eyes almost closed. "Why would a Somali biker gang call themselves that? The Nile doesn't flow through Somali. And why would a Somali biker gang be in Zimbabwe? Are you sure about this, Periwinkle?"

"Positive." He turned the leader's bloody face toward him. His tone rose an octave. "This is their leader, Jaafi Sharmarke Kumar, better known as The Angry Hyena. This is going to score us huge points with the CIA. And Interpol." He smiled at me. "Well done."

I brushed off the praise and mild ego boost, for I had a bone to pick with these two. "What took you so long? You left me on my own to fight not only Grandma and her grandsons, but these Nile Crocodile dudes."

"It's a long way back to the plane. And why didn't you radio in for help?" Agent Orange glanced at my ears. "You're not wearing your earpiece, are you?"

"Don't twist this into being my fault. You abandoned uthh."

"Well, from where I stand, it looks like you did pretty good on your own," said Agent Periwinkle as he surveyed the fallen with nodding approval.

"But the old woman and her grandsons got away. And they took the cat."

"Did they find the vials?" asked Agent Orange.

"No," I said.

"Good, then the vials are still here. I'll check the silo." Agent Orange grabbed a circle of rope with a grappling hook tied at one end.

"There still may be time to catch Grandma Marjorie and her grandsonthh."

"No time for that. The vials are our top priority," said Agent Orange as he did a test swirl with the grappling hook.

"You don't even care that the cat is gone. It doesn't matter to you. All you care about is those stupid vials." I hated the shrill that had crept into my voice. Tears pooled in my eyes. I wished for hands or at least the dexterity to wipe my eyes on my shoulders. "You're an unfeeling robot."

His head snapped towards me. He stormed up to my snout with fury blazing in his eyes. "You think I don't grieve for those we've lost? In the past week, I watched three GIBOD agents get vaporized into goo, two get devoured by zombie butterflies, and two more have their eyes pecked out. I failed to prevent any of that. You don't think that gets to me? Well, it does. So, don't lecture me about loss." His eyeball flames had diminished to a smolder. His brow had unfurrowed. He stepped back and tightened the knot on the grappling hook. "Put your emotions aside and do your job, because if we don't, millions more will die." He trudged toward the silo.

The groan of a Nile Crocodile, resembling a Texas rancher with a beard which rivaled those of Southern rock band ZZ Top, broke the awkward silence. He pushed himself up. With only a slight deviation in his path, Agent Orange slid over and gave the biker a swift kick in the head. A tooth flew as the Nile Crocodile collapsed.

I sat down in silent protest and refused to help with the search.

This lasted all of about a minute before Agent Orange yelled at me. "Cow, grab a flashlight and get searching. There may be more of these guys coming. There's no time for sulking."

Agent Periwinkle walked up and strapped a coal miner's hat on my head. He flipped the light on and patted my neck. "There you go."

The director searched inside the silo as Agent Periwinkle and I searched through the piles of rock. We found nothing. Next, Agent Periwinkle dug holes while I served as the anchor for the rope that lowered Agent Orange into the well. With the rope cinched around my waist, my blood boiled over his lack of compassion for my friends. The job always came first for him. I dreamed of untying the rope around my waist. I imagined the splash he'd make. Reaching back, I licked the knot. Knot tying was part of our training. Only the pig, thanks to his karate-clench hooves, had the dexterity to master knot tying. The chicken came close to tying simple knots with her claws, but the rest of us didn't stand a chance. Yet, I had learned to identify knots. This was a bowline knot. With a tug of a loop, the knot would fall apart.

"There's nothing down here. Cow, pull me up,"

I clamped my teeth onto the loop and prepared to pull, when a voice deep inside of me spoke up. *You knew the job was dangerous when you took it. There's no turning back now. If you want to save your friends, you need to do your job.* I released my grip, sighed and then pulled Agent Orange up by walking away from the well.

"Periwinkle. You find anything?" asked Agent Orange as he pulled himself over the well wall.

"No. I've got nothing." Agent Periwinkle sighed and sat down on a pile of rocks.

"Cow, are you sure they didn't leave with the vials?" asked Agent Orange as he brushed off his black suit coat and pants.

"I'm positive. She said they only came for the cat."

"So, the old woman and her freaky gang of grandsons didn't find the vials, but what about these guys?" Agent Periwinkle poked his foot at the long-bearded biker Agent Orange had kicked earlier. He let out a faint groan.

"I forgot. That one's still alive." Agent Orange grabbed a bottle of water and dumped it on the face of the not quite dead yet biker.

The biker's legs squirmed as he wiped the water off his face and long beard. He rolled over on his side, but never opened his eyes.

Agent Orange kicked him onto his back and dumped another bottle of water over his face.

The possible ZZ Top band member coughed and spat up water, but still didn't open his eyes.

"Wakey, wakey," said Agent Orange as he bent down, grabbed the man's shirt, and yanked him to a sitting position.

The burly biker opened his eyes.

"Hello. Good morning. What have you done with the vials?" asked Agent Orange.

The biker said nothing as he stared at his fallen comrades.

Agent Orange shook the biker with every syllable he spoke. "We need answers. What happened to those vials? Where are they?"

The potential member of ZZ Top spat in his face.

Agent Orange stood up without wiping off the spit, pulled his pistol out, and pointed it at the biker's head. The biker showed no emotion. He closed his eyes and awaited death.

Agent Orange lowered his weapon.

The biker peeked with one eye before opening them both. That's when he saw me coming up behind Agent Orange. He yelled "*Ibliisku Lo'da. Ibliisku Lo'da. Ibliisku Lo'da,*" as he scrambled backward into a stone wall of the Great Enclosure.

"What the heck is he saying?" asked Agent Orange as we advanced on the biker.

"It'thh Somali," I said. "He'thh saying 'the devil bovine, the devil bovine.'"

Agent Orange pulled his head back in bewilderment. "That white guy speaks Somali?"

Agent Periwinkle shook his head. "I told you, they're a Somali biker gang. Of course, they're going to speak Somali. The better question is, how does the cow know Somali?"

"Hector Spector'thh device must have –"

Agent Orange raised his hand. "It doesn't matter. We need answers from this ZZ Top wannabe, and I believe we found his weak spot. Cow, look menacing."

I snarled, bared my teeth, and put a hoof on his chest. His eyes popped even farther out of his head.

Agent Orange gave me a confirming nod. "Good. Now ask him about the vials."

I did. The long-bearded biker squirmed. I applied a bit more pressure with my hoof, and the squirming stopped. I asked again.

In Somali, he said, "Our orders were to collect the vials and give them to Robert, the crazy American who spends his days experimenting on birds."

I enjoyed the power I had over him. I asked more questions. "Who'thh left at the camp, besides the American?"

"Just the cook. Nobody else."

"Where'thh the camp?"

"I'll take you there. I'll take you there."

***

AFTER A SHORT TREK through the woods, we arrived at the camp. A well-worn path ran between two rows of A-frame single-person tents, and led to a larger house-shaped tent. A motorcycle stood outside each of the twelve A-frame tents, while a Land Rover sat beside the tiny house tent. The constant hum of a generator answered the question of what powered the light above the cook's firepit and the lamps inside the tiny house tent.

The cook waved us into the camp and offered us malawah and eggs. Agents Orange and Periwinkle accepted the offer and ate this traditional Somali breakfast while they tied him up. They left the cook and Guure, the lone survivor of my rampage, tied up by the fire pit, while we went for the American.

We found Robert outside his tent, leaning over a bird caught in the netting of a bird trap. He wore a white lab coat over his khaki shirt and cargo pants, removing any doubt that he was a scientist.

His head bobbed side-to-side, but I didn't see the white cords dangling from his ears until we got closer. He never heard us coming, but the bird squirmed and squawked as we approached. "Calm down, little birdie. Nobody's going to hurt you."

Agent Orange gave me strict orders to not speak, yet insisted I get Robert's attention, telling me to make it memorable and creepy. So as the scientist pulled the bird free, I licked the back of his neck.

The scientist sprang to full size and spun to face me. His eyes popped wide open. He staggered backwards and tripped over tent strings.

The bird pecked its way out of Robert's hands and flew away.

"Dang it. You made me lose my bird. Who are you people?" From the ground, he looked up at me as he yanked his earbuds out. "And what the heck is that?"

"That's a cow, Robert." Agent Orange offered a hand, but the scientist didn't grab it.

Robert eyed me up and down. "Yeah, I can see that. Why did it lick me?"

"Forget about the cow. We have other matters to discuss." Agent Orange motioned for Robert to enter the tent.

Agent Periwinkle had already gone inside. He hovered over Robert's desk at the back of the tent, counting the swallow zombie virus vials.

Robert scrambled to his feet, rushed into the tent, bounced across his bed, and tried to grab the vials. "Don't touch those. They're very dangerous."

Agent Periwinkle shouldered Robert away from the vials. "All the vials are here." He stuffed all but two vials into a satchel. "But two are empty."

"Seriously. You need to leave those alone. You don't understand what that stuff is." The skinny scientist made a wild grab for the satchel, which Agent Periwinkle casually blocked with a forearm.

While I stayed in the doorway, Agent Orange strolled around the bed, past the mini-fridge, coffee pot, and microwave. He squeezed between the bed and Agent Periwinkle, then pulled out the desk chair and motioned for Robert to sit.

"I'm good. I prefer standing." Robert snarled at Agent Orange.

"That isn't an option, Robert." Agent Orange forced him into the chair. "There, isn't that better?"

"No, it isn't." Robert sat in the chair like a pouting child. "And how do you know my name?"

"There is much about you and your Somali biker friends we know, including your connections to the terrorist organization, the Havarti Travel Bureau." Agent Orange paced behind Robert, who squirmed and twisted in his chair to make sure he maintained eye contact with him.

"One man's terrorist is another man's liberator."

"Are these your logs?" asked Agent Periwinkle as he flipped through the pages of a leather-bound notebook on Robert's desk.

The scientist threw his hands up in the air. "That's my stuff. Put it down!"

"Now, Robert, you know that's not going to happen." Agent Orange gave him the classic disappointed teacher glare.

Robert huffed, crossed his arms, and glared at Agent Periwinkle.

As the pair of agents rummaged through his tent, empathy for Robert crept in. I suppressed the emotion by reminding myself he worked for the people who had kidnapped my friends.

"Is this true?" Agent Periwinkle continued to flip through the notebook pages. "You've been testing this virus on swallows for the past week and a half, with no positive results?"

Robert scowled and shifted his stare to the dirt floor. "I'm not saying anything until I talk to my lawyer."

Agent Periwinkle motioned toward the stacks of bird cages piled next to the desk. There had to be over thirty cages. "You infected all these birds, and not one of them shows any signs of zombiism."

Robert groaned and stared down at his shoes. At one point, he bent down and flicked off a speck of dirt.

Agent Orange picked up the near-empty vial. "The label says swallow virus. The other viruses have been very specific."

"Sort of," said Agent Periwinkle. "What's your point?"

"Well, is this an African or European swallow virus?"

"Huh, I don't know that," said Agent Periwinkle.

"Oh great. Monty Python fans." The scientist rolled his eyes.

Dr. Hash Browns loved Monty Python and had us watch The Holy Grail over a hundred times. But I couldn't imagine either of the agents ever watching it. They had no sense of humor. They wouldn't have lasted to the first swallow reference.

Agent Periwinkle twisted up the left side of his mouth and squinted his left eye. "European swallow. African swallow. What's the difference?"

"Don't encourage him," said the scientist, as he scuffed at the dirt, the scowl still plastered on his face.

Agent Orange paced over to the cages. "Well, the African swallow is non-migratory. The virus won't spread very well with a non-migratory bird."

"How do you know so much about swallows?" asked Agent Periwinkle.

"Well, you've got to know these things when you're director of GIBOD."

"Stop it. Stop it." Robert doubled over, with his hands folded together on top of his head. "Enough with the Monty Python routine. Is this your new form of GIBOD torture?" He kept his head down as he squirmed in his chair.

Agents Orange and Periwinkle smiled at his misery, though I doubt they had a clue how well they parodied the movie.

Robert released the grip on his head, but continued to gaze at his shoes. His eyebrows, cheeks, lips, and ears all drooped, as he exhaled a heavy sigh. "You do bring up a good point. I wish I'd thought of that a week ago." He scanned his collection of healthy African swallows and sighed. "You don't happen to have any European Swallows with you?"

Agent Periwinkle strolled to the stack of bird cages that lined the far wall. "Have you infected any other birds besides these in the cages?"

"Just those and, as you've noticed, none of them are actually infected."

"What about the one that flew away?" asked Agent Orange.

"I hadn't infected him yet. I'd just trapped him."

"Well, let's pack it all up and bring it with us," said Agent Orange.

"Be my guest. It's all useless, anyway." Robert's face still drooped, and his shoulders slumped.

"We're taking you with as well," said Agent Orange as he started gathering up the scientist's notebooks.

"I figured as much." The scientist raised his sad eyes toward Agent Orange. "You got any chips with you, like Doritos or even pretzels? There is a lack of decent chips in this country. I've been craving chips for days."

Agent Orange blamed me for what happened next. Though he had not ordered me to be the lookout, he insisted I should have known that to be my role, seeing as I stood outside the tent. My focus was on the events inside the tent, so I never saw the cook free himself, sneak into the woods, and pop out with a rifle.

Shots ripped through the tent and into Robert.

I gasped, involuntarily cloaked, and dropped to the ground.

Agents Orange and Periwinkle drew their weapons and returned fire with deadly force.

Robert slid off his chair, clutching his chest. He coughed up blood that dribbled down his chin as he curled into the fetal position. "I'm not quite dead yet. I'm good to go with you."

Agent Periwinkle kneeled next to Robert, who coughed once more, spraying blood on Agent Periwinkle's face. Robert's eyes drifted into a blank stare at a random spot on the tent ceiling.

Agent Periwinkle, blood still splattered across his face, checked for a pulse. He shook his head and closed Robert's eyelids.

15: A Cow's Paradise

WE FOUND GUURE, THE lone "survivor" of my rampage in the Great Enclosure, dead. I stood over his body, apologizing as the mangled corpses of the bikers paged through my brain. The images faded as I convinced myself I had no choice. It was either kill or be killed. I forced the despair into the dark recesses of my consciousness. My focus needed to remain on saving my friends. I groaned as I looked down at Guure one last time, bemoaning the lost chance to interrogate him.

Agents Orange and Periwinkle collected Robert the Scientist's research notes and the vials of zombie virus, leaving the birds and deceased Nile Crocodiles for the GIBOD cleanup crew. Back on the plane, Agent Periwinkle entered the coordinates for the last batch of stolen zombie viruses, and we were off to India. Along the way, Agent Orange lectured me about paying attention to my surroundings. When he finished, I pushed for us searching for my kidnapped friends. Neither of us really listened to what the other said.

The sun shined brightly as we landed in a field of browned grass in northern India, but my body and mind thought it should be nightfall. Agent Periwinkle pointed out the Martand Sun Temple ruins on our descent. A subdivision sat between our field and these ruins.

As we walked down the ramp, Agent Periwinkle patted my neck.

"You're going to like India. Trust me. You won't even have to cloak."

"It'thh broad daylight. I can't just waltz around the ruins."

Agent Periwinkle smiled, which he did more often than Agent Orange, but it still creeped me out. "Have you never heard of the sacred cow?"

"I've been cooped up in a space station laboratory for several hundred yearthh, so excuse me if I haven't heard of the sacred cow."

"The Hindu religion reveres and worships cows. They'll treat you like royalty. There'll be no need for cloaking," said Agent Periwinkle.

"I thought the mad alien scientist that experimented on you taught you all about humans and Earth," said Agent Orange, rummaging through a duffle-bag.

"He didn't teach uthh religion. Anyway, I'll believe it when I see it."

Agent Orange pulled up an aerial image of the Martand Sun Temple ruins on a tablet. "Here's the plan." He pointed at the rectangular wall around the temple. "Agent Periwinkle and I will pose as tourists, which grants us access to the gardens, the courtyard, and the temple itself."

Agent Periwinkle pointed at unkempt fields at the sides of the courtyard walls. "But we won't have access to these fields."

"That's where your special status as the sacred cow comes in. You'll be able to roam these fields, with no questions asked," said Agent Orange.

"Again. I'll believe it when I see it." I'd grown tired of them talking up this sacred cow story.

Agent Orange shoved an earpiece into my ear and activated it with a tap. "Keep it on, and shout out if you find the vials. Got it?"

"Yethh, thhir," I said with the enthusiasm of a dog on their way to the vet.

We weaved through a rural neighborhood. The streets and houses resembled those of any small rural town. Only the golden-brown skin of the locals and the high-ratio of motorbikes and three-wheel vehicles to automobiles provided a clue to our location. Those locals judged us with unwelcoming and quizzical gawks. Murmurs hung in the warm morning air.

As we passed a mom and her two pre-school children out for a walk, the oldest child pointed at me. My jaw clenched as I waited for cries of, "Mad Cow! Mad Cow!" I froze and planned my escape route back to the plane.

The mother, in a bright red and yellow sari, locked her disapproving frown on us. My jaw-clench ran down my neck and back, ending in a tight butt scrunch. But as Agents Orange and Periwinkle kept walking, her stare followed them. Ahead of me and across the street, two boys held their soccer balls and pointed at the agents.

Three houses ahead, a cow munched grass by the side of the road. No one pointed or glared at her. They saved that for the two white guys in black suits and sunglasses. My stiff jaw relaxed into a smirk. The agents were the ones out of place, showing no resemblance to tourists on their way to the Martand Sun Temple ruins.

The mother still glared at Agents Orange and Periwinkle as she handed her daughters a large feedbag. They ran across the street towards me. The younger daughter hugged my leg. My butt cheeks relaxed, resulting in the release of gas. I feared this social embarrassment had ruined the moment. Instead, the girls chuckled, and the younger daughter tightened her squeeze. A warmth flowed down my spine and into my hooves as the older girl opened the feedbag full of grains and grass hay. The smell brought me back to my days on the farm. A simpler time, when a feedbag provided my greatest joy. I plunged my snout into the bag and began devouring the contents.

The mom shuffled across the street while monitoring Agents Orange and Periwinkle, who were several houses ahead. She placed her hand on my neck, closed her eyes and in Sanskrit said, "Just as every raindrop that falls from the sky flows into the Ocean, in the same way, every prayer offered to any Deity flows to Lord Krishna."

A tear dripped into the feedbag. I was unworthy of their adoration. The aura of positivity engulfing me did its best to force self-forgiveness, but I refused. I'd failed to protect my friends. I'd failed as their leader.

Unconscious stress eating took over, and I finished the grains and hay without savoring its pleasures.

"Cow, enough of the lovefest," said Agent Orange in my earpiece. "We've got a mission to complete."

I wanted to tell him where he could stick his mission, but knew if I spoke, the positive vibes that kept me from sobbing uncontrollably would turn sour in an instant and it would be back to "Devil bovine! Devil bovine!"

The oldest daughter pulled the bag away. The family bowed as they headed back across the street. I sighed and trotted up to Agents Orange and Periwinkle.

***

THE GROUNDS LEADING TO the temple resembled the entrance to an English castle. Manicured lawns and precision trimmed hedges flanked a modern stone walkway that ended at stairs to the temple's courtyard. At the top of the stairs, giant pillars resembling classic chess rooks announced the entrance to the courtyard. The series of archways forming the outer rectangular wall showed flashes of its former glory.

The locals and tourists regarded Agents Orange and Periwinkle with suspicious looks as we approached the temple grounds. Meanwhile, I waltzed across the manicured lawn in front of the ruins without even a sideways glare.

As instructed, I made my way to the unkempt fields outside the walled off ruins, while Agents Orange and Periwinkle headed for the entrance. I had no intention of searching for the stupid vials of zombie virus. As soon as I passed through a cluster of trees, into an area where no one could see me, I smacked my earpiece into a tree trunk, deactivating my mic. My emotions smashed the dam, releasing the flood of tears. I assumed my failures as a leader and losing my friends triggered the tsunami, but instead the bloody faces of the bikers scrolled in my head. I'd killed them all. A suppressed anger had erupted from the depths of my soul. A rage I didn't know I owned. Sure, they threatened to butcher and eat me, which Agent Orange insisted made my self-defense actions excusable, but I didn't have to kill them all. Agent Periwinkle claimed the Nile Crocodiles deserved fates far worse than death at my hands and I shouldn't waste a moment grieving their deaths. But neither of them had the biker gang's blood on their hooves.

My body heaved in waves as I saw no end to the sobbing. But for every action, there's an equal and opposite reaction. In this case, the heavy sobbing forced air out my backside. An image of the girls broke the chain of bloody faces. As if they were still with me, the warmth of the hug flowed up my leg, across my chest, up my neck, and dried my eyes. A chuckle snuck in amongst the weeps as I relived their laughter at my fart in their presence.

The sobs stopped, though despair still ravaged me. I blew my snot on the ground, so I could take a few deep breaths through my nostrils. It took several to shift the energy to positive pursuits. I could still make things right. I could still save my friends.

My eyes opened. As if on cue, the billowing blackness streamed up to me. It circled my head before the crow plopped on my back. He dug his talons into my leathery hide.

My cloak instinctively flickered on. I forced it off. "Take me. Take me to the others."

"That's the flan," he said in English, with a raspy folk singer voice akin to Bob Dylan.

He gave his wings a strong flap before I asked him what this meant.

We didn't move.

He took a deep breath, repositioned his grip, and flapped his wings again.

This time, my front hooves lifted an inch off the ground. The crow grunted. We rose another inch, then dropped back down.

"What does 'That'thh the flan' mean?"

He walked back and forth on my back, shaking his wings out. "Stupid misaligned beak. Sometimes my P's sound like F's. It's so annoying."

"I know what you mean," I said as I figured out that flan meant plan.

"So, the flan changed. Something about studying your indestructibility when cloaked."

"If you're taking me to the other animals, I'm in. Let'thh do it."

"Okay. Let's do this." He waddled up between my eyes, took several deep breaths, and grabbed my cowlick. He shifted into hyperspeed and blurred away with a claw full of my hair.

I chased after him, running through the cluster of trees and onto the temple's manicured front lawn. There was no sign of the crow.

"Cow, we found the vials," said Agent Orange in my earpiece. "Meet us by the entrance road in five. It's time to go home."

A black dot in the sky turned into a blur. It came straight at me. A moment later, the crow perched himself on the top of my head.

"Cow, if you want to come with me, you're gonna have to help. I need you to jump when I blast into hyperspeed."

It came out as, "...have to helf. I need you to jumf when I blast into hyfersfeed." It took a moment to translate. "Got it. I need to jump when you blast into hyperspeed. I'm ready when you are."

He hopped on my back and dug his claws in. "On the count of three."

I crouched, ready to launch.

"One. Two. Three."

I pushed off with all my power. We got about six inches off the ground. We hovered. He tightened his grip. He panted. He wheezed. We rose another inch. He let out a primal scream. We rose another half an inch before he lost his grip, tumbling me to the ground.

The crow landed on my back, where he paced and caught his breath. He didn't notice the families of tourists making their way toward us, yelling, "Shoo, crow, shoo!!"

A rock thrown by a child fell well short of us.

"How about this? You do a running start."

The crowd had moved within adult rock throwing distance of us, yet the crow still hadn't seen them. I liked it that way. I needed him to stay focused.

"Okay. Let'thh do it."

The crow straddled my neck as if he was riding a horse and dug his claws in. I bucked up on my hind legs like a wild mustang. When I came down, I started my sprint.

The crowd split in half just in time to let us charge between them. They yelled at the crow. They threw their rocks. I got pelted twice, but they missed the crow.

We raced past the gauntlet. I galloped faster than ever before. I imagined the world around me blurring away. The crow tightened his grip. Skin pulled up on the back of my neck. The bird flapped his enormous wings, again and again. After a moment of weightlessness, every fiber in my body, natural or unnatural, felt this was it; we were about to rocket off. I pounded out a couple more gallops and pushed off with all four legs.

I flew. There was nothing but air below me. I pumped my legs like I had seen in cartoon versions of Santa's mythical flying reindeer. Then I spread my legs out in the classic aerodynamic flying cow pose; front legs straight in front of me and back legs extended behind. The whoosh of the crow's flapping wings flowed through the handful of hairs left on my head. One more flap of the crow's mighty wings and the world around me would disappear.

But it didn't. We didn't blast into hyperspeed. I tried to pump my legs again. Have you ever reached the bottom of the stairs thinking there's still one stair to go? That's what it felt like when my legs smacked hard into the manicured lawn of the Martand Sun Temple ruins. My front legs spiked hard into the grassy surface. Momentum kept my backside moving while my face remained smashed into the dirt. My butt flipped over my head. The world around me became a blur as I tumbled into a series of uncontrolled cartwheels. The crow tried to separate, but got caught up in my cartwheel vortex. We crashed through the hedges before coming to a stop on the stairs of the Martand Sun Temple ruins entrance. I remember smacking into him, and him smacking into me at various points in my spiraling fall. When we came to a stop, the crow lay upside down next to me on the stairs.

As the crowd rushed toward us, the sight of their feet made me realize I was the one upside down.

"Did you see what that raven did to the cow?" said someone in Hindi.

"A raven attacked my herd last week and nearly killed a calf," said another.

"Get that raven," said third.

I righted myself and nudged the crow.

The crow backed up a stair as he glared at the crowd. "Where did all these feople come from? This isn't good. I'm not supposed to be seen. Feople aren't supposed to know about me yet. Cow, sorry, but I've got to go."

The crowd gasped as the crow shot straight up and blurred away.

I dropped to my knees and plopped my chin on the top step. My ride to the others had left without me.

Slow clapping came from behind me. Agents Orange and Periwinkle approached. They smiled and waved to the crowd. Agent Orange motioned for me to turn around.

I reluctantly obeyed.

The agents flanked me and put their arms around my neck. The three of us took a bow.

A small percentage of the crowd clapped.

"Thank you, ladies and gentlemen," said Agent Orange, standing at the top of the stairs. "Please give it up one more time for the amazing magician and animal training stylings of Dr. Perry Winkles." Lucky for Agent Orange, most of the crowd understood English.

He stepped aside to let Agent Periwinkle take center stage for more bowing. The entire crowd applauded, including some of the temple's security guards. Agent Periwinkle smiled and blew kisses to the crowd.

Agent Orange had to grab him by the shirt collar and drag him away.

"Cow, good job fending off the crow. We found the vials, so let's get out of this oven and head home." Agent Orange marched down the steps with Agent Periwinkle behind him. They waved to the tourists, who still held rocks and sticks, but didn't throw them.

I stayed put, as competing voices vied to decide my next move.

Forget it all. Stay here in the Cow's Paradise. Be pampered and loved every day and do whatever you want.

Wait for the crow. When the coast is clear, he'll come back for you. He'll take you to the others.

You need to refuse to move until you have a guarantee from Agent Orange to search for the chicken, dog, and cat. Make a big scene. He'll have to agree.

Activate berserker mode, destroy Agents Orange and Periwinkle, steal their plane, and go find your friends. It's the only viable option.

Too many options. I needed more time to decide. I needed pros and cons. A decision matrix.

"Cow! Let's go." Agent Orange had walked back to me and dragged me by the ear.

A couple of tourists raised their rocks.

I shook off his grip and sighed. Creating a scene would disrupt the locals' positive views of cows. Besides, I'd sworn an oath to GIBOD. With a heavy heart, I followed Agents Orange and Periwinkle to the plane, leaving a Cow's Paradise behind.

16: The Journey Home

ON THE WALK TO the plane, I had become numb and resigned to my fate. We would head back to the base. I feared I'd never see my friends again. I stayed in the cargo bay as Agents Orange and Periwinkle headed for the lounge.

If not for the boast of unconditional love from the mom and her daughters, I would have plopped to the floor. Instead, I took several laps along the walls, then added a diagonal crisscross to my meandering. Perhaps this was my attempt to escape the trap I found myself in. I couldn't give up on my friends, but I had no plan. No leads. No idea where they were. Neither did Agent Orange or Agent Periwinkle. I pinned my hopes on the crow coming to find me. In what I assumed to be a major rationalization, I concluded returning to the base to be my best option. The crow knew where our base was. He would expect me to be there. Perhaps heading home was the best strategy. It wasn't proactive, but it appeared to be my best plan. Satisfied with this rationalization, I joined Agents Orange and Periwinkle.

When I entered the plane's lounge, Agent Orange stood up and put his arm around my neck. "It's party time."

I slipped out of his neck embrace. "It doesn't feel like a time to party. Agents White and Eggshell got permanently blinded. The chicken, dog, and cat are missing. Grandma Marjorie and her grandsonthh are still at large."

"Cow," said Agent Orange as he sparked up a cigar, "in this business you've got to celebrate even the minor victories. And this isn't a minor victory. We saved the human race and several species from extinction-level events... potentially. Sure, we had setbacks, but at the end of the day, we came out winners."

"Well, I don't want to party." I may have concluded that returning to the base was the best way to find my friends, but it didn't mean I was happy about it.

Agent Orange puffed his cigar as he eyed me up and down. "What's the matter? Why the long face?" He paused, looked at Agent Periwinkle, and then broke into laughter. "You get it? She's got a long face, because of the snout, but she's also sad. It works on multiple levels." Agent Orange had smiled three times in my presence, but this was the first time he'd laughed.

It left me bewildered, especially since I saw no humor in the so-called joke.

Agent Periwinkle didn't provide a courtesy chuckle or even a smile, but gave me a subtle eye-roll.

Agent Orange swirled a brown liquid in a glass and then gulped it down.

"What'thh that you're drinking?"

"Single malt Scotch whiskey," said Agent Orange. "Good stuff. You want some?"

If it made this sourpuss happy, I figured it might improve my mood. "Sure. I'll try it."

"Periwinkle, pour this cow a drink."

Agent Periwinkle pulled a whiskey glass from a cabinet in the lounge and poured a shot of Scotch. He held the glass up to me and said, "Sorry, I forgot. No hands. You want it in a bowl, or should I just pour it in your mouth?"

"Pour it in." I didn't want to deal with licking it out of a bowl.

"I'll give you just a sip." He poured a small taste into my mouth.

It burned the instant it landed on my tongue. "My tongue'thh on fire. It'thh burning my esophagus. It'thh boiling my stomachs. Why do you humans enjoy melting yourself from the inside out?"

"It's good for you. It grows hair on your chest," said Agent Orange.

"Why would I want hair on my chest? It still burnthh. It still burnthh. Get me some water!"

The agents laughed wildly, but Agent Periwinkle brought me a large bowl of water. I lapped it up in an instant.

"How do you drink this stuff? Have you got cast iron throatthh and stomachthh?"

Agent Orange examined the whiskey in his glass. "It's Bowmore, one of the smoothest single malt scotch whiskeys in the world." He took another sip, showing no signs of it burning his mouth, throat, or stomach.

"The first sip is always the worst. It's smoother after that," said Agent Periwinkle as he held the glass in front of me.

I eyed the glass, but kept my mouth shut.

"You don't have to drink if you don't want to. No pressure." Agent Periwinkle pulled the drink back.

I took another look at Agent Orange's smiling face. "Fine. I'll have another."

Agent Periwinkle waited for me to tilt my head back and open wide. He poured the liquid fire down my throat.

I managed to swallow the toxic beverage before the coughing fit kicked in. "I thought," *cough, cough,* "you said," *cough, cough,* "the second shot would be," *cough, cough, cough, cough,* "smoother?"

Agent Orange came over and put his arm around my neck again. His jovial, laughing face had vanished. "Cow, I empathize with what you're going through. It's tough when you lose a friend in battle." He paused, wiped his eye, and sniffed.

Another first for Agent Orange. He demonstrated true empathy. These were emotions I didn't believe existed inside him. It was nice to know he wasn't always an emotionless robot, even if single-malt whiskey was the key to invoking these emotions. And for his sudden mood swings.

"I wish I could tell you it gets easier. It doesn't. But it is part of the job. We aren't greeters at Walmart. This is dangerous work."

"Yethh, we knew the job was dangerous when we took it."

"But you took it anyway. That shows guts. I may have misjudged you all. Well, not the duck and rabbit. I'm pretty sure I'm spot on with those two idiots. They're hopeless. Lost causes. But the rest of you, you've shown me something. You're not always the sharpest blades in the butcher shop, but very brave." He paused and covered his mouth. "Oh, sorry, probably not the right phrase to use in front of you."

"It'thh okay. No worries." His sudden change of heart and unexpected praise shocked me to the point where his offensive butcher shop comment hadn't registered with me.

"Anyway, I mean it. You guys showed me something out there. I'm back to being glad I talked you all into joining the agency. You're gonna need more training, 'cause like I said, not the sharpest tools in the... forget I said that. Anyway, we're going to find your lost friends. I promise."

"Thank you, thhir." His commitment to finding the others left me stunned. But I had no time to process this new Agent Orange, because he stuffed his lit cigar in my open mouth.

"Take a few puffs on this."

I took a toke and immediately coughed the cigar out of my mouth. "Are you trying to kill me?"

"You realize who you're dealing with, right? I mean, if we were trying to kill you, you'd already be dead," said Agent Orange, picking the burning cigar up off the floor.

"There are holes burning in my first and second stomachthh."

Agent Orange shuffled to the table, grabbed the bottle, and poured another drink for Agent Periwinkle and me. He looked surprised when he saw his own glass still had whiskey in it. He slugged it down and refilled it. "We haven't done a toast yet." He handed two glasses to Agent Periwinkle and held his up high. "We raise our glasses in honor of our comrades lost in the line of duty. Agents Maroon, Burgundy, Crimson, Cranberry, and Coral. We toast to those maimed or captured in the course of this mission. Your sacrifices have not been in vain, for we have secured the vials and foiled the Havarti Travel Bureau's evil plans."

Agent Periwinkle raised his glass. "May those who have passed find peace. May those injured heal quickly. And may we find those lost to us."

The two agents lowered their drinks and bowed their heads, so I did the same, bringing Agent Orange's smoldering cigar into view. I flashed back to the start of our mission when Agent Orange passed out the cigars. Back then, the thought of Agents White and Eggshell not finishing the mission never crossed my mind.

The agents raised their heads. Agent Orange held his glass high. Agent Periwinkle did the same with the two glasses he held. They clinked the glasses and as they slammed their drinks, Agent Periwinkle poured mine into my open mouth. The throat burn wasn't as bad as the first two shots.

"Cow, do you have any clue how far back Periwinkle and I go? I mean, I don't go as far back as he does. He's been around FOREVER. All I'm saying is we've seen a lot of bad stuff." Agent Orange filled the three glasses with what remained of the bottle. "Do we got another one of these?"

"I'll check." Despite having matched Agent Orange shot for shot, Agent Periwinkle's aloof demeanor hadn't changed.

As Agent Periwinkle took a step toward the kitchen, Agent Orange grabbed him around the shoulder and spun him to face me. "Listen to this man. He's wise. He was my first partner. Did you know that?"

"I was unaware, thhir."

Agent Periwinkle squished half his face as he gave his boss a sideways glare. Agent Orange released him, and he headed off to the kitchen.

"I owe that man everything. I wouldn't be director of GIBOD if it wasn't for Periwinkle. Actually, I'd be dead if it wasn't for him." Agent Orange plopped onto the sofa, spilling half of his drink. He didn't notice. "I was still a rookie. Periwinkle and I stumbled onto a group of real psychos. They believed squirrels were attempting to take over the world." He sat up and waved a pointed index finger. "Let me make this perfectly clear: there is no Great Squirrel Conspiracy."

Agent Periwinkle returned with a fresh bottle.

"Periwinkle, remember the Squirrel Conspiracy wackos?"

"Total nut jobs. By the way, we're out of Bowmore, so I settled for Glenmorangie Signet."

Agent Orange nodded his approval before continuing with his story. "They had built up an arsenal to fight what they thought was the imminent squirrel uprising. Crate after crate of semi-automatic weapons, ammunition, bazookas. They had frickin' bazookas to fight squirrels. And let me make this clear, there is no Great Squirrel Conspiracy."

"You mentioned that before," I said.

Agent Orange motioned for Agent Periwinkle to fill his glass. "Cow, I bet you don't know squirrels, on average, only live one year."

"I was unaware, thhir."

As Agent Periwinkle filled his boss's glass, I remembered the rabbit and duck calling him Agent Orange's man servant. They had a point.

"Well, it's true. And how much can they learn in one year? Humans, the smartest animal on the planet, are still pooping in their pants at a year old. All I'm saying is there's no way squirrels are smart enough to take over the planet."

"Agreed, thhir."

"Anyway, the point is, it was our job to disarm these whack-jobs. They got a little goofy around non-believers of the Great Squirrel Conspiracy and started firing at us. Well, this crazy old man jumps in front of me and takes a bullet. He took a bullet for me, right in the shoulder. Show her the scar."

"I'm sure she doesn't want to see my scar," said Agent Periwinkle as he sat down on the couch next to Agent Orange without spilling his drink.

"You saved my life. I love you, man," said Agent Orange, giving Agent Periwinkle a man-hug.

"I love you, too, my friend." Agent Periwinkle held his glass at a distance to avoid spillage and grimaced when a portion of Agent Orange's whiskey splashed on his neck.

"Sounds like crazy timethh."

"You don't know the half of it," said Agent Orange, his eyes now slits.

"Am I supposed to feel different, because I don't feel different?" I asked.

"At your size, it'll take a lot more to get you drunk," said Agent Periwinkle, shifting forward on the couch. "I'll pour you another one."

Agent Orange motioned for Periwinkle to stay seated. "Just let her drink from the bottle."

"Fine. Cow, have at it. I'm going to check on the cleanup of the Great Enclosure." Agent Periwinkle set the bottle on a counter as he slid past me.

My tongue, throat, and stomachs had gone numb, so I figured why not have another. I spilled a few ounces, working out the right method. I gripped the bottle with most of its neck in my mouth and snapped my head up.

When I turned to get Agent Orange's approval of my new whiskey drinking skills, I found him passed out on the couch.

After polishing off the bottle, I felt no different. On advice from the robot flight attendants, I tried tequila next. Then vodka. I finished by polishing off a bottle of rum as the plane touched down in the GIBOD compound.

***

I SLID OPEN THE barn doors. "Rabbit. Duck. Have you ever tried something called tequila? But now that I thhay that out loud, I'm afraid you'd like it too much, and with your tiny little bodies, it'thh a good idea you stay away from tequila." I looked up at their empty loft. "And whiskey. Stay away from whiskey."

No one responded. I headed out the back entrance, expecting the rabbit and duck to be working on their half-pipe. The half-pipe remained unfinished and the construction site empty.

I reentered the barn. "Fish, have you ever tried tequila? Though I suspect you would be more of a whiskey fan."

Again, no one responded.

I walked past the computerless office. "Cat, I haven't forgotten. I will enter your IT request." I dropped my snout and sighed. "Of course, you're not here and I have no idea what to enter or how to submit an IT request, thho …that will have to wait until you return, assuming you return."

I passed the chicken and dog's stall. Several images popped into my head, which I truly wish hadn't. "They're just good friends. They're just good friends."

I continued strolling around the barn, remembering how it used to be full of noise and activity. I chuckled about how the cat hated that. She complained about requiring peace and quiet to concentrate, and lobbied several times to get her own office or lab space somewhere else on the campus, far away from the rabbit and duck. She would have loved this quiet.

As I entered my office, a BarnYard Heroes group photo on my desk caught my eye. Agent Orange took the picture on the day we moved into the barn and started our training. The rabbit and duck gave me the photo the day before our training mission. Tears welled up. I had failed them. I promised to keep them safe.

The barn door opened.

I dashed out of my office. "Pig! I am so happy to see you." I raced to give him a hug, realizing too late that I'm not built to give hugs, only receive them, and ended up standing awkwardly close to him.

He gave me the stink eye and pushed me away. "You okay?"

I scoffed. *What a jerk.* "Geez, I'm just happy to thhee you. And where'thh everyone else? Where'thh the rabbit and duck? Where'thh the fish?"

"I haven't seen the fish in days, but that's not unusual. As for dumb and dumber, they took off two nights ago to, and I quote, 'Do superhero stuff and things.' Morons. They think if they do a heroic deed or two, like save a baby from a burning building, the agency will beg them to become agents. Idiots."

"And you just let them leave? Did you even try to stop them, or were you off making googly-eyes with your girlfriend? If anything happens to the rabbit and duck, that's on you."

The pig took a menacing step toward me. "One, she's not my girlfriend. Two, those idiots made their own choice."

"You abandoned uthh to hang out with your humans."

He poked me in the chest. "I never abandoned you. Everything I did was to protect all of you. Somebody had to. You gave into all their delusions of grandeur, letting them run off on dangerous missions, unequipped and unprepared. By the way, do you want to explain where the dog and cat are?"

At the mention of the dog and cat, my anger turned inward. "It'thh a disaster. Why did I talk everyone into joining the agency? It'thh far too dangerous. We could be living the simple life on a farm, watching the sunset. But, NOOOO. I had to push for uthh to join a secret agency. What was I thinking? There were no illusions. The agency never promised to protect uthh. All they offered was danger and death."

"So, it's true, they're both missing, and you didn't find the chicken?"

"She's gone. They're all gone. The dog. The chicken. The cat. Gone. The crow took them all."

The pig backed away, grumbled, and crossed his front hooves. "We had everyone assigned to safe duties on the base. Why were you and the others on this mission?"

A sharp pain pierced the pit of my stomachs. "Exactly. I'm an idiot. Stupid! Stupid! Stupid! I never should have brought uthh here."

The pig sighed and let his front hooves drop. "Bringing us here wasn't a bad idea. Going on missions, *that* was the bad idea."

"What do you mean?"

He put a karate-clench hoof on my shoulder. "Cow, we never would have been able to live the simple life. The agency, the Havarti Travel Bureau, French Toast; they all marked us long before we came to Earth. They would have hunted us down wherever we went."

"You don't know that. India loves cows. They worshipped me there. They'd protect me. I bet we could find a country like that for every one of uthh. I heard the French love chickens." Several deep breaths did nothing to calm my stomachs.

"That would never work."

"Maybe not for you. I doubt there'thh a country that reveres pigs."

He took a deep breath and looked away. I could see his lips counting, though no sound came out. After reaching ten, he said, "My point is, this is the safest place for us. You were right to encourage us to come here."

My eyes pooled. "Thankthh. That means a lot coming from you." I stepped forward to give him a hug, forgetting once again that I was incapable of giving hugs.

"Seriously, what's wrong with you?" He took a couple of sniffs. "Have you been drinking?"

I sniffed up my snot and wished for hands to wipe my eyes. "It's conceivable I had a couple of celebratory sipthh on the plane ride back."

He glared into my eyes. "A couple sips?"

"Thho, I had a few drinks and maybe a couple of puffs of a victory cigar. What'thh the big deal? If you had gone on an actual mission, like I did, you'd understand victory cigars and victory shots."

The pig snarled.

"You know, my stomachs don't feel so good."

"I'm not surprised. Come on. I think there's antacids in the office."

I followed the pig to the computerless office, and as he rummaged through the cabinets, he asked, "So, where were you guys? What were you up to?"

"I can't tell you that. It's classified."

The pig pulled a bottle of liquid antacid medicine out of a cabinet, shook it, removed the cap, and placed it on the table. "I heard Agents Eggshell and White got blinded. Why didn't the director bring an entire team of agents?"

I picked the bottle up in my teeth and chugged it. After spitting the empty bottle to the floor, I said, "Agent Orange has his reasons, but I'm not at liberty to discuss them right now."

"I'm not surprised." The pig did a casual scan of the area. "You know, I think there might be a sunset happening right now. Perhaps it would be a good idea for us to enjoy a relaxing sunset like you suggested earlier."

"I suggested watching the sunset? I don't remember that."

"You're drunk. You must have forgotten. But you did, so let's go." The pig took a couple of steps.

I wasn't sure what was going on, so I didn't follow him.

The pig stopped and gave me a stern look with an aggressive motion for me to follow.

Though still confused, I followed him out of the barn to the nearby silo.

The pig had to shout for me to hear. "We can assume they've bugged the barn, but we should be safe here."

"Okay. Thho?"

"I've heard things, things about Agent Orange. Let's just say, the man has a lot of secrets and is prone to irrational behavior. No one understands why your mission had such a small crew. And no offense, but everyone is wondering why half of that crew consisted of animals who had failed their cadet training."

I agreed with him and should have told him so. Instead, I went in a different direction. "You're just jealous he didn't take you on the mission."

The pig's face scrunched. "That has nothing to do with it. My focus has always been on the safety of you and the other animals. And you were all safe. You all got jobs which kept you out of harm's way. Then you stole a plane which somehow led to you being included in a mission, where several animals disappeared. Speaking of which, why hasn't Agent Orange sent out a search party for the chicken, dog, and cat?"

"He did promise to do that."

I thought that would please the pig. Instead, his face scrunched further, forcing out a growl.

The fury in the pig's voice. The fire in his eyes. That was me a few hours earlier. But after witnessing Agent Orange smile, crack jokes, and cry, I no longer pictured him as an emotionless robot. My anger had faded. But the pig reminded me how heartless and reckless Agent Orange had been. Back on the space station, when Dr. Hash Browns took things too far, I stepped in to protect the others. "It'thh like we swapped Dr. Hash Browns for Agent Orange. They both have good intentions, but disregard our safety. It was my responsibility to protect the others. You should be mad at me, not Agent Orange."

The tension in the pig's face eased, widening his eyes and relaxing his jaw line. "Cow, none of this is your fault. Agent Orange is unhinged. Did you know he locked up those old women from that church's knitting club?"

"One of them *did* pull a laser gun on uthh."

"The rest of them didn't. He left one of them tied up to a dentist chair when you all went off on your secret mission. She was there two days before anyone found her."

"Blanche! I forgot about her. Agent Orange was torturing her when the crow busted Grandma Marjorie out." This sparked the memory of Grandma Marjorie's rant about Blanche. "Blanche'thh son is a high-powered attorney, and her daughter is a United States Congresswoman. That'thh not good."

"Exactly. You see what I mean. The man is out of control."

"I have my issues with Agent Orange, but there is a method and reasoning to his madness. Someday I'll be able to explain it all."

"That's the thing. That's what everyone who goes on the director's secret mission says. They trust the director without question, and they'll tell the full story when the time is right. The problem is, they end up dead or missing before the time is right."

The pig looked over my shoulder. "Speak of the devil."

"What doethh the devil have to do with this?"

"Geez, you're as bad as the chicken sometimes. It's an expression. It means the director is coming up behind you."

"That'thh an oddly specific expression."

"Forget about the expression. The point is the director is coming. Act casual."

"Cow, there you are." Agent Orange kept his eyes on the pig as he approached. "Wow, it's noisy here. Why are you guys standing here?"

"We were getting ready to watch the sunset," said the pig.

Agent Orange's eyes ping-ponged between the two of us. "You do realize it's morning?"

The pig glanced at the sky. "It is? We're still trying to get used to the whole daytime, nighttime thing and how the sun sets at different times each night. It's very confusing. And what's the deal with daylight savings time?"

"I can't explain daylight savings time or why it's still a thing. Anyway, good to see you, but we've got a bit of an emergency. I need the cow."

"Of course, sir." The pig bowed. "What's the emergency? How can I help?"

"Your services are not required. Just the cow's."

"She has admitted to being intoxicated. I'm not sure she's mission ready, sir."

A black cargo van with tinted windows pulled up next to us. The front window rolled down to reveal Agent Periwinkle at the wheel.

"She'll be fine." Agent Orange opened the back doors. "Cow, let's go."

The pig turned away from Agent Orange and gave me a stern, squinty eyed glare.

I shrugged and climbed into the back of the van.

17: Mad Cows on the Loose in Western Illinois

I TEETERED BETWEEN THE walls as the van bounced out of the GIBOD compound. Of course, the only other occupants were Agents Orange and Periwinkle. I'm sure that worried the pig, but I'd grown to expect it.

"Are we going in search of the chicken, cat, and dog, like you promised?"

Agent Orange turned in his passenger seat. "No. You need to watch this."

He placed a tablet on the van's cargo floor. I poked at it with my hoof as it slid around, failing to get the video clip to start. Agent Orange reached back and tapped the play icon.

The video opened on what appeared to be the aftermath of a farm ravaged by a tornado. In the background stood a tiny country church with three giant satellite dishes.

"It'thh the church?"

"Correct, a day after our raid," said Agent Orange.

"What happened to the farm?"

"Just keep watching," said Agent Orange, cranking up the volume on the tablet.

"Kyle Branson, a resident of Rock Falls, a small Midwest town in central Illinois, describes the scene he encountered at 2:00 AM. Warning: some of what is described and shown is of a graphic nature."

The newscast cut to an interview with Kyle, a middle-aged man in a DeKalb corn hat and a 'Have You Hugged Your Farmer Today' T-shirt.

"I got woken up from a sound sleep by a loud crash," Kyle said to the reporter. "I come outside. The chicken coop is destroyed. Chicken guts everywhere. The barn is knocked over. I thought a tornado come through, but it wasn't rainin' or even windy. Heck, it wasn't even cloudy. I walks out toward the barn and I hears this hideous groaning moo. I looks over, and one of my cows is eating a chicken. It's eating a chicken! And it got worse. There was a group of cows eating one of my pigs. My cows had gone crazy. They'd gotten that mad cow."

The video panned away from Kyle to show five people in hazmat suits surveying the carnage of deceased farm animals.

"I ran into the house and grabbed my shotgun, but dang, those suckers were hard to kill. It took ten police officers with rifles, plus me, my wife, and my boy with our shotguns to bring all them mad cows down. Craziest thing I've ever seen."

They cut back to Kyle, wiping away a tear. "I lost everything, my barn, my cattle, my pigs, my chicken coop. All that's left is one chicken. I'm ruined."

"That'thh not mad cow," I said.

"We don't know that for sure," said Agent Periwinkle as he merged the van onto the highway.

"I know a thing or two about mad cow or what they call bovine spongiform encephalopathy." That's what I meant to say, but the name came out 'boo-fine spongy-foam and-see-fail-patchy.' I carried on as if I'd pronounced it correctly. "BSE for short. I felt lightheaded after one of our more intense training sessions and thought I might have it, thho I did some research. Cowthh with BSE don't eat chickens and pigs. Besides, cowthh get it from contaminated feed when they're babies, and it takes years before they show signs. There'thh no way an entire herd gets BSE overnight."

Agent Orange grabbed the tablet. "This isn't the only reported incident. Similar cases have been reported from neighboring farms. So, what do you think it is?"

"A zombie virus."

"See," said Agent Orange, hitting Agent Periwinkle in the shoulder, "she agrees. It's a zombie virus."

"I double checked. None of the bovine zombie virus vials are missing," said Agent Periwinkle.

"What else could it be?" asked Agent Orange.

"Good question," said Agent Periwinkle. "There's a chance it's just a new strain of mad cow. That's why we need to investigate and collect samples."

***

I REMAINED IN THE van as Agents Orange and Periwinkle approached the farmhouse. Although annoyed they dragged me along only to leave me in the van, a headache brewed in my skull, and my stomachs had turned sour, apparently caused by my heavy drinking on the plane. On my own, my mind drifted to images of the chicken, dog, and cat strapped to operating tables with countless probes attached to them.

I shifted focus. Thought about my training. *Know your surroundings.* I scanned the farmland. Little had changed on farms in the hundreds of years since I lived on one: a main dwelling, barns, a silo, grazing fields, a small vegetable garden, and fields of crops. Even the collapsed barn wasn't unique, though the police tape surrounding it was new. I could find no animals, living or dead. Burnt patches of grass gave the lawn a spotted cow hide look.

The two-story farmhouse's porch stretched across the entire front and wrapped around the side. Agent Periwinkle peeled a strip of loose paint off the railing as he climbed the steps. On his way to knocking on the front door, Agent Orange kicked aside a used engine part and a pot of wilted plants. When no answer came, Agent Periwinkle slid an unraveling wicker chair aside to peer through the picture window. After a shrug from Agent Periwinkle, Agent Orange knocked again.

Still, no one answered.

"Cow," said Agent Orange via our communicators, "get up here. We need you to kick down this front door."

"I thought we all agreed it was best I stayed in the van. The last thing these people need to thhee is a cow stalking around their house."

"There doesn't appear to be anyone home," said Agent Periwinkle.

"So, get up here and knock the door open," said Agent Orange.

"Why can't one of you knock the door down?"

"Stop arguing and get up here."

"Yethh, thhir." I opened the van's back doors with my hoof and jumped out.

"Cloak yourself!" yelled the agents.

"If no one is home, why do I need to cloak?"

"Just do it," ordered Agent Orange.

My cloak fizzled twice before activating.

Agent Orange stepped aside as I approached. I prepared to kick the door down with my hind legs, when a man inside shouted, "Get off my porch!"

The door flung open with authority. Kyle, wearing a 'Don't Fear the Reaper' T-shirt, came onto the porch and blasted a shot at our van. Agent Orange ripped the shotgun out of his hands while Agent Periwinkle wrestled him to the ground. They had him in handcuffs a second later.

"You just shot at a special agent." Agent Orange glanced back at the van, which had a dozen tiny holes in it.

"I wasn't shootin' at you. I was shootin' at the cow." Kyle lifted his head up from the porch floor. "I could have sworn I saw a cow out there."

Agent Orange gave me the stink eye. "There's no cow out there, Mr. Branson."

Kyle dropped his head, bonking his forehead on the porch floor. "I guess not. I'm sorry, but if you had been here. If you had seen them cows. I'm tellin' ya, you'd be a little jittery, too."

"We came here to ask you a few questions about your incident with the cows," said Agent Orange, motioning for Agent Periwinkle to help Kyle up. "If you cooperate, we'll forget all about this little incident. Okay?"

"Absolutely. I'll tell you everything," said Kyle, as Agent Periwinkle directed him into the house and sat him on their sagging couch, with his hands still cuffed behind him. His wide-open and bloodshot eyes darted from the agents to his wife and son in the kitchen.

I stayed on the front porch and watched through the open front door. Stacks of magazines and newspapers covered the coffee and end tables and spilled over onto the floor. Dirty plates and half-empty cups crowned the stacks. A layer of dust coated the farm animal knick-knacks scattered on the bookshelves. A cow in a glass milk jug caught my attention. I couldn't figure out how they got the cow figure into the bottle.

Kyle's wife paced in the kitchen, carrying on a conversation with herself. She pushed up the sleeves on her John Deere sweatshirt, tightened her ponytail, and stormed up to Agent Periwinkle.

"So, you're special agents. Then tell us what you're all doin' about this mad cow business? You're here terrorizing my husband when you should be out hunting down them crazed cows. A herd of 'em rampaged Southpark Mall. They trashed the Denny's. They almost killed the manager and a couple of waitresses, and you're wasting your time harassing this innocent man who just lost his entire livestock."

Agent Orange forced his way in between Agent Periwinkle and the woman who stood a full head and a half shorter than him. "Now, ma'am, let's stay calm." He motioned for her to take a seat on the couch next to her husband.

"Our goal is to get to the bottom of this. We just need to ask a few questions first," said Agent Periwinkle.

Kyle nodded for her to sit. "Everything's okay, Karen. These guys are here to help."

She released a low-pitched groan and glared at the agents as she took a seat next to her husband.

The son stepped out from the kitchen. "I heard the mad cows tear people's limbs off and then eat them while the victims watch."

Kyle shook his head. "Kevin, there's no proof of that."

"It's true. I read it in one them newspapers." The son walked to the coffee table and grabbed a newspaper off the top of a stack. "It's in here." He held the thin tabloid-sized newspaper up for all of us to see before he began flipping through it.

"The Weekly World News? Now there's a reliable source," said Kyle with sarcasm so obvious even the chicken would have gotten it.

"Actually, they do some of the best investigative journalism in the world," said Agent Periwinkle.

Karen shot him a side-eyed glare. "You're kidding, right?"

"Agents of GIBOD do not kid, ma'am." Agent Orange shuffled toward Kevin.

Kevin flipped through the newspaper. "Here it is." He pointed at the article. "The other night, this guy was on Interstate 74, over by the airport, when something came running out of the woods. He figured it was a deer and it sort of was and it sort of wasn't. It was a deer being dragged out of the forest by one of them mad Black Angus cows."

He held up a photo of a Black Angus cow with a deer hanging limp out of its mouth.

"That's obviously a fake picture," said Kyle.

"That doesn't mean the story is entirely fake." Agent Orange took the newspaper from the boy.

I thought the same thing. Deciphering the truth in articles from the Weekly World News and similar publications was part of our GIBOD training.

Agent Orange read from the article. "Lloyd Law, who witnessed the attack, said, 'The crazed cow had it by the throat, and tossed the still twitching deer into the middle of the highway. I slammed on my brakes. My tires squealed as I stopped just in time. The Black Angus never flinched. It never looked at me. It remained focused on devouring its fresh kill.'"

"Does that sound like the cows you encountered, Mr. Branson?" asked Agent Periwinkle.

"No, sir. My cows were moving slower than a three-toed sloth with a hangover. There's no way on earth one of them there cows could have caught a deer and tossed its still twitching body onto the highway."

I cringed on the front porch. Not because I questioned the validity of the story, which I found riveting. I took issue with the story's use of pronouns. Specifically, how the article consistently referred to the Black Angus as an 'it'. That's demeaning. I understand the gender of a Black Angus isn't easily apparent, but in that case, the proper pronoun would be 'they' instead of it.

"There's more," said Agent Orange. "'Once the beast had picked the bones clean, its head jerked up, and it stared at me with whitewashed eyes. It growled. It didn't moo. It didn't snort. The frickin' cow growled at me.'"

"They did have whitewashed eyes," said Kyle, "but I don't remember no growling. They still mooed, but it was a groaning kinda moo."

"Like a dying clown horn," said Karen.

Kevin hovered over Agent Orange's shoulder. "Read the part about how hard it was to kill the Black Angus." He pointed farther down the page.

Agent Orange read on, though his tone lacked the animation of his earlier narration. "'As the cow looked ready to attack me, National Guardsmen came sweeping out of the forest. They surrounded the beast, flooding it with spotlights and peppering it with bullets. The beast wouldn't die. It kept coming at them, growling and howling. Then a Guardsman pulls out a huge machete. The others ceased firing as the Guardsman, with the machete, approached the cow. With one fell swoop, he lopped the cow's head off.'" He shot Agent Periwinkle a side-eyed glance with his mouth scrunched to the left, closing his left eye.

Agent Periwinkle responded with a shrug. "There's always a level of exaggeration in the Weekly World News articles, mixed with the truth. Deciphering fact from fiction can be tricky."

My training suggested that Lloyd encountered zombie cows, but fabricated the Black Angus prowess. These publications never fact-checked eyewitness accounts, and the more fantastical and embellished the tale, the better the odds they will print it.

Kevin pointed at his father. "Now that sounds like our cows. Remember how hard it was to kill them?"

"They were hard to kill, son, but we didn't have to cut any heads off."

"Hmmm." Agent Orange shifted his scrunched mouth to the right. "The article goes on to say the cow bled black blood. Quote, 'A black darker than its hide.'"

Kyle vigorously shook his head. "That's definitely false. The cows bled red."

"I know, Dad, but this was a Black Angus."

"Son, just because their hide is black, it don't mean their blood will match. I think we've wasted enough of these men's time with this article.

Let's let them ask their questions."

"It was not a waste of time, Mr. Branson," said Agent Periwinkle as he examined a flat cartoon cow wall hanging. He tapped the tiny clock in its stomach, but the second hand remained motionless. "We cannot discount the entire story. Portions of the account match the description of the attack you encountered, but of course we will need to crosscheck the facts with the Illinois National Guard account."

"Kevin, can you close that window?" said Karen, pointing to the window next to the bookshelf of dusty knick-knacks. "I swear I can still smell the stench of them diseased cows."

Once she mentioned it, I couldn't help but notice the awful mix of skunk and litter box in the air.

"So, Mr. Branson, did you notice anything strange about the cows prior to the incident?" asked Agent Orange.

"Nothing. I'd milked them earlier in the evenin' and they were all fine."

"What time did you milk the cows?" asked Agent Periwinkle.

"I milk them the same time every evenin', five o'clock."

Agent Orange fumbled through his suit coat pockets. "And by two in the morning, they all had mad cow?"

"Every last one of them," said Kyle. "This is some crazy mad cow strain. Like my wife said, this thing is spreadin' fast. The Andersons, the Connors, the Parkers. Same thing happened to all of their cows."

Agent Orange showed Kyle and his wife pictures of Grandma Marjorie and her grandsons. "Do you recognize any of these people?"

"I don't recognize any of them." Kyle turned to his wife. "Honey, you recognize any of them?"

She shook her head no.

"Son, do any of these boys go to your school?"

Kevin stood by the window but hadn't closed it yet. "Does anyone else hear that?"

"Hear what?" asked his mom.

Kevin looked to the sky. "I'm not sure. Maybe it's just a flock of geese."

I heard it too and looked up, expecting to see the familiar V-shaped pattern of flying geese overhead, but the skies were clear.

Kevin closed the window, and walked over to Agent Orange, who held up the picture of Nick. "He's a couple of years older than me, but, yeah, he went to my school. I've seen him around. He's kind of a loner."

Agent Orange put the picture back in his pocket. "Have you seen him hanging around your farm in the past week or so?"

"No. I haven't seen him in weeks. What does he have to do with this?"

"We're not sure. We're just gathering the facts. Now, do you attend the church at the edge of your property?" asked Agent Orange.

"No, we're not church folk," said Kyle.

The skunky poop stink intensified, as did the flock of geese squawks. I walked to the edge of the porch. The noise grew louder and clearer. It wasn't geese squawking. This was a unique sound, best described as a chorus of grunts and, dare I say, moos?

My heart raced, adding a throbbing to my hangover headache. The alcohol already had my stomachs churning, and I feared another whiff would trigger an expulsion. I inched back towards the front door, never taking my eyes off the edge of the cornfield and epicenter of the mooing grunts. A swarm of flies swirled above the corn.

The first cow emerged. She raised her head and sniffed the air the way a cat does when it smells a freshly opened can of tuna. I wondered how she could smell anything other than the overwhelming skunk-poop stench of her own rotting flesh. Three more made their way out of the corn like a scene from Field of Dreams.

The lead cow sniffed the air once more and then directed her frosted-eyed stare right at me. Two things occurred to me at that moment. One, my cloaking power had worn off. Two, I was the freshly opened can of tuna.

18: The Cow Zombie Apocalypse Begins

I STOOD ON THE Bransons' front porch, frozen in place. Another four zombie cows staggered onto the front lawn. They gave no heed to the flies jockeying for position on their open sores. The herd dragged their mangled limbs toward the house like an angry mob, minus the torches and pitchforks. Mooing grunts emanated from the herd as if every step caused excruciating pain, though the blank stares on their faces showed no evidence of agony.

Once again, I failed to follow my agency training. I hadn't identified my exit points.

Another four zombified cows stumbled out of the corn. The herd leader had dragged her mangled carcass halfway across the front lawn.

I swiveled my head rapidly, though my panoramic vision allowed me to see all my potential exit points at once. If I'd identified my exit points earlier, before panic clouded my brain, I would have leaped off the porch and made a beeline for the van or simply ran away. Instead, I fixated on getting inside the house.

The mooing groans had become a chorus.

I reached for the doorknob of the screen door with my mouth.

"Holy Mother of – MAD COW! There's a mad cow on the front porch!" Kyle attempted to stand without using his handcuffed hands, but fell back into the sunken couch pit.

I lost my grip on the doorknob, and the screen door banged closed. The zombie herd leader had stumbled halfway across the lawn. "They're coming!! Let me in!!"

Kyle had freed himself from the couch, but ended up on his knees. His wife, Karen, stood by his side. Both their mouths hung open.

"Did... did that cow just talk?" she asked.

Agents Orange and Periwinkle glared at me.

There was no time to worry about blown covers. "Yethh, I can talk, but that'thh not important now. There'thh a herd of zombie cows, I mean mad cows coming out of the field."

Kevin ran to the front window. "INCOMING!!"

Another eight zombified cows emerged from the corn. I gagged on the skunk-poop stench, which churned with the whiskey and tequila festering through my stomachs. The overwhelming urge to vomit faded as I released a slow exhale.

Agent Orange scurried to the window, pushing Kevin aside. "What the –"

"I'm coming in!" I flung the screen door open and charged into the doorway. My shoulders slammed into the door frame. The jolt caused a tiny amount of milk to squirt out my utter. I rocked back, gathered my momentum, and took another go at ramming through. After this failed, I took two steps back and readied myself for ramming speed.

Agent Periwinkle rushed to block my path. "Stop! You're gonna break the doorframe."

"That'thh my general plan."

"If there's no door, we can't keep them out."

He made a good point, but the herd leader was only a couple limps from the porch, close enough to reveal blood dripping down both sides of her mouth. I inhaled. Big mistake. The revolting taste of rotting flesh triggered stomach convulsions. I clamped my mouth shut.

Agent Orange glanced around. "Kyle, do you have a wider entrance?"

Kyle's mouth still drooped open as he nodded his head toward the kitchen. "There's a cellar door in the back."

Karen's eyes then locked onto me. "Wait. You're not letting that cow in our house."

Agent Orange stepped into her view. "No need for concern, ma'am. She's a good cow. She's one of us."

Her face recoiled, her hands flew up, and she blinked six times in a single second. "Don't tell me what to not be concerned about."

I didn't wait around for further discussion. The lead zombie cow had her hoof on the first front porch step. I held my breath, jumped past the stairs, and kicked her with my hind legs. Her back legs snapped. She let out a moo-groan, heavy on the groan, and collapsed. I hesitated at the base of the stairs, feeling bad for inflicting harm to a fellow cow. Then I inhaled the rotting skunk-poop flesh. My stomachs could take no more. I puked all over the lead zombie without an ounce of regret. I spit the remnants of my vomit at her and took off for the back of the house.

Agent Periwinkle leaned out of the front doorway. "Cow, double-time to that back door."

What did he think I was doing?

The front door slammed shut, followed by the click of the deadbolt.

When I reached the back, my eyes locked onto the cellar doors. Four zombie cows stood in my path. I attempted to cloak. It sputtered on for only a second. Cloaking on the front porch had drained my power. My natural fighting powers would need to carry the day.

I spun around and kicked the first cow in the ribs, toppling her to the ground. The next received a devastating kick to at least three of her stomachs. She toppled backward, knocking down the cow behind her, who smacked her head against a boulder. Thick red blood streamed onto the lawn, causing my stomachs to churn anew. For the first time, I wished Dr. Hash Browns had not corrected my inability to see red. When the putrid stench of decaying blood hit my nose, my stomachs once again revolted, and I puked.

I had no time to dwell on my nausea. One zombie cow stood between me and the cellar doors. Her whitewashed eyes showed no fear. She moo-groaned as she inched her way toward me. I stood up on my hind legs and punched her with my front hooves. Her head snapped backward with every punch, then wobbled right back into position. I sprang to my forehooves and spun my hind legs up to deliver a blow to the zombie cow's head. Her skull caved in like a rock hitting a watermelon. Blood and brains splattered the outside of the house, yet the zombified cow remained standing, unfazed.

Bones snapped as the other three wiggled to their hooves. They let out tiny moo-groans with each break, then resumed their dogged pursuit. I flanked the stubborn fourth zombie cow and delivered a powerful roundhouse kick. She crashed into the others, toppling them over like bowling pins.

I rushed to the wooden cellar doors. A dozen specks of peeling paint provided the only clue the doors had once been white. I grabbed the door handle with my teeth and yanked. The handle slid off my teeth as the double doors rattled and thudded back into place. *NO!! It can't be!*

The four zombie cows drew closer. Their legs bent in the wrong directions and popped with every step, making it sound like they walked on bubble wrap.

I kept a firm grip on the handle and made gentle tugs. Lots of clattering, but the doors didn't open. I spit the handle out and stomped on the door.

"Hey! Anybody there? I can't open the door! It'thh locked."

The herd had caught up and bumped the four maimed cows aside.

I pounded on the doors with both front hooves. "Somebody, OPEN THE DOOR!"

"Cow, is that you?" asked Agent Periwinkle.

"Of course, it'thh me! Open the door!!"

Agent Periwinkle flung the double cellar doors wide open. I scampered down the steep railingless concrete stairs. He pulled the doors shut and replaced the wood block that locked them. The agent hopped down the stairs and bent over with his hands on his knees. He took several deep breaths. "Geez, those things smell awful," he said.

"I know. Like a skunk infused cow pie," I said.

"It burns the nostrils."

Loud thumping began on the double doors above us. The doors quivered, and the wood block bent a little more with each thud.

"Cow, are you in the house?" yelled Agent Orange from the kitchen above.

"Yethh, thhir, I am."

"Good. You and Periwinkle better get up here. We need your help."

Agent Periwinkle ducked under I-beams as he headed for the wood stairs leading to the kitchen. "If she couldn't fit through the front door, what makes you think she can make it through the skinnier basement door?"

"Cow, you'll be safe down here," he said before sprinting up the stairs.

The pounding on the cellar doors continued. I glanced at the wooden stairs to the kitchen. Railed and too narrow for my wide body. The cellar doors provided the only escape route. I'd trapped myself. We'd watched dozens of zombie horror movies on Dr. Hash Browns' pirated satellite TV. Being trapped in a confined space with the zombie horde surrounding you never ended well.

Thump. Plump. Thump, thump.

The cellar doors wouldn't hold for long. I surveyed the basement's open floor plan for something I could use to prop under the doors.

A furnace and ping-pong table occupied the middle of the room, with a washer, dryer, and utility sink against one wall, and makeshift shelves of concrete blocks and boards, stuffed with decades of collected knick-knacks and old mail, lining the other walls. I raced to the shelves and sunk my teeth into a board. I pulled the shelf away from the wall, scattering its contents.

Agent Periwinkle poked his head in the doorway to the kitchen. "Everything okay?"

"All good," I grunted through teeth clutching the board.

I spun toward the cellar doors, ignoring that the end of the board wiped out a set of ceramic pots on a lower shelf. I trotted for the cellar doors, and tripped over a toilet that, for reasons I cannot explain, had been installed in the middle of the basement. No walls around it. No pooping privacy that humans cherish. No adjacent sink. Just a toilet in the middle of the room.

I shook off this annoying conundrum, adjusted my grip on the board, tilted my head, planted one end of the board on the first concrete step, and raised the other end toward the cellar doors. It didn't reach.

Exploding wood startled me, and I dropped the board as splinters showered down on me.

A mangled cow hoof crashed through the middle of a cellar door. The bloody leg hung at eye level. The zombie cow let out a puzzled moo-groan as she tried to pull her leg out. Her moo-groans grew louder the more she struggled. She came down hard with the opposite hoof. Wood splintered. Her hoof smashed through the other cellar door. The beast let out a sad, mooing-grunt as her zombified brain realized she'd become immobilized.

Stomps from other zombie cows popped out a doorframe nail. It clanged on the concrete basement floor and rolled toward me.

My head smacked into low hanging ductwork when I turned to yell up the stairs. I shook it off. "I don't think I'm safe down here. These cellar doorthh won't hold much longer!"

"Deal with it. Do your super-cow thing," yelled Agent Orange.

"I can't. I'm out of power."

"We can't help you. We've got problems of our own up here," yelled Agent Orange.

"Here comes one!" A crash of breaking glass followed Agent Periwinkle's warning.

"That stench. Wow! It's like a skunk and fox had a baby and now we've got to clean its poopy diaper," said Kevin.

"Kevin James Branson, watch your tongue," said his mom.

A shotgun blast rattled the house, followed by a short moo-groan squeal. Dust rained down from the basement ceiling. A second blast rang out, followed by a thud and another shower of dust.

"Ma'am, can you reload the shotgun?" asked Agent Orange.

"You betcha." I heard Karen snatch the gun from Agent Orange. The ejected shells clanged on the floor above.

"Kyle, grab all the guns and ammo you have," ordered Agent Orange as feet shuffled above me.

My attention shifted back to the cellar doors. Thump. "Moo-groan." The pattern repeated, thump... moo-groan, thump, moo-groan, as the zombie cow alternated which leg she attempted to pull out of the cellar door. Another nail fell to the floor.

"Keep an eye on that picture window," said Agent Orange. "We're in big trouble if they break through that."

A giant crash came from upstairs.

"You had to say it, didn't you?" said Agent Periwinkle.

The sounds of breaking and falling glass lingered in the air before a shotgun blast drowned it out. The zombie cow let out one last moo-groan before she plopped onto the floor above me. Another shower of dust rained on me.

"Mr. Branson!" Agent Orange cocked a shotgun. "We're going," shotgun blast, "to the," shotgun cock, "basement," shotgun blast.

Kyle and his family were the first down the wood stairs. Several more shotgun blasts rang out before Agents Orange and Periwinkle followed. They closed and locked the door. I wondered why, since the cows couldn't fit through the doorway, anyway.

Agent Orange gave the door a stern tug. "We should be safe down here."

"Are you kidding me?" Kevin's nose wrinkled and his eyes widened. "Have you never watched a zombie movie? This is how they all die. Trapped in the house."

"We're not dying today." Agent Orange's words lacked conviction as he focused on the cow legs protruding through the cellar doors. He cocked his head when he noticed the real problem. One side of the cellar door frame hung on by only two loose nails.

Thump, moo-groan… thump, moo-groan.

"Periwinkle, where's that backup you ordered? Where are the emergency response teams from our 911 call?"

Agent Periwinkle checked his phone. "Sir, our closest operatives are still an hour and a half away."

Agent Orange whirled around to face Kyle. "Did you find more shells?"

"No. I'm out. I didn't have time to restock after the other night."

Agent Orange dumped the empty shells from his shotgun onto the ping-pong table. He searched the pockets of his black suit. He searched his pants pockets. "Did anyone think to grab the boxes of shotgun shells on the couch?"

No one responded.

He looked up the stairs to the kitchen. Thumping had begun on that door. "Cow, how's that recharging going?"

My cloaking power sputtered three times, but didn't activate. "Not good, thhir."

The Branson's collectively backed a step away from me. "What did that cow just do?" asked Kyle.

"Don't worry about it." Agent Orange patted Kyle's back. "You'll love it when she fully activates."

Thump, moo-groan... moooooooo-groan.

CRASH!

The cellar doors, with the zombie cow still stuck in them, slid down the concrete cellar steps, skidded across the floor, wiped out the ping-pong table, and slammed into the furnace.

We stood mesmerized by the struggles of the zombified cow stuck in the cellar doors. The cow stood upright, in what resembled an M.C. Escher drawing. Her forehooves punched through the two cellar doors up to her knees. The doors angled down, with her hind legs atop the doors. When she attempted to take a step, her front leg pulled a door open, causing her hind hoof to slide off. The doors flapped open and closed as the cow and doors toppled over.

Kevin laughed wildly as he captured the entire incident on his phone. "Stupid cow."

The rest of us remained stone-faced, as the zombie cow defied logic, and got back on her hooves. Then two zombified cows tumbled down the cellar stairs, knocking her over again.

Kevin erupted in a new fit of hysterical laughter.

Periwinkle let off a couple of rounds, dropping the two new zombie cows.

At the top of the cellar stairs, a dozen zombified cows jockeyed to be the next to tumble into the basement. The agents blasted them as they tripped down the stairs one-by-one. Within a minute, the pile of bloody and smelly cows became a dividing line. The Bransons stood near the kitchen stairs, with the agents and me stuck on the other side of the basement.

Rhythmic pounding on the upstairs door intensified.

Periwinkle searched the pockets of his black suit. "I've got no more shells."

A series of eerie creaks drew our attention to the upstairs door. Cracks formed on the wall surrounding the doorframe. Drywall dust flowed from the growing cracks.

BAM!

The door, the frame, and a good chunk of the wall came sliding down on top of the wood railing with a zombie cow riding it like a snowboard.

Agent Orange flipped his shotgun around and bashed the head of a zombie cow with the butt end. "Everybody, grab anything that can be used as a weapon."

Agent Periwinkle whacked a cow with the butt of his gun. "We've got to clear the stairs."

Kyle grabbed a meat hook and stuck it into a zombie cow. She let out only a muffled moo-groan when Kyle pulled the hook out. His son grabbed a milking stool and smacked the cow in the head. Karen delivered a second blow to the head with an old metal milk can.

The zombie cow staggered back, regrouped, and headed back for them.

It could have been adrenaline or the fear of death, or maybe the charging cycle completed. Whatever the reason, my cloaking power zipped across my hide. I nudged Agents Orange and Periwinkle out of the way. "I'll take the lead."

I charged up the concrete stairs, plowing into a row of the diseased beasts, knocking them down like a row of empty garbage cans.

They couldn't stop me.

They couldn't even contain me.

I blazed a path of destruction through the slow-moving zombie cows.

"Follow the cow," yelled Agent Orange from the basement. "COW! Head to the van."

The zombified beasts waddled toward me. They would open their mouths wide when I got close, but I never gave them a chance to bite. My confidence grew with every attacker I dispensed. I turned the corner of the house, sending zombie cows flying in all directions. For every ten I disposed of, twenty took their place. I reached the front yard. I noticed only attacking zombie cows and our van.

Agent Orange continued yelling orders, but all I heard was "van" and "keep moving".

I cleared a perimeter around the black van. Agent Orange jumped into the driver's seat and revved up the engine as Agent Periwinkle flung open the back doors. The Bransons and I piled in. I decloaked and collapsed to the floor of the van. I didn't bother checking for wounds.

Agent Orange stomped on the gas pedal. With the car accelerating, Agent Periwinkle hopped into the passenger seat.

Zombie cows bounced off the van as we plowed through the herd. The Bransons and I bounced off each other and the van walls. Once we got down the road, Kyle and his family sat down on the benches that lined the walls of the back of the van. They still held tight grips on their improvised weapons. None of them spoke. They just stared at me in my decloaked state, their mouths wide open. They didn't ask where we were going or question the talking cow that rampaged through a herd of zombie cows while in a semi-invisible state.

Agent Periwinkle turned his head toward us. "We told you you'd love it when her power fully activates."

19: The Search for the Human Zombie Virus

AGENT ORANGE DROVE THE van down country roads, altering our path with three-point turns when herds of zombie cows blocked the road. Mounds of smoldering cattle had replaced pastures of grazing cows. We drove past boarded or trashed and looted bars, gas stations, and pizzerias of rural towns, with every dollar store appearing to have been the victim of a terrorist attack.

Once we escaped the war zone, we dropped the Bransons off at a truck stop where they could wash up, get something to eat, and phone for help while we drove to an automated car wash.

"You realize this won't get all the cow guts off the van," said Agent Periwinkle, multitasking on a laptop and a tablet.

Agent Orange shrugged. "It'll get the bulk of it off." The van's wheel locked into the track, and he took his hands off the wheel.

"Sir, I've been running some simulations and they're very disturbing." Agent Periwinkle held out his tablet so we could see. It displayed a map of the Midwest with a repeated time lapse of pink and red blobs that rapidly overtook the entire region.

"What are you showing us, Periwinkle? An approaching storm?" asked Agent Orange as suds covered the van.

"In a manner of speaking, yes; the approaching cow zombie storm." Agent Periwinkle paused the video loop when it displayed a small pink blob and no red. "Based on the reported cases, I've been able to create a model. It's spreading fast, so it has to be an airborne virus. The pink shows areas where the airborne virus has spread, and the red shows the cows exhibiting signs of the zombie virus. That was two days ago." He advanced the loop. "And this is today."

The pink area grew to cover all of Iowa, most of Nebraska, Missouri, Illinois, and large portions of Wisconsin, Minnesota, and Indiana. A red dot marked the Branson's farm and neighboring communities we had driven through.

"Look how far the virus has spread already. All cows in the pink areas will show signs of the virus in the next three days." Agent Periwinkle advanced the map five days. Pink filled the entire screen and red covered most of the Midwest. After a week, red covered the entire map.

"We've got to stop this. We've got to slaughter all of these cows," said Agent Orange, as large rotating brushes attacked the van.

"Sir, wiping out caterpillars, butterflies, and chipmunks is one thing. This is different. GIBOD can't contain this. We don't have the resources to complete an operation of this scale."

The director pounded his fist on the dashboard. "This was the Havarti Travel Bureau's plan all along. They had us chasing Grandma Marjorie and her creepy grandsons all over the globe while they started the cow zombie apocalypse right in our backyard. How could I have missed this? How was I so blind?" He pounded his fist once more. "This can't be it. We haven't lost yet. We will stop this!"

My head retracted as I recalled the pig calling Agent Orange unhinged. This got me questioning why we'd joined the agency, which triggered memories of what brought us to Earth, and that sparked an idea. "Mr.

Steak&Eggs! He zapped all the cows into his spaceships. How about we get him to zap up all the zombie cows?"

Agent Periwinkle shifted to stare at me with squinted eyes. "Who's Mr. Steak&Eggs?"

"He's that nut job who stole all the cows. He planned on making a fortune selling milk and beef to the Cheddarians. Well, you know what? He can have them. He can take all the zombie-infected cows. Cow, brilliant suggestion." Agent Orange reached back and ruffled the bit of hair left on the top of my head.

"Thank you, thhir." Any thought of him being an unhinged maniacal dictator vanished for that moment, as I preened with the pride of him praising my idea.

"Oh, that guy. We turned him over to Intergalactic Tactical Security. He violated several dozen intergalactic laws and a dozen or more Cheddarian laws. He tried to activate a nuclear weapon here on Earth. They locked him up in a penal space station, circling one of Brie's moons. It's not like we can just phone someone up and say, hey, it's all been a big misunderstanding."

"Can't we use the same transporter technology Mr. Steak&Eggs used?"

Agent Periwinkle pulled his mouth back as if he faced a tremendous G-force. He leaned out of Agent Orange's sight and waved fingers across his throat.

Agent Orange growled and slammed a palm into the steering wheel. "We don't have that kind of tech. We're horribly outgunned every time. We're bringing slingshots to laser blaster fights."

The water jets blasted the sides of the van, rinsing off the soap and cow blood.

After giving Agent Orange a moment to simmer, Agent Periwinkle cleared his throat. "Sir, you're forgetting, the agency motto of always being one step ahead of the Havarti Travel Bureau."

"Well, it doesn't look like that's true today."

My head recoiled again, expecting Agent Orange to explode.

"The Havarti Travel Bureau doesn't win by starting a cow zombie apocalypse. GIBOD may lack the resources, but eventually, the human race will eliminate the zombie cows." Agent Periwinkle turned to me. "No offense, but slaughtering cows is one of the things humans do best."

"None taken." In truth, I did take a bit of offense. Kind of hard not to.

"Periwinkle, what's your point?"

"The cow zombie apocalypse just covers their tracks. The Havarti Travel Bureau's ultimate goal is to unleash the human zombie virus. That's what we need to prevent from happening."

"Periwinkle, tell me the human form of the virus is still in the vault and without a single drop missing," said Agent Orange as he drove the van through the air dryers.

"Sir, the human form of the virus isn't in the vault."

Agent Orange let out another growl. "It's stolen!? Why didn't you tell me that earlier?"

"Sir, we never stored the human form of the virus in the vault. We deemed it far too dangerous and stored it in a secure location that only the director of GIBOD knows about."

"I don't remember a human zombie virus being on the list of items in the Director's Warehouse. That should have stood out. Then again, the entire list is nothing but the craziest and most dangerous stuff ever." Agent Orange looked at the two of us. "I shouldn't have said that out loud."

"No worries, sir. The existence of the Director's Warehouse is one of the worst kept GIBOD secrets."

Of course, I knew nothing about it. But I bet the pig knew all about it.

"Trust me, sir, the vials were sent to the Director's Warehouse. I know, because I placed the order to send them there. We need to verify they're still there."

"Agreed." He stopped the van right after we exited the car wash and looked back at us. "You two have a choice. Either I tie you up and put bags over your heads, or I drug you, tie you up, and put bags over your heads. Sorry, it's protocol." Agent Orange got out, then poked his head back in. "And I'm going to need your phone, the tablet, and the laptops."

Agent Periwinkle held out his phone. Agent Orange snatched it and smashed it on the pavement. He then crushed the broken parts with the heel of his shiny black shoes.

"What are you doing?" asked Agent Periwinkle.

"Sorry, it's protocol. Give me the tablet."

Agent Periwinkle clutched it to his chest and shook his head.

"Periwinkle, hand it over."

He slowly unclutched his grip and held it out. He didn't watch as Agent Orange destroyed the tablet. I expected him to cry when Agent Orange ran the laptop over with the van.

"All right. Have you made your decisions?" asked Agent Orange.

***

Agent Orange had me lie down in the back of the van. Then he hog-tied my legs together.

"Sorry. It's protocol," he said. "Periwinkle, you'll need to lie down next to him."

Agent Periwinkle stood outside the back of the van. "You're kidding, right? And don't say it's protocol."

"But it is, so get in," said Agent Orange, tying Agent Periwinkle's hands behind him.

"The cow takes up the whole back. Where am I supposed to lie down?"

"In between her legs. You can use her front legs as a pillow and her back legs as a footrest."

Agent Periwinkle climbed into the van and got into position. "This is so degrading."

"Suck it up, big boy," said Agent Orange as he tied Agent Periwinkle's legs together. He began closing the door and stopped. "Wait, I forgot to put the bags over your heads."

The power drain from using my cloaking powers coupled with my recent alcohol consumption left a dull ache in my forehead, a serious lack of saliva in my mouth, and a sour churn in my stomachs. So, despite the lunacy of the agency's protocol, I welcomed sleep and passed out soon after he put the bags on our heads. Agent Periwinkle's head bouncing off my shin bone on every bump failed to disturb my slumber.

When we stopped, I awoke and figured we would get out. Instead, we heard the unscrewing of the gas cap and the beeps of self-serve gas pumping.

When Agent Orange returned to the car, Agent Periwinkle said, "I need to use the bathroom."

"Shut up. You can't talk," said Agent Orange. "And you should have thought of that before we left."

"You didn't give us a chance," said Agent Periwinkle.

When Agent Orange left the van on the second stop, I tried to sleep, but Agent Periwinkle kicked me and said, "Cow, I really need to go. Is there any way you can untie me?"

"Agent Orange is following very strict protocol. I really don't think we should."

"Forget the protocols. I need to pee."

"I couldn't untie you, even if I wanted to. No handthh."

He slammed his head into my thigh. "I wish I had taken option B."

Agent Orange returned with snacks and drinks, which he kept in the front.

On the third stop, Agent Orange came back smelling like cigarette smoke and beer.

He returned quickly on the fourth stop with a pizza. The blend of melted cheese and fresh baked bread smelled amazing. I wanted to devour the entire pie, but he didn't even offer us a slice or a bite.

On the fifth stop, we parked by what I imagined to be a waterfall. Car horns, emergency vehicle sirens, and the stench of car exhaust dominated the next stop. Hundreds of chirping birds are all I heard at the seventh stop. At the last stop, Agent Orange removed the hoods and untied us.

We were back at the car wash. The broken cell phones and laptops still littered the pavement and sparkled reflections from the parking lot lights.

"So, was it worth it?" asked Agent Periwinkle. "What did you find? Are the human vials safe?"

Agent Orange shut his eyes and rubbed them with a forefinger and thumb. He reopened them and glanced between the two of us. "No." He sighed and stared at the broken electronics. "Several vials are missing. The arrogant thief left a note." Agent Orange pulled a handwritten message out of an inside jacket pocket and read it. "Need these vials for the moment. I'll bring them back after we've saved the world. Signed, A One."

"Who'thh A One?"

Agent Orange threw his arms up. "I have no idea."

"Let me see that note." Agent Periwinkle snatched it from Agent Orange's hand. "It's not A One. It's capital A, capital L."

"What doethh that stand for?"

"Agent Lime, a former director of GIBOD," said Agent Periwinkle.

"Where do we find him?" I asked.

"We don't. He's dead."

"That's typically how us directors lose our job."

"If he was the director, why do you call him Agent Lime? Why isn't he Director Lime?" I turned my head to address Agent Orange. "For that matter, why aren't you Director Orange?"

"We call everyone Agent, so our enemies can't figure out our hierarchy."

"Once they identify who's in charge, they can cut off the head and watch the rest of the body die," said Agent Periwinkle, still staring at the note. "I remember him; Agent Lime. I worked with him. And for him." Agent Periwinkle wiped under his eyes, though he had stopped short of producing tears. "He was a good man. And a good friend." He fixed a stare at Agent Orange. "He would be proud of you."

"I doubt any former director of GIBOD would be proud of me. I'm going to be the director at the helm when the Havarti Travel Bureau finally exterminates the human race."

Agent Periwinkle squinted at the note, then flipped it over. "It's written on the back of a gas station receipt for snacks."

"It's all part of the protocol," said Agent Orange.

"There's a date: March 25th, 1989." Agent Periwinkle looked up at the night sky and wiped away tears. "I remember that date. That was the day he died." Agent Periwinkle took a couple of deep breaths. "We never found the killer."

"So, the Havarti Travel Bureau killed him, took the vials, and now we're all gonna die. Great." Agent Orange kicked the remnants of the tablet across the parking lot.

"That was twenty-five years ago." Agent Periwinkle waved the note over his head. "If they had the vials, they would have used them by now. I have confidence in Agent Lime. He was clever; very clever. I bet he hid the vials before they got to him."

"Assuming that'thh true, the vials could be anywhere. Where do we begin?"

Agent Periwinkle snapped his fingers. "We need to think like him. Where would Agent Lime hide the vials?"

Agent Orange pointed at Agent Periwinkle. "You're the only one who met this guy. This is all on you."

With one eye closed, Agent Periwinkle cocked his head toward Agent Orange. "Actually, that's not true."

Agent Orange glanced at me numerous times while Agent Periwinkle continued to glare at him. "What is wrong with you, Periwinkle?"

I wondered the same thing.

Agent Periwinkle smirked. "Agent Lime had a son."

"Great. So, where do we find his son?" asked Agent Orange.

Agent Periwinkle raised his eyebrows and gave a subtle shrug.

Agent Orange responded with an aggressive shrug.

The two shifted into a prolonged stare down.

Then it hit me. "I got it." I pointed a hoof at Agent Orange. "You're his son."

Agent Periwinkle smiled and did the magician's voilà motion with his hands.

"Oh, give me a break." Agent Orange did a dramatic eye-roll. "We're not living in some stupid Hollywood movie, where everybody is surprisingly related. I suppose the cow is my sister. Don't be ridiculous. My father was a computer programmer, not a secret agent."

Agent Periwinkle pointed at the receipt. "Look at the date."

Agent Orange snatched the receipt. He studied it. His eyes narrowed. He studied it some more, then leaned his head back. The moonlight gleamed off his water-filled eyes. "I *do* remember that date." His eyes were full buckets, but no drops spilled. "They told me they died in a car crash. They brought me to the scene."

All thoughts of Agent Orange as this emotionless robot disappeared, as I recalled watching my mother herded away, never to be seen again.

With both hands, Agent Orange shoved Agent Periwinkle in the chest. "You knew all this time, and you never told me."

"And as far as anyone else knows, I never have. Revealing this information breaks the most fundamental rule of the agency. We never reveal an agent's true identity."

Agent Orange curled his lip. "Maybe I should bring you up on charges."

"I had to tell you. You're our only hope. Think. Where would your dad have hidden the vials?"

"How would I know? I thought he was a computer programmer for a small modem company."

"Did you ever visit his office?" asked Agent Periwinkle.

"A handful of times. It was always late at night."

"Do you remember where it is?"

"Maybe." Agent Orange rubbed his chin. "I think so."

"Let's start there. I'll drive."

20: Who Still Uses Modems?

THE FIRES HAD SHIFTED into my third and fourth stomachs by the time Agent Periwinkle pulled the van down a road behind a Home Depot. My head throbbed to the rhythm of my heartbeat. I wondered how long hangovers lasted.

"Sir, are you sure we're in the right town?" asked Agent Periwinkle for the fifth or sixth time.

"I'm sure. I mean, I'm pretty sure." Agent Orange scanned the small, boxy office buildings and warehouses which lined both sides of the street. "It's been a while. I was ten the last time I was here. Things have changed a lot." He pointed ahead of us. "That strip mall and the Home Depot, none of that was here."

"Maybe they tore the office down and replaced it with the Home Depot," I said.

"No, this isn't the right place. There were houses surrounding it. Look for a small strip mall office building in the middle of a residential area."

Agent Periwinkle turned the van back onto the main road. "I know a place that fits that description, but I doubt it's where your dad used to work."

He drove us through a series of curving residential streets until we came upon a boring rectangular building, which looked similar to dozens we had driven past earlier. No business signs hung above any of the three doors. If it wasn't for the packed parking lot, you would have assumed the entire complex was vacant.

"This is it. I remember this." Agent Orange bounced in the passenger seat.

Agent Periwinkle pulled the van into the parking lot but found no spot available.

"What'thh the deal with this office? It'thh Friday night. I thought humans didn't work on Friday nights."

"This isn't an office anymore. It's a bar. Well, and a restaurant. And a brewery. But aren't they all nowadays?" Agent Periwinkle shook his head. "Microbrewers love this nondescript office-warehouse motif."

"Thho, this isn't where his dad worked."

"No. This is it. I know it." Agent Orange had his face plastered to the passenger window.

Agent Periwinkle parked the van on the street.

I cloaked myself as we exited the van. "I'm confused. If Agent Lime was head of GIBOD, why did he also work for a modem company? And I thought you all couldn't have families."

"Things worked differently back then," said Agent Periwinkle, pointing for us to head to the paved alleyway that ran behind the building. "The rules we have in place now were a direct result of what happened to Agent Lime."

A row of evergreens lined the alley and blocked the view of the brewery from the residents who lived behind. Agent Orange peeked in every window of the building as we passed.

"Any of this triggering memories?" asked Agent Periwinkle.

"Not yet. We need to get inside."

As if on cue, the garage style door at the far end of the complex opened. A man with long hair and a bushy beard wearing a flannel shirt, overalls, and fishing waders came out and lit up a cigarette. He leaned against the wall and took a few puffs before he noticed us.

He pushed himself off the wall and walked toward us. "The entrance is around front."

As the agents greeted him, I stayed in the shadows so he wouldn't see the cow outline.

"We know. I dragged my friend here for a walk down memory lane. My dad used to work here long before it became a brewery," said Agent Orange.

"Before my time. Now, if you're heading inside, you need to go around front."

"Wait." An older man in torn blue jeans and a flannel shirt over a tie-dye T-shirt popped his head out of the building. He, too, had a full beard, but he pulled his long hair into a ponytail. He only wore galoshes and not full fishing waders. "I used to work here before it became a brewery."

He scampered out of the building and rushed up to Agent Orange, invading his personal space. At first, I thought he was sniffing him. Then he took off his glasses, and through squinted eyes, examined the director's face.

Agent Orange took a step back, glancing at Agent Periwinkle for help. Agent Periwinkle shrugged, then motioned with his head for Agent Orange to respond.

"Yeah, my dad was a software programmer for the modem company that used to be here."

"Harry! You've got to be Harry's boy, Joey. You're the freaking spitting freaking image of him. Hey Frankie, I know these cats."

"Did you seriously just call them cats?" Frankie rolled his eyes, tossed his cigarette on the pavement and headed inside.

"I'm Charlie, by the way." He smiled and aggressively shook Agent Orange's hand. In an instant, his face drooped. The smile vanished. He pulled Agent Orange toward him. "Your parents' death. What a tragedy. Horrible. I'm so sorry for your loss."

"Thank you," said Agent Orange as he eased his hand free.

Agent Periwinkle raised an eyebrow. "So, you're still working here even though it's now a brewery?"

"Yep. The universe works in mysterious ways, my friend." Charlie wiggled his hands in the air, then abruptly stopped. "The modem business crapped out, and these guys bought the place. I went to school for chemical engineering, so I hooked up with this lot and became a brewmaster. Cool, eh?"

Agent Orange leaned toward Charlie. "Look, the reason we're here is..." he looked inside the brewery, "we're looking for something my father might have left behind."

Agent Periwinkle stepped up to speak into Charlie's left ear. "Something he might have hid on the night he died."

"Anything you can remember about that night might help," said Agent Orange into Charlie's right ear.

Charlie took a couple of steps back, put his glasses back on, and crossed his arms. He scanned the two agents up and down three times, snarled and scratched his chin. "Who are you guys, for real?"

Agent Orange hesitated, then said, "We're agents of GIBOD."

Agent Periwinkle glared at the director.

Charlie recrossed his arms. "Show me your badges."

"We don't carry badges. If you knew my father the way I think you did, you'll know agents of GIBOD don't carry badges."

Charlie's eyes sprinted between the two agents, then he lunged and whacked both of them on the shoulder.

Each agent grabbed an arm and slammed him to the ground. Charlie smiled and chuckled as his chest met the pavement. "Okay. You're definitely real. Sorry, but I had to make sure. It's been twenty-five years. I started thinking I imagined everything. So GIBOD really frickin' exists?"

"It does," said Agent Orange as he and Agent Periwinkle released their grip.

From his knees, Charlie rolled to his feet and jumped in the air, smiling as if he'd won the grand prize of a game show. "Hot damn. It's real. It's all real." He paced in front of the garage door entrance, then whirled to face us. His smile had vanished and his eyes glazed. "You've seen the movie *A Beautiful Mind*, right? The guy who imagined people and a giant conspiracy. I thought that was me." He rushed up to Agent Orange. "I started thinking your father never existed, except in my mind. I thought I was completely insane. But I'm not." Charlie pushed between the agents, and skipped to the middle of the alley, forcing me to back up. He threw his hands into the air and shouted, "I'm not crazy!"

He spun back to face the agents, his eyes popping out of their sockets. "This is really happening. I've got something to show you guys." He sprinted back to the garage door, slicing between the agents along the way. He stopped and spun around. "Holy crap, it's why you're here. This is so amazing. AAHHH!" He ran up to Agent Orange and put his hands on his shoulders. I thought he was going to kiss him, but instead jumped up in the air four times.

He took a step back from Agent Orange, closed his eyes, crossed his arms, pulled them to his chest, and took a deep breath. "Calming down. Calming down." When he opened his eyes, they still looked ready to launch from his head. He kept his crossed arms tight to his chest as his eyes darted from side to side. "Follow me." He pivoted and marched into the brewery in a mini high-step fashion.

Agent Orange followed until Agent Periwinkle grabbed his arm. "This guy seems a bit off. I don't think we should trust him."

"He has to be my dad's one. The one who knew his true identity. So, if my dad, aka Agent Lime, trusted him, I say we should trust him, too." Agent Orange strolled into the brewery, with Agent Periwinkle following, shaking his head. I caught up, being careful not to clump my hooves on the pavement.

Charlie took us past the beer kettles and into a small office area. I stayed back, keeping most of my semi-transparent body behind a wall. I worried the sight of my cow outline would send this guy over the edge.

He uncrossed his arms to unlock and open a walk-in supply closet. Inside were shelves filled with stacks and stacks of boxes and various electronic components. After looking behind us several times, he rummaged through the boxes. He made no reaction when he knocked a couple of boxes to the floor. Two empty boxes got tossed over his shoulder before he said, "Aha!" He waved a box triumphantly over his head, then pulled a modem out and tossed the box aside. The power cord dragged behind him as he headed back to the office area. His head frantically scanned the room. He found a desk he liked, and shoved several stacks of paper to the side, knocking a cup of pens and pencils to the floor.

The agents exchanged raised eyebrows and started picking up the mess.

Charlie reeled the power cord up and plugged it in. He grabbed the phone off the desk, yanked the cable out, and plugged in the modem. "Dang it. I need another cable."

"Can we help you?" asked Agent Periwinkle as he placed the cup of pens back on the desk.

"I got it." Charlie dove under the desk. He popped up, twirling the telephone cable above his head in celebration. He hurried back to the first desk and connected the cord to the phone and modem. "I just hope this thing still works. It's been years since I used it." He tapped the side of his head. "If I could just remember the number. What's the number? It's one of those numbers you'll never forget, except now I forgot it. Wait, wait, wait. I've got it on my phone." He pulled out his phone and started scrolling with his finger. "Now, if I could just remember the contact name. There it is. Secret Lair." Using the desk phone, he dialed the number. The obnoxious tone of a failed phone call emanated from his phone. "Oh, no, no, no, no. This can't be happening. The line is no longer in service. Well, of course it's not. Who would have paid the bill? I mean, of course, nobody's paid the bill. There's nobody left to pay the bill. Who would the telephone company even send the bill to? That telephone company probably doesn't even exist anymore. How could I be so stupid?"

Agent Orange came up behind Charlie and placed a hand on his shoulder.

Charlie flinched away with his arms flailing about his head like a Muppet. Then he jerked himself still. He slowly peered around Agent Orange, then yanked his head back. He rubbed his eyes, rapidly blinked, and then closed them tight. "Four, three, two, one." He sprang his eyelids open and groaned. His face turned steel cold. He grabbed Agent Orange's suit jacket with both hands. "Slap me!"

Agent Orange recoiled. "What?"

"Slap me. Slap me in the face. Slap me hard."

Agent Orange brushed away Charlie's grip on his jacket. "What's wrong with you?"

"Maybe nothing. Maybe everything. That's why you need to slap me." He dropped to his knees and begged.

Agent Orange looked at Agent Periwinkle, who shrugged and pantomimed a slapping motion. Agent Orange rolled his eyes and lightly slapped Charlie across the face.

"Oh, please. You call that a slap? Put some muscle behind it. You're a frickin' agent of GIBOD. Now SLAP me!"

Still on his knees, Charlie put his hands behind his back and closed his eyes.

Agent Orange shook his head, sighed, and shrugged before he wound up.

SLAP!

The solid thud of the slap impacting Charlie's face made Agent Periwinkle cringe.

Charlie snapped his head back straight. He slowly opened his eyes and leaned around Agent Orange. His head and shoulders crumpled. "Well, that didn't help."

Agent Orange helped him stand up. "What's going on, Charlie?"

"It's happening again. It's been nice playing with you, imaginary people, but I've got to get back to work." He stepped toward the brewery.

Agent Orange grabbed him by the arm. "What are you talking about?"

Charlie fought off Agent Orange like he was in a child's hand slap fight. "You're not real. I'm imagining all of this. I thought it was different this time, but no."

Agent Orange let go of his arm.

Charlie's arms slumped, pulling his upper half into a serious slouch. He began to sob.

"Look at me." Agent Orange lifted Charlie's chin up. "We're real people. I just slapped you in the face. Your lip is bleeding."

Charlie's crying slowed as he wiped the side of his mouth with his thumb. He examined the blood. He licked the side of his mouth. "I'm bleeding. So, the slap was real. But that doesn't explain the cow." He pointed at me.

I looked down at my visible legs. "Thhorry. My cloak deactivated."

Charlie's hands swung to his head as if his head had become a powerful magnet and he wore metal gloves. "Oh great, the cow talks this time. I'm gonna need a new prescription." He headed for the brewery with his hands still glued to his forehead.

Agent Periwinkle blocked his path. "Wait. This is real. This is all real, even the talking cow. I swear, she's real, she can talk, and she's an agent of GIBOD."

Charlie looked back at me, dropped his head, and tried to push past Agent Periwinkle.

He grabbed Charlie. "Forget the cow. Look at me." Charlie's bug eyes looked up at Agent Periwinkle. "We need your help. The world needs your help. We need you to show us whatever it was you planned to show us."

"So, you see the cow, too?"

"Yes, I see the cow," said Agent Periwinkle.

"And you hear the cow talking? English?"

"Yes. The cow is a friend of mine and I'm sure she'd love to be a friend of yours."

My head cocked as I processed Agent Periwinkle calling me a friend. I'd always viewed him as a boss. An authority figure. But we'd been through quite an ordeal the past few days. We'd laughed and drank together. We'd been tied up in the back of the van together. Perhaps we *had* become friends.

"No! I don't need a cow friend." He sneered and eyed me up and down.

All the warmth of my new friendship with Agent Periwinkle disappeared. Oh, how I missed India. But I knew it was unrealistic to expect all humans to shower me with unconditional love. I would have to earn Charlie's trust. I didn't know how, but I was confident I would overcome his irrational prejudice of a talking cow, and build a lasting friendship.

Then his eyes went wild as he walked backward and pressed himself against a wall. "He's not one of them mad cows, is he?"

"I don't have whitewashed eyes. I'm not drooling excessively. And I don't stink like skunk poop. Thho, no, I'm not one of them zom–, I mean, mad cows."

Charlie puffed his chest. "No offense, but that's exactly what a talking mad cow would say."

Agent Periwinkle spun Charlie to face him. "Don't worry about the cow. Let's focus on what you were about to show us."

"Yeah, well, that's the thing. To open the door, I need to call the analog modem on the other side, but they disconnected that phone line, so I can't show you what I planned to show you." He crossed his arms and huffed. "Wait a minute." He raised his hand up to his chin. "I've got an idea. I can make this work. Some quick rewiring, which I can totally do. I used to do this all the time."

He ran back to the storage closet and shuffled through the shelves. "Tools. Tools. Where are my tools? Ah, found you." He grabbed a bag off the top shelf and ran to the nearest desk. My head flinched when he slammed the bag down. Tool after tool got tossed onto the desk until he found one resembling the love child of a glue gun and a power drill.

He darted across the office to a closet door and pulled an enormous set of keys out of his pants pocket. It took several tries and a couple of swears before he found the key that unlocked the door.

Bang. The door flung open. He patted his pockets until he found his reading glasses. His head bobbed up and down as he scanned the rows of wire connections. "Read me the number for that phone."

Agent Periwinkle walked over to the desk where Charlie had connected the modem. "NO! Not that one. The other desk. Over there." He pointed to the desk from where he had pulled the extra phone cable.

This was my chance to get in Charlie's good graces. I beat Agent Periwinkle to the table. "Six, three, zero."

"Not the cow. Someone else. Anybody else."

With a dropped head, I shuffled away from the phone. Agent Periwinkle gave me a loving pat on the head and read the phone number several times before Charlie said, "Okay. Got it. That should do it."

He ran back to the desk with the modem, picked up the phone, and dialed. A second later, we heard a muffled ring coming from below the floor of the storage area.

"Huzzah!" Charlie waved his jazz hands high in the air.

After a single ring, a series of ear-piercing beeps emanated both from the modem on the desk and the floor of the storage area. The staticky sounds of an untuned radio came next, followed by more unpleasant beeps. Oddly enough, the noises sounded like the Cheddarian phrase, "Make love, not peanuts."

Charlie grinned as if the sounds were music to his ears. The beeps and static stopped. Charlie ran over to the storage closet entrance. The rest of us crowded behind him. A short, pleasant-sounding beep came from below the floor, followed by the swooshing sounds of escaping air. Then came the stale smell of your grandparents' house. The floor of the tiny storage area began sliding away from right to left.

Charlie looked at the shelving units to the right. Then the left. And then straight ahead. "We should have moved those first."

21: The Lair, the Vials, and the Virus Keeper

Agent Periwinkle squeezed around Charlie and reached for one of the closet shelves. The closet floor slid away in an instant. As if I watched a cartoon, the three shelving units hung in the air for a second. Agent Periwinkle lunged for the one on the right. The metal shelves dropped. They tumbled down a winding metal staircase, with Agent Periwinkle along for the ride. Banging and clanging echoed in the dark spaces below. Boxes flew in all directions. Agent Periwinkle had grabbed onto one shelf and launched off a curve in the railing like a luge rider flying off the track. Motion lights activated as Agent Periwinkle, the shelves, and multiple boxes skidded across the floor, revealing Charlie's secret lair, which resembled your typical unfinished basement.

I expected brewery workers to run into the office to check on the noise. But no one came.

Charlie glanced down. "I hope he's okay, but he should have just let the shelves fall." He motioned for Agent Orange to head down the stairs, then gave me a squinty-eyed glare before moving aside to let me by.

Fortunately, the staircase was wide enough for me. I looked down once and snapped my head up before vertigo and fear of stepping on metal grates took hold. With my head held high, I navigated the spiraling steps. My hooves slid off the tiny steps once, but thankfully the sturdy railings held tight, and guided my recovery without me having to look down. Once I made the final turn, I leaped off the steps, clumping onto the concrete flooring.

Above us, Charlie closed the closet doors and clanged down the steps.

"So anyway, your dad and I were neighbors growing up. Neighbors and best friends, so when he got into this secret spy business, he needed someone on the outside he could trust. That was me. And I helped him build this underground lair to do super-secret agency things. Important things. As I say it out loud, it sounds crazy, which is why I've spent the last twenty-five years thinking I had imagined everything."

Agent Periwinkle, still sprawled out on the floor, groaned and rubbed his elbow.

"It sounds like you and my dad were close. Why would you ever doubt this wasn't real?"

"I'm still doubting it. I mean, there's a talking cow in my secret lair. That's not right." He cocked his head at Agent Orange. "Speaking of which, why didn't I see her right away?"

"She can turn invisible."

"Well, virtually invisible. It'thh more of a cloaking technique."

Charlie threw a palm up, closed his eyes, and rubbed his forehead with his other hand. "An invisible talking cow. Great. That's not helping. Cow, I'm gonna have to ask you to not talk. I can't handle that. You can moo. That would be fine. Just, no words."

I shrugged and said, "Moo." I could moo for a while, if that would lead to acceptance and eventual friendship.

"Nope. Don't moo. That was pathetic. Not convincing at all. So, nothing from you. Just silence. Actually, if you could go back to being invisible, that'd be great."

I opened my mouth to explain how I didn't have the power to cloak, but figured it'd be best to remain silent. The path to friendship would not be easy, but I had confidence in my likability. I would eventually win him over.

When he reached the bottom of the stairs, he announced, "Welcome to GIBOD's secret lair. That's what I call it. I know I'm not a part of the organization, so it's not an official agency lair. Anyway, welcome. It's not much, but we added plumbing. Look, there's a sink and a bathroom. We planned to add a bar, but never got around to it."

As he advanced, the motion lights revealed more of the space beneath the brewery. "There's a fridge, a kitchen table, and a ping-pong table. Your dad and I used to play all the time. Oh, yeah, and there's my chemistry lab." He picked up a dusty beaker and gazed at it. "Those were the days." He placed it back down on the table with other beakers, burners, test tubes, a scale, a microscope, and a variety of glass containers connected via an intricate array of tubes. He repositioned the beaker to fit in the dust-free circle, marking its position.

Agent Orange had followed Charlie and stood behind him. His shoulders slumped. "I didn't get to spend a lot of time with my dad. I was just a kid when he died. What memories I have are fragmented and fading. So, I'm sorry, but I don't remember you. I mean, you were my dad's best friend, but I don't remember meeting you."

Charlie stared at the beaker. "Secrets. Once your dad joined that agency, there were all these rules. I couldn't know anyone else in his life. No one was supposed to know we were friends. So many stupid rules. When I explained the rules to my therapist, I had to admit it sounded cuckoo."

Agent Orange patted him on the shoulder. "The rules are real and necessary. Those rules kept you safe all these years."

"I suppose." Charlie drooped as he expelled all the air from his lungs.

Agent Orange opened his mouth twice without speaking, before he said, "I'd love to hear more stories about you and my dad, but there's an urgency to why we're here. We're looking for something my father would have hidden on the day he died. Did he bring you something that day?"

With a clap, Charlie spun on his heels. A beaming smile had erased all signs of sadness. "Yes. That's why we're down here. He brought me some vials. Charlie the Virus Keeper, he called me." He put his hands on his hips and pointed his nose in the air. He held the pose for a second, then started walking toward the kitchen. "I loved that name. Anyway, very dangerous stuff."

The corners of Agent Orange's lips curled up into that rare occurrence of a smile on his face. "That's what we're looking for. A set of vials."

Charlie stopped and scratched his chin. "It's all real. A zombie virus that can wipe out the human race really exists." He clapped his hands, spun around via a single foot hop. "I cannot wait for my next therapy session. I am going to throw this in my therapist's face." He leaned into Agent Orange. "Listen here, you so-called psychiatrist with all your fancy degrees, well how about sucking on these apples, all those hallucinations you say I was having, well they weren't hallucinations. It's all real, baby. And you can thank me for the fact that you're not a zombie."

"Please, don't tell anyone about the vials," said Agent Orange, backing away.

Charlie waved a dismissive hand. "She's a therapist. She's taken an oath of confidentiality." His face melted into a frown. "Of course, I know what she'll say." He placed a hand on his hip. His pitch rose an octave, adding a condescending tone. "How convenient that these people show up out of the blue and just happen to be looking for exactly what you've imagined storing for all these years. What a coincidence."

Agent Periwinkle had gotten back on his feet. He brushed off his suit and straightened his tie. "Charlie, can you please show us the vials?"

Charlie kicked fallen boxes and spare parts out of his way as he headed to an old refrigerator. "I assumed they needed to be kept cold, though, now that I think about it, I doubt it mattered." He reached into the refrigerator and pulled out a rack of vials identical to the ones we had been traveling the globe to recover. He set them down on the kitchen table.

Agent Orange picked one up and examined the label. "Human zombie virus. Charlie, I could kiss you. GIBOD and the entire planet, thank you for keeping these safe all these years."

"No worries. My pleasure, though I honestly thought I'd gone nuts."

I nudged Agent Orange and whispered, "Why did Harry entrust Charlie with the zombie virus vials instead of keeping them locked up in the Director's Warehouse?"

Charlie flexed his fingers in and out of fists. "I told you not to talk!"

"Thhorry."

Agent Orange held an open palm toward Charlie. "Easy. She brings up a good point. But one that I can easily answer. My dad didn't know who in GIBOD he could trust. I've got the same problem. Some days, it feels like everyone else in the agency is a double-crossing Havarti Travel Bureau accomplice. But my dad could trust his lifelong friend, Charlie. You must have been his one."

Charlie did a palms up shrug. "No idea what that means."

"When you join the agency, you're allowed to let one person know. It can't be a blood relative. It can't be your spouse. Only that person knows you've joined GIBOD."

I steamed over just learning this now. Me and the other animals never got a chance to name our one. I mashed my teeth but kept quiet. I didn't want to receive another round of Charlie's wrath.

Agent Orange picked up another vial. His eyes narrowed as he cocked his head. "Wait, these aren't all human zombie viruses. This one says Leporid."

"That's the rabbit form," said Charlie.

Agent Periwinkle snagged a different vial. He held it at arm's length as he scratched his temple with his free hand. "This one says feline, and that isn't my handwriting. I thought I'd labeled all the vials."

"There's several types," said Charlie. "Feline, fowl, swine, canine, and some kind of fish."

"Salmon," said Agent Orange, holding up a vial.

Charlie glanced at me. "Oh. And bovine."

My head jerked at hearing this last one and it made me ponder the rest. The list of viruses had the entire Barn Yard Heroes gang covered, as if we were being targeted.

Agent Orange held up a half-full vial. All red hues vanished from his face. "Why is some of the human zombie virus missing from this vial?"

Charlie plucked it out of Agent Orange's hands. "I did some testing with it."

Agents Orange and Periwinkle locked eyes, as if telepathically deciding which of the two would ask the obvious follow up question. Agent Orange broke eye contact and took the lead. "So, what kind of–"

The closet doors to the office opened. A lone set of footsteps clanged onto the spiral staircase.

"Put the vials back in the fridge," said Agent Orange, as he and Agent Periwinkle scrambled to slide the vials back into the rack.

"Who's there?" asked Charlie as he slid the rack into the refrigerator.

The footsteps continued.

I attempted to cloak. It flickered and sizzled, but I lacked the power to fully activate.

The agents drew their pistols and hid them behind their backs as they tried to look as casual as two secret agents in black suits in a secret basement lair could.

I moved off to a dark corner, which activated the lights, making it no longer a dark corner. I decided my best option was to stand perfectly still and pretend to be a statue, but I struggled to keep my tail from twitching.

Frankie stepped onto the basement floor. He put his hands on his hips and surveyed the room. He had the look of a cop surveying a crime scene. No smile. No frown.

Charlie walked up to greet him. "Hey, Frankie. Sorry about the mess and all the noise. Don't worry, we'll clean it up."

Frankie smiled, kicked a couple of boxes out of the way, and stepped through one of the fallen shelving units. "I've been looking for this room for fifteen years. I started to think it didn't exist."

Charlie watched him pace around the lair. "I'm not following you, Frankie."

"You think I kept you around for your brewing skills? Your beers are awful. Nobody wants a chai tea curry IPA. It was a horrible idea and literally made people sick. And the turnip and radish beer. Disgusting. Didn't you notice I never sold your beers in the restaurant?" He stopped pacing when he reached the table.

"You always said you loved my beers."

"Well, I didn't, and I don't have to pretend anymore." He removed a side bag strapped around his shoulder and tossed it on the table. "Put the vials in."

The agents drew their pistols and pointed them at opposite sides of Frankie's head.

"Hands up, mister," said Agent Orange.

Frankie raised his hands above his head as he glared at Charlie. "Friends of yours?"

"Yes, they are."

"Are you sure?" asked Frankie.

Charlie wasn't given time to answer.

Agent Periwinkle shifted his aim to Charlie and fired a shot into his head.

Frankie grabbed Agent Orange's arm and dragged him to a support pole, where he repeatedly smacked his hand into the pole until the weapon dropped to the floor. He then kicked the director in the groin.

With Agent Orange doubled over, Frankie followed up with a hard knee to his head. Agent Orange collapsed to the ground.

I charged at Frankie with the rage of a rhino.

Frankie spun to face me. He jerked his head back into a triple chin, then he popped it forward, eyes wide. "Is that a–"

I sent him flying. The satisfying ping of his head smacking a metal post lingered as he spun around the pole before crumpling to the floor.

In my extended peripheral vision, Agent Periwinkle aimed his pistol at me. "Cow, this is nothing personal. I like you. I really do." He pulled off three rounds.

My ears fluttered as the bullets whizzed by. I fixed a stern glare at him. This had become personal.

"Your stupid cloaking shield." Any hint of compassion or signs that he cared about my wellbeing had disappeared. "Do you even realize it's activating?"

I hadn't. I searched for a mirror, seeking confirmation I didn't have bullet holes in my head.

Agent Periwinkle's signature hunched shoulders and drooped head had disappeared. He stood tall, looking ten years younger. He took aim once again.

I dove and rolled across the floor.

He shot off another couple of rounds. The bullets ricocheted into the basement walls.

I sprang to my hooves. "You're going to pay for your treachery." I shifted my hooves, preparing to launch into a gallop. A fallen shelving unit lay sprawled out between him and me. I smiled and charged, channeling my inner-athlete running the tires or ladder drill. The first step between the shelves was perfect. I glanced at the agent. He aimed at my head. I took a peek down, but too late. My right front hoof caught the top of a shelf. I tried to adjust and get my hoof down, but failed.

Two more bullets buzzed past me.

As I fell and rolled, I became one with the shelving unit. My legs, head, neck, and torso weaved through the bent shelves and posts. I tried to wiggle a leg free, but only made things worse. When the shelf and I stopped tumbling, I hung intertwined with the rack, staring at the floor.

His footsteps approached. His feet came into view first. He bent down and smiled at me as he put away his gun, so he could give me a round of applause. "Cow, that was impressive." He patted my face.

The shelving unit shook as I tried to muscle my way free. "Why are you doing this? How could you betray GIBOD?" I glanced at Agent Orange's limp body. "How could you betray your best friend?"

"Cow, you have no idea what you've gotten yourself and your little animal friends into."

For the first time since we'd left the GIBOD base, I pictured the chicken, dog, and cat strapped to operating tables, with their chests sliced open. The horror of the image paled compared to my shame at having forgotten about their plight. I'd become Agent Orange. The mission had consumed me.

"You also have no clue how helpful you've been. But it is time to say goodbye." He pulled out his pistol and placed the barrel right between my eyes. "Let's see if your cloak shield can stop this."

I closed my eyes and waited for the piercing pain. My only solace was knowing it wouldn't last long. I felt the barrel move as he pulled the trigger. I heard the dull thud, but no blast. There was no searing pain. He lifted the gun off my head and pulled the trigger once more. Again, only a dull click.

"Dang it. I must have lost track of my bullet count." His suit coat ruffled. "Are you kidding me? I don't have a spare–"

BONG!

Thud.

I slowly opened a single eyelid. Agent Orange towered over the collapsed body of Agent Periwinkle. "Take that, you double-crossing piece of trash." He tossed away a long metal shelving post. It clanged across the floor until the table leg stopped it. He grabbed the side bag Frankie had tossed on the table and flung open the fridge. The bag had pouches designed for test-tube sized vials. He stuffed the vials in the pouches, then slammed the fridge closed. "We've got to go."

I wiggled my legs to demonstrate my entrapment.

Agent Orange examined me and my interconnectedness with the shelving unit. He cocked his head, then pushed me and the shelves over. The unit busted apart when the intertwined mess of me and shelves hit the floor. I stood up and shuffled two steps to make sure my legs worked.

Faint sounds of sirens came from above. Agent Orange glanced at Charlie, a pool of blood around his head. He sighed. "We've got to go."

22: The Cow and Agent Orange on the Run

AGENT ORANGE OPENED A garage style docking door in the office area. As we exited the building, he straightened his jacket, adjusted his tie, and ran his fingers through his hair. Emergency vehicles filled the parking lot and the street. Police escorted patrons from the restaurant and brewery. I activated my cloaking power as we made our way along the parking lot perimeter.

A police officer spotted Agent Orange and headed toward us. "Sir. Sir! Hold it right there. Where are you coming from? Were you in the restaurant?"

"I was in the bathroom when the commotion started. Were those gunshots? Is this an active shooter situation?" Agent Orange motioned with his hands behind his back for me to keep moving toward the van.

As I passed the director, I noticed a pickup truck doing a slow drive-by. The grandsons stood in the cargo bed.

"We're sorting it out. You'll need to come with me." The officer positioned himself sideways and motioned Agent Orange toward the line of police cars in the parking lot.

I whacked Agent Orange with my tail to get his attention. He glanced at the truck, then dropped his head and covered his face. The truck screeched to a halt, almost rocking the grandsons off.

"Sir," said Agent Orange, "I'd like to get as far away from this building as possible."

I went behind a line of shrubs on the edge of the parking lot. I had a plan. In my best farmer's voice, I yelled, "Oh no! It'thh one of them there mad cows." I dropped my cloak and ran out of the shrubs with my tongue flopping and my eyes crossed. Well, as cross-eyed as a cow can get. I headed straight towards Agent Orange and the police officer.

As the police officer took off running, Agent Orange yelled, "Mad cow on the loose! Everybody run."

I lowered my head as I ran up to Agent Orange. "Grab on."

He wrapped his arms around my neck and I helped bounce him onto my back like we were part of an Old West show.

He kept up the rant as we ran through the parking lot. "Mad cow! Everybody run. Mad cow!"

Officers and patrons scattered as I weaved around the police cars to the van.

Agent Orange jumped down. "Cow, excellent improvisational problem solving." He pulled the keys out of his pocket and as he reached for the back door, we heard the screeching tires of Grandma Marjorie and her grandsons speeding toward us.

I walked into the middle of the street and let out a menacing snort. I lowered my head and pawed at the pavement with my front hoof. The tires squealed to a stop. She had seen this act before and wanted no part of it. Out of the corner of my eye, I saw the van rolling. The back doors were open. I turned and jumped in. As soon as my hooves landed in the back of the van, Agent Orange floored it. I stumbled, but regained my footing before falling out.

We sped down the residential street, with Grandma Marjorie and her grandsons in hot pursuit. Behind them, the police cars mobilized, sirens blaring.

Agent Orange glanced over his shoulder. "Close the doors."

The two van doors waved back and forth. I looked down at my hooves. "I don't think I can do that, thhir."

He glanced back with a stern glare.

I lifted a hoof. "No hands."

He rolled his eyes and returned his focus to driving.

Bullets zipped through the van and got lodged in the bulletproof windshield. "Was that granny or the cops?" asked Agent Orange.

The flashing lights made it hard to focus, but the grandsons had rifles pointed at us. A couple more bullets whizzed through the van, once again lodging in the windshield. "It'thh granny's boys."

"Hang on."

I braced my four legs against the sides of the van. The director weaved the van back and forth. Another round of bullets lodged into the sides of the van.

Police cars pulled up on either side of Grandma Marjorie's truck.

"Put down your weapons and pull over." The command bellowed out of the lead police car.

Grandma Marjorie ignored the warning and sped up.

The parade of our van, granny's truck and the squadron of police cars zigzagged through traffic and ran red lights.

"Pull your vehicle over, or we will open fire," bellowed the police.

Another volley of bullets came from the boys, this time directed at the cops.

The police responded with an eruption of gunfire. Tires squealed. Metal crunched. Glass shattered.

The chaos faded.

"There'thh still two squad cars following uthh, with their sirens off."

"I see that. I've got a plan." Agent Orange slowed down, pulling onto the gravel shoulder. "Keep up the mad cow routine. I've got an idea." After he brought the van to a halt, he leaped out of the driver's seat, ran to the back, and slammed the back doors shut.

One squad car stopped in front of the van, and the other behind. The two cops came out of their cars with weapons drawn as Agent Orange headed back toward the driver's side door.

"Stop right there! Hands on the van," said the cop in the front.

"Thank you, guys, so much for taking care of those nut jobs shooting at me. I'm eternally grateful. I'm from animal control. As I'm sure both of you are aware, there was a mad cow on the loose. Crazy stuff, eh? Well, I've got that beast trapped in the van." He pounded the side of the van.

I took that as a cue to act crazy. I banged back and forth against the walls, rocking the van.

"The beast is totally bonkers. I've got orders to get this thing to the processing center in DeKalb."

"We're gonna need backup," said the cop in the back.

It sounded like they weren't buying the director's story, so I ratcheted up the crazy. I slammed the sides of the van, bucked the front chairs, and kicked a back door open. To end the show, I let out a mooing growl.

The three scrambled to slam the door shut.

"See what I'm on about. I've got to get this thing to the center now," said Agent Orange.

"We'll give you an escort," said the cop from in front.

"I don't have time for this," said Agent Orange.

Bang. Thud. Crunch.

The officers still groaned as Agent Orange jumped into the driver's seat. "We need to dump this van."

"Shouldn't we call for back up?" I rocked into the walls, as he bounced the van back onto the road, spitting stones at the cops and their cars.

"We need to go dark; very dark."

"But we've got to warn the agency about Agent Periwinkle."

Agent Orange closed his eyes for less than a second, but it still unnerved me at the speed we traveled. "I trusted him. He was my mentor. My advisor. My best friend. He saved my life." Tears pooled, and jagged red lines formed star patterns in the whites of his eyes. "But it was all a lie. That double-crossing snake." He wiped his eyes. "He was the only agent left I thought I could trust. Let this be a lesson. Trust no one."

"There'thh good people in GIBOD. They wouldn't turn their backthh on you, thhir."

"We cannot afford such optimism. At this point, you and your little animal buddies are the only agents I can trust."

My already deflated mood sank lower. "They're all gone, thhir. We can't get a hold of any of them."

"What about the pig?"

"I'm not sure we can call him one of uthh anymore." My legs gave in to depression, and I plopped to the floor.

His eyes lingered in the rearview mirror, watching me. The tears and redness had vanished. "Don't worry. We'll get this straightened out and get the rest of the animals back." He slapped the blinker on. "But for right now, we're going to have to rely on each other. We're all we've got."

"What'thh our move?"

"First, we need a new vehicle. One big enough for you." He swung the van into a forest preserve, without touching the brake.

Luckily, I had dropped to the floor, so I slid into the wall instead of tumbling and banging into it.

***

AGENT ORANGE AND I ditched the van in the forest preserve lake, walked over to a campsite, and stole an elderly couple's RV, equipped with a handicap entrance lift. I scared the couple off with the old mad cow routine.

As Agent Orange pulled the RV out of the campground, I tried to get comfortable in the cramped camper living space.

"Thho, where are we headed, thhir?"

"Well, it's for times like this that agents have their one contact in the outside world. They're your last hope when you can't trust the agency. We're headed to visit mine."

I'd been waiting to question him about this. "How come I didn't get the chance to pick my one person? None of us animals did." Without realizing bolts locked the kitchen table to the floor, I tried shoving it aside. The stationary tabletop dug into my ribs.

"Cow, who would be your one person? All the animals you know are already part of the agency."

He made a good point. I hadn't even considered who would be my one. "It still would've been nice to have had the opportunity." I decided Dr. Hash Browns would be my one, even though we didn't know how to get in touch with him. "Anyway, who'thh your one person?"

"I can't tell anyone that, especially another GIBOD agent."

"It all soundthh silly to me." He made a sharp turn, banging my butt into the refrigerator. Contents inside toppled and clanged.

"Well, I'm glad the policy exists, because we need a safe place to hide these vials."

"Wait. If we're meeting your one, I'll know who they are. Isn't that against protocol?"

Agent Orange grumbled through a closed but wiggling mouth. "We're not playing by GIBOD rules anymore. We're on our own. Now get comfortable, it'll be a couple hours' drive." He pulled onto the highway entrance ramp.

I kneeled the best I could in the cramped quarters. "That workthh for me. All the cloaking and super-cow attacks have left me exhausted. My brain hurts, my stomachs churn. I need a good lie down."

"That sounds like a hangover. How much did you drink on the

plane?"

"I finished the bottle of scotch and then drank a bottle of tequila. Oh, and a bottle of vodka." I lowered my head onto my knees.

"Definitely a hangover. You'll feel better after some rest."

"I hope thho," I said, and fell fast asleep.

***

CRUNCHING GRAVEL, CHIRPING CRICKETS, croaking frogs, and the occasional hoot of an owl provided the soundtrack as Agent Orange weaved the RV down a gravel road through the woods. We passed several dirt driveways before we turned down one. With the headlights off, we drove for at least a minute with no sign of a house or even a tent. He stopped the RV, took several deep breaths before rolling the RV forward, then stopped again just a few feet later.

"Is everything okay, thhir?"

"Yes. Everything is fine. It's all good. It's just that I haven't seen... this, this..."

"Your one. The only person in the world you told your deepest secret to." Someone had to finish his sentence.

"Yes, my one. I haven't seen her in quite some time."

"Oh, it'thh a lady friend. Is she your girlfriend?"

"She was. It's complicated." He gazed straight ahead, never popping up to give even a glance at me in the rearview mirror. "I asked her after we broke up." He rolled the RV forward a couple of feet and stopped again. "The breakup was kind of ugly."

"Thithh is getting interesting. What happened?" I relished Agent Orange opening up to me, even if he never made eye contact.

"She caught me and her best friend... well, you know."

I was glad he wasn't looking at me, for my eyes bulged and my jaw dropped. "And after that, you still asked her to be your one?"

"That's how the story goes."

"Wow. I'm not a relationship expert, being a cow and all, but that doesn't sound like a good idea."

"I didn't have many choices. My contacts on the outside are limited."

The joy of Agent Orange sharing details of his personal life beamed from my eyes and smile.

He glanced in the mirror. "What are you so happy about?"

"It'thh nice to get to know you better. Learn a bit about your life."

He frowned as he pulled out his cell phone and stared at the blank screen. "Well, don't get used to it. We're not in a buddy cop show where we're going to have regular heart-to-heart crying sessions."

"Understood, thhir." I did my best to reign in my happy face, even though I bubbled with glee, believing there would be more heart-to-heart sessions.

He tapped his phone to life. "Do you think I should call her and let her know I'm coming?"

"That would be the right thing to do, but you should have made that call at least an hour ago, not when you're parked in her driveway."

"So, you think I should call her?"

I shrugged. "Better late than never."

"Okay, I'm gonna call her." He shifted his blank stare out the windshield to his phone.

A thought occurred to me. "Wait, you still have your cell phone? I thought you smashed all the devices thho we couldn't be tracked?"

"This phone is untraceable. I didn't need to smash it."

"Who told you that?"

"Agent Periwinkle." As Agent Orange's own words brought him enlightenment, floodlights lit up the night sky.

"Agent Orange, former director of GIBOD," boomed Agent Periwinkle through a megaphone, "as the new director of GIBOD, I am here to inform you that we have a warrant for your arrest. We have you and the cow surrounded. There is no hope of escape. Exit your stolen recreational vehicle with your hands up."

23: Agent Periwinkle: Director of GIBOD

AGENT ORANGE SCOWLED OUT the RV's windshield. Somewhere out there stood Agent Periwinkle, the new self-proclaimed Director of GIBOD. I took a glance, but the blaring lights assaulted my eyes, and I averted my gaze. Yet, Agent Orange continued to stare into the light, his face stiffening harder with every passing moment.

"Thhir, what should we do?" I was curious about our plan of action, but more importantly, I wanted to distract him so he'd look away.

It didn't work. His head remained fixated straight ahead. "That snake dares to call himself Director? I once regarded him as a father-figure. Now this king of all liars has turned my agency against me. I should have killed him when I had the chance."

His head dropped, and the tension in my neck eased slightly. I prayed he'd looked away in time to avoid blindness.

He turned and rested his glistening, bloodshot eyes upon me. "I couldn't believe it. I couldn't believe he'd been lying to me all these years. Even now, I cling to the hope this is just a misunderstanding. Like somehow the Havarti Travel Bureau is forcing him to do this. Or perhaps they've hypnotized him or taken over his brain. Maybe this isn't the real Agent Periwinkle. It could be a clone."

The bellowing of Agent Periwinkle returned. "Ex-Agent Orange, you've reached the end of the line. It's time to give yourself up."

A sternness returned to Agent Orange's face. "Or perhaps he's been a jerk this entire time." He popped out of the driver's seat, grabbed the bag of vials, and motioned for me to back up. "We need to hide this. Do you think you could swallow it?"

"What? The whole bag?" I took two steps back before banging my butt into the bathroom door at the back of the RV.

"Is that a problem?" said Agent Orange as he squeezed between me and the kitchen cabinets.

"Yethh, that'thh a problem. I can't swallow the entire bag."

In rapid succession, he opened all the cabinet doors. "There's nowhere to hide it. What if you swallowed them vial by vial?"

"You want me to swallow zombie viruses? Are you crazy?"

"They're in vials. You'll be fine."

The booming voice of Agent Periwinkle interrupted us. "Ex-Agent Orange. Cow. Let's end this ordeal peacefully. Come out with your hands up."

"He *does* realize I don't have hands?"

Agent Orange looked at the tiny RV bathroom. His eyes lit up. "We can flush them down the toilet."

"Won't that dump them out the bottom of the RV?" I turned my head toward the back and whacked it into an open cabinet door.

"Cow, that's not how it works. That'd be gross. It goes into a storage tank that gets emptied later." He tossed the bag at my feet. "I'll stall them. You flush."

"Assuming I can turn around to get to the bathroom, I'd doubt I could fit my head through that tiny door."

He ignored me and ran up to the driver's seat to yell, "This RV is a residence! It's private property. You can't come in without a search warrant."

"I already said I have a warrant. That's like the first thing I said."

"Besides, you're trespassing on *my* property," said a female voice.

I moved to the front of the RV. A petite woman with a black-haired ponytail draped halfway down her back, wearing a light jacket over rainbow unicorn pajamas, stood next to Agent Periwinkle. She pulled his arm down so she could talk into the megaphone. "What are you doing here, Joey?"

"Is that your girlfriend?" I asked.

"Ex-girlfriend. Abigail. Now get to flushing the vials down the toilet."

I tried to make a three-point turn, using the space by the wide handicap exit door, but couldn't get my butt past the stove.

A rock pinged off the windshield. "You're a real piece of work, Joey. I haven't heard a word from you for twenty years and then out of the blue, in the middle of the freaking night, you bring the holy wrath of your insane secret agency down upon my house, you freaking jerk!"

Agent Orange closed his eyes, scratched his cheek, and shook his head. "I'm sorry. I shouldn't have shown up unannounced. I should have called first."

"You shouldn't have shown up at all." She rushed the RV, with the megaphone in one hand and a baseball-sized rock in the other. Agent Periwinkle waddled behind her but didn't catch up to her in time to stop her from whipping the rock, cracking the windshield. "Honestly, I didn't think you'd show. I pegged you as a coward, too afraid to face me."

"Sorry I dragged you into this, Abigail." Agent Orange had his head down and his eyes still closed.

Agent Periwinkle lunged for the megaphone, but Abigail did a quick sidestep and scurried to the side of the RV. Something semi-large clanged into the siding. "I never understood this whole business of me being your one. You made it abundantly clear I was not your one when you slept with Stacey."

Agent Orange shuffled to the door, leaning against it. "Abigail, I'm sorry for everything that happened. I really am. But you've got to believe me, I'm the good guy. That old man out there is evil. He plans to kill us all. Wipe out the human race. You've got to help me."

"I don't believe a word you say. You know what? I'm going to enjoy watching whatever your secret agency friends plan to do to you and the farm animals you're harboring in that RV."

A high-pitched reverb joined another clang into the RV siding.

After a blow into the megaphone, the voice of Agent Periwinkle boomed once more. "Enough is enough, Ex-Agent Orange. If you and the cow are not out of that RV in ten seconds, we will open fire."

Agent Orange turned to me with wide eyes. His arms and hands flailed. "What are you doing? Why aren't you back there flushing vials?"

"I can't get to the bathroom." I banged into the stove and kitchen table to demonstrate I couldn't turn around. But the truth is, I'd gotten sucked into the Joey-Abigail saga, forgetting all about flushing the vials.

"You have eight seconds."

Agent Orange squinted and focused on a random cabinet doorknob. He took a slow, meditative breath. Then his head jerked toward me. He had the classic Agent Orange stoic and stern glare. "Fine. Forget flushing. We'll move on to Plan B. Follow my lead." He flung the RV door open and yelled, "We're coming out!"

"What about the vialthh?"

"Leave 'em there," he whispered to me.

I left the bag on the kitchen floor and followed him down the steps.

The lights had lit up the driveway and the surrounding forest like a Friday night high school football field. Abigail stood behind ten GIBOD agents, who formed a semi-circle around us, blocking all escape routes, except back into the RV. I had trained with all of them, but now they stood against us. Worst of all, the pig was among them, blending with the humans in his GIBOD black military uniform.

Agent Periwinkle walked up to us alone, with Agent Orange scanning him from the tips of his black leather shoes to the top of his gray hair.

When he stopped, Agent Orange leaned toward his left ear. "Whatever it is they've got on you, we can fix it. We've just got to work together."

Agent Periwinkle rocked backward, chuckling. "Son, I've been twenty steps ahead of you your entire life." His laughter stopped in an instant as he snapped his head to glare Agent Orange in the eyes. "Now hand over the vials."

"So, your loyalty was an act all along?" Agent Orange stepped up to be nose-to-nose with his former Number One. "Give me one good reason why I shouldn't kill you where you stand."

"Because that will confirm your guilt to the others." Agent Periwinkle broke eye contact and looked in the windows of the RV. "Now, where's the bag?"

"I should have killed you when I had the chance."

"You should have. But you didn't. And now you've lost. So, let's get this over with and perhaps I'll show you some mercy."

Agent Orange brushed past Agent Periwinkle to address the other agents. "Don't believe anything this man says. He's working for the Havarti Travel Bureau, and plans to wipe out the human race with a zombie virus."

"Interesting accusation," said Agent Periwinkle, pacing in front of him. "Yet, you're the one who attacked the special agents protecting the zombie virus, attempted to kill me, stole the virus, and is driving around in a stolen RV."

"Lies. All Lies. I'm protecting the vials," said Agent Orange.

Agent Periwinkle pulled out a gun and pointed it at the former director's head. "Tell us where the vials are."

"Go ahead, shoot me. Then you'll never know where they are."

Agent Periwinkle dropped his arm. "Search the RV. The bag is in there."

Agent Orange gave me a wink. A wink where the other person should instinctively know what the winker meant. I was the other person, or in this case, creature, and I had no idea what his wink meant. I shrugged my shoulders.

He rolled his eyes. He winked again and added a nod. I still had no idea what he wanted me to do, but figured I better do something, so I kicked Agent Periwinkle where it hurts. Based on Agent Orange's raised brow and wide-open eyes, this was not what he wanted. I didn't care. I enjoyed it.

Agent Orange followed up with a swift kick to Agent Periwinkle's head and then pushed him to the ground. "Back in the RV," said Agent Orange, bounding up the stairs.

I activated my cloak and followed. The agents opened fire. Bullets deflected off my cloaking shield and ripped into the sides of the RV. Agent Orange dove into the driver's seat. He started the engine and slammed it into gear in a single motion.

I squeezed inside and pushed between the captain's chairs as Agent Orange hit the gas. With my snout touching the windshield, I wiggled my butt out of the entryway and backed up into the living space.

Someone clanked up the metal stairs. The door flung open. I got ready to kick the agent out of the RV, but stopped when I realized it was the pig.

"Cow, I'll give you one chance. Apprehend the former director right now, and you won't go down with him." The pig had no weapon, but stood in a combat-ready position.

Agent Orange backed over the floodlights behind us, causing mini explosions.

"Pig, you've got it all wrong. Agent Periwinkle is working for the Havarti Travel Bureau." I looked the pig straight in his eyes, so he'd know

I spoke the truth.

The pig scoffed and nodded toward Agent Orange. "Is that what he's been telling you?"

"No. I figured that out on my own when Agent Periwinkle tried to kill me."

The right side of the pig's mouth curled up to meet his squinting eye. If he had a corncob pipe in his mouth, he could have passed for Popeye. "Come on. The evidence doesn't support that story."

I understood how guilty Agent Orange and I looked, but I thought the pig would believe me. That hope evaporated, as if I were a giant bouncy house that someone had pulled the plug on. "Why would I make that up?"

His face straightened out. His eyes narrowed. His mouth tightened. "I have no idea. But you leave me no choice. I'm bringing you two in."

"Cow, we don't have time for this," said Agent Orange, backing the RV down the dirt driveway. "Get rid of him."

I gathered as much energy as my collapsed morale could, bucked up, and punched the pig in the chest.

The blow forced the pig to lean back slightly. He smiled, then stretched his neck side-to-side until it cracked. "Cow, you don't want to mess with me." He smacked me in the head, then grabbed my front legs. I ended up flipped over on the floor wondering how he had space to do that. The pig stood upright and prepared to deliver a blow.

We hit the end of the driveway. Agent Orange spun the RV onto the gravel road. This sent the pig flying out the open door.

"Close the door! Close the door," said Agent Orange. The headlights were on this time as we sped down the gravel road, spitting rocks out behind us.

"Why do you keep asking me to close doors when you know I don't have hands?"

"Use your mouth and grab the doorknob. Geez, do I have to tell you everything?"

The bolts ripped out of the floor as I banged the table, toppling it over. The door flopped toward me. When the doorknob swung within reach, I stretched out, grabbed it with my mouth, and slammed the door closed.

"See, you can close a door." He looked in the rearview mirror. Multiple sets of headlights pulled onto the gravel road.

Agent Orange put the pedal to the floor. The RV sped away, but soon the sounds of motorcycles and a Jeep tearing through the gravel road got much louder.

"They're gaining on uthh."

"I know, but this behemoth doesn't go any faster," said Agent Orange as we bounced onto the paved road and skidded across. By the time he straightened the vehicle out, the motorcycles rode beside us. "I thought I had trained these agents better."

"What do you mean, thhir?"

"Watch." He swerved the RV to the right. The motorcycle on the right veered onto the shoulder, wobbled, and toppled into a ditch. Agent Orange swerved hard left, sending the second motorcycle into the ditch on the other side. "Idiots."

Behind us, Agent Hunter Green stood up in the convertible Jeep. "They got a rocket launcher," I said.

"I see it. Hold on tight."

I'm a cow. I cannot hold on tight to anything, so when Agent Orange slammed on the brakes and our tires squealed, I shot between the captain's chairs and did a face plant into the windshield, while my backside fishtailed into the kitchen cabinets.

The Jeep crashed into us without a squeal of its tires.

My face pressed harder into the windshield.

"The stupid Jeep is stuck on the back of our RV." Agent Orange pumped the gas, but the van slowed down.

This was a gross understatement. The Jeep was not just stuck, it had rammed through the RV's bathroom. The front bumper rested on top of the toilet.

Agent Orange swerved down the road, attempting to dislodge the Jeep.

I wobbled backward, planning to push the Jeep off, but noticed something of higher importance. "Slow down the swerves! We've got a problem." I banged into the refrigerator. "There'thh vials of zombie virus rolling everywhere."

"Scoop 'em up, and put 'em in a safe spot," he said while continuing to jerk the steering wheel back and forth.

"That'thh what I'm trying to do, but that'thh difficult for me, even on solid footing."

As a vial rolled in front of me, I snagged it with my tongue. I scanned the RV for a safe spot to deposit it and settled on the sink. It should hold the vial even with the constant swerving. As soon as I set it down, Agent Orange jerked the steering wheel to the right, and the vial flew out of the sink. With a quick snap of my head, I snatched it out of the air. The bag slid over by me, and I stuffed the vial in.

I bent to grab another tumbling vial, but ran into a pair of black boots. The cocky smile of Agent Yellow greeted me as I raised my view, wondering how he got there.

With his fists together, he raised his hands above his head as if he was swinging an ax, and came down with a double-fisted blow to my head. I do not know why he thought that would be effective. Sure, I felt it, but it's not like it hurt. I responded with a swift kick from my right front leg, which sent him into the cabinets above the sink. The cabinet door cracked in half. The bottom third of the cabinet smashed into pieces. A box of pancake mix exploded, spraying powder across the stovetop and the tiny counter space. Boxes of cereal tumbled down and spilled their contents across the floor. A plate slid out of the broken cabinet and wobbled into the sink before a second plate crashed into it. The sounds of breaking ceramic increased as each subsequent plate smashed into the sink.

"I hope those aren't the vials breaking," said Agent Orange, as he yanked the steering wheel in the opposite direction, causing coffee mugs to become projectiles. One of them nearly smashed a rolling vial of zombie virus.

Agent Yellow hopped to his feet and kicked me in the head. The blow got my attention, but had little effect other than leaving him wide open for a kick to his stomach. He flew into the refrigerator. The impact dented the door and left the agent dazed. I took the opportunity to grab another rolling vial, collecting a couple of shards of coffee mug in the process.

As I put the vial into the bag, Agent Yellow regained his sea legs and jumped on my back. He wrapped his arms around my neck, locked his hands together, and squeezed as hard as he could. I thought he wanted to hang on to me like a cowboy on a bucking bronco. Then I realized he intended to choke me. I visualized Agent Orange shaking his head in disgust, wondering where he had gone wrong with his training. I faked a gasp for air, rose on my hind legs, and wiggled my hoofs.

Agent Yellow snickered and tightened his neck hug.

I clenched my lips to suppress a smile while I waited for one of Agent Orange's patented weaves, so it coincided with my body slam of Agent Yellow into the refrigerator, making it super effective.

Agent Yellow slumped to the floor.

"What's going on back there?" Agent Orange continued his serpentining, but the Jeep remained affixed to the back of the RV, pivoting on the toilet.

"Just having a little row with Agent Yellow. It'thh over now.

I bent down to grab another vial, when Agent Orange broke his serpentining rhythm. He started to swerve left, then reversed directions, jerking the RV to the right. I missed the vial, slamming my head into a cabinet. The blaring of a semi-trailer truck's horn mixed with our wheels spitting up shoulder gravel. Agent Orange hugged the shoulder until we passed the truck, then lurched us back onto the road.

"It'thh time to get rid of this Jeep," I said, waddling backwards. I gave the Jeep a hard kick with a hind leg. The Jeep dislodged, but took the bathroom with it. "The Jeep is gone. You can thhtop swerving."

"Thank you," said Agent Orange, pressing the gas pedal to the floor. The RV lurched forward. The plethora of items littering the floor rolled toward the back, including cereal, chunks of broken plates and coffee mugs, a bouncy ball, an eclectic assortment of silverware and, of course, the vials of the deadly zombie viruses.

Items started falling out onto the road behind us. I dove to my stomach, locked my back hooves into what remained of the back corners of the RV, and spread my legs out butterfly style. Four vials rolled toward me. The first one rolled straight down the middle. I snatched it up with my tongue. The next one rolled down my right leg like a pinball down the outlane and rested between my neck and shoulder. The third did the same, but down my left leg.

This left only one vial, which wiggled behind a chunk of a broken coffee mug until Agent Orange hit a bump. It ping-ponged off a plate, a fork, a box of cereal, a broken glass, and then rolled right for me. I lifted my snout, allowing it to roll underneath, and trapped it under my chin. I exhaled a sigh of relief.

My relief was short-lived. A no longer motionless Agent Yellow groaned and rubbed his eyes with his open palms. After a couple of head shakes, he pushed himself up. He wobbled, rubbed his eyes again, and rattled off a quick ten blinks in half a second. Then he saw me lying spread-eagled on the floor and smiled. "Well, well, well. What do we have here?" He made a fake lunge towards me. "Careful. One false move, and you fall out the back of the RV."

He leaped into the air and came down with a classic elbow drop to my head. My skull inflicted more damage to his elbow than his elbow did to my skull, but his elbow drop crushed not only the vial in my mouth but the one under my chin.

I spit the broken glass and poisonous liquid into the agent's face. "You idiot. That was a vial of zombie virus!"

24: We're Camping

AGENT ORANGE STOMPED ON the RV's brakes. "Did you say a vial broke?!"

The RV skidded to a sideways stop. Agent Yellow stumbled backward, fell on his butt, and slid to the front of the RV. I followed, sliding just short of him. The vials of the deadly disease rolled ahead of me, past Agent Yellow, and stopped by the captain's chairs. Agent Orange spun and picked them up in a single motion.

Both agents stood up and had the briefest of stare downs before Agent Orange pulled Agent Yellow's head down while bringing his knee up. Nose cartilage crunched. Blood splattered. Agent Yellow's watery eyes rolled up into his forehead. He blinked them back to normal, but too late to block Agent Orange's vicious knee to the groin. Agent Yellow dropped to his knees.

As they fought, I scrambled to the sink and spat out the broken vial and zombie virus. I knocked the faucet handle up and lapped at the streaming water. This did nothing to get rid of the black licorice mixed with beet infused Brussel sprouts taste.

Agent Yellow gasped for breath. Agent Orange grabbed him by the shirt collar, dragged him to the side door, yanked it open, and tossed him out.

I spat a dozen more times, then flung open the refrigerator door. "I need something to kill my taste buds. And like forty shots of Benadryl."

"What is wrong with you?" asked Agent Orange, slamming the RV door shut.

"A vial broke in my mouth!" I grabbed the first drink I could find; a half gallon of milk. Not my usual choice, but this was no time to be fussy. I bit the cap off and spit it on the floor. I picked the bottle up with my mouth, then tilted my head up. Once I had a mouth full, I slammed the bottle down on the counter, gargled, and spat the milk into the sink. Then I repeated the process.

Agent Orange gazed out the missing back of the RV. Headlights approached in the distance. "We need to get out of sight, then figure out which vials broke. There's a campsite up ahead. I'm heading there."

With a high-pitched shrill I didn't think my oversized stiff vocal cords could reach, I said, "I need a doctor."

***

After making sure no one followed us, we drove past the sleeping ranger at the campground's entrance, thankful we did not have to explain the missing back end of our RV. After winding down a labyrinth of dirt roads with our lights off, Agent Orange found an open campsite, and parked.

I finished my fifth milk-wash gargle, which had added a sour tang to the lingering licorice, beet, and Brussel sprout mixture. In between rinses, I scoured through the broken vials littering the floor. My breath shortened, and my heart raced. "The vials are in a million pieces. I can't read the labels. I have no idea which one broke in my mouth."

Agent Orange squeezed between the captain's chairs and walked to me with his palms down. "We'll figure this out by process of elimination." He dumped the vials from the side bag onto the couch.

"So, there were twelve vials of the human virus?"

"Only ten, thhir."

"That's good, because I only count ten."

"Bovine! Bovine! Do you thhee a bovine vial?" My pounding heart vibrated my ribs.

"Yes, I have the bovine vial." He waved it over his head.

"Oh, thank goodness." I released a good portion of my stress with a long breath. The pulsing blood in the veins of my forehead eased.

"So, what were the other viruses?" He lined the vials up on the couch.

"Okay, let'thh thhee. Besides bovine, there'thh feline, fowl, swine, salmon, canine, and leporid." Stating the list out loud caused my neck to shiver. Had *the Havarti Travel Bureau known decades ago about the Barn Yard Heroes and prepared viruses to kill us?*

"Leporid. I don't see the leporid vial."

"It'thh right there," I pointed my snout at a vial in the middle of the row.

"Okay, good. Swine, we've got swine. We've got feline and salmon."

"And canine," I said.

"That leaves fowl. That's not so bad. We can contain this." He smiled for just a moment, then dropped his shoulders and frowned. "Except I'm not the director of GIBOD anymore. So, maybe not."

"Thhir, isn't fowl just another word for bird? It seems rather nonspecific for these viruses." I hoped the answer would ruin my theory that the viruses targeted the BarnYard Heroes.

"It said domestic fowl, which would be chickens, turkeys, ducks, maybe pheasants." He slid the vials into the side bag, which he flung over his shoulder before hopping out the back of the RV.

I followed with my worrisome theory still intact. "Thhir, why do you think the Havarti Travel Bureau had zombie viruses targeted for each of uthh animals?"

"The Bureau had zombie viruses for hundreds of species. The

question you should be asking is why did my dad pull a set of vials matching you and the other animals? I don't know the answer to that, nor do we have time to ponder it. We need to find a new vehicle." He checked the campground road before motioning me to follow.

We looped through the woods along a dirt road, with unattended smoldering campfires providing the only light, but enough to grant glimpses of the spacious campsites, each nestled under its own private canopy of trees. Questions about why Agent Lime had collected viruses to kill the BarnYard Heroes rattled through my brain. Had he seen us as a threat?

"Cow, can you fit in the back of that Jeep?"

His question snapped me back to the present. I glanced at the Jeep. "Not a chance."

"Who'd have known it would be so hard to find a vehicle in a campground?"

I suffered an involuntary gag attack. The stench was faint, but undeniably the skunk-poop stink of rotting zombie bovine flesh. "They're coming."

"Who's coming? Campers?" asked Agent Orange as he checked out an oversized pickup truck.

"No. Not campers. Can't you smell that?"

He took a deep breath. "Nothing but smoldering campfires."

"Zombie cowthh. They're coming, so let'thh pick a vehicle already."

"What do you think of this pickup truck? Plenty of room in the bed."

It's a good thing the owner parked the truck near the road, well away from the campsite's tent, because Agent Orange whacked the side of the truck with his open palm to demonstrate the vehicle's sturdiness.

I needed no convincing. "It'thh great. Let'thh go."

Agent Orange scavenged around the campsite. "Help me find something to break the window."

I kicked the driver's side window in with my right front hoof.

"That'll work." Agent Orange reached in and opened the door. He dove under the dashboard.

I caught a stronger whiff of the skunky rotting flesh. I scanned the trees marking the edge of the campsite. No zombie cows were in sight, but a shirtless man flew out of his tent. "Hey, what did you do to my truck?!"

Fireworks sparked under the stirring wheel, causing Agent Orange to flinch. "Dang it. I never was good at this. Cow, you don't happen to know how to hotwire a car?"

"Of course not." I waved a hoof in the air. "No hands." I nodded toward the campsite. "Plus, we've got company."

"What?" was all Agent Orange said before the angry camper yanked the truck door wide open.

"You're going to pay for that window with your blood." He pulled Agent Orange out and tossed him to the ground. He then pulled Agent Orange up by his tie and dangled him like a limp stuffed animal.

"Cow! A little help."

I walked up behind the man and nudged him with my snout.

He spun around, dragging Agent Orange with him, and punched me in the jaw.

I smiled at the man's feeble attempt to hurt me. I raised my front right hoof and placed it on the man's chest. He dropped Agent Orange as I pressed him against the truck.

The man grabbed my hoof with both hands. As he took an exaggerated inhale, he shifted his footing. Then, with a loud grunt, he strained to move my hoof. His face turned lobster red. Veins protruded from his forearms and zigzagged across his forehead.

My hoof didn't move.

"Thank you," said Agent Orange, straightening his tie and suit coat.

"You're welcome," I instinctively said, not thinking about the fact we had a civilian present.

The man's eyes bulged, and his mouth gaped wide open.

Agent Orange sniffed the air and made a sour face. "I smell it, now. They've got to be close. Sir, we need to commandeer your vehicle. Give us the keys."

With his eyes popped and his mouth drooped, the man nodded agreement. He checked his pajama pockets and then said, "They're in the tent."

"Well go get 'em," said Agent Orange.

I let the shirtless man go, but followed close behind as he crawled into his tent.

A young man ran through the neighboring campsite, screaming, "Mad cow stampede! Run for your lives!"

Four more young men charged out of the woods, a couple of them carrying beers. They plowed into the shirtless man's tent. Beers spilled as they toppled over. The man fought his way out of the collapsed tent, ready to bust heads, but the young men were gone.

"There's a cow over here! They're surrounding us," yelled a mom coming out of the neighboring tent, clutching her toddler.

Six or seven cars zipped past, racing for the exit.

The dad grabbed the child. "Everybody in the car!"

As the family piled into their SUV, a Black Angus with frosted eyes stumbled into their campsite.

"We've got to go," I said to the shirtless man. "We'll take you with uthh."

He rustled his way out of the collapsed tent. He eased himself to full height, raised a handgun, and pointed it at my head. "I don't know what you are, but I ain't going nowhere."

The family's SUV spit out a dust storm as they sped away.

I used the diversion, bucked up, and gave the man a swift kick. He flew backwards, then skidded across the dirt until he banged into rocks lining his smoldering campfire. With a humph, he pushed himself up and gathered himself into the classic single-handed pistol shooter's pose.

I shuffled through the wreckage of his tent, looking for the truck keys.

Keys jingled.

The man grinned and dangled the keys in his unarmed hand as Agent Orange walked up next to me. The man narrowed his glare at him. "You're going to stand nice and still while I call 911." The man reached into his pajama pants pocket and exchanged his keys for a mobile phone.

"Mad cow! Look out!" Agent Orange pointed at the Black Angus staggering through the trees and into the man's campsite, sniffing for flesh.

Moo-groan. Moo-groan.

"I'm not falling for that trick." He worked the touchscreen on his phone while monitoring us.

Agent Orange waved his arms above his head. "Seriously, don't you smell them? Don't you hear the hideous groans? Why do you think everyone is running?"

The man did a brief, shifty-eyed glance around his wrecked campsite. Rustling leaves and moo-groans provided the only soundtrack, as everyone else had fled the scene. His nose wrinkled when he took a mini sniff. "I don't care about what's got everyone else spooked, bud. You and your robot cow are going to jail."

He raised the phone to his ear.

Moo-groan.

The Black Angus shuffled up behind him as two more hobbled through the trees.

"Nine, one, one. Where is your emergency?" said a female voice on the man's phone.

The zombified Black Angus chomped, engulfing the phone and the man's hand.

He spun and shot the zombie cow in the head.

The Black Angus wobbled back a step; their teeth still clenching the man's hand.

He screamed as he pounded on the zombie cow's skull with his gun.

Moo-groan. Unphased, the Black Angus continued to gnaw on his hand.

He pumped three more bullets into the Black Angus's head.

Moo-groan. Gnaw. Gnaw. They refused to let go.

Four more zombified Black Angus zeroed in on him.

"Should we help him?" I asked.

The man jabbed the barrel of his gun into the zombie cow's eye. A muffled shot rang out.

Agent Orange shrugged. "Not sure what we can do."

A second zombified Black Angus engulfed the man's hand and gun in their mouth.

A couple of muffled gunshots went off.

Moo-groan. Om nom nom.

The second zombified Black Angus twisted their head.

Bones cracked.

The man wailed.

His arm twisted at the shoulder until it popped. His screaming intensified.

A third zombified Black Angus moved in and snagged the man's head in their mouth.

Pop.

The screaming stopped.

The man went limp as two more zombie cows joined the feast.

Agent Orange and I stood motionless, watching the carnage.

"So, did you find the keys?" asked Agent Orange.

"He'thh got them in his pocket."

We watched the zombie feast for another couple of seconds.

"Forget the truck. Run!" said Agent Orange.

We sprinted for the campground exit, but a limping herd of twenty to thirty zombified Black Angus blocked the road. We took a sharp right.

Another band of slow-moving zombified Black Angus greeted us around the next bend.

The first herd staggered toward us. They had us hemmed in.

Agent Orange pointed at two small structures. "Quick, head to the bathrooms."

As we approached the campground bathrooms, the skunk-poop stench gagged us both. We turned back. Frosted eyes bobbed toward us from all directions.

Agent Orange backed into the wall of the campground bathroom. "Time to do your super-cow thing."

"I'm not sure I can defeat this many."

Agent Orange glanced at the bathroom roof. "Do you think these things can climb?"

"No."

"Good. Let's climb up on the roof. We'll be safe there and we can just wait 'em out."

"The reason I know they can't climb is because *I* can't climb."

"Fine. You got any bright ideas?"

I didn't.

"I'll try the super-cow thing. Get on my back like you're riding a horse." It took Agent Orange several tries and the use of the bathroom building's wall to get on my back. "Grab onto my neck and hold on tight."

There were hundreds of zombie cows, mostly Black Angus. I scanned for the weakest link in the chain. Thank goodness the zombie Black Angus were nothing like the one fabricated in the Weekly World News article. They all looked to be the weakest link. These once proud and powerful Black Angus cows nearly fell with every step. I spotted one with a broken bone protruding out of their hide. The bloody bone stuck out farther with every step they took. I lowered my head as I scuffed the dirt with my right front hoof. I unleashed a loud snort and galloped full steam at the Black Angus zombie with the compound fracture as my cloak zipped across my hide. He toppled and rolled like an empty garbage can on a windy day. I rammed through the herd, sending zombified cows tumbling.

The wall of cow zombies grew thicker the farther I plowed into the herd. It got harder and harder to fight my way through. My tactic of shoving one cow to the right and one to the left no longer worked. I reared up and began beating the cow zombies with my front hooves. I followed up with a series of spinning bucking bronco kicks until only three zombie cows stood between us and an open field. With one kick, I sent them flying off to the right and galloped to safety.

"Cow! Stop!"

"Why?"

"I dropped the bag."

25: Save the Bag, Save the World

I skidded to a halt in the open field. Agent Orange slid off my back as I spun around to face the wobbling herd of zombified Black Angus. The cows changed direction with the grace and speed of a semi-trailer truck, making an eight-point U-turn on a side-street. The bag of zombie virus vials lay on the edge of the herd.

"How could you drop the bag?" I asked, initially hoping I hadn't used a how-could-you-be-such-an-idiot tone but reversed that wish mid-sentence. Based on the eye daggers Agent Orange shot my way, the tone was clear.

"It wasn't easy hanging onto your back, with you flailing all over the place. Bucking up and down."

"If I hadn't been flailing and bucking, the zombie cows would have eaten uthh."

"Look, *you* try staying on your back. It's not easy."

Zombified Black Angus staggered all around the bag.

Agent Orange's shoulders heaved. "One of us better go fetch that bag before they crush it."

"I'm lucky I escaped without getting bitten. One bite and I'll turn into one of them."

"It's an airborne virus. If you were going to turn into a zombie, you'd be one already."

"Are you sure? In all the movies, the zombies have to bite or scratch you." I hated how much I sounded like the rabbit and duck. This triggered immediate regret for having forgotten about my friends. Plans for their rescue hadn't entered my mind for hours. My transformation into Agent Orange was complete. I had only focused on the mission.

I tuned back to Agent Orange in the middle of his ranting response. "...movies. The reality of this virus is that it's airborne, and I'm guessing that, thanks to your altered DNA, you're immune. Besides, that cloak of yours is like some sort of impenetrable force field. Now stop being such a baby, activate your cloaking shield, and fetch the bag."

Attempts to reactivate my cloak sputtered like a lamp with a loose wire. "Well, my power isn't working, so you do it. You're small and nimble. I'm big and bulky. You'll be able to zip in and out with no problem. Besides, you're the one who dropped it."

A zombified Black Angus's legs snapped. They crashed down inches away from the bag.

Agent Orange snarled at me, but after another zombie cow almost crushed the bag, he ran into the herd. Agent Orange made a sliding grab, inches before a gnarly hoof came down on the bag. But he ended up under a zombified Black Angus. They wobbled as they twisted to take a bite of him.

I charged in and knocked the cow over. As Agent Orange got to his feet, I reared up and beat our closest attackers with my front hooves, until my hind legs gave way. After dropping to all fours, I spun and kicked a few more zombie cows before stumbling and collapsing. The moo-groans intensified as the zombie herd closed in on us.

Hope danced in the field in the form of gleaming headlights. "Look, someone is coming to save uthh."

"Cow, we have no friends left. It's just the two of us. Whoever is in that vehicle is not coming to save us." Agent Orange shot two of the attacking cows in the head.

I sprang to my feet. "Well, right now it'thh our only hope."

Zombie cows nipped at my tail, so I pulled it underneath me. Only a handful of zombified Black Angus stood between us and the open field. They snapped at us. I kicked their mouths away.

The headlights grew closer.

I plowed through the zombified Black Angus like a lead blocker, with Agent Orange behind me holding the side bag like a football running back. We screamed with anger and joy as we ran into the clearing, feeling as if we had scored a touchdown.

Our celebration was short-lived. A military truck bounced past us, with Grandma Marjorie at the wheel and Nick in the passenger seat. Noy and Bugbear stood in the bed with weapons ready.

"I told you we didn't have any friends," said Agent Orange.

Thanks to my exceptional peripheral vision, I monitored them and the herd as we sprinted across the field.

The moo-groans increased when the headlights flashed in their whitewashed eyes, then turned to high-pitched screams as flames streamed from Noy and Bugbear's flamethrowers. Despite the screams and flames, the Black Angus continued their limping, stumbling charge.

The truck beeped as Grandma Marjorie crammed the truck into reverse. I was several strides ahead of Agent Orange when they caught up to him. Noy and Bugbear hopped down and aimed their flamethrowers at him, as Grandma Marjorie and Nick climbed down from the truck. Collectively, they formed a semi-circle around Agent Orange.

I trotted to Agent Orange's side, stomped to a stop, and snarled my lip.

Bugbear's excessive body spray greeted me, providing a slight upgrade from the skunk-poop stench. He also greeted me by aiming his flamethrower at my head.

"Hand over the bag, Joey," said Grandma Marjorie.

Agent Orange growled, and his face morphed into a squinty-eyed Clint Eastwood scowl as he removed his handgun from his shoulder holster and aimed it at the old woman. "I told you, that's not my name."

Grandma Marjorie brushed off his rage-filled tone with a shrug. "I figured, since you are no longer an agent, you'd go back to Joey."

"Never call me that name again." Agent Orange straightened his aim at the old woman's head and increased his squint. One eye quivered to a close.

Grandma Marjorie shrugged once more and gave Agent Orange a half smile. "Go ahead. Shoot me. I'll die happy, knowing you're dead and I've secured the safety of my grandsons. So, go ahead. Shoot."

"Fine." Agent Orange shifted his aim to Nick. "He dies first."

Without a change in his straight-lipped, stoic expression, Nick pulled his handgun and pointed it at Agent Orange.

Grandma Marjorie's snarky smile disappeared, replaced with a sneer and an unwavering glare at Agent Orange.

Noy and Bugbear exchanged scrunched-face looks and shrugs.

The stench of smoldering, rotted flesh stung my nostril hairs, distracting my focus on the tense scene. The herd had stumbled to within a truck length. Thin strands of charred flesh were all that covered the teeth and jaw of the lead Black Angus. Whiffs of smoke rose from its head.

Noy wiggled his flamethrower, which was still pointed at Agent Orange. "Shall I light him up, Grandma?"

"That's a great idea," said Agent Orange, keeping his stare glued to Nick. "Light me up. Let's see what happens when these glass vials melt."

Grandma Marjorie nodded in my direction.

Noy shifted his aim to me.

She glanced at the approaching herd. Flames still blazed on four of the zombie cows, but they didn't notice or care. "You're running out of time, Joey."

"I warned you to never call me that again."

Shots rang out. My cloak instinctively activated. Flames engulfed me, but I felt no heat. I charged Noy and Bugbear and kicked the flamethrowers out of their hands. Errant flames scorched the field behind me.

Grandma Marjorie kneeled next to Nick's limp body, with her mouth hung open and a quivering bottom lip. Her head whipped toward Agent Orange. Her mouth snapped closed, though her lower lip still quivered. In an instant, her ghost white face turned pomegranate red. She gradually rose and took aim at Agent Orange with her tiny laser gun as he examined a hole in the shoulder of his black suit.

Words failed me. "Muraaagghh!!!" I'm not sure what word of warning I intended to shout. But at least my brain didn't completely freeze. I charged, sideswiping Noy and Bugbear with my backside, as I slammed the old woman into the truck. Her blaster sailed into the air.

The commotion broke Agent Orange's focus on his jacket bullet hole. He quickly surveyed the scene. "We're taking the truck. Get in the back."

I jumped in the back as he climbed into the driver's seat. He pounced on the gas pedal as he spun the truck around.

Behind us, Grandma Marjorie dropped to her knees and cradled Nick's head, sobbing uncontrollably. Noy and Bugbear tugged at her as the zombie herd of Black Angus shuffled closer.

I decloaked and, despite the bumpy ride across the field, passed out.

***

AN ANNOYING PECK AT my ear, along with a garbled cluck, woke me up. I wiggled my ears and flicked my head to shoo away the pesky chicken that had hopped onto me. She came right back and bit a chunk of my ear off. She leaned in for seconds. I snapped my neck, swatting the chicken with the side of my head. She sailed across the truck bed.

I curled up as best I could between the benches in the bed of the military truck and rested my head on my front legs. The garbled clucking returned before I closed my eyes. The chicken waddled toward me with her head flopping like the top of a broken tennis racket.

"Good, you're awake." The truck door clanged into a tractor. Agent Orange squeezed out and navigated the clutter crammed into the barn.

"I don't remember us pulling into a barn," I said.

"You were out cold." He climbed onto a riding mower, a step in the process of getting into the truck bed. "You feeling better?"

"Not really. I'm tired, my head is pounding, and my stomachs are churning. How long are hangovers supposed to last?"

"You're past hangover time. But you have been using your power a lot. It seems to take a lot out of you," he said, hopping into the truck bed.

"I guess thho. How long have we been here?"

He grabbed the zombie chicken and tossed her across the barn. "About four hours."

I examined the deceased chicken. "It didn't take long for the virus to spread."

"That's only the half of it." Agent Orange nodded toward the other side of the barn.

A row of stalls lined the wall, each containing a black and white dairy cow, with frosted marbles for eyes. They pounded into the wood stall doors as if they didn't know they were closed.

He dropped the tailgate. "Those doors won't hold much longer. We've got to go."

"We're not taking the truck?"

"They'll be looking for it. We need to find something new."

He navigated the lawn mower and tractor obstacle course, grabbed the bag of vials out of the front seat, and headed for the barn door.

I popped up and hopped out of the truck bed. The floor wobbled. The barn walls vibrated. I floated for a second before crumpling into a support post. The wood post cracked, bending like a knee. Creaks and pops echoed in the rafters of the old barn. At least three of my stomachs churned. I staggered over to a pile of hay and discharged the contents of those churning stomachs.

Agent Orange stood by the barn door. "Cow, come on. We've gotta go."

I staggered past the zombie dairy cows banging into their weathered stall doors. Once I joined Agent Orange, he pushed the barn door open. Grunting-clucks greeted us. Feathers dropped off several dozen zombie chickens as they limped toward us. "Gluckyuck. Gluckyuck."

"Let's grab that truck up there." Agent Orange motioned to a rusting pickup truck parked up a short hill leading to the farmhouse. He kicked the first couple of waddling zombie chickens, sending them flying over the rest of the flock. "Cow, I wanted to..." He kicked a zombie chicken into a tractor. "Well, first of all, I think we make a good team. Secondly, I wanted to apologize for dragging you into this mess."

I was in double shock. The compliment sent my head spinning, but the apology sent it flying. I didn't think he knew the word apologize existed, let alone how to pronounce it.

He stopped in the middle of the zombie chicken flock. "I'm a terrible leader, and I've made a big mess of everything." The chickens converged on him.

It was refreshing to hear him self-reflect, but he didn't need to stop walking. My legs struggled to keep me upright, and my stomachs wanted another round of vomiting, but I needed to catch up to him and kick away the zombie chickens nipping at his ankles.

"Gluckyuck. Gluckyuck."

His head hung low, and his shoulders slouched as he nudged away the zombie chickens that pecked his pants.

He'd gone through a lot in the last few days. Betrayal by his most trusted advisor. The wound of his parents' death reopened. Losing his role as Director of GIBOD. Revisiting his failed relationship. My heart went out to him. But I wished he'd kept moving. "This isn't your fault, thhir. You're the victim. It'thh that jerk Agent Periwinkle's fault. He'thh been using you." I swept away zombified chickens waddling toward the stationary Agent Orange.

"That's my point. How could I be so blind? I thought he was my friend. I thought he had my back. Instead, he was using me the entire time, and I fell for the whole thing. I'm so stupid."

"Gluckyuck. Gluckyuck." The zombie chicken pecked Agent Orange's ankle, who responded with a swift kick.

"You're not stupid, thhir," I said, though he had a point. He should have sniffed this out. And frankly, he had been a horrible leader. He should never have taken a small team of inexperienced agents on a dangerous mission. Then again, what kind of leader had I been? Maybe we deserved each other. "Besides, we still have the vials. That jerk hasn't won yet."

He lifted his head and looked at me. "You're right. We can still fix this. We WILL fix this. Thanks."

The grunt-clucks intensified as the flock scattered away from us.

"That'thh odd," I said. Then I saw the rooster.

He stood in our path, half his feathers gone, and those that remained were the color of cream cheese. Yet, he still stood proud. With his head tilted up, he bellowed what sounded like a cock-a-doodle-do while gargling. After he finished, he charged at us at zombie speed.

I trotted up and kicked him into the pasture.

We continued our stroll to the truck.

"Cow, once we straighten this mess out, we're getting your friends back. It was selfish of me to bring you on that mission. I'm done exploiting you all. Once the gang is back together, we'll find a safe place for all of you to stay. Maybe a peaceful farm out in the middle of nowhere."

"That sounds nice, thhir." I found myself winded after the short walk and stopped a couple of steps from the truck.

The farmhouse front door flew open and banged against the house siding. A man yelled, "City slicker, I'm gonna give you five seconds to get away from my cow, and get off my property." He cocked his shotgun.

"I'm a federal agent investigating the mad cow catastrophe," said Agent Orange, strolling toward the farmer. "I just inspected your barn, and they've all gone mad except this one."

"They were fine when I milked them last night," said the farmer.

"Go look yourself, but you'll have to get past the mad chickens first. I suggest you vacate the premises immediately."

The man stepped toward the barn, then stopped. He surveyed the flock of zombie chickens waddling toward him. As he stood motionless, his barn let out a steady stream of creaks and cracks. Then the far wall gave way. Puffs of dust billowed around the barn, which stabilized in a half-collapsed fashion that resembled a ramp.

The farmer squinted at the scene. "That looks repairable." A soft creaking noise quickly increased in volume, then abruptly stopped.

We collectively took a sigh of relief.

Then the entire barn crashed down with a resounding thud.

As the dust cloud engulfed the remains of the barn, Agent Orange walked up to the man. "I am commandeering your vehicle. You and your family can come along."

The man gazed at his collapsed barn and the army of zombified barn animals methodically advancing toward us. He opened fire at his flock of zombie chickens and marched toward them. "Go in the front door. There's a key rack above the small table on the right. The Packers keychain has the keys for the truck. I wish you luck." He loaded new shells, cocked the weapon, and let out a couple more blasts.

"He should save some shells for the cows. Those are the ones he'thh got to worry about."

"I don't think it'll matter," said Agent Orange, standing next to me watching the farmer continue down the hill.

The farmer waded into the flock and ran out of shells before getting halfway to the barn. The chickens encircled him. They attacked his feet and legs first. He swung the gun like a golf club and took a few heads off. The headless chickens continued their assaults, clawing at his ankles. He dropped his gun, grabbed a chicken, and wrung her neck. He bent down to grab another. Chickens attacked his arms. The groaning-clucks intensified. The man dropped to a knee. He shot a glare at us. "What are you doing? Get out of here!"

We snapped out of our trance. "Packers keychain," said Agent Orange, before he dashed into the house. I kept one eye on the action down the hill while heading for the truck. I planned to open the tailgate with my tongue but couldn't position my head to get a good grip.

From his knees, the farmer pulled zombie chickens off him and broke their wings and legs.

Agent Orange returned with the keys. "Quit wasting time and get in the truck."

"I can't get the latch open."

I moved out of the way as he opened the tailgate. It dropped with a creak and a thud.

The farmer screamed. He collapsed face first into the dirt. The groaning-clucks crescendoed as the flock swarmed on top of him.

"Let's go," said Agent Orange, heading to the driver's side door.

I got my front hooves on the lowered tailgate, but my hind legs wobbled. I tried to push myself up, but my legs did not have the strength. My front hooves slipped off the hatch, and I tumbled to the ground.

"Cow, what's wrong with you?" asked Agent Orange, about to get in the driver's seat. "Get in the truck."

"I'm trying, thhir. It'thh weird. I don't have the strength. Last night must have taken too much out of me." I picked myself up, and once again strained to get my front hooves on the tailgate.

He slammed the door closed and stomped toward me. He rammed his shoulder into my backside. I didn't move. "Work with me. Come on. Put some effort behind it. On three, let's do this. One, two, three."

I pushed with all the strength I had left, as Agent Orange drove his shoulder into my butt and powered me up into the bed of the truck. I collapsed, panting like a dog having a heart attack. Agent Orange closed the tailgate and sprinted to the driver's seat.

The farmer's rust-bucket kicked over on the first try, which was a considerable relief. The clutch clanked as Agent Orange jammed it into gear and stomped on the gas pedal. Gravel sprayed out behind us, but then we skidded to a halt.

A standard issue GIBOD black Suburban had pulled into the farmer's dirt and gravel driveway, blocking our escape.

26: Farmhouse Showdown

THE BLAST OF THE shotgun and explosion of the truck's windshield occurred simultaneously. Thousands of glass pellets rained down the dashboard. I ducked for safety in the back of the truck.

A glance through the cab's back window exhausted me. The remnants of the truck's windshield still rolled down the hood. Agent Orange brushed away glass pebbles and peeked above the dash.

Agent Periwinkle ambled toward us and took aim for a second shot. I ducked down as another shot rang out. Shattered pieces of the back window pelted me like a tiny hailstorm. He cracked open the shotgun to dump the empty shells.

With a break in the shooting, Agent Orange sprang out of the truck. "You double-crossing jerk!"

As the former director of GIBOD charged at him, Agent Periwinkle reached into his sport jacket, pulled out two shotgun shells, calmly slid them into the chamber, and slammed the gun back together. He raised the rifle to his shoulder just as Agent Orange plowed into him. The gun fired harmlessly into the air.

Agent Orange wrestled the gun away and smacked his foe in the head with the butt end. He turned the gun around, but before he could take aim, Periwinkle kicked him just below his gut.

Agent Periwinkle grabbed the shotgun with both hands. The former director refused to let go. The pair rolled on the ground, each with their hands glued to the weapon.

I wanted to help, but it took all my strength to hold my head up and follow the action.

When the rolling stopped, Agent Orange kneeled on top. He removed a hand from the shotgun to deliver a punch.

Absorbing the blow to his jaw, Agent Periwinkle yanked the gun from Agent Orange's single-handed grip.

The former director responded with a flurry of punches. Agent Periwinkle fought through the onslaught and stuck the gun barrel in Agent Orange's face, who dismissed it with a swift chop of his arm. He added another punch to the face before standing to stomp on Agent Periwinkle's stomach, causing him to curl up like a roly-poly bug.

The gun dangled in his hands. Agent Orange kicked it away and followed up with a series of hard kicks to the gut. I loved the groan Agent Periwinkle made with every blow. He rolled to his knees, spat out a tooth, and crawled for the shotgun. Agent Orange waltzed up and delivered a devastating kick to his jaw. Blood sprayed across the lawn. Agent Periwinkle collapsed. It took all his energy to lift his head up.

Agent Orange sauntered over to the shotgun and picked it up. He cocked the weapon as he walked back. With the barrel of the shotgun, he lifted Agent Periwinkle's head.

"Go ahead. Do it. Shoot me."

"That's exactly what you want me to do. You've got everyone convinced *I'm* the traitor. So, if I kill you, that confirms your story," said Agent Orange.

"You don't have the guts to do it."

"Oh, please. I've got the guts and you know it."

"Then do it. Do it now."

A headless zombie chicken waltzed in front of Agent Orange. He kicked it toward the flock that staggered up the hill. Zombie dairy cows, acting like a pack of slow-moving hyenas, had claimed the remains of the farmer.

"You're not going to goad me into killing you. I'm bringing you in." Agent Orange kept the gun pointed at Agent Periwinkle's back as he grabbed him by the collar, pulled him to his feet, and shoved him toward the agency's standard issue black Suburban.

Agent Periwinkle stumbled and slouched over like he had fallen asleep standing.

"How did you find us?" asked Agent Orange, giving him another push.

Agent Periwinkle laughed as he staggered a couple of steps forward. "You still carrying that cell phone?"

My cheeks flushed with angry heat at the news that Agent Orange still carried his cell phone. They had already tracked us once. If I had the dexterity and energy to execute a face palm, I would have.

Agent Orange poked the gun into Periwinkle's back. "You're gonna pay for all your treachery. I'll make sure of it. Now, move it."

I saw Agent Periwinkle reach inside his coat. A flash of the early morning sun glimmered off the blade. I didn't have time to pick proper words of warning, but I never expected to make the noise I did. In the panic of the moment, I mooed.

This drew Agent Orange's attention. Not the outcome I wanted. He never saw it coming. The knife plunged into his gut. Agent Periwinkle gave it a twist before pulling it out.

As Agent Orange howled in agony and dropped to his knees, Agent Periwinkle wiped the blade clean on his victim's shoulder, then placed the clean knife back into its hidden holster.

With both hands over the wound, Agent Orange gasped for air, then spit out blood. Agent Periwinkle tapped him with the tip of his black leather shoe. Agent Orange toppled to his side.

"Hmmm, where have I seen this before?" Agent Periwinkle paced around his fallen opponent, scratching his chin. His eyes rolled up to the sky. Then he pointed a finger in the air and smiled. "Oh, yes, I remember. It was that night twenty-five years ago. The night your father died. How Lion King of me."

Fighting through the pain, Agent Orange got to his feet. Hunched over and clutching his stomach, he glared up at Agent Periwinkle.

Hope pumped through my veins, giving me the strength to twist my torso into a better view.

"What are you going to do? Bleed on me?"

Agent Orange tried to stand straight, but winced, coughed up blood, and doubled over.

"That's the thing about stomach wounds," said Agent Periwinkle as he circled around behind the former director. "It can take a long time, but trust me, you will die. There's no stopping that now."

Agent Orange spotted the shotgun six paces away from him.

"Go ahead. Grab it," said Agent Periwinkle with a smirk. He took a step back and spread his arms to show the path was clear.

The blood flow from Agent Orange's gut increased with every cough. He fell to his knees. He crawled toward the gun, but collapsed well before reaching it.

My head and shoulders sank, as hope fled from my cardiovascular system.

"I'll help you," said Agent Periwinkle in an exaggerated bubbly tone that even the chicken would recognize as sarcasm. He walked over and kicked the gun to Agent Orange.

He stared at the gun resting inches from his nose, then closed his eyes.

"This has been a nice little chat, but I think we're done here." Agent

Periwinkle turned and walked to the truck.

"Cow," said Agent Orange in a weak voice, his eyes still shut. "It's up to you now."

Fueled by anger, I wiggled my knees. My vision blurred as I planted my front hooves on the truck bed one-by-one. I rested for a moment, then pushed with all I had left. The world wobbled, and I thought the truck was tipping over. But it wasn't the truck. It was me. I collapsed in a heap, clanging to the metal trunk bed.

Agent Periwinkle whistled as he grabbed the bag of vials, then came by me. "Cow, you don't look so good," he said, patting me on the head.

I pulled my double image of his smirking face into one. Rage kicked in. I opened wide to bite his hand, but Grandma Marjorie and her grandsons, Noy and Bugbear, appeared at the end of the rocky driveway, diverting the focus I needed to complete the attack.

Grandma Marjorie waltzed up to the truck. "She don't look the ticket." She then spotted Agent Orange and frowned. "But she looks better than Joey."

Agent Orange coughed twice, bubbling blood out of his mouth each time.

Noy smiled wide, revealing a missing front tooth, and pointed to the farmer getting devoured by zombie dairy cows. "And they both look better than that guy."

"Why are you here, old woman?" asked Agent Periwinkle.

"They sent me to congratulate you on a job well done." With the frown of an angry librarian, she glanced between Agent Periwinkle and a wheezing Agent Orange. "As much as I enjoy witnessing his demise, I wish you'd have left him to me. I had a score to settle."

"He's not quite dead yet. I'll grant you the privilege of finishing the job," said Agent Periwinkle.

She walked over to Agent Orange, her cheeks tightening with every shuffle step. She lorded over him until he rolled his eyes up to greet her.

Then she spit in his face and pressed her heel on his wound.

His mouth sprang open, and his neck constricted, but only a gurgling moan emanated from him.

She lifted her foot off him and wiped the blood off in the grass. Her cheeks, forehead, and frown eased. "He can't even scream properly. Killing him would be merciful. I prefer to see him suffer."

As she walked away, he closed his eyes, gagged, and coughed up more blood.

With the tight-lipped expression of a corporate executive, she walked up to Agent Periwinkle, with Noy and Bugbear flanking her. "Let's get straight to business. Our orders are to take it from here, so hand over the vials."

Agent Periwinkle crossed his arms. "Those aren't my orders."

She furrowed a brow at the parade of zombie chickens staggering up the hill. "There's no time for debate. You've been to all the meetings. You know the plan. Now hand over the vials." She motioned for Noy to get the bag from Agent Periwinkle.

"You think I take orders from the Havarti Travel Bureau, those piles of cockroach dung?" Agent Periwinkle chuckled, yet his face remained serious.

"Knock it off, Bradley, and give Noy the bag."

Noy walked up to Agent Periwinkle and held out his hand.

Agent Periwinkle wrinkled his nose at the boy's skunk stench, then spit on his outstretched hand. "I spit on the Havarti Travel Bureau."

Noy's head repelled and scrunched. "Bro, that's gross. What's wrong with you?"

Agent Periwinkle hissed at him and clutched the bag to his chest.

Grandma Marjorie did a double-handed rub of her closed eyelids. "Bradley, it's been a long and devastating evening for me and the boys. Now stop this nonsense, and hand over the bag."

"I will do no such thing. And stop calling me Bradley."

"Surely you're not still going by Periwinkle."

"Of course." He puffed his chest, straightened his shoulders, and tilted his head up. "For I am Agent Periwinkle, Director of GIBOD."

The haggard droop of Grandma Marjorie's jowls flipped to a scowl. "Why you rotten little snot. You've been loyal to GIBOD this whole time." She pulled her tiny laser gun out of her handbag.

"Oh, please. I'm not loyal to GIBOD." He chuckled, though his face again remained stern.

With her scowl intact, she aimed her weapon at him. "Then who are you working for?"

"The Travel Bureau of Havarti."

Grandma Marjorie's jaw dropped, and she lowered her gun. "You're kidding, right?"

"I do not kid."

Agent Orange coughed and gasped his last breath. No one noticed. Except me.

Noy wiped his hand on his pants and, with an expression of genuine bewilderment, said, "Bro, there's no difference between the Havarti Travel Bureau and the Travel Bureau of Havarti."

"Oh, dear little Noy, you're so naive." Agent Periwinkle shook his head and patted Noy on the shoulder. "The Havarti Travel Bureau are blood-sucking greedy fiends, whereas the Travel Bureau of Havarti is a noble business run by creatures of honor."

"Are you listening to the words you're saying?" Grandma Marjorie's neck disappeared into her raised shoulders. "Both companies do the exact same thing. They secretly commit genocide in order to buy a planet cheap, then turn it into a high-class vacation paradise. There's no difference."

Agent Periwinkle pinched the bridge of his nose. "If all you care about is saving your own skin and the allure of getting rich, sure, there's no difference. But the Travel Bureau of Havarti is the only one that will restore this planet to its original beauty, the wonder it had before humans destroyed it with their giant cities, mountains of garbage, and devastating pollution."

"And then they'll open it to their obscenely rich clientele, just like the Havarti Travel Bureau. There's no difference," said Grandma Marjorie.

"Those HTB hacks will turn the planet into a Vegas-like cesspool. The Travel Bureau of Havarti will correct the centuries of human abuse this planet has endured."

With a single eyebrow raise, Bugbear asked, "You do realize you're a human?"

"Of course, but I've become self-aware. We're the problem. Think about what we've done to the planet in the last two hundred years. The staggering list of species we've brought to extinction. Islands of plastic floating in the oceans. Global warming. Fracking. Ranch Dressing Flavored soda. We're an abomination. A parasite. A planetary virus that must be stopped. But not by those jerks at the Havarti Travel Bureau, who'll turn the planet into a giant amusement park for the obscenely rich."

Grandma Marjorie rolled her eyes. "Yet, you were a willing participant in the plans to exterminate cows, caterpillars, chipmunks." She sneaked a peek at the army of zombie chickens staggering up the hill. "And now chickens."

Agent Periwinkle glimpsed at the flock of diseased chickens with a shrug. "Domesticated livestock are major producers of methane gas. The caterpillar and chipmunk outbreaks have been contained. My conscience is clear."

"Enough talk." Her cheeks clenched, and she once again aimed her weapon at Agent Periwinkle. "Hand over the bag."

"You're a fool, old woman." Agent Periwinkle sighed. "The Havarti Travel Bureau leaves no witnesses or collaborators alive. You and your grandsons will perish with the rest of the humans."

Noy took a step back and pulled a handgun on Agent Periwinkle.

Bugbear, standing next to his grandmother, pulled his gun out as well.

"Last warning. No counting this time. Hand over the vials," said Grandma Marjorie.

Agent Periwinkle dove into the beat-up pickup truck's front seat.

I ducked my head and curled up like a snuggling cat.

The laser gun made a faint puff, and a moment later, the roof of the truck cab blew off.

The gears clanked as Agent Periwinkle stomped on the gas of the already running truck.

Bugbear and Grandma Marjorie scattered as Agent Periwinkle drove right at them. Noy blasted a couple of harmless rounds into the cab as Agent Periwinkle accelerated the truck past them and bounced it onto the road.

I gazed at the lifeless body of Agent Orange as we drove away. I expected overwhelming sadness, but found I had no emotion. All I felt was an uncontrollable urge to eat my former boss while he was still fresh.

27: Is This Slaughterhouse Really Temple Grandin Approved?

AGENT PERIWINKLE WOKE ME up with a slap on my butt. I sprang to my feet, skidded around the slick truck lining, toppled out of the truck bed, and threw up.

The top half of the sun rested at the end of empty fields. I wondered if this meant the start or the end of the day.

Corrals of docile cows spanned out past the truck. One cow greeted me with a moo.

"A fitting end for a cow, don't you think?" said Agent Periwinkle, pointing to the only building in sight. The sign above the double-door entrance read Slaughterhouse 5.0. In smaller lettering, it read, "Temple Grandin Approved."

"You big fat piece of—" I lunged at him, intending to sink my teeth into his juicy thigh.

He did a quick sidestep and threw a lasso around my neck.

"You haven't looked in a mirror for days, have you?" he asked, tightening the loop around my neck, and pulling me away from the beat-up pickup truck. My legs struggled to keep up.

He walked into the blind spot in front of my snout. "You haven't seen your eyes. Those once majestic dark brown and black eyes are now blobs of milky white."

"I know what I'm becoming, but I'm fighting it. I'm fighting the cravings, though I might make an exception for you."

He walked into my side vision, starting a circling trek around me. "You are one tough animal. A true beast among beasts. Dr. Browns should be very proud of his work. You've fought the virus off for weeks. I knew you would. The perfect carrier. But even you can't fight it forever."

I wanted to tell him how much I hated his guts, but all that came out was a moo-groan.

"I'm not enjoying this." He smiled. "Okay, maybe just a little. But, the truth is I do like you. Honestly. Take solace from the fact you have played a key role in restoring this planet to its original glory and grace. Not only helping to exterminate humans, but rid the planet of cows and their menacing methane gas. Oh, and a bonus... you started the demise of chickens and their lethal farts. I thank you."

I glared at him with contempt as he came near my head. With my mouth ready to chomp, I lashed out. But with a tug of the rope, he yanked my head away.

"You did thithh to me. You gave me the virus."

"Yes, but I'll leave all the glory to you. You'll be famous. The cow who started the Great Cow Zombie Apocalypse. The fame will be short-lived, of course, since cows and humans will soon be extinct."

"Why you piece of—" I attempted to activate my cloak, but it didn't even flicker. "If I had just five percent of my power, I'd destroy you where you stand."

"But, you don't." He yanked the rope hard, and I staggered away from the truck.

I snarled at him. "I don't get it. Why did you need me to spread the virus? Why didn't you just let Grandma Marjorie and her boys spread it?"

"Do I really need to explain my entire plan? That's so cliché." He yanked the rope hard, but I stayed on my feet.

I drooled.

Fresh meat.

Tasty love-handles.

Must devour. So hungry.

Agent Periwinkle wiped tears from his eyes as he expelled a couple of quick breaths and stopped laughing.

"What'thh with you?"

"Welcome back. Sorry for laughing, it's just, you should see yourself. It's hilarious. 'I'm a zombie. I'm not a zombie. I'm a zombie.' It's cracking me up. Anyway, I ought to get going."

He tugged me toward the corral. I dug the heels of my hooves into the loose dirt. After a roll of his eyes, he gave a harder pull. My knees buckled, and I stutter-stepped into the corral.

Hungry.

Eat the human. Eat his arm.

Clang!

The gate snapped shut. Agent Periwinkle stood snickering on the other side.

I lunged for his face, but the gate stopped me hard. The rattle rippled down the fence line in both directions. A murmur of moos rose from the herd as they shuffled toward me.

"Enjoy your zombification for the short time you have left." He waved and headed for the truck.

I banged against the gate, then threw up the remaining contents of my stomachs, which amounted to a tiny amount of liquid bile. "I will hunt you down, Agent Periwinkle, and destroy you."

He didn't bother to turn around as he said, "I applaud your optimism. Keep that up as you're led to a slow and painful death." He sighed. "Actually, it will be quite peaceful, ending with a swift and painless death. A bit disappointing. Anyway, enjoy the ride, zombie boy."

As he hopped in the truck and drove away, I couldn't stop thinking about him calling me zombie boy. I'm a female, not a male. I'm several hundred years old, so I'm clearly not a child, and even if I was a child, they call baby cows calves not boy or girl. The proper phrase would have been zombie calf. What an idiot. Then I got mad at myself for going down this ridiculous line of thinking, especially considering my predicament, and hoped this was not my last rational thought.

I stood shoulder to shoulder, crammed in a pen with the other cows. They had no clue of their fate. I banged my head against the gate and shouted, "We're all gonna die! Help me break down the fence. We have to escape." But it came out as, "Moo-groan, moo-groan, mooooo-groan. Snort. Mooooo-groan."

A smattering of "Moo" and "Moo, moo" responses came from the herd. I banged my head against the gate a couple more times.

"Moo-groan."

Head hurts. Fence bad. Fence mean.

Herd move. Follow herd.

Through gate. Follow curve.

Curve take herd back to corral.

Hunger. Must bite tasty cow butt.

A cow's tail slapped me in the face as if it challenged me to a duel. I backed off and trotted alongside a herd of Herefordshire cattle heading down a four-cow-wide curving hallway. I wondered where we were going as we shuffled like humans in line for an amusement ride. A happy, peppy song played on an endless loop.

We've got the curves

And non-slip floors

We're the best design in comfort and grace

The familiar melody soothed me as I followed the winding high concrete walls, yet the lyrics didn't mesh with my memory of the tune. Ignoring this disconnect, I took the next curve, confident it would lead me and the herd back to where we came from.

Where did we come from? This isn't my herd. All I see is cattle. Where are the dairy cows? Wait! I know what this is. PERIWINKLE!!!

"Run. Everybody run! They're going to slaughter uthh."

The herd responded with half-hearted moos.

I couldn't turn around. Too many cows in the narrow passage. I banged the cows next to me until I had room.

The half-hearted moos turned angry as I pushed against the flow.

A man popped his head over the top of the wall. His eyes locked onto me as he revealed his cattle prod.

The herd grew thicker and pushed me backwards.

"Out of my way! Move it."

One cow responded with an indifferent "Moo."

The man swung the metal rod with swift precision. Pain seared through my hindquarters.

The herd spun me around. "Moooo! Mooo!"

I responded with a moo-groan.

Follow the herd. Follow the curve.

Happy song.

Meat. Need meat.

Beef. Big beef butt. Eat. Eat tasty beef butt.

Chomp. Hate tough skin. Chomp.

Ow!!

I stopped. I spit blood. The cows behind me mooed, like drivers honking as soon as the light turns green. I shuffled forward with the rest of the herd. We entered a circular opening. I strolled away from the cow I bit and tried to blend in with the others. But I didn't belong. I couldn't put a hoof on it, but I knew I had to get out of there. Images from a Temple Grandin documentary flashed through my brain. *SLAUGHTERHOUSE!!*

I plowed through the docile cattle, fighting to escape the circular courtyard.

The joyful tune droned on.

> *Serpentine ramps shield your views*
> *Semicircles are natural moves*

I recognized the tune. They played it in Wrigley Field whenever the Chicago Cub's win. But the lyrics didn't match. The dichotomy ached my brain.

"Moo-groan."

Follow the herd.

Leave the circle.

Curve ahead. It will take us back.

Hooves in water.

Keep moving.

Water deeper.

I flailed my legs in random patterns after becoming submerged. *Get to the surface. Get to the surface.* I bobbed up and stretched my head out. I breathed in as much air as I could, before plunging underwater again in mid-breath, inhaling a mouthful of chemicals. My legs galloped in place until I popped to the surface, where I coughed out the bitter metallic water.

I sank. My legs frantically paddled to no avail. I was going under again. But as if by divine intervention, a giant strap of fabric gently wrapped around my belly and lifted me out of the water. It politely placed me on a conveyor belt.

"Moo-groan."

Bouncy ride.

Hooves dangling.

Happy Song.

Tunnel.

Scary Tunnel.

My heart raced as the vibrating slots of the conveyor belt jiggled my stomachs. As I rode into the darkness, I wondered if this was an amusement park ride. That would explain the peppy song.

> *Don't stamp your hooves*
> *And you'll be fine*
> *Enjoy the Temple Grandin design*

The name buzzed through the recesses of my mind until it connected Temple Grandin with slaughterhouse design.

I'M IN A SLAUGHTERHOUSE!!

The tunnel walls closed in on me. This was the final stage. The stun bolt awaited.

I banged the ceiling and slammed the walls. The belt wobbled but kept chugging forward.

> *Go, cows, Go!*
> *Go, cows Go!*
> *Hey, you bovines, what do you say?*
> *Y'all gonna stay calm today*

The cow in front of me stayed calm as she rode into the restrainer.

I smacked the ceiling and walls with all the power I could muster.

The belly and chin lifts locked the cow in place.

I bit the conveyor belts but could not stop it.

The stunner hissed, preparing to deliver its deadly payload.

I kicked at the belts, but my legs just waved at the air.

The rush of air propelled the steel bolt into the cow's head.

I was next. My breath shortened. I needed a plan.

The conveyor deposited me into the restrainer. Every muscle and every tendon in my body flexed, but I could not break free. I kicked at the lifts and pushers, but they still locked me in place.

My cloak. Agent Orange called it an impenetrable force field. I need to activate my cloak.

With gritted teeth, I strained and groaned, but my cloak only sparked like a lighter out of fluid.

The stunner warmed up with a hiss.

I made one last effort to activate my cloak, to no avail.

I closed my eyes and took a deep breath.

Who's going to save my friends now?

28: Brains, Brains, Brains

The stunner hissed.

POP!

The bolt unleashed.

A rush of air wiggled my ears as a fizzy tingle waved down my spine, springing my hide hair to attention along the way.

A steady alarm beep joined the peppy song.

Go, cows, Go!

Beep

Go, cows, Go!

Beep

The restraints loosened as the stench of burning motor oil filled the air. I opened my eyes to smoke billowing out a giant crack in the middle of the bolt stunner.

My hide hair relaxed.

The fizzy tingle down my spine. The raised hide hair.

I knew those sensations. My cloak had activated... on its own.

Thank you, cloaking powers.

Giant hooks streaming through the smoke interrupted my celebration shuffle. I ducked just in time to avoid them.

I turned and kicked the restrainer frame apart before it could lock in its next victim.

The next cow in line strolled past as the stun gun choked on its own oil. The cow looked at me and gave an emotionless moo. It angered me. Her moo contained no hints of gratitude for saving her life.

Realizing my anger was misplaced, I collected myself with a deep breath.

> *Hey, you bovines, what do you say?*
> *Y'all gonna stay calm today*

Stopping the annoying song would be a good redirection of my ire. I spotted the speaker above the other cow's head. I pushed her aside and ripped the stun gun off its mechanical arm with my mouth. Sparks flew out from what remained as I hurled the broken gun at the speaker.

I missed.

While searching for something to hurl at the speaker, my eyes locked onto a line of cows dangling on hooks. Tears rolled into my mouth.

Sad moo-groan.

Why sad?

Angry humans approach.

Tasty humans.

Happy song.

Wandering cows. Tasty beef.

Chomp!

Angry cow. Angry herd.

STAMPEDE!!

BANG! BANG!

Keep up with herd.

Doors smash.

Humans scream.

Cows groan.

Walls fall. Fences topple.

Herd is free.

Herd slows.

Want tasty beef.

Only rotting beef here.

Hungry.

Eat rodents.

Eat frogs.

Need more meat.

Pork. Follow the smell of pork.

Moo-groans. Moo-groans.

Tasty pork.

More flesh.

Cow thud.

BLAST!

Cow thud.

No blast.

Tasty human flesh.

More flesh. More flesh. More flesh.

More flesh.

Follow the scent of flesh.

Herd grows.

Ravage farm. Ravage town.

Follow the scent of flesh.

Herd grows.

Ravage farm. Ravage town.

Follow the scent of flesh.

Pig flesh.

Familiar pig flesh.

Must eat the pig.

Human flesh. No.

Me want pig.

Fog. Can't see.

Follow pig scent.

Drool.

Pig close.

Can't breathe.

Fog thick.

Cough. Cough. Cough.

Lost pig scent.

I dropped to my front knees. A chemical cloud overflowed my lungs. I let out a coughing hack like the cross between a hippo snort and a donkey bray. The cloud poured back in.

The pig and his human companions lorded over me in their gas masks. I mumbled an expletive and vomited in their general direction.

29: The Cure and the Rescue

THE PIG TOSSED ME onto his shoulder. "Come on. We're going to the truck."

Images of carnage raced through my head. So much feasting. So much carnage. The mental slideshow flashed to Agent Orange lying in a pool of blood. I popped my eyes open. The images disappeared, replaced by dense gray fog. I couldn't even see the pig. *Where did he say he's taking me? A truck. He's arresting me. I need to break free.*

I twisted and flailed my legs, but the pig tightened his karate-clench grip. "Where are you taking me? You shouldn't arrest me. Agent Periwinkle. He'thh the bad guy. You should go after him instead."

"Yes, I know," said the pig, as he repositioned me on his shoulder.

"He killed Agent Orange," I said.

"We know," said the pig, and Agent Lavender in unison.

I rolled my head toward the sound of her voice, but couldn't spot her through the fog. Her location didn't matter. I needed to tell them the full story. "Agent Periwinkle has the other zombie virus vialthh; including the human form."

"We know," said the pig, Agent Lavender, and a chorus of other agents, lost in the fog.

"Cow, do you think you can stand?" asked the pig.

"I guess. Probably."

"I'm placing you in the back of the truck with the others." The pig bounced me off his shoulder and clutched me like a sack of peat moss. The canopy covering tickled my ears as he plopped me in the truck's bed.

I staggered on wobbly legs and stepped on a few boots, overreacted, toppled into agents sitting on the benches that lined the military cargo truck.

"Thhorry. Thhorry. I'm still adjusting to normalcy."

"No worries," said Agent Garnet, as he and a couple of other agents pushed me back to my feet.

"Thho, how do you know what Agent Periwinkle did?" A horrifying explanation came to me. "He unleashed the human zombie virus already."

"No. He hasn't released the virus," said Agent Lavender from the passenger seat of the truck's cab.

"I activated your earpiece during our fight in the RV," said the pig, heading for the driver's seat. "We've been listening ever since."

"Thho, you did believe me. You knew Agent Orange and I weren't the bad guys. "

"Well," said the pig as he started the truck. "I had my doubts about Agent Orange, but I knew you wouldn't intentionally do anything evil, so I had to learn the full story."

I hadn't had much time to reflect on our last encounter, but I feared we'd be enemies forever. All remnants of this concern disappeared, replaced with a twinge of guilt for having been concerned. "Well, thank you. And then you rescued me. And cured my zombiism. You're my savior. And Agent Lavender. And all the other agents in the truck, who I can't see because of this fog. Why is it so thick? Even in the truck. How can you drive in this stuff?"

"Cow, there's no fog." The pig cranked the truck into gear.

I stumbled as the truck lurched into motion and stepped on someone.

The person moaned, then said, "You're blind. More specifically, you have severe cataracts. A symptom of the zombie virus."

There was no mistaking that voice. "Charlie! Charlie the Virus Keeper. It'thh you! But how? How are you alive? You got shot in the head."

"Funny thing. Apparently, surviving a bullet wound to the head is quite common. Who knew?"

"It'thh so great to see, well, hear you. Give me a hug."

"No. I may have gotten used to conversing with talking animals. Sort of. I mean, it's more of a developed tolerance for talking animals. But hugging. No. That's a step too far."

"Hold on. *You* found the cure for zombiism. That'thh what you were working on."

"It was my promise to Harry. My purpose. My obsession. I had to find the cure. Granted, I focused on the human vaccine for all these years. Luckily, it works on cows, too. And chickens. We'll be able to put an end to the Cow Zombie Apocalypse and stop the Chicken Zombie Apocalypse before it begins. I mean, I wouldn't eat the meat of a former zombie cow. Or chicken. Or drink their milk. Definitely don't eat the eggs. But, yeah, I did it. For years, I thought I was crazy. Wasting my time. But I wasn't crazy. It wasn't a waste of time."

I definitely wanted to give him a hug, but restrained myself. "Well, I thank you."

The pig made a sharp turn, and I stumbled into him. "Get off me. Get off me, you smelly bovine. I said no hugs." He aggressively shoved me off him.

"Thhorry." I stabilized my footing as the truck rolled down the road, wishing I could see more than gray, which got me wondering. "I could thhee when I was a zombie. Why can't I see now?"

"You'd have to ask your cat friend. I'm assuming she's your friend. I assume all you talking animals are friends. Now that I say that out loud, it sounds presumptuous. Anyway, the cat predicted this would happen. She rambled on about symbiotic cataract compatibility with zombie vision. Honestly, I think she was making it all up."

I'd been prancing my front hooves from the moment Charlie mentioned the cat, waiting for him to take a breath so I could interject. "You found the cat?!" My voice cracked, which I thought was impossible for a cow.

"I was unaware you'd lost her," said Charlie.

"She was kidnapped by a hyperspeeding crow."

"Great. Another magical animal." His sarcasm came through clearly, even for a recent zombie. "I suppose the crow talks as well?"

"Of course. But that'thh not important. Where'thh the cat?"

"On some spaceship, somewhere. We had a video chat. It was annoying. She's very pompous and condescending."

"That's definitely her. Were the dog and chicken with her?"

"No, they're here on Earth. Living in the GIBOD barn. Another disturbing encounter. They're like a bickering old couple. If I'm going to keep working with you animals, I'm gonna need some help working through my anxiety issues with talking animals. But it's not like I can bring this up to my therapist. She'll have me committed."

My brain danced and sang. They cured my terminal disease. The pig didn't hate me. The cat, chicken, and dog were all ALIVE! This was the best day ever. But I had more questions. "How did you find them? Where were they? Are they okay? Why is the cat on a space station? Is she safe?"

The pig answered by yelling from the truck cab. "It's a long story. Do you remember Dr. Hash Browns talking about that French Toast guy?"

"Yethh." He was Dr. Hash Browns' rival and had kidnapped the rest of the animals before we'd joined GIBOD. That's also a long story.

"Well, the crow brought the three of them to him. He hauled them up to a space station and put them to work experimenting on sheep. He's got all of Dr. Hash Browns' old equipment. Even the Mambomatic 5000. Anyway, he soon realized the cat was the only one who could help. She worked out a deal. She agreed to help him enhance the sheep, if he sent the chicken and dog home."

"Thho, she'thh a prisoner?"

"Yes and no. She can't leave, but she's a willing lab assistant, and happy as can be."

As we drove along, I rattled off a series of questions: *Who is the crow working for? French Toast or the Havarti Travel Bureau? Or maybe the Travel Bureau of Havarti? Where's the crow now? Who gave the crow his hyperspeed power? Why did they want to capture me and then didn't? Shouldn't we be worried about what French Toast is doing to the sheep and why?*

Eight agents sat in the back of the truck, four on each side. Agents Bronze, Garnet, Poppy, and Warm Sienna sat to my right, and Agents Capri, Merlot, Rust, and Scarlet sat on the left. They took turns answering my questions with responses such as, "We're looking into that," or "We're not sure," or "Good question."

Finally, I hit upon a question that someone could answer. "You all spoke to the cat. And the chicken and dog. Thho, they spoke English?"

Charlie answered right away. "Yes, they did. But why does this surprise the talking cow?"

"It means she got the translator working. That'thh great news. Agent Orange will..." The euphoria of knowing my friends were alive drained out of me. "I mean, it would have made him happy." The memory of Agent Orange taking his last breath flashed through my mind. On the bright side, I no longer felt the urge to eat him.

I closed my eyes. The grayness dimmed and mildly brightened when

I reopened them. "Will I ever thhee again?"

"That pompous cat friend of yours thinks you will. She said energy drinks should speed the healing." Charlie's tone indicated skepticism of the cat's claim.

I figured it was worth a shot. "Do we have any energy drinks on board?"

"Of course," said Charlie. "I got one right here."

A pop preceded the satisfying pressure release, but I didn't get a chance to take a sip.

CRASH!

I toppled onto the agents to my right. Tires squealed as we skidded across the pavement until we smacked into the curb. As the truck tipped on its side, the can smacked me three times, dumped an ounce or two into my left ear, and sprayed carbonated energy juice into my eyes. When we stopped, it felt like I laid on a cluster of exposed tree roots, with a couple of fallen branches on top of me.

"Get off," said Agent Bronze, exhaling the only breath I hadn't squeezed out of him.

"Thhorry." With the truck on its side, I couldn't stand up. I raised enough for Agents Bronze, Garnet, and Poppy to squeeze out from under me as bullets riddled the truck's undercarriage.

Charlie dove into my midsection and curled his knees into my gut as agents scrambled over me toward the upright floor of the truck bed. "I shouldn't be here." His voice had raised an octave, and he increased his already rapid pace. "I should have stayed behind. But I was worried about last-minute adjustments to the vaccine fog dispenser? If something went wrong, who'd fix it? Now look what I've gotten myself into. Cow, activate your super cloak thing, and go kick their butts."

My hide tingled, and my hair stood on end, but my cloak wouldn't activate. "It'thh not working."

Another barrage of gunfire pelted the truck.

The agents stood up and returned fire.

"The cat warned that might happen. I hate how she keeps being right." He stretched his arm out, but snapped it back when bullets rattled the truck. When the flurry stopped, he extended for an instant, then rolled back into me and popped open a beverage can. "Let's pump energy drinks into you."

He stuck the can in my mouth.

I guzzled it.

A new volley of bullets sprayed our way.

"Who'thh shooting at us?"

"How am I supposed to know?" shrilled Charlie, burrowing himself further into me.

The bellowed phrase, "You're gonna die. You're all gonna die," preceded the next round of gunfire.

"It'thh Grandma Marjorie."

"And her grandsons," yelled the pig from the cab of the truck, blasting a round of shots off.

"And there's a bunch of double-crossing agents with them," said Agent Lavender, also from the cab, and also blasting shots at Grandma Marjorie and crew.

A faint puff, like the rush of air when opening a new pickle jar, preceded the obliteration of the back two feet of the truck.

"Ew, ew, ewww!" Charlie shuffled his feet, wishing to scurry from the carnage, but only pressed himself further into my gut. "There's nothing left but her hand."

"Who did we lose?" ask the pig.

"Agent Warm Sienna," said Agent Bronze.

"She was a good agent. We need to make sure this crazy old lady gets the justice she deserves." Agent Lavender started a long volley of shots. The other agents joined the blitzkrieg.

When the barrage of bullets ended, the team fell silent, except for the clicks of reloading.

"Now that I have your attention, let's discuss the terms of your surrender," said Grandma Marjorie, with the assistance of a megaphone.

"We'll never surrender," shouted the pig.

"Ok, then the cab gets laser blasted next, on the count of five, four…"

"What do you want, old woman?" asked Agent Lavender.

"The vaccine."

"What vaccine?"

"Pig, don't play stupid with me. Hand over the vaccine."

"If you kill us, you'll never find where we hid it," said the pig.

I felt Charlie tighten his squeeze on the bag of vials clutched to his chest.

"A reliable source informed me you have it with you right now."

"The joke is on you. The vaccine was in the part of the truck you just obliterated."

"Pig, again, stop playing dumb with me. Your ADHD chemist is clutching a bag of the vaccine as he cowers behind the cow."

How did she know Charlie was here? Could she read my mind? No. That's crazy talk. A mole. There must be a mole. But who?

"There's no chemist here," said the pig.

"Well, there's definitely no ADHD chemist, because I don't have ADHD," mutter Charlie at a volume only I could hear.

"Pig, just stop. Send the chemist out with the bag, or I destroy the truck cab in five, four…"

A boot brushed my leg on its way to kicking Charlie. "Come on, out you go," said Agent Rust.

Mole identified.

"Why, you double-crossing jerk," yelled Agent Merlot.

The Agents scrambled, pulling the canopy that lay under me in multiple directions. Uniform accessories jingled. Weapons swished and cocked. I imagined all their weapons aimed at Agent Rust, but then

Agent Merlot asked, "Whose side are you on, Agent Capri?"

Charlie curled into a baby, hugging its precious toy. "Activate your cloak! Activate your cloak!"

It flickered, but nothing more. On the plus side, my eye-fog cleared enough to see figures pointing guns at each other, though I couldn't identify who was who and who pointed their gun at whom.

"Trust no one," said Agent Capri.

Then, the shootout began.

***

FOUR SHOTS ECHOED IN the back of the tipped-over truck, along with one long scream from Charlie. An agent collapsed on my neck. Two more fell on my midsection. Four agents stood around me with their weapons pointed at each other in sequence.

"Is there no one we can trust?" asked the pig.

"Trust no one," said Agent Lavender in a robotic style.

"But who's on whose side?" asked the pig.

"I'm with you and Agent Lavender," said Agent Capri. "We're stopping this zombie apocalypse right here and now."

Agent Merlot kept his gun aimed at Agent Capri. "Now I definitely think you're one of them. That's why you shot Agent Garnet."

"I shot him because he was about to shoot Agent Poppy."

"Thanks, but he wouldn't shoot me."

"I thought Agent Garnet shot Agent Scarlet," said Agent Merlot. "And who shot Rust?"

"How would you know Agent Garnet wouldn't shoot you?" asked Agent Bronze.

Through blurred vision, I saw him shift his aim to Agent Poppy. This prompted the other three to re-target and maintain the equilibrium of everyone pointing a gun at someone.

"Pig, are you ready to turn over the vaccine?" asked Grandma Marjorie with the aid of her megaphone.

"NO," replied the pig and Agents Lavender, Capri, Merlot, and Bronze in unison. Agent Poppy was the sole agent to answer, "Yes."

Agents Capri, Merlot, and Bronze shifted their aim at Agent Poppy.

"It's a fair cop," she said, sounding content with her fate, but then Charlie got yanked away from me, and she said, "Everybody, drop your weapons or the chemist gets it."

The others opened fire, Charlie squealed, and someone collapsed on my stomach.

"Tell me that'thh Agent Poppy."

Charlie dropped to my side, his body quivering like a subwoofer. "It is."

"I'll give you another minute to finish shooting each other. It makes my job easier," said Grandma Marjorie.

The three remaining agents aimed at each other as the hum of motorbikes approached. Tire squeals preceded the fading engines. It had been nonstop threats, attacks, and near-death experiences for the past... I don't know how many days, since I didn't know how many days I was a zombie. I had grown tired of it and feared what horrors approached via motorbikes. Then they talked.

"Dudes, what are you doing?"

"Aren't you all on the same side, man?"

"They've got a point," said Agent Bronze. "We all shot Agent Poppy. That proves we're all on the same side." He lowered his gun.

Agents Capri and Merlot followed suit.

I stretched my neck to get a glimpse of the duck and rabbit, but could barely make out their forms. "Guys, it'thh great to see you, but why are you here?"

"We rushed over as soon as we got the pig's distress signal, dude."

The pair hopped and flew over. They jumped on me and hugged my neck.

"For the record, it was not a distress signal. It was just an informative message," said the pig.

They tugged my ear and lifted my lip before jumping off me.

"So, dude, we heard you were a zowbie."

"Looks like the cure worked, man."

"Zowbie? What's a zowbie?" I asked.

"It's a mash-up of cow and zombie, man. Zowbie," said the rabbit.

"It's what all the cool kids are calling a cow zombie, dude."

"It's the stupidest thing ever," said the pig. "Zombie cows are terrorizing every corner of the globe, but we call them by a cute name."

"Dude, the planet is round."

The rabbit mimed a circle with his front paws. "It doesn't have any corners, man." He turned towards me. "So, how cool was it being a member of the undead?"

"That had to be awesome, dude."

"And now you're like, un-undead, man."

"Dude, if she was un-undead, she'd be dead."

"I never got that whole undead thing, man. Doesn't being undead just mean you're alive?"

"Then we would all be part of the undead, dude."

"That's my point, man."

"I think you have to die and come back to life. That's what makes you *undead*, dude."

The rabbit and duck's heads jerked toward me. In unison, they said, "Dudeman, did you die?" Their tone oozed enthusiasm. Not a hint of concern that I might have died.

I shrugged. "I don't think thho, but maybe?"

Charlie slid across my belly, creating distance between him and the rabbit and duck. "I can't believe I'm joining this discussion, and by no means does this make us friends, but no, she didn't die. She had a virus.

A zombie virus. But she was very much still alive."

As they often did, the rabbit and duck had distracted me with nonsense. "Enough about zowbies. You two shouldn't have come. It'thh far too dangerous."

"Agreed," said the pig. "You shouldn't be here."

"You should have stayed–" I realized I didn't know where they'd come from. "Where did you come from?"

"Chicago, dude."

"We were doing superhero stuff, man."

"And, dude, we're onto something big."

I wanted to ask more questions, but Grandma Marjorie interrupted. "It's been a while since I hear shooting." Her tone had a mix of disappointment and annoyance. "I assume you stopped shooting each other. So, time to hand over the vaccine, or we attack."

The duck looked at me. "Dude, what's your orders?"

"Get out of here. Get someplace safe."

The rabbit turned toward the agents. "Man, don't we have grenades or something?"

"Good point," said Agent Capri. She pulled a grenade off her belt, peeked around the tipped-over truck, pulled the pin, and let it fly.

Two screams accompanied the explosion.

"That got their attention," said the pig.

A roar bellowed from Grandma Marjorie. "Now you've made me angry. You're all gonna die."

The middle of the lamppost behind the truck exploded. The top crashed harmlessly behind us.

"I take out the cab next," said Grandma Marjorie.

"Hey, dude, we hear you're bulletproof."

"Why don't you use that to kick their butts, man?"

"It'thh not working. I'm still recovering from zombiism." I pushed the bodies off me as I stood up. "And why are you two still here?"

Charlie popped another can. I opened wide and let him empty it in my mouth.

"We're putting an end to this." The pig punched a hole in the cab's roof and ripped it wide open. He grabbed the top of the fallen lamppost and charged Grandma Marjorie, her two remaining grandsons, and the agents loyal to the Havarti Travel Bureau. Agent Lavender followed his lead.

The now empty truck cab disappeared in a laser blast explosion.

Agents Capri and Merlot poured out from behind the cover of our capsized truck and joined the pig's Civil War style charge. The rabbit and duck mounted their tiny motorcycles, popped wheelies, and joined the attack.

The sound of an opening parachute preceded a pig squeal and a single gunshot.

"What'thh happening?"

"I have no idea," said Charlie.

I poked my head around the side of the truck. "My eyesight still stinks. You need to look."

"Not going to happen." He popped the tab of another energy drink.

"That stuff is not working. You need to peek."

"Look, I saved you and your entire species, so you owe me. Now, open wide."

I groaned before downing another can. I closed my eyes, took several deep breaths, and focused on listening.

No hum of the rabbit and duck's motorcycles.

"Cow, chemist, and whoever else is left behind the truck," said Grandma Marjorie, "Agents Charcoal and Beechwood are coming to collect the vaccine."

My eyelids lifted. "I can see! I can see!!"

"Great. Activate your power. Activate your power," said Charlie.

My cloak zapped on. Charlie squealed when I knocked away the sideways truck that protected us. I charged at Agent's Charcoal and Beechwood. They shot a couple of rounds at me before fleeing back to the truck.

Charlie shrieked again. Still clutching the vaccine bag, he dove behind the repositioned truck.

I bucked up, wailed like a starving hyena, and charged the old woman's truck.

The pig lay in no-man's-land, struggling to escape from a giant net. The body of Agent Merlot sprawled out next to him, surrounded by a pool of blood. Agents Lavender and Capri kneeled several paces past the pig. Agent Bronze stood behind them with a gun in each hand pointed at their respective heads. Noy stood in front of the truck, chuckling as he banged the rabbit and duck together like a pair of cymbals. In the middle of the action strolled three blind, recovering zowbies. They sniffed the pig, but were no longer interested in his flesh, and moved on. What stood out most to me amid this chaotic scene was how the rabbit's fur had filled in. No bare patches or scars. She appeared fully recovered from her zombie caterpillar attack.

Agent Bronze eyed me as I charged by, instead of keeping watch on his prisoners. Agents Lavender and Capri struck in tandem, leaving him unarmed and bloody. They grabbed his guns and unleashed a flurry of bullets.

The betraying agents ducked for cover. I slammed into their military grade steel-reinforced truck headfirst.

A sharp pain radiated from my skull to my hooves. I staggered backward. I wished I'd noticed my cloak had worn off before ramming the truck. Two images of the truck swayed in front of me. Cloak or no cloak, I prepared to charge the spot where the images overlapped. Before I got the chance, the pig jogged past me at full speed for him. He picked up the truck, shook it, and dumped the agents out like a set of Yahtzee dice.

Noy dropped the rabbit and duck, who instantly attacked and disarmed Grandma Marjorie. The pig glared at Bugbear, who dropped his weapon and raised his arms, an action that pulled his T-shirt up, exposing his ample belly.

I saw the white Roadrunner style blur of the chicken cruising toward us. My heart exploded in the form of a giant smile.

Before they knew what hit them, the chicken secured Grandma Marjorie, Noy, Bugbear, and all the agents loyal to the Havarti Travel Bureau with duct tape.

"Chicken, it'thh great to thhee you back safe and sound. And I'm glad you remembered the duct tape."

She zipped over and hugged my ankle. "Thanks. It's great to see the cure worked, and you're unzombified."

The pig cleared his throat in a manner that demanded attention. "Don't get me wrong, I'm thankful for the help securing the assailants, but why are you here? You were supposed to stay in the barn."

"Once I saw your distress signal, I zipped over. Oh, I should go get the dog and fish. They're still in the barn." The chicken disappeared in a flash.

The pig grumbled. "It was not a distress signal. It was a for-your-information message."

Similar to the pig, Grandma Marjorie cleared her throat to gain our attention, except hers had the rhythm of Beethoven's fifth. Once the pig and I turned our heads toward her, she slowly raised her head, revealing her watery eyes. "All I ask is you give my grandsons the vaccine."

"No. We need to ration and preserve the small quantities we have," said the pig.

"Why do you sentence my grandsons to death? What have I ever done to you?" She dropped her head and let the tears drip off her cheeks.

Her theatrics did not phase me. "You kidnapped the chicken, dog, and cat."

"They are safe now. And unharmed," she said, with a steady tone, while still staring at the ground.

"You killed half a dozen agentthh."

"In self-defense."

"You left me to be eaten by Somali piratethh."

She lifted her head. The tears had stopped. "They weren't going to eat you."

"You didn't kill Agent Orange, but you wish you had."

She shrugged. "I didn't think you two were that close."

Faint sirens put an end to our tiff.

Agent Lavender walked up to us. "Cops. We need to get out of here."

"What do we do with them?" I nodded toward Grandma Marjorie and her entourage. "Turn them over to the intergalactic authorities?"

Flashing lights had become visible.

"We don't have time to deal with intergalactic authorities. We'll leave it to the local police." The pig surveyed the intersection; cornfields on three sides and a gas station on the other. "There's got to be surveillance cameras at the gas station. They'll see who's to blame here."

Grandma Marjorie smiled. "They'll see a band of superpowered barnyard animals attacking a little old lady, her grandsons, and the agents who tried to defend them."

Agent Lavender pointed a finger at the old woman. "They'll see you ramming into our truck."

"It doesn't matter. We'll leave it to the authorities to sort it out," said the pig, hopping into the driver's seat of their truck.

I had a hoof on the back bumper of the truck, when Grandma Marjorie called to me. "Cow." Her smile faded.

A blind cow mooed and walked headfirst into the truck.

"I usually say you're fighting on the wrong side, but not today. Bradley is going to unleash the virus at O'Hare. He's on his way there now. You've got to stop him. You've got to save my boys."

"We should have guessed that's where he'd spread it," said Agent Lavender, as she climbed into the passenger seat of the military truck cab. "It's one of the busiest airports in the world. I bet he plans to unleash it in the international terminal."

"No! Not the international terminal, Ethel." Flying spit punctuated the old woman's harsh tone.

"My name is Agent Lavender, and that's the most logical spot to have it spread worldwide."

"No, it isn't, Ethel. The international terminal only has incoming flights and US customs. International departures leave from the other terminals."

The sirens grew louder.

Another blind cow staggered into the truck.

"Fine. So, where does he plan to spread the virus? And stop calling me Ethel."

"The tunnel in the United terminal, between the B and C Concourses."

"It's a high traffic bottleneck. Perfect place to unleash the virus." The pig tapped his earpiece. "Cat, we suspect Agent Periwinkle is in the O'Hare airport. Terminal one. See if you can locate him."

The flashing lights danced across the rows of corn.

"We've got to go," said Agent Lavender. "Now."

The pig started the truck.

"Dude, who's Bradley?" asked the duck, as he flew into the back of the truck.

"Bradley is Agent Periwinkle's real name," said Agent Lavender.

"How does she know that?" The pig turned his head and glared at Agent Lavender. "How *do* you know that?"

"I didn't. I figured it out from context."

"Does that mean your real name is Ethel, man?" asked the rabbit, hopping into the back of the truck.

"If any of you ever call me that, I'll kill you," said Agent Lavender.

None of us said a word, as Agent Capri, Charlie and myself climbed into the bed of the truck.

"So, how do we get to O'Hare?" asked the pig.

"Go straight. I'll tell you when to turn," said Agent Lavender.

30: Dude, I Don't See the Tunnel

As we sped toward O'Hare Airport, I attempted to process what had just happened. "I need a recap," I said. "Agents Bronze, Poppy, and Rust, bad. Agent Merlot was with us. What'thh the deal with Agents Warm Sienna, Scarlet, and Garnet?" This had bothered me the entire ride.

"It's hard to say," said Agent Capri. "I thought I could trust Poppy, so I shot Agent Garnet because he looked ready to shoot Poppy. Who knows who's on whose side at this point? Trust no one."

"We can trust the group in this truck," said the pig.

"And, dude, we need clarification," said the duck. "Is it true that Agent Orange's manservant is really an evil genius?"

The pig huffed. "Agent Periwinkle was never a manservant. But, yes, he's the evil mastermind plotting to wipe out life on this planet."

"Technically, he only wants to wipe out humans. He'thh okay with other species. Except cows. He doesn't like cows, either. Or chickens."

"Whatever," said the pig, tapping his karate-clench hooves on the steering wheel. "We need to stop him. The cat confirmed Agent Periwinkle's presence in the airport. We need to get there ASAP."

While en route to O'Hare, the chicken caught up to us. Multiple times. First, she dropped off the dog, sprinting away before I could order her to stay away. The dog licked my snout, and I ruffled the fur on his head with a hoof. Despite the joyous reunion, I wish he'd stayed in the barn, away from danger.

The chicken returned moments later with the fish contained in a waterless fish tank. "It keeps him from flying out of the truck."

I enjoyed seeing the fish again, though we didn't learn what he'd been up to, since the rabbit and duck dominated the discussion with tales of their superhero adventures, followed by the chicken and dog telling us how French Toast's experiments had killed or severely disfigured dozens of sheep, and that despite him being an evil idiot, the cat loved his lab and would never leave.

The conversation pushed my recent trials and tribulations to the background, and soon the pig eased the truck down a side street on the outskirts of the airport, parking along the side of Wolf Road. An 18-foot fence with a barbed-wire top separated us from the airport grounds. The truck's canopy rattled and flapped as a plane rumbled over us.

Charlie rose from the bench. His legs wobbled, and his hands shook, though he still kept a firm grip on the vaccine bag. "Um, I probably should have mentioned this earlier, but shouldn't I be heading back to the base?" His voice cracked. "Storming O'Hare airport sounds like a grand time, but there's a lot of work to be done distributing this cure across the globe. Got to put an end to the Cow Zombie Apocalypse."

"Zowbie Apocalypse, dude."

The pig glanced at Agent Lavender, who nodded her approval. "I reckon so, but how are you going to get back?"

Charlie staggered toward the back of the truck. "I'll just get out here and order a ride share."

"Nonsense. I'll zip you back to base." The chicken sprang into action before Charlie could protest. His scream lingered longer than the white streak of him and the chicken departing.

The chicken hauling Charlie away got me thinking. "Shouldn't uthh animals be heading back to the safety of the barn?"

Agent Lavender twisted. Her face filled the tiny back window of the truck cab. "Agent Periwinkle needs to be stopped. The fate of this planet depends on it."

"But we're not cleared for these types of missions," I said. "We're not official agents of GIBOD."

"I say otherwise." Agent Lavender was firm in her conviction. "You are ready for this moment. The world needs you. The world needs the BarnYard Heroes."

Her words inspired me, but didn't diffuse my concerns. Nor did the eager faces of my fellow barnyard friends. They didn't understand the risks. But what choice did we have? There weren't enough agents left to fight this battle. We needed to be the heroes Dr. Hash Browns built us to be.

The chicken zipped back into the truck. She jerked her head from the pig to Agent Lavender to me. "So, what's the plan?"

"We storm the airport!" shouted the rabbit and duck.

"We can't storm an airport," I said. "They're like the most heavily secured locations on the planet."

The duck waved a wing toward the airport. "Dude, I don't see any guards."

"Exactly, man. I say we drive right up to the gate."

Agent Lavender pointed out the passenger window toward the O'Hare terminals. "Grandma Marjorie said he'd be heading to the tunnel between the B and C Concourses. That's between those two well-lit buildings in the distance."

We fought each other to the front of the truck bed to get a glimpse out the passenger window. Several runways and service roads stretched out between us and the glowing buildings.

"Dude, I hate to be the one to tell you, but there's nothing between those two buildings."

"It's a tunnel," said the pig.

"I heard you, dude, but I don't see a tunnel."

"Of course you don't see the tunnel. It's underground. That's why they call it a tunnel!"

The duck's eyes rolled around his head. "I guess that makes sense. So how do we get there, dude?"

"We drive." The pig cranked the truck into reverse and bounced back up onto the road. He positioned the truck perpendicular to the fence. He revved the engine. "Brace yourselves."

***

THE TRUCK LURCHED FORWARD fast enough to send Agent Capri staggering into me, but not enough to ram through a fence. In the movies, they smash through these types of wire mesh fencing, sending chunks flying, but in our case, the fence around O'Hare Airport bent but refused to break. The pig had the pedal pinned to the floor. The back wheels spit out divots.

"Pig, this is a terrible idea," said Agent Lavender, clutching the dashboard.

I agreed with her.

The pig backed the truck up. "You've got a better plan?"

Agent Lavender scanned the lights that illuminated and marked runways in front of us, but didn't say a word.

I had no better ideas, either.

"That's what I thought. We're sticking with this plan." The pig stomped on the gas pedal. We still came nowhere near ramming speed before slamming into the wire mesh. The fence bowed easier this time. Our wheels spit out less earth. The fence kept giving way. Finally, a satisfying snap announced its release from the posts. The pig cranked the gear shift and revved the engine as we bounced over the fence remains.

We four-wheeled down an embankment and spun onto a runway. The pig shifted into top gear, which for the large military truck was just over 60 miles an hour.

"You seriously think we can just drive up to the terminal?" Agent Lavender had one hand glued to the dash, and the other clutched the grab handle above the passenger door.

The pig waved his hand toward the windshield like a game show hostess displaying a prize. "I don't see anyone stopping us."

Agent Lavender groaned like a mother hearing her know-it-all teenager say they don't need to study for finals.

The pig flipped on his right blinker and turned onto a new runway, which led to Concourses B and C. That's when the sirens first became audible.

The dog circled the truck bed, looking through every crack in the canopy. "Where... where... where are the sirens coming from?"

"Dog, look out the front windshield," I said.

"Oh, there, there they are." A squadron of emergency vehicles rushed straight toward us.

"And I told you so," said Agent Lavender.

The chicken relayed the message I'd just heard in my still active earpiece. "The cat says Agent Periwinkle is heading toward TSA screening."

"If, if, if he's headed... headed for security, why don't we just call TSA and have him detained?" asked the dog.

"We're not dealing with those pinheads from TSA," said Agent Lavender, glaring out the front windshield. "Unless he's carrying liquids over three ounces, it's not their problem."

The emergency vehicles grew larger out the front windshield. I stretched my neck to see the side mirror. Another squadron approached from behind. The authorities would have us surrounded in a matter of seconds, yet the pig barreled full speed ahead.

"Pig, how long do you intend to play this game of chicken?" asked Agent Lavender.

"Don't worry. I've got this." His eyes darted from the driver's side mirror to the front windshield to the passenger side mirror.

I had no confidence he had this covered, and I'm sure Agent Lavender didn't either.

The chicken's beady eyes narrowed. "What's this game of chicken?"

"It'thh a game to see who will chicken out... I mean, who will back down first."

The chicken crossed her wings. "So, you're saying it's common knowledge that chickens back down easily? We're just a species of cowards?"

"It'thh just an expression."

"Expression or not, I'm offended. I don't back down easily."

"Pig!" Agent Lavender had a double-handed death grip on the grab handle. "Seriously. What game are you playing here?"

We all looked out the front. A head-on collision with a firetruck was imminent.

"I've got this." The pig tightened his grip on the steering wheel and glared at the firetruck driver.

"Pig! You're gonna get uthh all killed."

The fireman blasted his horn.

Agent Lavender reached for the steering wheel, but the pig pushed her arm aside.

"I know what I'm doing." The pig cracked his neck and answered the fireman with a long blast of our truck's horn, which, to our surprise, resembled a clown horn. This embarrassing response to the firetruck's loud blasts didn't faze the pig. Though he already had the gas pedal plastered to the floor, he pressed down harder.

The firetruck driver chickened out, swinging to our right, causing the flanking ambulance to swerve off the runway. The other emergency vehicles followed the firetruck's lead, creating a clear path for us. Once we passed them, the pig made a slight left. The concourses were directly ahead of us, with no emergency vehicles in between.

Tires squealed behind us, and more than one crash occurred. The vehicles resembled a flock of sheep scrambling away from a herding dog.

"Punch it, man. We're almost there," said the rabbit.

"I've been punching it the whole time. This is as fast as this beast goes."

The cat reported that Agent Periwinkle was currently being screened by TSA.

The pig was leading us into an airport catastrophe. I pictured our faces plastered on every newscast in the world. Worst yet, we would be too late. "Make the call to TSA. Periwinkle is in line. It'thh our last chance."

"I already told you, we're not calling those TSA clowns," said Agent Lavender. "Besides, we're almost there."

As we entered the space between the terminals, the pig swerved the truck sharply to the right, avoiding a plane backing away from a gate. Then, he almost ran over a man in an orange vest frantically waving oversized flashlights.

"Dude, I get this tunnel is underground, but like, where underground?" asked the duck.

The pig honked the clown horn at a food truck and a baggage vehicle that occupied the road in front of us. "Get out of the way!"

The vehicles separated just in time, and we passed between them without sending food trays and luggage flying.

The pig slammed on the brakes. We all stumbled forward as the truck lurched to a halt. "The cat said it should be here, at the midpoint of the concourses."

Dozens of workers preparing planes for their next trip gave us the stink eye. Once they noticed the swarm of approaching emergency vehicles, they dropped their tools and ran away.

The pig scanned the scene. "We'll have to go in through that catwalk, B-9. There's no plane blocking it." He flung his door open and hopped out.

"Pig, the gate is on the second floor. How are you going to get up there?" asked Agent Lavender.

A handful of travelers gathered by the windows on the second floor. The pig ran as fast as he could and leaped. He grabbed a corner of the catwalk, ripped the door off its hinges, and tossed it to the ground.

The travelers by the windows scrambled for emergency exits.

The pig waved for us to follow and disappeared into the catwalk.

"How are we... how are we supposed to follow him?" asked the dog.

"We can't. He's an idiot." Agent Lavender pointed to a door with an awning entrance. "We'll use that door."

As Agent Lavender reached for the passenger door, flashing lights danced off her face. The cocking of forty to fifty weapons echoed. She groaned and stared at the truck ceiling. "This is ridiculous. The police are not our enemy. Stay here. I'll straighten this out."

She deposited her weapons on the front seat before hopping out with her hands folded behind her head.

I doubted Agent Lavender could talk her way out of this, so I figured we better take matters into our own hooves, wings, paws, and fins. "Chicken, catch up to the pig. Scratch that. Head straight for Agent Periwinkle, and get those vials."

"But she told us to stay here," said the chicken.

"You move thho fast, she'll never notice you."

"Sure thing, boss." She hopped into the truck's cab, and blasted into hyperspeed, soaring out the passenger door and up into the entrance to the terminal B-9 catwalk.

The dog, fish, duck, rabbit, and I scrambled to find an opening or mirror where we could watch Agent Lavender. She walked up to the police. Within seconds she was face-down on the pavement, a police officer's knee on her back and two others with guns pointed at her head.

"I'm an agent of GIBOD," she said. She did not resist as the officer pulled her arms behind her.

"GIBOD? What's that?" asked the officer, slapping cuffs on her.

"I think it's an insurance company, captain," said a cop who had his gun pointed at Agent Lavender's head. "They have those funny commercials."

"We're not an insurance company. We're a secret agency."

The captain still had his knee on her back. "Well, I've never heard of a secret agency called GIBGOB."

"It's GIBOD, the Global Intergalactic Bureau of Defense. And of course, you've never heard of us. That's one of the key facets of being a 'secret' agency."

A couple dozen cops encircled the truck.

The cat gave another update. "Agent Periwinkle has exited the security check and is in the process of reattaching his shoes."

"What do you want us to do, man?"

"Hide," I said. We might be the only hope of stopping Agent Periwinkle. We needed to avoid getting captured.

The rabbit, duck, and dog hid under the bench. Agent Capri rolled her eyes and readied her weapon. The fish swam into the glove box.

"Do you have a badge or an ID?" The captain took his knee off Agent Lavender's back and stood up.

"We don't carry badges or IDs."

"Well, that's going to make things difficult, isn't it? Now, please explain what your friend in the pig costume is up to inside the terminal?"

"He's securing our flight arrangements," said Agent Lavender.

"You expect me to believe that?" The captain grabbed the walkie-talkie off his belt and brought it to his mouth. "Have you detained the assailant inside the airport?"

"We're moving in on him now, captain," responded a female voice.

In the terminal above, authorities directed fleeing passengers, but I couldn't find the pig.

"Look, we're the good guys," said Agent Lavender as she rolled over and sat up.

Guns cocked, and the captain gave her a shove in the back. "Get back down, with your face pasted to the pavement."

Agent Lavender flopped back to a face-down position. "We're not the enemy here. You've got to listen to me."

My cloaking power sparked, but I remained visible as the captain motioned to the officers surrounding the truck. Doors flew open. The back flap flew up. The flashing lights turned the truck bed into a dance floor.

"Captain Johnson, you've got to see this," said an officer standing on the back bumper with his weapon pointed at us.

31: Animals? There's Animals in the Truck?

CAPTAIN JOHNSON STOOD OUTSIDE the back of the truck. "Animals?" He cocked his head to the side. "Biff, why do they have a cow, a dog, a duck, and a rabbit in their truck?" He removed his police hat and ran his fingers through his gray, yet surprisingly thick, hair.

"I can't answer that, sir," said Biff. He stood on the back bumper and hadn't taken his eyes off us.

Why did I tell them to hide? Except for the fish, we remained in plain sight. I wish I'd told them to sneak out the side or stumble out of the truck like real animals and wander aimlessly around.

The captain looked at Agent Capri and sighed. "I suppose you're an agent of GIBGAB, as well?"

"It's GIBOD. And yes." She'd dropped her weapon and put her hands on her head as soon as the truck's back flap flew up.

"Get on the ground with your friend," said the captain with disdain. Then he spun on his heels and marched to Agent Lavender. "Agent... what did you say your name was?"

"Lavender. Agent Lavender."

"Agent Lavender, can you please explain why you have a bunch of animals in the back of your truck?" His tone had a mix of bewilderment and mild amusement.

Officer Biff hopped down from the bumper and readied his weapon when me and the other animals crept up to listen.

"They're important in the fight against the animal zombie outbreaks. They're immune to the virus. We have orders to get them on a plane to New Mexico ASAP. We need to get to Concourse C immediately."

"I guess that's plausible." The captain's doubt almost turned his statement into a question. He rubbed his temples and returned to a stern authoritative tone. "But that doesn't justify crashing through the airport fence and driving down runways."

"We were attacked. There are forces who want the zombie virus to spread. We had no choice but to take drastic measures," said Agent Capri, as a couple of cops pushed her down next to Agent Lavender.

"So, you expected to drive up to the terminal gates, drop off these farm animals, and have them loaded onto a plane?" He rolled his eyes and paced away from the agents without waiting for a response. He raised the walkie-talkie to his mouth. "Tell me some good news. Tell me you've got the assailant under custody."

There was no reply. The captain removed his hat and once again ran his fingers through his wavy gray locks.

"Agent Periwinkle has completed the security screening process and is proceeding toward the B terminal gates," said the cat in our earpieces. "He will approach the tunnel to Concourse C in less than two minutes."

Biff kept his eyes glued to us. "Captain, I know this is going to sound crazy, but I think these animals are up to something."

"Biff, don't be stupid." The captain never looked our way.

Agent Lavender still had her earpiece in, so I knew she heard the cat. "Captain," she said. "It's imperative we get these animals on the next plane to Albuquerque."

"Keep kissing the pavement." His tone had turned harsh. "And stop talking. I don't want to hear any more of your nonsense. In fact, get these two out of here. Take 'em to security. They can tell their lies down there."

As officers pulled Agents Lavender and Capri off the ground and escorted them to police cars, Captain Johnson raised the walkie-talkie to his mouth and pressed the talk button with a heavy thumb. "Cooper, are you there? Give me an update on the guy who ran into the airport." Still no response.

I feared the body count the pig had racked up.

The rabbit, duck, and dog shuffled to my front hooves. They appeared to await orders. Panic attempted to shiver up my hooves, through my legs, up my spine and scramble my brain, but it fizzled out around mid-thigh. I'd grown numb to danger, for I'd faced worse and survived. With my thoughts clear and calm, a plan germinated.

Biff tilted his head, keeping his eyes on the smaller animals. "Captain, I'm serious. I swear these animals understand what we're saying."

The captain rolled his eyes behind Biff's back. He tried the walkie-talkie again. "Cooper! Give me an update."

This time, the crackling voice of Cooper responded. "Sorry, sir, but this pig-man is difficult to apprehend."

"Pig-man?" asked the captain.

Gunfire, grunts, and thuds buzzed through the walkie-talkie.

"Yes, sir. I know it must be a costume, but dang, it looks real. At least the face. But more importantly, he's well trained. Very well trained. I've never seen anything like it. It's like–" The crackling noise along with Cooper's voice stopped.

"Cooper! Cooper!" Captain Johnson raised the walkie-talkie over his head, ready to slam it to the ground, but stopped himself with a deep breath. "Get in there and get this pig mask guy," he said to a nearby group of officers. "Be careful. Apparently, he's dangerous."

I tried to justify the pig's actions as acceptable loss, but he would never get to Agent Periwinkle this way. I wished Biff would stop staring at us, so I could tell the others my plan.

"Captain, this pig-man, you don't suppose he's a real pig?"

"Biff, walk away from the truck and stop staring at the animals," said Captain Johnson.

Biff gave us several looks over his shoulder as he joined his captain.

"Agent Periwinkle is less than 200 meters from the tunnel," said the cat.

With Biff's back turned, I whispered in Cheddarian, "Dog, do you think you can dig your way down to the tunnel?"

"Well, no. I mean, yes, but no. It's, it's just that, that I can't get through the pavement."

"Rabbit can do it, dude," said the duck.

"Remember, the doc said he gave me Thunder Stomp, but I could never get it to work? Well, man, I figured it out, and it's freaking awesome. I can crack this pavement wide open."

"Do it," I said, thrilled at how quickly we'd resolved the issue.

"How will I, how will I know which way to go to get to the tunnel?" Biff glanced back at us.

"Act casual," I said.

We stood still. I was thankful for the break. It gave me time to think of a solution. When Biff looked away, I said, "Fish, get out here. We need you to swim through the ground and find the tunnel. Then guide the dog there."

"Sure thing, boss." The fish swam out of the glove box, through the floor of the truck, and into the pavement. No cops noticed him.

"Agent Periwinkle has stopped," said the cat. "He's within a few meters of the tunnel, but has deviated from his destination to join a queue for what I can best determine to be an opportunity to purchase expensive gourmet coffee or tea."

I nodded for the rabbit and dog to move out.

They hopped out of the truck.

Biff spotted their movement, pointed his gun at them, and shouted, "Put your hands in the air!"

I cringed as the dog sat down and raised his front paws. The rabbit smacked him, and the dog dropped his paws.

"Biff, did you just tell the animals to put their hands in the air?" asked Captain Johnson, giving Biff a side-eyed glare.

"Yes, but didn't you see that? The dog put his hands in the air." Biff nodded toward the dog.

The captain glanced at us, then raised an eyebrow at Biff.

"He put them down now, because the rabbit nudged him. But I swear, he had them raised."

"Biff, back away from the animals."

Biff huffed and fixed a squinted glare on us, as he shuffled backward between the police cars.

I wondered what was taking the fish so long, as the cat reported, "I will determine a new estimated arrival time for Agent Periwinkle to the tunnel between Terminals B and C based on average wait time observed at the gourmet coffee shop. The subject is currently in queue position six."

The fish popped his head out of the ground to the rabbit's left. He gave the pair a nod before diving back underground.

"Did you see that?" Biff nudged the officer next to him. "A fish head popped out of the pavement." He had no bewilderment in his voice, just joy and excitement.

"Biff!" Captain Johnson shot laser eyes at him. "Do you realize how crazy you sound?"

"I know, but..." Biff glanced around at the blank stares of his fellow officers. His shoulders drooped. The joy fizzled out of his voice. "Come on. Nobody else saw that?"

The other officers shook their heads.

I gave the rabbit a nod.

He crouched and wiggled his butt before leaping five feet into the air. After hanging in the air, he blasted down in a karate pose. He smashed into the pavement.

A slight crack appeared.

The rabbit hopped on one leg, shaking his other foot and yelling in Cheddarian. "Wrong foot! Wrong foot!"

Biff pointed while prancing in place. "You heard that? You all had to have heard that. Rabbits don't make high-pitched crackling noises like that."

"What the…" said Captain Johnson with his mouth hung open.

The rabbit jumped ten feet straight up and came down like a bullet on his right foot. A rush of air tickled my hide. The duck staggered back a couple of steps. Despite the dramatic move, only a tiny bump, half the size of the rabbit, formed on the blacktop. But the bump grew. Asphalt buckled. The lump of broken blacktop grew to the size of a beer barrel and rolled toward the officers, who watched in awe.

Officers exchanged glances but didn't move.

Biff waved a finger. "I told you they were up to something. I told you!"

The pavement wave grew to the size of a tumbling Volkswagen Bug.

Captain Johnson pushed Biff out of harm's way as he dove in the opposite direction. Chunks of asphalt showered them as they rolled on the ground.

The wave reached the size of a railroad tank car as it cut a pie wedge path of destruction, tipping over police cars, ambulances, food trucks, and luggage carts. Officers in the path either toppled to the ground or scrambled for cover.

I breathed a sigh of relief when I saw the police van carrying Agents Lavender and Capri driving away well past the disaster zone.

"Dude! That was awesome. Do it again," said the duck who had flown down next to his buddy.

Before I could yell stop, the rabbit turned to his right, leaped in the air, and sent a second wave toward the cops parked there. He didn't bother to watch its effect before turning and sending another wave in the opposite direction. The waves grew to the mass of steamrollers as they plowed through the squad cars and blew garage-door-sized holes in the terminal buildings. Windows shattered in the terminals a floor above us. Screams of the last few travelers scrambling for emergency exits blended with blaring car alarms.

"Enough!" I snatched the rabbit by the scruff of his neck before he sent another wave.

The duck rolled on his back with laughter. "That was amazing. Look at their faces, dude."

Captain Johnson got back to his feet and surveyed the destruction. Enormous fire trucks lay on their sides. Ambulances stood upright. Water sprayed everywhere. The sweet stench of airplane fuel filled the air.

"Agent Periwinkle has moved up to queue position five," said the cat in our earpieces. "The first customer took one point seventeen minutes to complete her purchase. Assuming the other customers average equivalent times with their purchases, Agent Periwinkle will reach the tunnel in six point zero five minutes."

I had to calculate the stupid cat's metric time into the actual time of about eight and a half minutes. I dropped the rabbit. "Dog, dig that tunnel, now," I said, as I jumped off the back of the truck.

"Sure thing, boss." His front paws attacked the cracked pavement until he found a soft spot. Pavement chunks and dirt streamed out through his hind legs like a broken fire hydrant. In less than a second, his head disappeared into the hole.

Captain Johnson's head stretched forward. He did a couple hard blinks, then rubbed his eyes.

"I told you. I said, 'There's something wrong with these animals.'

Nobody would believe me. But I called it."

"Shut up, Biff." The captain took a couple of unsteady steps onto the destroyed pavement.

"Follow me," said the fish before diving into the pavement in front of the dog's hole.

The dog disappeared below the pavement. Dirt streamed out as if a snowblower burrowed down the hole, raining debris onto the officers.

Cops brushed themselves off, readied their weapons, and fell in behind the captain, who had stopped. His head retracted. His eyebrows shot up.

A dull thud, followed by an "Ow," echoed out of the hole. The dirt stream stopped. After a series of grunts, the dog popped out of the hole. "I've, um, I hit some sort of... some sort of wall."

"Good. That's the tunnel," I said as I kept an eye on the cops that gathered behind their motionless captain. "Rabbit, get down there and Thunder Stomp a hole in the tunnel ceiling."

"It will be my pleasure, man." After a brief struggle to squeeze past the dog, the rabbit slid down.

THUD.

The ground shook.

This snapped Captain Johnson out of his trance. He surveyed his troops.

The rabbit climbed out. "It's the tunnel alright."

Captain Johnson stared back at us. "I can't believe I'm about to say this," he muttered, before raising his voice. "Animals or droids or whatever you are, I need you to cease and desist whatever it is you're doing." His confidence started strong, but disappeared by sentence's end.

"Go, go. Everybody, down the hole and into the tunnel." I pointed my hoof into the hole.

The rabbit slid down.

Captain Johnson's face scrunched. His eyes blazed. Confidence returned to voice. "Stop it. Stop diving into that hole."

I paced toward the cops and in front of the hole as the duck and dog dove in.

The fish levitated out of the pavement, a couple steps behind me, but in my extended peripheral vision. "What are you going to do? You won't fit down that hole."

"Don't worry about me. Just stop Agent Periwinkle any way you can."

The fish nodded and disappeared into the road.

I continued my slow walk toward the police, with no plan, yet no worries.

"Do you think it's a zowbie?" asked Biff.

"That lady agent said it was immune to the virus," said a cop.

"I don't care what it is, cow, zowbie, or a person in a cow suit. I want it kneeling," bellowed the voice of Captain Johnson. "Now!" He stood behind an upside-down police car. Dozens of other officers crouched behind their disheveled vehicles, with pistols, rifles, machine guns, and one rocket launcher.

"The subject is now in queue position four. Time to complete the second customer's purchase was one minute and thirty-seven seconds. The revised estimate for Agent Periwinkle's arrival at the entrance to the tunnel is four minutes and eighty-one seconds."

I looked up at the deserted second-floor terminal. Something didn't add up. How could Agent Periwinkle be casually waiting for coffee when they evacuated the terminal?

"I'm running out of patience. Get on the ground or we will open fire," said the captain. "In five, four, three..."

32: Animals on the Loose in O'Hare

RED LASER DOTS FRECKLED my hide. My cloaking power sparked like a stove top burner with no gas.

"... two, one. This is your final warning," said Captain Johnson.

Following Dr. Hash Browns' training, I focused my energy on activating my cloak, but only faded in and out like poor television reception.

"Is it just me or is that cow disappearing?" asked Biff from behind the cover of a sideways ambulance.

"I think it's a hologram," said another cop. She poked her head around a vertical slab of asphalt, walked out, picked up a chunk of concrete, and threw it at me.

I watched it fly towards me, concentrating on igniting my power. My cloak flickered. The concrete chunk bounced off my head.

"It's not a hologram," she said.

Then, magically, my cloak activated.

Biff stepped out. "Where did he go?"

I sprinted for the opening, as Captain Johnson said, "I see an outline of a cow. It's making a break for the terminal. FIRE!! Fire at the cow outline!"

Knocking over cars and officers along the way, I galloped through the opening created by one of the rabbit's Thunder Stomps. Officers fought each other to reach the building first, as I ascended the terminal staircase with the grace of a giraffe climbing a ladder. At the top of the stairs, I kicked garbage cans and a bench down toward the officers.

"The next customer completed their purchase in eighty-seven seconds," said the cat. "I now estimate Agent Periwinkle will enter the tunnel between Terminals B and C in three minutes and sixty-one seconds."

I wondered what video screens the cat watched. How could Agent Periwinkle be standing in line to buy coffee when the terminal was being evacuated?

My hooves slid on the smooth tile floor, causing me to resemble a dog trying to run on a loose throw-rug. The cop swarm reached the top of the stairs as I reached full stride. They held their fire, as a handful of travelers were still being herded out emergency exits.

Three TSA agents stood in my path to the tunnel stairs. They squinted and rubbed their eyes.

"Is that some sort of hologram?" asked one of the TSA agents.

"It sounds like a trotting horse," said another.

My cloaking power ran out, and I became visible.

"It's a zowbie!" screamed the third. "RUN!!"

But they didn't run. They remained wide-eyed and paralyzed.

My attempt to change directions sent me into a spin. I left four hoof skid marks on the tile before slamming sideways into them. Together, we slid about five yards, then toppled over.

"Thhorry." They squirmed and groaned as I tried getting up without stepping on them.

The police caught up and encircled me and the crushed TSA agents.

"There is a disturbance occurring in the B terminal," said the cat in my earpiece. "Authorities are attempting to apprehend a resisting assailant."

I wanted to tell the cat that the assailant was the pig, and the disturbance happened about five to ten minutes ago, but didn't want to freak out the TSA agents and police with the talking cow routine.

A white blur appeared behind the officers. A moment later, the chicken rocked back and forth in front of me. The TSA agents stopped wiggling out from under me to gawk at the chicken.

"Hi, boss. Looks like you could use some help."

So much for not talking in front of humans.

She hopped on the back of my neck and dug in her claws. The terminal blurred away. I caught a glimpse of the escalators as we flew over them and down into the tunnel between Terminals B and C. When we came to an abrupt halt, my four stomachs fought to be the first up my throat. I focused on the green lit tunnel walls as I wobbled to stability and waited for my stomachs to settle back to their natural positions.

The tunnel reminded me of a subway terminal with side-by-side moving sidewalks instead of tracks. Thin tubes of neon lights snaked across the ceiling, resembling stalactites. They changed colors and patterns along the way, cascading on and off to the beat of *Rhapsody In Blue*. My shoulders loosened as I soaked in the soothing music and captivating light show. The tunnel would definitely be Temple Grandin approved for humans. Those jerks from Slaughterhouse 5.0 should come here and take notes.

"Are you okay, boss?" asked the chicken.

"I'm fine." I wasn't, of course, but vastly improved from how I felt moments before. "How did you do that? The crow couldn't pick me up. I was too heavy."

"It's a phase shift thingy I do. Weight doesn't factor into it. The crow must be doing it wrong."

We walked to the break between the moving sidewalks, where

passengers walked a dozen steps to catch the second half of the tunnel ride that takes you from one set of escalators and stairs to the other. An announcement about the moving walkway ending played on an endless loop, drowning out the relaxing orchestra music. Either end of the tunnel provided the obvious exit points, but officers would soon come down the stairs and escalators of Terminal C. I didn't see any other exits, so Terminal B provided our only escape route.

The rabbit and duck rode opposing hand railings of the walkway that scrolled toward us from Terminal C. The dog sat at the end of that sidewalk, with the fish hovering above.

My shoulder muscles tightened. "What have you guythh been doing?"

"Um, waiting for, for you," said the dog without taking his eyes off the end of the moving walkway, as the rabbit and duck approached. They stuck their necks out when they reached the end, like sprinters crossing the finish line. The moving railing looped down, and the pair stumbled off.

"Dude, I beat you by at least four inches."

The rabbit shook his head. "No way, man. I won by at least a foot."

The duck turned to the dog. "Dude, who won?"

"The, the duck won, but only because he can, he can stretch his neck out further."

"That's not fair, man. Next time we're going by whose chest crosses first."

"Idiots!" I paused to rein in my anger. "You were supposed to be looking for Agent Periwinkle, not doing whatever this is."

"Travelator races, dude."

"What'thh a travelator?"

The fish hovered into view. "It's another word for these moving walkways." He turned toward the rabbit. "And I agree with the dog. The duck won thanks to stretching his neck out."

"That's not fair, man. I demand a rematch."

"No rematch. We need to find Agent Periwinkle!" In that moment, three epiphanies came to me. One, Agent Orange had been right in not making us agents. Two, I sounded exactly like him. Three, I understood why he had been so hard on us.

"I searched inside and outside the terminals, but could not locate Agent Periwinkle," said the chicken.

I revised my previous thoughts to exclude the chicken. She might have what it takes to be an agent of GIBOD. But the others? No.

My earpiece crackled. "The assailant appears to be the pig. Repeat, the assailant causing the disturbance appears to be the pig."

"Why is the cat just now talking about the pig'thh rampage?"

"She's on a slight delay," said the fish. "She's in another galaxy. It takes time for communications to travel through space."

"That would have been good information to know earlier. Why didn't anyone tell me?"

The dog shrugged. "We thought, thought it was common knowledge."

"Thho, how much of a delay?"

"We figure about ten to fifteen minutes," said the fish.

"The cat'thh updates are useless. Chicken, get this thing out of my ear."

"Sure thing, boss," she said as she flew up and pecked my earpiece out.

When it hit the ground, I stomped on it. "Thho, Agent Periwinkle probably dumped the virus already and left. We're too late."

"It's possible that after all the commotion, he decided to abort," said the fish.

"You think I would give up that easily?"

We all spun around.

Agent Periwinkle stood on the travelator from Terminal B, riding toward us.

My hooves clenched, pressing into the tile floor. *What a pompous jerk.*

My cheeks flared into glowing hotplates. I imagined engulfing his head in my mouth. I'd chuckle as I squeezed, relishing his screams, until – SNAP.

The dog's voice brought me back to reality. "Where, where did he come from? I mean, how, how did he get there without us seeing or smelling him?"

Agent Periwinkle shook his head. "You remember nothing from your training. None of you marked the tunnel's emergency exit doors."

As if he wielded evil mind control magic, my anger over him killing my mentor, poisoning me, and leaving me at a slaughterhouse morphed into defensive rage. "I checked. There'thh no emergency exits down here."

"They're behind those giant maps of the airport," said the fish.

The map case hid the doors from my view, but I should have seen the exit sign hanging from the ceiling when I scanned for escape routes. *How could I expect to lead this band of misfits if I failed at such a basic yet critical task? But also, if the fish spotted the emergency doors, why wasn't he watching them?*

"That's stupid, dude. Why would they hide the emergency exit?" asked the duck.

"Worse yet, man, let's say there's a mass emergency exodus. Everyone has to get around that stupid display case."

"People will die because of this poor emergency exit door placement, dude."

"I'd forgotten what a bunch of idiots you all are," said Agent Periwinkle, stepping off the travelator.

I hated how much I agreed with him and how frustration with my team had lessened my fury towards Agent Periwinkle.

He looked me over from hooves to snout. "I see Charlie's vaccine has worked its magic. That is good to know, for those of us who've taken it."

His arrogant tone refueled my anger as hut-huts and stomping boots came from both ends of the terminal. The officers chasing me raced toward us from Terminal C as a new crowd of officers charged down the escalators and stairs from Terminal B.

"Fortunately, this will all be over soon." Agent Periwinkle pulled vials from both pants pockets and held them high over his head. "Thank you for showing up, though. I needed a scapegoat."

Instinct kicked in. "Chicken, grab the vials!"

Agent Periwinkle's arms came down.

The white blur zipped toward him.

The vials left his hands, headed for the tile floor. They disappeared in a blur of white.

Two vials flew out of the blur.

"Here, take these," said the chicken. I didn't notice she hovered in front of me until she spoke, for my eyes focused on the two vials spinning toward me. I didn't have time to respond before she stuffed four vials into my mouth.

"Mrrmph, mrrph, mrp mph?" is what came out. I meant to say, "What are you doing?"

It didn't matter. The chicken never heard me. She had blasted back to hyperspeed. The spinning vials disappeared and before I knew what happened, she'd stuffed them in my mouth.

Agent Periwinkle closed his eyes, cranked his head to the left, and grumbled, "I had forgotten what a pain in the butt you meddling animals are." After a deep breath, he opened his eyes, straightened his neck, and adjusted his suit coat. He then pulled a badge out of his coat pocket with one hand and a pistol out of his shoulder holster with the other. "No problem. On to plan B," he said in a calm demeanor. He pointed his gun at me and took a couple of steps toward the onrushing officers with his badge held high. He cleared his throat, and in a serious FBI agent tone said, "Officers, we need to detain these animals. They are part of a covert operation to spread the zombie virus across the globe. Inside the mouth of this cow, you will find vials of a new zombie virus; one made to infect humans."

"I thought the agents of GIBOD didn't carry badges?" said the chicken in Cheddarian.

I shrugged my shoulders as I focused on swallowing the vials one at a time.

"Who are you?" asked Captain Johnson, who led the mob of officers.

"I'm an agent of GIBOD. We've been investigating these animal zombie outbreaks."

Captain Johnson rubbed his mouth as he closed one eye. "GIBOD? I've got a couple of your agents locked up downstairs." He motioned for a couple of officers to grab Agent Periwinkle. "They said agents of GIBOD don't carry badges."

Agent Periwinkle scoffed. "Don't trust them, and keep them locked up. Those agents went rogue. They're the ones behind this worldwide cow zombie outbreak." His eyes bounced from officer to officer, then to his gun being confiscated and his hands being cuffed, and finally rested with a glare at Captain Johnson. "What's the meaning of this? We're on the same side."

"If that's true, we'll get it sorted out in the security holding pen." Captain Johnson waved a dismissive hand. "Get him out of here."

An officer motioned for Agent Periwinkle to walk toward the stairs.

Agent Periwinkle shouldered the officer aside and nodded toward me. "Check the cow's mouth. You'll see what this is about."

I couldn't tell if his panicked voice was genuine or an act. Regardless, it worked. Captain Johnson sighed, rolled his eyes, and then sent a couple of officers to check my mouth. I had swallowed four vials and was working on the fifth when they approached. They stood on either side of my head as the fifth vial slid down my throat. Without time to swallow the last one, I maneuvered it under my tongue.

"So, how do we get this thing to open its mouth?" asked the officer on my left. With his head cocked, he walked in front of me. As soon as his hands touched my lips, I let out a guttural growl. The pair leaped backward and threw their hands in the air.

"For crying out loud." Captain Johnson shook his head as he holstered his weapon and came toward me. "I grew up on a farm. I know how to do this."

The captain put his arm around my neck as I maneuvered the vial out from under my tongue and tried to swallow it. It traveled halfway down, but wouldn't go further. Involuntary muscles took over, and I coughed the vial back up.

Agent Periwinkle broke away from the officer holding him. "Get her mouth open now. She's trying to swallow the vials." This time, his panic was clearly real.

"Relax. I've got this." Captain Johnson wiggled his free hand between my lips and teeth, then stroked the roof of my mouth.

I opened wide, without time to resist.

"Grab hold, guys, and keep her mouth open," said the captain.

The two officers wedged their hands into my mouth, grabbing hold of my teeth. With all their strength, they pulled my mouth open a bit more. Determined to stop them finding that last vial, I chomped down on their puny little hands. Captain Johnson pulled his hand out in time. The two officers were not so lucky. They screamed as they ripped their hands out from my clenched teeth.

"Get it open. Get her mouth back open." Agent Periwinkle's voice had gone shrill.

Captain Johnson put up his palm. "Calm down." He re-established his hold around my neck. As he strengthened his footing, I slid the final vial down my throat. He once again jabbed his hand in and rubbed the roof of my mouth. When I opened, he jammed a flashlight in.

He grabbed a second flashlight from one of the other officers, flipped it on, and searched inside my mouth. He pushed my tongue around to look underneath before he yanked the flashlight out and said, "There's nothing in this cow's mouth."

"You took too long. She swallowed them." Agent Periwinkle stomped toward Captain Johnson. Officers grabbed his arms, but he ripped himself free. His eyes popped wide open, his face glowed chili pepper red, and he spit as he shouted. "You've got to get her to a hospital, a lab, or a butcher. Someplace where we can slice her open and get those vials."

Captain Johnson took a step back and wiped the spit off his cheek as two officers grabbed Agent Periwinkle's arms. A third stepped between the captain and the agent. With a side-eyed glare at Agent Periwinkle, Captain Johnson said. "Get him out of here." He glanced at me. "And round up these animals."

"What do you want us to do, boss?" asked the chicken in Cheddarian. "I can start hyperspeeding us out of here. Just say the word."

My focus rested on the six vials swimming in my first stomach. I swallowed them without thinking. Beads of sweat pooled on my forehead. My stomachs churned. *What if one of them breaks inside me? Will they pass through my digestive system? What if they get stuck sideways? Will I digest the glass? Will the vials pop open? How do we get them out? Do we wait for me to poop them out?*

"Did anyone else just hear a weird staticky noise?" asked Biff, moving toward us.

Agent Periwinkle nodded toward us. "It's them! The animals. That's their language." His rattled voice faded as officers and the moving sidewalk dragged him toward Terminal C. "They're plotting something!"

"I told you they were talking to each other," said officer Biff.

The captain rubbed his forehead.

"You want me to use Thunder Stomp, man?" asked the rabbit, also in Cheddarian.

Sweat dripped down my snout. I *was* thankful the others looked to me for leadership, but at that moment, I feared moving, worried I'd break a vial or pop a cork off. I couldn't focus on a plan and orders.

Agent Periwinkle twisted his head to give me a final glance. He smiled and winked.

Why was he happy? What was he up to? Wait. There're four vials of human zombie virus unaccounted for.

"He'thh still got vials," I said in Cheddarian. "We've got to stay close to him. We need to go with the officers."

The officers had surrounded us with handcuffs ready. I wondered which of us animals they thought those would work on.

One officer inched closer and asked the cop next to him, "Which one of them created them earthquakes?"

The other officer shrugged.

Captain Johnson scanned the officers and tossed his arm up. "Grab them already."

Before they took a step, I cleared my throat and said in English, "There is no need to worry, Captain Johnson. We'll go peacefully."

In unison, the officers took two steps back. Their gaze darted between each other, the captain, me, and the other animals.

Captain Johnson's mouth gaped as he rubbed a knuckle in ear. He glanced at the retreating officers. "Am I going crazy or did that cow just talk?"

Biff grinned and pointed at us. "I told you. I told you they could talk."

Captain Johnson shrugged. "You heard the cow. The animals are ready to go. Round 'em up."

Three officers lassoed ropes around my neck in quick succession. Two other officers ignored the dog's deep growl as they snapped a collar around his neck and hooked on a leash.

"I said we'd go peacefully." I gave a mild tug of the ropes.

"And if you don't resist, it will be, but we're not taking any chances." Captain Johnson rubbed his eyes and blinked. "I'm reasoning with a cow. This is not how I thought this day would go."

As an officer picked him up, the duck asked, "Dude, where did you get the rope?"

"And the dog collar?" asked the rabbit as the same officer scooped him up.

An officer swung a fish net over the fish, but he passed straight through.

"Sorry. I'm not entirely solid," said the fish.

"Why does that not surprise me?" said Captain Johnson.

"Because we saw him pass through the pavement and into the ground," said Biff.

With slumped shoulders, Captain Johnson stared at the floor.

"Look, I won't cause any trouble. I'll come along with the rest of them," said the fish.

"Whatever." Captain Johnson gave a half-hearted wave toward Terminal C. "Let's go."

They led me onto the travelator first, followed by the dog, the officer holding the rabbit and duck, and another holding the chicken. The fish hovered above us. The sensation of the rolling sidewalk flashed me back to the conveyor at Slaughterhouse 5.0. Images of hooks dug into the stunned cows played in my head as clear as if it were happening live.

I nudged Captain Johnson. "You've got to listen to me. We're the good guys."

The captain scrunched his face until he resembled a bulldog. He pointed at the hole in the tunnel ceiling. "You've got to be kidding me. And I suppose you're going to tell me you're an agent of GIBOD."

"Well, actually, yethh. All of uthh animals are agents of GIBOD. Okay, technically, the rabbit and duck aren't full agents. Not yet, but I'm betting they will be soon. Anyway, the point is, the rest of uthh are." I hated how my nerves had me rambling.

"Cow, I've heard enough."

"But it'thh important you know I swallowed six vials of the human zombie virus, but I did it to stop Agent Periwinkle from activating them.

He'thh the real bad guy, and he'thh still got four vials."

The captain massaged his temples. "We'll sort this out in lockup."

The officer leading us backed up into the captain, pointed toward Terminal C, and said, "Those aren't our guys."

An unhandcuffed Agent Periwinkle stood at the top escalator, flanked by uniformed agents of GIBOD.

33: Showdown at O'Hare

HALF A DOZEN OFFICERS lay on the floor above us with Agent Periwinkle and a dozen GIBOD agents standing over them. Agent Yellow kicked an officer down the stairs. His limp body tumbled four steps before coming to a halt.

Captain Johnson rubbed his eyes with his left thumb and index finger. "Who are those guys?"

"I think they're TSA," said Biff.

"No, they're agents of GIBOD," I said. "Bad agents of GIBOD." The police had no clue about the trouble coming their way. My attempt to cloak flickered on and off like a failing fluorescent light bulb.

"I'm really getting sick of agents of GIBOD," said Captain Johnson.

Bullets shattered both sides of the walkway's glass railing.

The walkway conveyor glided us, animals and officers, towards the GIBOD agents like targets in a carnival shooting game.

Shots from agents and officers echoed off the tunnel walls, providing the illusion shots came from all around us.

The first three officers in front collapsed, exposing the officer holding the rabbit and duck. He released them and drew his weapon.

"Head for the map cases!" The airport map cases near the break in the moving sidewalks provided the only cover in the tunnel. I meant it as an order to my barnyard companions, but the officers obeyed as well, releasing the ropes, leashes, or hands that bound us.

We scattered right and left off the travelator. Ten officers joined us to the left, providing cover along the way. Across the tunnel, the rest of the officers, including Captain Johnson and Biff, fought each other for the limited cover. It was a high stakes game of musical chairs, with several officers losing out. They fired back, but the agents were far better shots.

The dog yelped. He spun as his backside fell to the floor. With my mouth, I grabbed him by the scuff of his neck and pulled him behind the protective case. Bullets pummeled the case and flew just over my head. I reeled in my tail after a bullet clipped off a clump of hair.

Blood trickled down the dog's quivering leg. "I'm bleeding, I'm bleeding. Apply direct pressure. Who's got a first aid kit?" His leg shaking intensified into full body tremors. His panting progressed to hyperventilating. "I'm, I'm fading. It's all, it's all going dark." His pupils rolled into his forehead.

The duck examined the bleeding leg. "It don't look that bad, dude. I think it only grazed you."

"I've got this," said the chicken, as she whipped out her duct tape. After a quick white blur spun around the dog, she had bandaged the wound.

The dog's pupils returned to their normal position. His panting slowed. His shakes lessened to a shiver. He examined the chicken's work with a cocked head. "Are you sure that's, that's sanitary? I mean isn't, isn't there supposed to be gauze on the wound? The, the tape, the sticky part of the tape is on the wound. And won't the duct tape take my fur off?"

"Quit your whining. It stopped the bleeding, and that's the important part," said the chicken.

The officers huddled with us exchanged hand signals. Two popped up at opposite corners of the map case, blasting a steady stream of gunfire.

The others sprang out. "Huzzah!!!"

Gunfire erupted, rattling my ribs and jostling my lungs. I ducked further below our protective map case, feeling immersed in a fireworks grand finale.

The huzzahs turned to screams of agony. Bullets felled the officers providing cover. The gunfire slowed. The screams faded.

I peeked.

No officer made it over three steps.

The animals and I were all that remained behind our map case. Across from us, Captain Johnson, Biff, and the others continued to fight for safety behind their map display.

On their perch in Terminal C, the agents of GIBOD remained unharmed.

Before I could suggest we escape through the emergency exit behind us, the chicken held up her roll of tape and announced, "It's duct tape time." She never got the chance to blur into hyperspeed. She took one step out from behind the case. Bullets rattled the tunnel. She collapsed.

The dog scampered out on three legs, clutched a wing in his mouth, and dragged her to safety. "She's, she's hit. She's bleeding. Help! Somebody, somebody help." He cradled the chicken in his front paws.

"Duct tape it! Duct tape it! Duct tape it," she yelled, holding out her bleeding leg.

"I've got this, man." The rabbit grabbed the roll of tape and spun it rapidly with his paws. "I can't find the beginning. "

The duck pointed at the tape with his wing. "Dude, you just passed it."

The rabbit spun the roll back. "Got it." With his paw, he poked and swiped at the tape's start line.

"Hurry up!" He stared at the chicken's wound with watery puppy eyes. "She's, she's bleeding out. Look at, look at all the blood. She's tiny. She doesn't have that much blood in her."

"Man, how do you get this thing started?"

"Dude, give it to me," said the duck, snatching the roll out of the rabbit's paws.

The fish looked at me and said, "I've been practicing. I can do this."

"Wait," I said, but he'd already swum off toward the agents.

Why do they all want to be heroes? Just a few minutes ago, they wasted time having travelator races, waiting for my orders. Now they all think they can win the battle singlehanded. I've lost control of my team.

As expected, the agents greeted the fish with a barrage of gunfire. The bullets harmlessly passed through him, shattering the neon ceiling lights, triggering sparks and a confetti-drop of rainbow glass.

The dog watched the shards of colored glass bounce on the floor. He clutched the chicken and buried his snout under her feathers. "Rainbow hailstorm. My, my, my vision of doom. We're all gonna die."

"No, we're not," I said, with strong conviction, despite my growing concerns. "Your visions do not mean doom." *I never should have led them into this deathtrap. We're stuck in a tunnel, with limited escape routes.*

The dog popped his head up. "Regardless, the chicken is going to die if you idiots can't figure out how to pull a strip of duct tape."

The chicken patted the dog with a wing and broke from his embrace. "Just give it to me." The chicken pecked the roll out of the duck's wings. Within a second, she had a strip of tape pulled and ripped.

The rabbit and duck helped adhere it to her wound. She then snuggled back into the dog's embrace.

My tiny friends huddled behind the protective case. At the top of the Terminal C stairs, the fish hovered at eye level with Agent Sangria. I sighed. *We're not cut out for this. We're a team of misfit barnyard animals with faulty powers.*

My umpteenth attempt to activate my cloak fizzled out.

A peaceful farm in the country. That's where we should be. Not here, about to die. This is all my fault. I encouraged them. I led them straight into this slaughter. I need to save them.

"Listen up. Once the fish comethh back, we're heading out the emergency exit."

The fish's tail swayed back and forth as he stared into Agent Sangria's eyes. With a snarl, she swatted the butt of her gun through him. She took aim and pulled the trigger. The bullets whizzed through the fish, shattering more ceiling lights and creating more rainbow hail. The fish flopped to his side and drifted toward the ceiling.

Agent Sangria pumped a fist into the air. "Take that, you bug-eyed freak." With a giant smile and a triumphant yell, she high-fived Agent Vermilion.

I did a double groan. Once for the misguided confidence of the agent's celebration and a second for the fish hypnotizing himself... again.

"I'll wait for the fish. You guys get out of here." I nodded toward the emergency exits.

Across the hall, Captain Johnson pointed toward their emergency exit door. While he shot at the agents, two cops dashed out from behind the display case. Sniper fire gunned them down within their first two steps.

"I'm, I'm not going anywhere," said the dog. "I'm, I'm staying behind this, this, whatever this thing is. It's safe here."

The duck flew on to my snout, where I couldn't see him. He grabbed my head with his wings. "Dude, it's time to go Super Cow."

"It'thh not working." I demoed how it flashed on and off like the failing neon lights above us.

The duck flew down. "Energy drinks, right? You need energy drinks, dude."

"Like, ten or twenty," I said, though I doubted any amount would help.

"I'm on it, boss. I know where there's some." The chicken stood up, took a deep breath, and tried to push off into hyperspeed, but collapsed, clutching her wounded leg.

Heavy footsteps echoed through the tunnel. A sixty-member troop of heavily armed TSA agents marched down the stairs from Terminal B like an advancing Roman regiment with their clear-glass shields up. I half-expected one of them to be carrying a giant TSA flag.

"Dude, who knew TSA owned weapons?" asked the duck.

"Whatever, man. We can use this as a cover to get them energy drinks."

"There's a fridge full of drinks up in Concourse B. Just make a right at the top of the stairs," said the chicken. "Do you know which cans are energy drinks?"

"Dude." The duck held up a wing. "We are energy drink connoisseurs."

"Guys, forget the energy drinks. Let'thh use this cover to get out of here. Live to fight another day."

"No way, man. We're doing this. We're getting you those energy drinks."

"Dude, once you go Super Cow, you'll put an end to this mess."

"You're, you're our only hope," said the dog, flashing his sad brown eyes.

Could they be right? Had I ignored our best weapon? Myself. Could I actually put an end to this?

On the Terminal C landing, Agent Periwinkle and henchmen agents pointed and laughed at the TSA assault team. I zeroed in on his smug face, remembering all he'd put me through. "Go. Go get me those drinks."

"You got it, dude."

"Anyone else need anything?" asked the rabbit.

"I'll take a, a, um, a bottle of water, or maybe, maybe an unsweetened iced tea. Yes, an unsweetened tea," said the dog.

"You got it, dude."

The rabbit and duck scurried off, hugging the tunnel wall.

A set of TSA agents kneeled on the travelator with their shields up and weapons ready. Others walked alongside, keeping pace to maintain the formation. When they reached the end of the first walkway, they formed a five-row choir arc of agents. With the formation complete, they chanted, "T-S-A," and stomped their right foot.

The agents of GIBOD laughed.

"Do you, do you think they rehearsed that entrance?" asked the dog.

The chicken and I shrugged. My thoughts had become consumed with memories of Agent Periwinkle ending Agent Orange's life. His lifetime of lies and betrayal. His sinister laugh as he sent me off to the slaughterhouse.

"Agents of TSA," boomed Agent Periwinkle through the tunnel's speakers. I couldn't decide what angered me more, his arrogant voice or losing the soothing *Rhapsody In Blue* melody. "We have no beef with you. Pun intended. We understand that you're just doing your job. Hand over the cow, and we'll be on our way. No more lives need be lost... tonight."

The heads of the TSA agents swiveled until they, one-by-one, locked in on me. I gave them a nod and my best cow smile, which is just me baring my teeth, so who knows what that looked like.

Two TSA agents moved towards us. I switched to my angry cow face. Closed mouth. Squinty eyes. I let out a snort and scuffed a front hoof on the tile.

They came no closer.

"Hello," said Agent Periwinkle, waving his arms. "We've got expert snipers with high-powered weapons aimed at your heads, and you're more afraid of a cow?"

The confused looks on the TSA agent's faces grew more puzzled when the rabbit and duck arrived, each carrying a bag full of drinks.

"Which one do you want, dude? Monster? Rock Star? Red Bull?" The duck pulled a can of each out of his bag.

The rabbit displayed another lineup. "5-hour Energy? Mountain Dew Kickstart? Starbucks Doubleshot?"

"I don't know. Which do you recommend?" I asked.

"You can't go wrong with 5-hour Energy, dude."

"Grab the cow," bellowed Agent Periwinkle, "and this will all be over."

Eight more TSA agents broke the choir arc formation and walked towards us.

"My personal favorite is VPX Bang Blue Razz." The rabbit pulled a can out of his bag and displayed it with his paws like a hand actor in a commercial. "It's loaded with all sorts of brain-boosting vitamins and some wild amino acids. Man, it's awesome. And sugar-free."

"I don't need a brain boost. I just need energy."

"Bang's got that too, man. It's got some crazy chemical that energizes your heart and muscles."

"Dude, it's not a crazy chemical. It's Coenzyme Q10, an antioxidant your body produces naturally. It's grossly overrated."

"Whatever, man. It will pump you up."

The ten TSA agents formed a semi-circle around us. They all looked ready to ask questions, but none of them did.

"For crying out loud," said Agent Periwinkle. "Grab the cow!"

The duck pulled a shiny blue can out of his bag. "I prefer Nos High Performance, dude. It provides a serious caffeine rush."

"There was a habanero watermelon flavored that worked great for me," said a TSA agent, receiving side-eyes from his TSA comrades.

"Gross, dude."

He pointed at the duck. "Don't knock it till you try it. That spice kicks the energy boost into high gear."

"We ain't got any of that, man." The rabbit opened his bag wide and hopped toward the TSA agent. "But, if you'd like one of these, be our guest."

He reached his hand out, but it got slapped away by another agent. "I'll pass. But, thanks."

I snorted to get their attention. "We don't have time for this nonsense. Just give me the Nos High drink."

"Don't take that one, man. All it has is caffeine. You might as well just grab a cup of coffee."

"Dude, it's got more than caffeine. It's got L-theanine, dude."

"That explains the headache I get from it," said the rabbit.

"Well, it tastes way better than that sugar-free Bang crap, dude."

"Guys, just give me one of each."

They popped open their cans and held them up to me.

I grabbed both in my mouth and chugged them. I spit the cans across the floor. My cloak sputtered like a car almost warmed up enough to start.

"Don't let her drink the energy drinks!" yelled Agent Periwinkle, his arms thrashing about.

The hair covering my body stood up straight. Blood pumped through my neck, giving me apple-red cheeks. "Hit me again."

The rabbit and duck had already popped open another round.

"Stop her, you idiots," said Agent Periwinkle as he took a couple of steps down the stairs.

A TSA agent raised her weapon and stepped forward. "I can't believe I'm saying this to a gang of barnyard animals, but here goes. Drop the energy drinks, and slide them over here."

"I may be your only hope. You've got to let me drink this." I guzzled the next two cans without waiting for a response. My cloaking power zapped across my hide before the last remnants of energy drink dripped down my semi-invisible chin.

The TSA agent lowered her weapon and took a step backwards, as did the others with her.

Agent Periwinkle waltzed back onto the Terminal C landing. "Well, you're all gonna die anyway, so it might as well be now. Open fire!"

34: The Showdown at O'Hare Continues

I ROSE LIKE A bucking bronco and screamed like someone lit my tail on fire.

Gunfire erupted. The tunnel walls rattled. The floor shook. TSA agents screamed. The mixed stench of rotten eggs and hot metal assaulted my nostrils.

I galloped through retreating TSA agents and sprinted down the travelator. All the while, bullets ricocheting off me.

"We're with you, dude!" yelled the duck, as he sprang into the air, then torpedoed the floor behind me.

Within a second, the travelator belt swelled, carrying me into the gunpowder haze. My head shattered the ceiling's neon lights as I surfed the wave of walkway, tile, and concrete toward Terminal C. The blare of bullets overwhelmed the music, but I hummed the *Rhapsody In Blue* tune in my head, as I focused on my target, Agent Periwinkle. The wave cracked like a whip when it reached the end of the walkway, launching me forward. I flew over the stairs. My hooves clacked the tile floor. I slid past the GIBOD agents, past Agent Periwinkle, and smashed through three rows of chairs before a United courtesy desk stopped me.

Bullets bounced off me as I untangled from the desk. Agent Vermilion stood closest. With a running start, I booted him like a field goal kicker. He sailed over the stairs and landed on a jagged edge of the glass railing. There was no scream as the glass wedge stabbed through his chest.

I charged at the next closest agent, who collapsed from ricocheting bullets before I had a chance to crush his skull. Agent Sangria approached, unleashing a barrage of gunfire. I brought my front hooves down on her head. I howled as I stood over her crumpled body.

Anyone wearing a black tactical suit got the full wrath of my rage. Blood splattered. Bones snapped. Limbs flopped.

I spotted my target among the collage of mangled and bloodied agents. Agent Periwinkle stood in front of me, a smirk on his face. I reared up and prepared to clobber him. He waved his index finger at me, like that would stop me. I couldn't wait for the satisfying thud of his limp body hitting the floor.

He pointed at the tunnel. "You should think about your friends."

Smash his skull and look later was my first thought, but I have exceptional peripheral vision. Down in the tunnel, agents of GIBOD held the chicken, dog, rabbit, and duck like prize catches. Agents had Captain Johnson, Biff, and three Chicago police officers lined up at the bottom of the stairs. They were on their knees, with their hands tied behind them and guns pointed at the back of their heads. Agents of GIBOD dragged ten TSA agents to the middle of the tunnel, adding them to the line-up.

The bodies of police officers and TSA agents littered the tunnel floor. The moving sidewalk I rode to Terminal C had crashed against the stairs and escalators below me. Walkway tread snaked down them like seaweed. Only two green tubes of neon remained to illuminate the ceiling. The groans of the wounded and dying, along with the chuckling GIBOD agents, removed all peacefulness from the *Rhapsody In Blue* melody, which, thanks to the lack of gunfire, once again graced my ears.

I dropped back to all fours, panting. My cloak remained active, but I feared not for much longer. I needed to end this fast. "Hand over the last four vials."

Agent Periwinkle chuckled. "Cow, you're in no position to bargain."

I didn't care. "Give me the vials."

"Here's the deal." Agent Periwinkle paced up to my snout. "You cough up those vials you swallowed, and I allow you and your animal friends to walk out of here alive. We'll set you up on a quiet farm in California, where you can roam free like your ancestors did."

I shook away concerns he'd read my mind and let snarkiness flow. "I don't think cows ever roamed free. Who would milk uthh in the wild?"

Agent Periwinkle strolled up to me, lightly shaking his head. "Cow, I'm making you a generous offer."

"And if I refuse?" I said, unintentionally imitating Batman.

His jaw stiffened as his eyes pierced through me. "One-by-one you will witness your animal friends die." He snapped his fingers.

Agent Hunter Green broke from the cluster of agents at the bottom of the stairs. He carried the duck at arm's length as he came up. The duck flapped his wings and flailed his legs, but couldn't break free.

"And what if I crush your skull right here, right now?" I said, channeling every Clint Eastwood movie I'd ever watched. Thanks to my cloak, my upper lip snarl didn't have the intimidating impact I'd intended.

"Do it, dude. Crush his skull," said the duck in the clutches of Agent Hunter Green who had reached the top of the stairs.

"Then all your friends die ... instantly," said Agent Periwinkle.

"Here'thh my deal. You hand over the vials, and I let you and all your double-crossing agents live."

"You tell 'em, dude. We don't negotiate with double-crossing murdering terrorists."

Deep down, I was thankful for the duck's support and applauded his courage, but I wished he'd have kept quiet. There would be repercussions.

"Shut him up," said Agent Periwinkle.

"Dude, I've got the right to–"

Agent Hunter Green squeezed the duck's neck. His bill kept flapping, but no words came out.

My nostrils flared, and my hooves clamped so tight, I swear they turned white. Every muscle prepared to strike, but my brain flashed the stop sign. Logic insisted I wouldn't be able to save them all. Anger, impulse, and heroism fought back, leaving me paralyzed.

Agent Periwinkle paced over to Agent Hunter Green and the duck. "Dr. Hash Browns gave you and your friends amazing abilities, but you all have your vulnerable spots. Take your friend the duck here. His legs and neck. I can snap them like twigs." He grabbed the duck's leg with two hands.

I took a step towards them, as anger, impulse, and heroism got the upper hand.

Agent Periwinkle stopped me with a simple shake of the head and an eye-roll toward the others.

The duck squirmed, trying desperately to yank his leg free.

Agent Periwinkle's grip tightened.

My neck tensed into slow twists, thumping with every rapid beat of my heart.

Agent Periwinkle grinned.

SNAP.

The duck's bill opened wide, but no scream came out.

My heart lurched, skipping a beat.

Anger rocketed to the lead. I visualized snapping Agent Periwinkle's arms and legs, one-by-one, and in multiple places. I readied the checkered flag, preparing to let angry rage consume me, with no care for the consequences. Then, like a rigged donut race on the ballpark big screen, the dark horse of despair sprinted past logic, impulse, heroism, *and* anger to claim victory. My muscles lost their form. I struggled to keep my head up. Tears flowed as I pictured the agents executing my friends, one-by-one. *I'd failed to protect them. I'd failed them worse than Agent Orange ever did.*

My cloak flickered. Despair shrugged, willing to let it drop. I brought anger back to a simmer, enough to keep the cloak powered. But not for much longer.

"Cow, you're out of time. What's it going to be? Death to all your friends, or a carefree life on a hundred acres of peaceful farmland?"

I wanted off my emotional rollercoaster. I needed this ordeal to end, and his offer provided the only viable option. And after all, I wanted this. We'd be safe, living the rest of our days frolicking on a peaceful farm. I scanned the fiery eyes and clenched mouths of my fellow animals as they struggled to break free of their captures. They'd be angry with me... at first, but they'd come around.

Agent Periwinkle paced to the side of my snout and stared into my eye. "What's it going to be?"

I glimpsed the humans held captive by the GIBOD agents. He'd execute them as soon as the deal completed. "I'll accept your terms under one condition. You also release the police officers and TSA agents you hold hostage."

Agent Periwinkle threw his hands up. He paced past me as if he was a coach, and I was a ref who made a bad call. "Why? Why? Why do you continue to protect humans? You've seen what humans do to your kind. You witnessed the slaughtering, the skinning, the butchering. You know they grind the extra bits up, form patties, cook it, and eat it. Yet, you still look out for them. Why?"

"There'thh good humans out there. Caring, kind humans."

"Stop it," said Agent Periwinkle.

"Those are good men and women down there just doing their job."

"Fine. We'll release them. Besides, a shot to the head would be merciful compared to the agonizing death by zombiism they will experience."

I'd sold out the human race to save me and my friends. My simmering anger vanished and with it, my energy reserves. Despair devoured me. I collapsed to the floor. My cloak zapped off.

Agent Periwinkle smiled. "Here's the new deal." He pulled out his revolver and aimed it between my eyes. "Cough up the vials, or I blow your brains out and carve them out of you."

35: Still more of the Showdown at O'Hare

AGENT PERIWINKLE WALTZED TOWARD me until the barrel of his pistol pressed into my forehead.

"I said I accept your deal." I rattled my brain to come up with a new plan of action.

"That deal is no longer available. Start coughing up the vials, or I blow your brains out."

Stall. That was the best idea I had. Stall until an actual plan formulated, though the chances of that happening given my current state of emotional chaos were slim. So, I performed a dramatic extended fake hack. I gagged. I wheezed. My face turned red.

Agent Periwinkle pushed the barrel deeper into my hide. "You cows cough your cud up as a regular part of your digestive process. So, knock off the act, and hack up them vials."

A flicker of movement at the far end of the terminal caught my attention. The pig emerged from a staircase. A tingle returned to my hide. My hooves jittered. A team of Chicago cops and TSA agents followed him. The calvary was on its way! I just needed to give them time.

"You know there'thh cameras everywhere. The cat is recording all of thithh from an undisclosed location off planet. She'll alert the intergalactic authorities. You're finished. You and the whole Havarti Travel Bureau."

"I spit on the Havarti Travel Bureau." Agent Periwinkle punctuated his statement by spitting on the floor.

"Oh, that'thh right," I said, knowing all along his true alliance. "You work for the other greedy jerks, the Travel Bureau of Havarti."

Agent Hunter Green snarled at me and tightened his grip on the duck's neck. "You better watch what you say. TBH rules."

I grinned. "Thank you for validating on camera who you work for."

Agent Hunter Green gave his boss the "oh crap" look.

"Oh, no," said Agent Periwinkle, though he didn't sound worried at all. "I've been outsmarted by a cow. I never thought there'd be cameras in the airport. If only you and your super brain were on our side."

I thought I struggled with the concept of sarcasm, but Agent Hunter Green's lack of understanding rivaled that of the chicken's. He still had the petrified eyes of a dog caught drinking from the toilet.

"Cow, you don't have your earpiece in, do you? You haven't gotten the cat's latest updates?"

I snarled and huffed. His needling about the earpiece hit a nerve.

He eased the gun back a bit. "Aren't you curious? Don't you want to know what she sees on the airport security cameras?" With his free hand, he motioned around the terminal. His head followed, turning toward the pig and his posse closing in behind him.

"She'thh watching all the crimes and horrible things you've done." I blurted this out to get his attention back on me.

It worked. He turned back to see my expression. "Nope, she's watching replays of classic television showing Celebrity Boxing."

Agent Hunter Green's smile returned with a hip-level arm pump.

"I'm glad you learned that tidbit before you died," said Agent

Periwinkle. "It would disappoint me if you died believing you had evidence on me and the Travel Bureau of Havarti."

What a jerk. But at least I'd distracted him. He had no clue officers sneaked in via the tunnel's side doors.

"Now, enough stalling." He cocked his revolver, which I assume he did for dramatic effect, since he didn't need improved accuracy with the barrel still pressed to my forehead. "Cough up the vials."

The pig and his team of heavily armed cops and TSA agents fanned out across the terminal. Agent Lavender and a group of officers readied themselves behind one display case in the tunnel, and Agent Capri led a group behind the case on the opposite side. I loved my near 360-degree vision.

Agent Lavender gave a wave.

Showtime.

My power levels had returned. My cloak zipped into action as I slid my snout back and chomped down on his arm. He tried to pull his arm out, but I had a firm grip.

"Cow, release my arm, or I will shoot."

I wanted to say, "Make my day," but I had his arm in my mouth. So, I snorted instead.

He pulled the trigger.

My expectation of spitting the bullet back into Agent Periwinkle's face was a gross miscalculation of my powers. The bullet burned its way down my esophagus. It ricocheted inside my first stomach. The vials exploded. Glass shrapnel bounced off the inner linings of my stomach. The bullet pinballed out of my first stomach. It lost speed, but still bounced around my second stomach before coming to rest. Shards of the shattered vials tickled the inner lining of my first two stomachs. On the plus side, the bullet hadn't ripped through the back of my head or tore my stomachs open.

I spit his arm out with the gun still in his hand and clamped my mouth shut. I couldn't let the gasses escape. Then I headbutted Agent Periwinkle.

He staggered back several steps before collapsing.

The pig and his posse swarmed Agent Hunter Green, who released the duck and threw his hands up. The GIBOD agents holding the animals and cops hostage never saw the teams led by Agents Lavender and Capri coming. Only Agent Onyx needed additional persuasion, via the butt end of a rifle to the head, to surrender. He dropped the rabbit and aimed his weapon at his attacker before fainting straight backwards. He got off one shot, which took out one of the two working neon ceiling lights.

The pig slapped me on the back. "It looks like it was a rough fight. It's good to see you all survived." His eye dropped. He scanned his hooves as he cleared his throat. "And, um, I'm sorry for being late to the party, and for rushing off half-cocked. That wasn't professional of me."

After getting past the shock of the pig apologizing, I wanted to tell him no worries. After all, he'd just saved the day. But I didn't dare open my mouth, so I nodded, looked him straight in the eyes, and held up a hoof for a hoof pump.

He obliged, then bolted off to secure rogue GIBOD agents in duct tape handcuffs. He didn't question my silence. I assumed he was thankful the moment ended quickly and didn't get sappy.

The rabbit bounced up the stairs to check on his buddy.

"I've had worse," said the duck, hopping over to me on his one good leg. "Dude, you swallowed a bullet. And lived."

"That was totally awesome, man."

To me, stupid provided a better description. I envisioned putting the gun in my mouth as looking tough and dramatic. But, if I had left the barrel of his gun pressed against my forehead, the bullet would have rebounded right off my active cloak, and I wouldn't have been standing there with a belly full of broken zombie virus vials. I kept telling myself, it's the human zombie virus. *I'll be fine. I'll be fine. But keep my mouth shut.*

Agents Lavender and Capri carried the chicken and dog up the stairs. Along with the rabbit and duck, they formed a semi-circle in front of me. The fish hovered above them, having snapped out of his self-hypnosis.

I wanted to explain the situation, but with my lips pressed together tight, all that came out was, "Mrr, mr, mrrr mrph mrrr mrrph."

"I think the, I think the bullet to her head turned her back into a normal cow. She can only moo," said the dog.

"Those aren't moos, dude. That's mumbling."

"Did the bullet destroy your vocal cords?" asked the chicken.

"Mrrrr." My disgruntled tone, along with a roll of my eyes and a shake of my head, clarified that mrrr meant no.

"I think, I think the shot sealed her mouth shut," said the dog.

I shook my head again as Agent Periwinkle struggled to his feet behind the others. He pulled a vial from his pants pocket.

"Mmmrr, mmmrr," I said as I did a stationary prancing shuffle dance and bobbed my head toward him.

The duck pointed a wing at Agent Periwinkle. "The dude's got more vials."

"I'm on it, boss," said the chicken as he jumped out of Agent Lavender's arms. She landed with a heavy thud. "Ow, ow, ow. That was stupid," she said, hopping around on her one good leg.

In his left hand, Agent Periwinkle held the vial high above his head. The duck flew at him, head down, wings out, and legs up, though his broken leg dangled. The rabbit leaped face first, with his mouth wide open, exposing his unsheathed vampire teeth. Agent Periwinkle swatted the duck away with his right hand, but his gun flew out. As he brought his left arm down, the rabbit clamped his pointy teeth into the agent's wrist. Agent Periwinkle screamed as he tried to shake the rabbit off. The duck rejoined the fight and attacked the agent's grip on the vial.

The vial flew out of the fight. It spun like a kicked football. The trajectory had it sailing left of my head. I took a step toward it before remembering if I opened my mouth, I would release the virus stewing in my stomach. "Mrr, mr, mrrr." I pointed my snout at the vial.

The heads of Agents Lavender and Capri snapped and locked onto the spiraling vial.

Agent Lavender sprang into action, taking a step toward the vial.

Agent Capri tossed the dog to the floor. Unfortunately, right in Agent Lavender's path.

The dog yelped.

Agent Lavender sprawled across the floor.

Agent Capri stepped on her arm, then tumbled on top of her.

The vial began its descent.

Captain Johnson reached the top of the stairs. He stepped onto the landing, gawking at the wounded dog, Agent Lavender, and Agent Capri fighting each other like football teammates vying for a fumble.

"Catch that vial!" yelled the chicken as she limped toward the vial. She would never get there in time.

Captain Johnson's head pivoted until he located the flying vial. He snapped his hat off his head, took two shuffle steps, and dove.

Agent Capri dug a knee into Agent Lavender's back and launched herself toward the vial.

Captain Johnson and Agent Capri converged on the vial, smashing into each other like two outfielders lunging for a pop fly.

The vial bounced off Agent Capri's hands. She twisted and tapped it up.

It bounced off Captain Johnson's forehead.

Agent Capri stretched, but it had gone out of her reach.

Captain Johnson flailed a hand toward it but missed.

It reached its apex, hung for a moment, then plummeted. My shoulders collapsed in synch with the vial's descent. A crash landing, triggering a human zombie apocalypse, appeared to be a second away.

But the chicken hadn't given up. She shuffled. She stretched. She extended a wing and batted it back into the air.

Captain Johnson scrambled and caught the vial in his hat.

I wanted to exhale a giant sigh of relief, but stopped myself before expelling the deadly fumes inside me.

Captain Johnson examined the vial while getting to his feet. "It's even labeled human zombie virus. How did you get through security with this?" While still examining the vial, he raised an enormous gun and pointed it at Agent Periwinkle. "Don't even think about reaching into your pockets."

Agent Periwinkle plunged a hand into his coat pocket.

Captain Johnson fired.

The bullet ripped into Agent Periwinkle's shoulder. He collapsed, dropping the last three vials. They rolled harmlessly to Biff as he reached the top of the stairs.

"You idiots. You think you've saved the planet," said Agent Periwinkle, clutching his bleeding shoulder. "Instead, you saved the parasites destroying it."

The pig rejoined us and helped Agent Capri grab Agent Periwinkle.

"You've doomed this planet," he said, as the pig and Agent Capri rolled him onto his stomach. "Don't you understand? Humans are parasites. They're destroying the planet."

The pig duct taped Agent Periwinkle's hands behind his back.

"Mrrr mrr mrrmmr," I said, trying to get them refocused on the bigger problem.

"Is that your language?" asked Captain Johnson.

"Dude, no," said the duck. "I don't understand a word she's saying."

"Mrrrph!" I pointed my hoof at broken glass on the floor and then at my stomach.

"What's she doing, man?" asked the rabbit.

"Dude, she's apologizing for the mess."

"That's not what she's trying to tell us," said the fish. He swam closer to me.

I nodded to the fish and pointed at the broken glass and my stomach again.

"I got it, dude. Her stomach is made of broken glass?"

"She swallowed some broken glass, man."

I shook my head yes, and no, and shrugged in the same motion.

"So, is that a yes or no, dude?"

"Man, that's a solid maybe."

I pointed at the vials in Biff's hands.

"We know you swallowed the vials, dude. We saw you do it," said the duck.

"Yeah, man, what does that have to do with broken glass?"

I exploded my cheeks while keeping my mouth shut tight.

"She's, she's, she's gonna hurl," said the dog.

After rolling my eyes, I pointed to the vials, the broken glass, and then my stomach.

"You have broken glass inside you?" asked the fish.

I emphatically nodded yes.

"And it's gonna make you barf?" asked the rabbit.

I shook my head and pointed at the vials.

"The vials are the broken glass," said Captain Johnson. I wanted to hug him, but as I've mentioned before, I'm physically incapable of giving hugs.

"The bullet must have broken open the vials in her stomach," said the fish.

I nodded my head like a bobblehead.

"Dude, if those vials broke inside of you, you'd better keep your mouth closed," said the duck.

"What do you think she's been doing?" said the fish.

"Mrph, mmrrmr." I thanked the fish for saying what I was thinking.

"Excellent point, dude, but just to be safe, we should duct tape her mouth closed."

"Agreed," said the rabbit.

Despite my reservations, their logic was sound. They needed to seal my mouth. I shrugged my approval.

With the chicken, dog, and duck out of commission, the gang turned to the pig to perform the duct taping honors.

"We've got to close every orifice," he said, wrapping five layers of duct tape around my mouth. "Don't breathe either."

I had figured that out on my own. Thanks to Dr. Hash Browns' enhancements, all of us animals could hold our breath for over a day.

Once he finished my mouth, the pig duct taped over my nose and ears.

"I think we should duct tape her butt closed, man," said the rabbit.

"Dude, even for you, that's pretty immature."

I wholeheartedly agreed with the duck.

"I'm serious, man. Cows fart a lot. I read once that cow farts are like the leading cause of this whole global warming thing."

"Dude, listen to yourself?"

It shocked me to consider the duck as the voice of reason.

"The stupid rabbit has a point," said Agent Periwinkle from his prone position on the floor. "Cows are the second greatest menace to Mother Earth, with their methane gas coming out of every orifice. Their belches are the worst offenders. I would have wiped them off the face of the planet if it wasn't for you meddling fools and your cow zombie cure. I was so close to victory. How? How did you misfits stop me? Your incompetence is beyond compare. This cannot end this way. I will not be defeated by the BarnYard Idiots."

The rabbit cocked her head. "So, you agree, we should duct tape her butt closed, right?"

"Let her fart all over the place. Let her start the great zombie apocalypse. Yes, be the stupid creature I've come to loath. Do it. Let her rip away, and give me my victory." Foaming drool formed on the corners of Agent Periwinkle's mouth.

The pig ripped off a lengthy piece of duct tape. "We're taping her butt closed."

After Agent Periwinkle's rant, I agreed.

The pig slapped tape across my butt hole, layering more on until I had what I assumed looked like a gray asterisk covering my butt hole.

"The planet will fight back. It will destroy you all," said Agent Periwinkle.

"Can you shut him up?" asked Captain Johnson.

"Sure thing," said the pig, as he slapped a strip of duct tape over Agent Periwinkle's mouth.

"Mrrr, mrr, mrrmmr," said Agent Periwinkle.

"Thank you," said Captain Johnson.

I wanted the attention back on me and the broken vials in my stomach. But, I couldn't talk or breathe. I could barely hear. And I had a plugged butt as if I prepared for hibernation. Fortunately, I rarely needed to poop, once again thanks to the enhancements of Dr. Hash Browns.

Agent Lavender walked over to Captain Johnson, who placed his vial into an evidence bag which already contained the three Biff picked up. "Is our truck still parked out between the terminals?" she asked.

"More than likely," said the captain, as he sealed the bag.

"Good. We've got to get the cow to a secure and quarantined location immediately," she said.

"We shouldn't risk taking the cow in that truck," said Agent Capri. "I radioed for an airlock transport. It will be here in five."

"Excellent work," said Agent Lavender. "I'll take the cow in the airlock transport. The rest of you ride in the truck."

Captain Johnson surveyed the carnage. "You all can't leave. You're coming with us."

"Do you have airlock transport?" asked Agent Capri, strutting up to him. "Do you have a quarantined facility large enough to house the cow, with expert scientific and medical personnel ready and waiting to extract the virus from her stomach?"

"Well... no," said Captain Johnson.

"I rest my case. And we'll take those as well." Agent Capri snatched the evidence bag of vials from his hands.

"Those are dangerous," he said, with his palms raised. "We need to make sure those are secure."

"Do you have a secure vault which assures the vials will never get damaged or lost?" asked Agent Lavender.

"I'm pretty sure we do. We handle evidence all the time." He reached for the bag, but Agent Capri pulled it out of his reach and stuffed it into her coat pocket. "How am I supposed to prosecute this jerk without evidence?"

"You won't," said Agent Lavender. "We're taking him too." She motioned for the pig and Agent Capri to grab Agent Periwinkle.

"Whoa, whoa, whoa." Captain Johnson blocked the pig and Agent Capri from dragging Agent Periwinkle away. "Who do you think you are?"

"We already told you," said Agent Lavender. "We're agents of GIBOD. This is what we do. We save the human race from this type of scum. We're the only agency on the planet equipped to contain these traitors and, more importantly, the only agency authorized to bring these criminals and their accomplices, the Havarti Travel Bureau, to intergalactic justice."

"Dude, he actually works with the Travel Bureau of Havarti," said the duck.

"Travel Bureau of Havarti or Havarti Travel Bureau, what's the difference?" said Agent Lavender.

"MRMMR MMRPH MRR MRR!!" Agent Periwinkle's face grew a deeper shade of red with every mumbling word.

I chuckled to myself, enjoying his duct taped mouth suffering.

Captain Johnson crossed his arms. "You're all crazy. You've got no badges and no jurisdiction. I mean, even he claimed to be an agent of GIBGOB. And aren't these guys who shot at us also agents of GIBGAB?"

Agent Lavender walked up to Captain Johnson. "It's GIBOD, and yes, they were agents, but we stopped them. We stopped them because we have a cow that becomes indestructible, a fish who can swim through the air, a dog who can dig giant tunnels in a matter of seconds, a pig with super strength, and a chicken who can fly around at hyperspeed."

She gave us praise? She bragged about us? No surprise she praised the pig, but the rest of us? It warmed my hooves.

"And that rabbit who can create mini earthquakes," said Biff, still standing at the top of the stairs.

"You're not helping, Biff." The captain turned to Agent Lavender. "What's your point?"

"We just saved the world from a zombie apocalypse that none of you even knew existed. That's the point."

"But it was one of your agents who masterminded it," said Captain Johnson.

Agent Lavender rolled her eyes and motioned for the pig and Agent Capri to move around Captain Johnson's one-person blockade.

I followed, wanting to get into that airlock truck as soon as possible.

"I haven't approved this," yelled Captain Johnson, as they dragged Agent Periwinkle toward the stairs. A group of officers led the Agent Periwinkle loyalists to the stairs, bumping into Captain Johnson along the way. "What are you guys doing? Where are you going with them?"

"The agents ordered us to take them to their truck," said an officer.

"You don't take orders from them. I'm the captain here."

"We're going to need a couple of you to help carry these animals," said Agent Lavender.

"It would be an honor to carry one of those barnyard heroes," said Biff.

"Dude, that's what we call ourselves, the BarnYard Heroes!"

"Cool." Biff ran over and picked up the dog bear-hug style.

"Thank, um, thank you," said the dog.

"My pleasure," said Biff.

"Has everyone lost their minds?" asked Captain Johnson, his arms waving above his head.

"After what we just witnessed?" said Biff. "Probably." He took a step and stopped. "Actually, most definitely, yes." He followed us toward the stairs, cradling the dog.

The dog gave Biff a quick lick on his cheek, then rested his chin on Biff's arm.

Agent Lavender tapped Captain Johnson on the shoulder and attempted to hand him the chicken. "Can you carry the chicken? She got shot in the leg. She can't walk."

"I'm not carrying your chicken." He stepped away in a huff, then sighed as he gazed upon the tunnel wreckage. "Sorry, it's just, how am I supposed to explain this? My superiors will need an explanation. The press will demand answers. How do I give them that without suspects in custody? How do I explain that giant hole in the tunnel ceiling? And the massive loss of life?"

"I'm not sure," said Agent Lavender. "But I'm sure you'll figure something out."

"Blame it on the dead agents," Biff shouted over his shoulder.

Agent Lavender gave Biff a thumbs up. "That's the spirit. We'll leave you the dead agents, so you can blame them." Clutching the chicken, she quickened her pace to catch up to the rest of us. "One more thing. You better cover up that hole before the next rain."

We left Captain Johnson staring in silence at the carnage in the tunnel.

36: It Wasn't My Fault, Entirely

THE AIRLOCK TRUCK ARRIVED at the same time we got outside. Crumbled pavement and tipped over cars littered the roadway, but amazingly a clear path for the arriving truck existed.

I figured once inside the safety of the airlock bed, they would remove the duct tape. I figured wrong. My sides brushed the walls. The closed door pushed my snout into the front wall and pasted my tail to my butt. Only the hairy tip could swish.

A brief suck of air announced the airlock had sealed.

Two clicks, a dull thud, and a loud clang made it clear they had locked me in.

Total darkness took hold. I closed my eyes, and images of skinned and decapitated cows from the slaughterhouse flashed through my mind, followed by the zowbie horde ravaging a chicken farm. I popped my eyes open and settled in for a long stare at the steel wall in front of me.

My legs wiggled. My hide twitched. *This must be how it feels to be buried alive.*

The instinct to hack up and chew the broken vials like cud kicked in.

Deep breaths typically squelched the urge, but the duct tape refused to let that happen.

I flashed my cloak on and off. The distraction worked for a bit, but then I became acutely aware of my beating heart. *Did it always beat that fast? And that hard? Too many energy drinks. It's going to explode.*

"MRRMMRPH. MRR. MRRPH!" I screamed, which translated to, "GET ME OUT OF HERE!"

I banged the side walls, stomped on the floor, headbutted the front wall, and kicked the back door. Whoever sat in the driver's seat responded with several solid thuds to the cab's back wall.

The engine turned over. Gears clanked. We finally moved.

The ceiling hissed. Stinging droplets assaulted my eyes. I caught a faint whiff of sweet vanilla infused paint thinner. I contemplated how this meant the duct tape hadn't provided a one-hundred percent airtight seal. My eyelids sagged. My legs wilted. As I wafted to the floor, my snout squeaked against the wall, and my butt stuttered down the back door.

A blissful sleep commenced.

***

A MUSTY DIRT SMELL filled my lungs as I stretched all four legs like a cat, crinkling the large white tarp I laid on. With my eyes still shut, I lifted and twisted my neck. I blinked until my eyes adjusted to the bare lightbulb dangling from the middle of the barn ceiling.

"Note, at hour five, thirteen minutes, and seventy-three seconds, the subject opened her eyes and lifted her head on her own." The cat hopped down from my desk, which someone had dragged out to the center of the barn.

She pulled up my already open eyelids as she talked into her handheld device. "Pupils show a minute dilatation. No visual signs of zombie cataracts." She flashed a light from her handheld device into my eyes.

I flinched my head away.

"Pupils are responsive, as are the subject's reflexes. I will attempt verbal communication." She sat in her customary regal pose. "Cow. Hello. How are you feeling?"

"Cat, what are you doing?" I asked, examining the fifty plus sensors stuck on me from head to hooves.

"Subject is conscious and demonstrates the capacity for verbal communication, but has provided an inappropriate response to the simple question of 'how are you feeling?' This indicates a sign of dementia or brain damage. I recommend a CT scan of the subject's brain, as well as tests of the subject's mental capacities."

"Cat, I'm fine." I stood and yanked sensors off with my mouth.

"Subject is uncooperative and displays mild hostile tendencies."

I rolled up and began the ungainly leg presses, shoulder rotations, and head counterbalances required for me to stand. "Cat, it's great to see you, but trust me, I'm fine. And I'm not hostile."

"Your self-diagnosis is an insufficient analysis of your current condition. I abandoned a volatile situation two galaxies away to attend to your predicament. A full examination is required in order to ascertain your current mental and physical well-being, which is precisely what I intend to do. Now, I must insist you lie back down."

"What'thh this volatile situation you abandoned?"

"My actions may have contributed to the creation of an aggressive army of sheep with delusions of grandeur and an intent to enslave the known universe. Now lie down."

"That doesn't sound good," I said, finally reaching full height.

"I thought I made that clear by my use of the word volatile."

"She's awake. She's awake," said the dog, charging out from his stall with his tail flapping. I lowered my head to let him lick my face.

The chicken zipped out behind him. "Cow, great to see you up on your hooves."

They each had bandages on their legs, but neither showed signs of limping.

"Chicken, I am glad you have returned," said the cat. "Please reconnect the sensors."

With her beak, she picked up a sensor I had torn off.

"Chicken, I'm fine. I don't need the sensors." I stretched to remove the sensors on my butt but couldn't reach them.

The chicken dropped the sensor in her beak and pulled the sensors off my butt.

"Subject has demonstrated disorientation, logic confusion, and an inability to follow simple instructions. Further examples of diminished brain functionality," said the cat into her handheld device.

"She looks, looks good to me," said the dog, as he sniffed my backside. "I'm just glad the procedure was a, was a success and we didn't have to cremate her."

"There were plans to cremate me?"

"If things went south, we were prepared to destroy the virus by any means possible," said the pig, entering the barn. "I'm sure you understand."

I understood the needs of the many outweighed the needs of the few, making my life expendable. But it would have been nice if he'd used at least a bit of tact in his words and tone.

He walked past me and took a seat in my office chair, which had been hauled out to the barn's common area along with the desk. I'm not sure why I had an office chair, since I was incapable of fitting into it. Regardless, it ticked me off to see the pig sitting in it.

"I'm glad I was unaware of this plan," I said, bending my head down so the dog could snag sensors off with his mouth.

The cat huffed with a twinge of a hiss. "Since you refuse to cooperate with your medical examination, I will depart. I have more pressing matters to attend to."

"You're back in the barn safe and sound. Why would you leave?"

"I explained my pressing matters earlier. Cow, your mental deficiencies are concerning. In my absence, I recommend a full cognitive assessment and a CT scan."

"Please tell me you won't do anything stupid to try and stop these killer sheep."

"Cow, I realize you are struggling with your mental faculties, but I would still expect you to know better than to suggest I could do something stupid."

"You helped create an army of killer sheep who want to enslave the universe," said the chicken. "That's kind of stupid."

The cat huffed and lifted her head high. "I intend to rectify the situation." She headed for the door.

"Cat, wait. We're, we're coming with," said the dog, as he and the chicken followed.

The cat kept walking and didn't look back. "I do not require your assistance."

"You're getting our help, whether you like it or not," said the chicken.

"Wait," I said. "You guys can't head off on your own. I mean, you're not full-fledged agents."

"Actually," said the pig, with a slight shrug of his shoulders, "they are agents of GIBOD now, and have orders to accompany her."

"We're her bodyguards," said the chicken.

"You both took bullets to the leg. You should both be resting in hospital beds, not getting sent off on missions."

They assured me they had healed and promised to stay safe. Their words did nothing to calm my fears. I watched in disbelief as they hopped and trotted toward the barn exit. *Why did GIBOD think they were ready for dangerous missions? And why is the pig on board with this?*

"Good luck saving the universe, dudes," said the duck, flying down from the barn loft.

"Man, we are so glad you're awake," said the rabbit, hopping off the ladder.

The duck hobbled up to me with a cast on his tiny leg. "We've been tracking something big, dude."

"Remember we told you about a gang of animals with superpowers, just like us?" asked the rabbit.

I didn't remember, but the duck didn't wait for my answer. "Well, they're up to something, dude."

"We're not sure what it is, but it's gonna be huge, man."

The fish swam into the barn. "Guys, she just woke up from a medically-induced coma. Let her catch her breath."

"But, dude, we're just so excited."

"If we stop 'em, man, Agent Lavender said she'd make us agents."

The pig took his feet off my desk and sat up straight in my chair. "She never promised you two would become agents. She said she'd consider letting you reapply to the training academy."

"We're going to be agents. We're going to be agents," chanted the rabbit and duck.

The questions had piled up, but one stood out. "Wait, I was in a coma?"

"Medically-induced coma, man."

"That's standard operating procedure for a dude in your condition," said the duck.

"Especially since you were out for two weeks, man."

"Two weeks?" I had no clue.

The fish shrugged his gills. "A month, actually. You know the cat. She needed to run tests, do research, crunch the numbers, run the projections, etc."

"Dude, be thankful you were out cold."

"You had tubes running in and out of every opening you've got, man."

"And a few new openings, dude."

I took a quick scan of my body. No tubes found, but a large bandage covered a section of my side. I also noticed a couple more sensors, which I flicked off with my tongue. "Maybe it'thh best I don't hear any more about this procedure."

"Man, have you got that right."

"Dude, you won't believe how they cleared out your system."

"It involved turpentine, gasoline, air guns, and a whole lot of flames, man."

"I'm not, not saying flames shot out your butt, dude."

"I've heard enough. New subject. Is Agent Lavender the new director?"

The pig leaned forward. "Yes, Agent Lavender is the new director of GIBOD. She wanted to check on you in person, but she's meeting with the Intergalactic Business Ethics representative to review the case against Agent Periwinkle and the Havarti Travel Bureau."

"And the Travel Bureau of Havarti," said the fish.

"Thho, we did it. We brought down the Havarti Travel Bureau?"

"Not yet," said the pig, resting his elbows on my desk, much to my dislike. "She's presenting our case, but it will be difficult to prove the Havarti Travel Bureau conspired with Agent Periwinkle."

"Or the Travel Bureau of Havarti," said the fish.

The pig did a mini eye-roll. "Of course. Anyway, it's doubtful they'll take the case, and the humans will have to prosecute him and his loyalists via US laws."

"Back when my microphone was on. At that farm and the slaughterhouse. He confessed to everything. That recording should prove it."

The pig rolled the palms of his hooves up. "They say that's not admissible evidence."

"The intergalactic court system is messed up, dude."

I didn't want to hear any more. "What about Grandma Marjorie?" I asked, hoping for better news.

"She's in police custody," said the fish, "but she has public opinion on her side."

"How can she have public opinion on her side? She'thh a murderer who tried to start a zombie apocalypse."

The pig cleared his throat. "Cow, I would like you to know what a fantastic job you did. You're a good agent. GIBOD is proud to have you on the team."

"Thank you, but the way you said it makes it sound like there'thh more to the story."

They all looked at one another in hopes someone else would talk.

"Just tell me."

The pig spun a computer monitor around on my desk. A news site displayed a wanted poster of a cow's head, with the caption, "The Cow Responsible for the Cow Zombie Apocalypse."

I scoffed and twitched my head. "That could be any cow. In fact, I bet it'thh a stock photo."

The duck shook his head. "Dude, that's definitely you."

"How can you be sure?"

The pig scrolled to a full-body cow picture.

"Because, man, there's no other cow with a giant 'Test Cow 42' tattooed on their butt."

"They have pictures of you all over the globe," said the fish, as the pig scrolled, revealing pictures of me in Ireland. "There are outlandish stories of you causing massive destruction and threatening children at a soccer match."

"Totally fake news, man."

"Well, that'thh not totally fake. There was an incident at a children'thh soccer match in Ireland."

"Dude! Why did you attack a kid's soccer game?"

"Not cool, man."

"I said there was an incident. I didn't attack children." I groaned at how quickly they'd turned against me. "They attacked me. The parents. Not the kids. Well, not most of them."

The pig scrolled down and highlighted a section. "That's not what they wrote in the article. They claimed Grandma Marjorie and her grandsons stopped your assault."

With my shoulders squared, I proudly proclaimed, "That'thh a lie."

"We gathered that. But there's more." The pig brought up a new article with an aerial photo of the dead Somali pirates.

My squared shoulders flinched, and I averted my eyes. So many horrible things had happened since that night, I'd forgotten my dreadful rampage.

"Dude, did you kill all those guys in Zimbabwe?" asked the duck.

"Yethh," I said with a whimper. I didn't want to believe I'd killed so many. "But it was self-defense." My tone conveyed sincerity, yet I hadn't forgiven myself.

"They were bad dudes."

"Nobody's upset over this incident, man."

"But folks are upset at me?"

"Dude, they're picketing."

The pig brought up a live surveillance feed showing a mob of fifty protesters with signs, such as "Death to the Demon Cow" and "The Only Good Zowbie is a Dead Zowbie" and "Free Grandma Marjorie, The Zowbie Slayer."

A scream festered inside me. *How could people believe such obvious lies?* As images of fields littered with cow corpses, regular and zombified, flashed on the screen, my inner scream faded to sorrow. I'd left a tidal wave of death and destruction. "I want to go back to India. They loved me there."

"Sorry, but not anymore." Despite using the word sorry, his tone contained not a shred of empathy. He brought up a video of Indian children beating a cow piñata with a "Test Cow 42" painted on it.

My perceived body weight doubled. I lacked the energy and will to keep my head up. My nose scraped the white tarp. "I want to go back into a medical coma."

"You don't want that, man."

"Dude, you'll be fine. The government will blame it on immigrants."

"Plus, humans have collective ADHD. Something new will grab their attention next week, man."

"Anyway, dude, we're glad to see you came through the surgery in one piece, but we've gotta get going."

"Yeah, man, we've got superhero stuff to do."

"But the duck'thh leg is still healing. You can't go on a mission with a broken leg."

"Dude, with this cast, I'm good to go." The duck hobbled a couple of steps. "Besides, I prefer flying." He hopped in the air and flew toward the barn exit.

"Surely, there'thh other agents who can stop these creatures?"

"Well," said the pig with a sheepish tone, "the rabbit and duck are attempting to infiltrate an all-animal gang. The human agents can't do that."

"We'll be wearing our black suits the next time we see you, man," said the rabbit, hopping to the exit.

They waved a paw and wing as they left the barn.

I panned the empty stalls. Zoomed in on the stairs to the loft. Followed the noiseless ceiling to the cat's computer room, which emitted only a single electronic beep. It's what they wanted. It's what we'd signed up for. Danger. Adventure. The chance to be a hero. Yet, as I focused on our group photo perched on my desk, I felt the same sorrow I did the last time I gazed upon it. They were all gone, and I'd failed in my promise to keep them safe.

Well, they weren't all gone. The pig still sat in my chair, and the fish still – "Where'thh the fish?"

"Who knows? He probably slithered through a wall when we weren't looking. That's what he does."

"True."

As I stared at the relaxed posture of the pig, my solemn face transformed into one of squished bewilderment. My solemn face transformed into one of squished bewilderment. "You lobbied to get uthh desk jobs. You said we weren't ready to become agents. You said the rabbit and duck would never be ready. Yet now you're fine with them all heading off on dangerous missions. Aren't you worried about them?"

He got out of my chair, walked to me, and put a hoof on my shoulder. "Of course, I'm worried. I've done everything I can to keep you all safe. But this wasn't my call. Agent Lavender made the assignments."

"How come you have less influence on her than you did on Agent Orange?"

He glanced at the ceiling, then focused on me. "She made compelling arguments about how far you've all come. She raved about the courage you all demonstrated in that tunnel, especially you." He poked me in the chest. "You swallowed zombie virus vials with no regard for your own safety."

"You thhay courage, I thhay fool's confidence. We all should have died in that tunnel. And I was one fart away from wiping out the human race."

"But you didn't die. And you saved the human race. The cows. The chickens. You're ready to be an agent of GIBOD. They're ready."

I ground my teeth as if chewing on cud. "Are we? I mean, what'thh changed your mind? To me, we're still the same bumbling fools who let the primary suspect escape on our training mission. The same dimwitted animals that were doing travelator races in the tunnel instead of locating the exits."

He patted my neck. "You're too hard on them. And yourself."

I shook my head, squished bewilderment still plastered across my face. "When did we swap roles? Desk jobs for everyone sounds great. I really don't think we're cutout to be agents."

The pig smiled. "You've been out of commission. You haven't witnessed their full growth. But you *have* seen them use their powers effectively. You've seen how they work together as a team, especially under your lead. They have amazing powers, resilience, and resourcefulness. They'll do fine."

"Even the rabbit and duck?"

He returned to my desk chair. "You'd be surprised. They're doing a great job on this assignment."

"But I won't be there to protect them. And neither will you. We can't guarantee their safety."

He chuckled, as he leaned back, wrapped his karate-clench hooves around the back of his head, and kicked his hind hooves onto my desk. "You're right. We can't guarantee their safety. But we knew the job was dangerous when we took it. We have to trust that we've given them the training and knowledge to succeed and be safe."

I shuffled off the tarp and kicked at the dirt. Leading was much easier when I just had to strap on a cowbell and the rest of the herd followed me everywhere. I couldn't shake the distress of helplessness, nor my imposter syndrome. "I've been an emotional wreck throughout this ordeal. One minute I'm weeping about the other's capture, and the next, I'm so obsessed with the mission I turn into Agent Orange and forget about rescuing the chicken, dog, and cat. That's not the type of leader they need."

The pig locked his eyes onto mine. "You're a good leader. You've always protected us. But in the special agency business, you can't afford to be our protective mother and our leader. You need to have a bit of Agent Orange in you. He stuck to his principles and the mission. He kept fighting, even when all seemed lost."

The vision of him fighting Agent Periwinkle and paying the ultimate price played in my head, followed by a montage of our adventures, from celebrating on the plane ride home to fighting zombie cows and chickens. I even managed a smile, remembering him retrieving the bag of vials he dropped in the middle of a herd of zombified Black Angus.

"Cow, you've been through a lot the last few weeks. Take time to reflect, relax, and recover. GIBOD is going to need your talents. The other BarnYard Heroes will need your leadership."

The pig had mentioned how much we'd all grown, but all I thought about was how much he'd grown. He'd never shown so much compassion and philosophical wisdom before. I assumed Agent Lavender's influence played a major role in his transformation. His words had provided mild comfort, and I thanked him for that.

As I waited for my emotional rollercoaster to climb its next crest, my gaze drifted to a video of protests playing on the computer screen. They were interviewing a woman with a "Save Test Cow 42" sign.

The pig turned his head to see what caught my attention. "Look at that. You've got a fan."

"I know that woman." It was the farmer, Karen Branson.

The pig turned up the volume.

"That cow, Test Cow 42. She didn't start no cow zombie apocalypse, and she ain't the killer you all make her out to be. She saved me and my family from the zowbies. She took on an entire herd of them zowbies and won. Test Cow 42 is a hero."

"Wow. You really do have a fan," said the pig.

The news clip cut to a group of middle schoolers beating, then burning a life-size papier mâché Test Cow 42. All the joy of Karen's praise drained out of me. "But the rest of the world hates me and blames me for the cow zombie apocalypse?"

"Don't worry about it," chuckled the pig. "Humans have the attention span of gnats. Like the rabbit and duck said, the humans will forget about you by next week."

I shrugged, not convinced.

He stood, patted my butt, and waddled toward the door. "Still, you should get that tattoo removed."

The barn door closed. I surveyed the quiet empty barn, resting my gaze upon my desk, wishing I'd gotten the others to move it back into my office before they'd all left.

About the Author

Absurd and fun are the most common words used to describe Samuel A. McAdams's writing. He focused on the former and anointed himself the 21st Century Absurdist. Samuel has no concerns that his writing does not match the traditional absurdist definition, insisting the term "traditional absurdist" is an oxymoron, therefore making the point moot.

Samuel wrote his first story in the third grade. As he read the story to his class, improvising to correct his poor grammar, the students, teacher, and even the school principal laughed. From that day forward, he became hooked on the craft of writing and obsessed with humor. His slow and below average reading level, horrendous spelling, and awful penmanship made writing a major chore. He did not let this deter him from continuing to write silly short stories that kept his classmates laughing. He soaked up humor in all forms, from Sunday comics, to standup comedians, sitcoms, and sketch comedy, but it wasn't until his teenage years when he discovered Douglas Adams, Hunter S. Thompson, and Kurt Vonnegut Jr that he developed a love for novels. Thanks to advanced grammar checkers, the emergence of self-publishing, and a well-paying day job that affords him to hire editors, Samuel is bringing his multiple rough drafts to life. He hopes you enjoy reading them as much as he enjoyed writing them.

Explore the inner workings of Samuel's mind at sammcadams.com, or learn more about the BarnYard Heroes at BarnYardHeroes.com. To hear about upcoming events and future releases, scan the QR Code below to follow Samuel on Facebook as The 21st Century Absurdist.

Acknowledgements

Friends and family have suggested that my wife, Emmi, is a saint. I agree with the sentiment, though her current relationship with the Catholic Church may throw a wrench in the canonization process. On top of her beauty and intelligence, she has embraced, and I dare say encouraged, my transformation into The 21st Century Absurdist. She tolerates my Thursday Night Shut Yer Trap & Write sessions, Saturday writing group meetings, and November Novel Writing marathons. She even abides with my efforts to push our annual holiday letter to levels of confusion and absurdity that leave our friends and family members not only questioning my sanity, but hers as well.

The BarnYard Heroes would never have been born without the assistance of my kids, Alexis and Ben. Our brainstorming sessions around the kitchen table gave birth to the characters that I've spent decades writing about.

BarnYard Heroes: The Havarti Travel Bureau Conspiracy or How I Learned to Stop Worrying and Love the Cow Zombie Apocalypse took fifteen years from conception to publication. There have been countless members of my suburban Chicago writing community, the Writing Journey, who provided valuable feedback and critiques of this novel. We had numerous debates on how to handle the cow's lisp and who my target audience was. I created a set of rules for the former. The latter is still up for debate, especially as the violence increased, making it no longer an all-ages novel.

This novel would never be what it's become without the incredible developmental feedback of my editor, Fiona. If you're looking for a developmental editor, go to Fiverr now and hire her services.

My friend, Tara Gillim, supplied the final copy edits, correcting my numerous grammatical errors. She is amazing at finding all the mistakes I and the AI grammar checkers missed.

Do you like the novel's cover art? I worked with Team Iconic to bring my concept to life. Hire them via Fiverr for your next book cover.

Last but not least, I would like to thank you, the reader. I had a blast writing and editing this novel. (Yes, I'm one of those weirdos that loves editing). Hopefully, you enjoyed the adventure and had a few laughs along the way. I have one request. Book reviews are the lifeblood of writers. Please take a moment to rate the novel and write a review. Scan the QR code below for links to where you can enter your review.

www.ingramcontent.com/pod-product-compliance
Lightning Source LLC
Chambersburg PA
CBHW031158310726
48969CB00001B/132